D1107081

DISCARDED

PRIZE STORIES 1968:

The O. Henry Awards

PRIZE STORIES 1968:

The O. Henry Awards

Edited and with an Introduction by

WILLIAM ABRAHAMS

Doubleday & Company, Inc., Garden City, New York

1968

COLLEGE OF THE SEQUOIAS
LIBRARY

Library of Congress Catalog Card Number 21–9372
Copyright © 1968 by Doubleday & Company, Inc.
All Rights Reserved. Printed in the United States of America
First Edition

CONTENTS

PUBLISHER'S NOTE

THE PRESENT volume is the forty-eighth in the O. Henry Memorial Award series. No collections appeared in 1952 and 1953, when the continuity of the series was interrupted by the death of Herschel Brickell, who had been the editor for ten years.

In 1918 the Society of Arts and Sciences met to vote upon a monument to the master of the short story, O. Henry. They decided that this memorial should be in the form of two prizes for the best short stories published by American authors in American magazines during the year 1919. From this beginning, the memorial developed into an annual anthology of outstanding short stories by American authors published, with the exception of the years mentioned above, by Doubleday & Company, Inc. Blanche Colton Williams, one of the founders of the awards, was editor from 1919 to 1932; Harry Hansen from 1933 to 1940; Herschel Brickell from 1941 to 1951; Paul Engle from 1954 to 1959 with Hanson Martin co-editor in the years 1954 to 1956; Mary Stegner in 1960; Richard Poirier from 1961 to 1966, with assistance from and co-editorship with William Abrahams from 1964 to 1966. William Abrahams became editor of the series in 1967.

Doubleday has also published First-Prize Stories from the O. Henry Memorial Awards 1919–1966.

The stories chosen for this volume were published in the period from the summer of 1966 to the summer of 1967. A list of the magazines consulted appears at the back of the book. The choice of stories and the selection of prize winners are exclusively the responsibility of the editor. Biographical material is provided by the contributors.

INTRODUCTION: PRIZE STORIES 1968

THAT violence has become a crucial element in American life and experience would seem to be inarguable. Each of us has some knowledge of it, the surge of violence in the heart and the street that we read about in our newspapers and watch on our TV screens, although for most of us it is still what happens in the next street (not yet in the next room) and in the heart of another (not yet our own). Even official rhetoric, which only rarely bears much relation to the reality of things as we know them, can't smooth over the existence of war and racial dissension, or get past the violence they do to human flesh and spirit. The least that can be said is that an awareness of violence, of something dark, threatening and irrational in the background of ordinary, everyday life, has become a part of the "human condition" in America in the closing years of the 1960s, and it is hardly surprising then that a great many American short story writers have made it their subject and concern.

I should admit, in making this last statement, that I am being wise after the fact. When I began to read stories for the present collection, it was not with the aim of finding illustrations for a pre-determined theme, e.g., Short Stories in an Age of Violence, or something similar. As in past years the search has been simply for stories of a certain excellence and durability, those that are not only readable but will also repay rereading, in which an original or personal note is sounded, authentic in style and feeling, where there is no appreciable gap between intention and achievement. I have deliberately omitted from the catalogue of what one looks for the question of subject matter, for it is not in itself a prime consideration. The hard truth seems to be that any subject, no matter how slight or unpromising, in the hands of a gifted writer can be made to yield a story of unquestioned value —which is the alchemy of art—whereas the converse unfortunately is not true: great subjects don't make great writers, and

an ambitious failure, however we may honor the ambition and
seriousness of its author, is no less a failure for being ambitious.
But as I made my way through the year's accumulation, so diver-
sified in form and style, in subject and sensibility—and I hope
the selection here will suggest something of that diversity—I was
struck by the occurrence of violence, the manifestation or impli-
cation of violence, in so large a number of stories, many of outstanding merit, that it could not be passed over in silence or dismissed as merely an odd coincidence. It had nothing to do with
the age and professional experience of an author, or where his
story appeared. (So much for the easy formulations beloved of
trend-spotters: the violent young, the brave new magazines, etc.,
etc.) No, it was there, for example, in a story by an established
master like Eudora Welty, and in the first-published story by a
young writer like Paul Tyner, and both of these stories appeared
in *The New Yorker,* which, justly or not, one doesn't think of as
especially receptive to violence.

Of course, stories of violence—gangster stories, murder stories,
war-blood-sex-and-sadism stories—have been for a long time now
a perfectly respectable sub-category of escapist entertainment, and
numerous magazines exist for their propagation. But the stories of
which I am speaking are of a different order. They belong to a
perhaps less glamorous but more central tradition where violence
is not the material of fantasy, an exotic inducement to chills,
thrills, and hot flushes, but a recognizable, disquieting aspect of
life as we know it to be. The shocks in these stories are shocks
of recognition, and what we recognize are insights that might be
our own, that, once encountered, have an absolute inevitability
and rightness, and stay in our minds thereafter. It is not for
nothing that, as V. S. Pritchett has remarked, "the short story is
above all the memorable form of writing . . . perfectly fitted to
the glancing, allusive, nervously decisive and summary moods
of contemporary life." Violence enters these stories in a natural
or organic way, not being imposed upon them to prove a point;
nor are violent episodes being written up, or down, for the sake
of the *frisson.* These stories are not documents, their concerns are
private; and so, if a newspaper were to report on what happens
in them—where the headline is—there would be significant omis-

sions and amputations, in effect (as Miss Welty makes clear)
cutting out the heart of the story.

I began by suggesting that war and racial dissension are in
the foreground of public consciousness, a background against
which a writer writes his stories, although he may make no
reference to them, at least not directly. Many do, however, and
find their subject in the relation between Americans of different
races, not the call for Black Power or for official days of Prayer
and Reconciliation, the strident or dulcet slogans that convert a
reality to a stereotype, but something more private, personal, and
truthful. It is a relation that is being explored, tentatively and
with full regard for its complexity, in the contemporary story.
But the war, whether in Vietnam or in America (in what once
upon a time would have been called "the home front") remains
in possession of newspapers, newsmagazines, broadcasters, ana-
lysts, and official rhetoricians. Thus, there are no "war stories" in
this year's collection, not, as one might properly assume, because
none were thought to meet a standard of excellence, but simply
because during the past year there were virtually no such stories
written or published. Of those that were, few got beyond propaganda, and fewer still beyond sentimentality. One can only speculate as to why serious writers have chosen not to write war
stories—in the case of "battlefield stories" there has been, I feel
safe in saying, a refusal to "invent" or "falsify" experience not
known at first-hand, and for that sort of story we shall have to
wait until some of the men now fighting in Vietnam return to
civilian life and become writers. (Though they may choose to
keep silent about what they have seen; after all, more than a
decade has passed, and no major writing has come out of the
war in Korea.) What one might more reasonably expect are
stories that originate in the longing for peace and an end to this
appalling war that so many Americans feel: such stories have yet
to be written. But the presence of war, hardly affecting the
material surface of American life, nonetheless makes itself felt:
it is part of the atmosphere in which the contemporary story is
being written, a scent of violence tainting the air and calling
into question all official platitudes and mock-heroic or mock-pious
postures.

It is the atmosphere of Miss Oates's story, where the sacred

text is the lyric of the pop song ("I'm gonna get you, baby"),
where the deity is the pop singer, his prophet the disc jockey,
and his temple the drive-in restaurant "shaped like a big bottle,
though squatter than a bottle." There, adolescent girls "sat at the
counter and crossed their legs at the ankles, their thin shoulders
rigid with excitement, and listened to the music that made
everything so good; the music was always in the background like
music at a church service, it was something to depend on." And
when one of these girls went home, "She went inside the house
and turned on the radio to drown out the quiet. She sat on the
edge of her bed, barefoot, and listened for an hour and a half
to a program called XYZ Sunday jamboree, record after record
of hard, fast, shrieking songs she sang along with . . ."

It is the atmosphere of Mrs. Broner's story, reducing and dis-
carding one by one the pieties of public speech and life, and
finding a brilliant image of civic obliteration: "One day, during
the summer session, after a long drought, while the children
suffered from prickly heat, Celia walked down a path where the
sun was merciless. A veterans' mall, in honor of students killed
in World War II, had been torn up to make room for classroom
buildings. The buildings shone white, pre-cast concrete, like more
sidewalk. Along the path the university had planted geraniums."

It is the atmosphere of Miss Welty's story, set in one of those
small towns in the delta South that she has made us familiar with,
seemingly timeless—"the telephone wires along the road were
hung with shreds of cotton, the sides of the road were strewn
with them too"—but the mood is no less anxious, disaffected, contemporary: "He thought he had been patient, but patience had
made him tired. He was so increasingly tired, so sick and even
bored with the bitterness, intractability that divided everybody
and everything." This is not all. As in life, unexpected and con-
tradictory, there comes a moment of piercing illumination: "And
suddenly, tonight, things had seemed just the way they used to
seem. He had felt as though someone had stopped him on the
street and offered to carry his load for a while—had insisted on
it—some old, trusted, half-forgotten family friend that he had lost
sight of since youth. Was it the sensation, now returning, that
there was still allowed to everybody on earth a *self*—savage,
death-defying, private? The pounding of his heart was like the

assault of hope, throwing itself against him without a stop, merciless." There is beauty in the writing of this, and courage unmarred by sentimentality: a declaration of life in a time of violence, when the self is not tender but "savage, death-defying," when hope comes to one as an "assault" and is not merciful but "merciless"—as the sun is merciless, shining down on the obliterated memorials of an earlier war.

WILLIAM ABRAHAMS

PRIZE STORIES 1968:

The O. Henry Awards

EUDORA WELTY lives and writes in Jackson, Mississippi. "The Demonstrators," which will be included in a forthcoming collection of her work, is the third of her stories to be awarded First Prize in this series. In addition to writing she has lectured and worked at numerous colleges and universities throughout the country.

The Demonstrators

NEAR eleven o'clock that Saturday night the doctor stopped again by his office. He had recently got into playing a weekly bridge game at the club, but tonight it had been interrupted for the third time, and he'd just come from attending to Miss Marcia Pope. Now bedridden, scorning all medication and in particular tranquillizers, she had a seizure every morning before breakfast and often on Saturday night for some reason, but had retained her memory; she could amuse herself by giving out great wads of Shakespeare and *"Arma virumque cano,"* or the like. The more forcefully Miss Marcia Pope declaimed, the more innocent grew her old face—the lines went right out.

"She'll sleep naturally now, I think," he'd told the companion, still in her rocker.

Mrs. Warrum did well, perhaps hadn't hit yet on an excuse to quit that suited her. She failed to be alarmed by Miss Marcia Pope, either in convulsions or in recitation. From where she lived, she'd never gone to school to this lady, who had taught three generations of Holden, Mississippi, its Latin, civics, and English, and who had carried, for forty years, a leather satchel bigger than the doctor's bag.

As he'd snapped his bag shut tonight, Miss Marcia had opened

"The Demonstrators" – Eudora Welty, *The New Yorker,* Copyright © 1966 by The New Yorker Magazine, Inc. Originally appeared in *The New Yorker.*

her eyes and spoken distinctly: "Richard Strickland? I have it on my report that Irene Roberts is not where she belongs. Now which of you wants the whipping?"

"It's all right, Miss Marcia. She's still my wife," he'd said, but could not be sure the answer got by her.

In the office, he picked up the city newspaper he subscribed to—seeing as he did so the picture on the front of a young man burning his draft card before a camera—and locked up, ready to face home. As he came down the stairway onto the street, his sleeve was plucked.

It was a Negro child. "We got to hurry," she said.

His bag was still in the car. She climbed into the back and stood there behind his ear as he drove down the hill. He met the marshal's car as both bounced over the railroad track—no passenger rode with the marshal that he could see—and the doctor asked the child, "Who got hurt? Whose house?" But she could only tell him how to get there, an alley at a time, till they got around the cottonseed mill.

Down here, the street lights were out tonight. The last electric light of any kind appeared to be the one burning in the vast shrouded cavern of the gin. His car lights threw into relief the dead goldenrod that stood along the road and made it look heavier than the bridge across the creek.

As soon as the child leaned on his shoulder and he had stopped the car, he heard men's voices; but at first his eyes could make out little but an assembly of white forms spaced in the air near a low roof—chickens roosting in a tree. Then he saw the reds of cigarettes. A dooryard was as packed with a standing crowd as if it were funeral time. They were all men. Still more people seemed to be moving from the nearby churchyard and joining onto the crowd in front of the house.

The men parted before them as he went following the child up broken steps and across a porch. A kerosene lamp was being held for him in the doorway. He stepped into a roomful of women. The child kept going, went to the foot of an iron bed and stopped. The lamp came up closer behind him and he followed a path of newspapers laid down on the floor from the doorway to the bed.

A dark quilt was pulled up to the throat of a girl alive on the bed. A pillow raised her at the shoulders. The dome of her forehead looked thick as a battering ram, because of the rolling of her eyes.

Dr. Strickland turned back the quilt. The young, very blackskinned woman lay in a white dress with her shoes on. A maid? Then he saw that of course the white was not the starched material of a uniform but shiny, clinging stuff, and there was a banner of some kind crossing it in a crumpled red line from the shoulder. He unfastened the knot at the waist and got the banner out of the way. The skintight satin had been undone at the neck already; as he parted it farther, the girl kicked at the foot of the bed. He exposed the breast and then, before her hand had pounced on his, the wound below the breast. There was a small puncture with little evidence of external bleeding. He had seen splashes of blood on the dress, now almost dry.

"Go boil me some water. Too much excitement to send for the doctor a little earlier?"

The girl clawed at his hand with her sticky nails.

"Have you touched her?" he asked.

"See there? And she don't want you trying it, either," said a voice in the room.

A necklace like sharp and pearly teeth was fastened around her throat. It was when he took that off that the little girl who had been sent for him cried out. "I bid that!" she said, but without coming nearer. He found no other wounds.

"Does it hurt you to breathe?" He spoke almost absently as he addressed the girl.

The nipples of her breasts cast shadows that looked like figs; she would not take a deep breath when he used the stethoscope. Sweat in the airless room, in the bed, rose and seemed to weaken and unstick the newspapered walls like steam from a kettle already boiling; it glazed his own white hand, his tapping fingers. It was the stench of sensation. The women's faces coming nearer were streaked in the hot lamplight. Somewhere close to the side of his head something glittered; hung over the knob of the bedpost, where a boy would have tossed his cap, was a tambourine. He let the stethoscope fall, and heard women's sighs travel around the room, domestic sounds like a broom being flirted about, women getting ready for company.

"Stand back," he said. "You got a fire on in here?" Warm as it was, crowded as it was in here, he looked behind him and saw the gas heater burning, half the radiants burning blue. The girl, with lips turned down, lay pulling away while he took her pulse.

The child who had been sent for him and then had been sent to heat the water brought the kettle in from the kitchen too soon and had to be sent back to make it boil. When it was ready and in the pan, the lamp was held closer; it was beside his elbow as if to singe his arm.

"Stand back," he said. Again and again the girl's hand had to be forced away from her breast. The wound quickened spasmodically as if it responded to light.

"Icepick?"

"You right this time," said voices in the room.

"Who did this to her?"

The room went quiet; he only heard the men in the yard laughing together. "How long ago?" He looked at the path of newspapers spread on the floor. "Where? Where did it happen? How did she get here?"

He had an odd feeling that somewhere in the room somebody was sending out beckoning smiles in his direction. He lifted, half turned his head. The elevated coal that glowed at regular intervals was the pipe of an old woman in a boiled white apron standing near the door.

He persisted. "Has she coughed up anything yet?"

"Don't you know her?" they cried, as if he never was going to hit on the right question.

He let go the girl's arm, and her hand started its way back again to her wound. Sending one glowing look at him, she covered it again. As if she had spoken, he recognized her.

"Why, it's Ruby," he said.

Ruby Gaddy *was* the maid. Five days a week she cleaned up on the second floor of the bank building where he kept his office and consulting rooms.

He said to her, "Ruby, this is Dr. Strickland. What have you been up to?"

"Nothin'!" everybody cried for her.

The girl's eyes stopped rolling and rested themselves on the expressionless face of the little girl, who again stood at the foot of the bed watching from this restful distance. Look equalled look: sisters.

"Am I supposed to just know?" The doctor looked all around him. An infant was sitting up on the splintery floor near his feet, he now saw, on a clean newspaper, a spoon stuck pipelike in its mouth. From out in the yard at that moment came a regular guffaw, not much different from the one that followed the telling of a dirty story or a race story by one of the clowns in the Elks' Club. He frowned at the baby; and the baby, a boy, looked back over his upside down spoon and gave it a long audible suck.

"She married? Where's her husband? That where the trouble was?"

Now, while the women in the room, too, broke out in sounds of amusement, the doctor stumbled where he stood. "What the devil's running in here? Rats?"

"You wrong there."

Guinea pigs were running underfoot, not only in this room but on the other side of the wall, in the kitchen where the water had finally got boiled. Somebody's head turned toward the leaf end of a stalk of celery wilting on top of the Bible on the table.

"Catch those things!" he exclaimed.

The baby laughed; the rest copied the baby.

"They lightning. Get away from you so fast!" said a voice.

"Them guinea pigs ain't been caught since they was born. Let you try."

"Know why? 'Cause they's Dove's. Dove left 'em here when he move out, just to be in the way."

The doctor felt the weight recede from Ruby's fingers, and saw it flatten her arm where it lay on the bed. Her eyes had closed. A little boy with a sanctimonious face had taken the bit of celery and knelt down on the floor; there was scrambling about and increasing laughter until Dr. Strickland made himself heard in the room.

"All right. I heard you. Is Dove who did it? Go on. Say."

He heard somebody spit on the stove. Then:

"It's Dove."

"Dove."

"Dove."

"Dove."

"You got it right that time."

While the name went around, passed from one mouth to the other, the doctor drew a deep breath. But the sigh that filled the room was the girl's own, luxuriously uncontained.

"Dove Collins? I believe you. I've had to sew him up enough times on Sunday morning, you all know that," said the doctor. "I know Ruby, I know Dove, and if the lights would come back on I can tell you the names of the rest of you and you know it." While he was speaking, his eyes fell on Oree, a figure of the Holden square for twenty years, whom he had inherited—sitting here in the room in her express wagon, the flowered skirt spread down from her lap and tucked in over the stumps of her knees.

While he was preparing the hypodermic, he was aware that more watchers, a row of them dressed in white with red banners like Ruby's, were coming in to fill up the corners. The lamp was lifted—higher than the dipping shadows of their heads, a valentine tacked on the wall radiated color—and then, as he leaned over the bed, the lamp was brought down closer and closer to the girl, like something that would devour her.

"Now I can't see what I'm doing," the doctor said sharply, and as the light jumped and swung behind him he thought he recognized the anger as a mother's.

"Look to me like the fight's starting to go out of Ruby mighty early," said a voice.

Still her eyes stayed closed. He gave the shot.

"Where'd he get to—Dove? Is the marshal out looking for him?" he asked.

The sister moved along the bed and put the baby down on it close to Ruby's face.

"Remove him," said the doctor.

"She don't even study him," said the sister. "Poke her," she told the baby.

"Take him out of here," ordered Dr. Strickland.

The baby opened one of his mother's eyes with his fingers. When she shut it on him he cried, as if he knew it to be deliberate of her.

"Get that baby out of here and all the kids, I tell you," Dr. Strickland said into the room. "This ain't going to be pretty."

"Carry him next door, Twosie," said a voice.

"I ain't. You all promised me if I leave long enough to get the doctor I could stand right here until." The child's voice was loud.

"O.K. Then you got to hold Roger."

The baby made a final reach for his mother's face, putting out a hand with its untrimmed nails, gray as the claw of a squirrel. The woman who had held the lamp set that down and grabbed the baby out of the bed herself. His legs began churning even before she struck him a blow on the side of the head.

"You trying to raise him an idiot?" the doctor flung out.

"*I* ain't going to raise him," the mother said toward the girl on the bed.

The deliberation had gone out of her face. She was drifting into unconsciousness. Setting her hand to one side, the doctor inspected the puncture once more. It was clean as the eye of a needle. While he stood there watching her, he lifted her hand and washed it—the wrist, horny palm, blood-caked fingers one by one.

But as he again found her pulse, he saw her eyes opening. As long as he counted he was aware of those eyes as if they loomed larger than the watch face. They were filled with the unresponding gaze of ownership. She knew what she had. Memory did not make the further effort to close the lids when he replaced her hand, or when he took her shoes off and set them on the floor, or when he stepped away from the bed and again the full lamplight struck her face.

The twelve-year-old stared on, over the buttress of the baby she held to her chest.

"Can you ever hush that baby?"

A satisfied voice said, "He going to keep-a-noise till he learn better."

"Well, I'd like a little peace and consideration to be shown!" the doctor said. "Try to remember there's somebody in here with you that's going to be pumping mighty hard to breathe." He raised a finger and pointed it at the old woman in the boiled apron whose pipe had continued to glow with regularity by the door. "You stay. You sit here and watch Ruby," he called. "The rest of you clear out of here."

He closed his bag and straightened up. The woman stuck the
lamp hot into his own face.

"Remember Lucille? I'm Lucille. I was washing for your mother
when you was born. Let me see you do something," she said
with fury. "You ain't even tied her up! You sure ain't your
daddy!"

"Why, she's bleeding inside," he retorted. "What do you think
she's doing?"

They hushed. For a minute all he heard was the guinea pigs
racing. He looked back at the girl; her eyes were fixed with
possession. "I gave her a shot. She'll just go to sleep. If she
doesn't, call me and I'll come back and give her another one.
One of you kindly bring me a drink of water," the doctor
continued in the same tone.

With a crash, hushed off like cymbals struck by mistake, something was moved on the kitchen side of the wall. The little boy
who had held the celery to catch the guinea pigs came in carrying
a teacup. He passed through the room and out onto the porch,
where he could be heard splashing fresh water from a pump. He
came back inside and at arm's length held the cup out to the
doctor.

Dr. Strickland drank with a thirst they all could and did follow.
The cup, though it held the whole smell of this house in it, was of
thin china, was an old one.

Then he stepped across the gaze of the girl on the bed as he
would have had to step over a crack yawning in the floor.

"Fixing to leave?" asked the old woman in the boiled white
apron, who still stood up by the door, the pipe gone from her
lips. He then remembered her. In the days when he travelled
East to medical school, she used to be the sole factotum at the
Holden depot when the passenger train came through sometime
between two and three in the morning. It was always late. Circling
the pewlike benches of the waiting rooms, she carried around
coffee which she poured boiling hot into paper cups out of a
white-enamelled pot that looked as long as her arm. She wore
then, in addition to the apron, a white and flaring head covering
—something between a chef's cap and a sunbonnet. As the train
at last steamed in, she called the stations. She didn't use a loudspeaker but just the power of her lungs. In all the natural volume

of her baritone voice she thundered them out to the scattered and few who had waited under lights too poor to read by—first in the colored waiting room, then in the white waiting room, to echo both times from the vault of the roof: ". . . Meridian. Birmingham. Chattanooga. Bristol. Lynchburg. Washington. Baltimore. Philadelphia. And New York." Seizing all the bags, two by two, in her own hands, walking slowly in front of the passengers, she saw to it that they left.

He said to her, "I'm going, but you're not. You're keeping a watch on Ruby. Don't let her slide down in the bed. Call me if you need me." As a boy, had he never even wondered what her name was—this tyrant? He didn't know it now. He put the cup into her reaching hand. "Aren't you ready to leave?" he asked Oree, the legless woman. She still lived by the tracks where the train had cut off her legs.

"I ain't in no hurry," she replied and as he passed her she called her usual "Take it easy, Doc."

When he stepped outside onto the porch, he saw that there was moonlight everywhere. Uninterrupted by any lights from Holden, it filled the whole country lying out there in the haze of the long rainless fall. He himself stood on the edge of Holden. Just one house and one church farther, the Delta began, and the cotton fields ran into the scattered paleness of a dimmed-out Milky Way.

Nobody called him back, yet he turned his head and got a sideways glimpse all at once of a row of dresses hung up across the front of the house, starched until they could have stood alone (as his mother complained), and in an instant had recognized his mother's gardening dress, his sister Annie's golf dress, his wife's favorite duster that she liked to wear to the breakfast table, and more dresses, less substantial. Elevated across the front of the porch, they were hung again between him and the road. With sleeves spread wide, trying to scratch his forehead with the tails of their skirts, they were flying around this house in the moonlight.

The moment of vertigo passed, as a small black man came up the steps and across the porch wearing heeltaps on his shoes.

"Sister Gaddy entered yet into the gates of joy?"

"No, Preacher, you're in time," said the doctor.

As soon as he left the house, he heard it become as noisy as the yard had been, and the men in the yard went quiet to let

him through. From the road, he saw the moon itself. It was above
the tree with the chickens in it; it might have been one of the
chickens flown loose. He scraped children off the hood of his
car, pulled another from position at the wheel, and climbed inside.
He turned the car around in the churchyard. There was a flickering light inside the church. Flat-roofed as a warehouse, it had its
shades pulled down like a bedroom. This was the church where
the sounds of music and dancing came from habitually on many
another night besides Sunday, clearly to be heard on top of the
hill.

He drove back along the road, across the creek, its banks
glittering now with the narrow bottles, the size of harmonicas, in
which paregoric was persistently sold under the name of Mother's
Helper. The telephone wires along the road were hung with
shreds of cotton, the sides of the road were strewn with them
too, as if the doctor were out on a paper chase.

He passed the throbbing mill, working on its own generator.
No lights ever shone through the windowless and now moonlit
sheet iron, but the smell came out freely and spread over the
town at large—a cooking smell, like a dish ordered by a man
with an endless appetite. Pipes hung with streamers of lint fed
into the moonlit gin, and wagons and trucks heaped up round as
the gypsy caravans or circus wagons of his father's, or even his
grandfather's, stories, stood this way and that, waiting in the yard
outside.

Far down the railroad track, beyond the unlighted town, rose
the pillowshaped glow of a grass fire. It was gaseous, unveined,
unblotted by smoke, a cloud with the November flush of the
sedge grass by day, sparkless and nerveless, not to be confused
with a burning church, but like anesthetic made visible.

Then a long beam of electric light came solid as a board
from behind him to move forward along the long loading platform,
to some bales of cotton standing on it, some of them tumbled
one against the others as if pushed by the light; then it ran up
the wall of the dark station so you could read the name, "Holden."
The hooter sounded. This was a grade crossing with a bad record,
and it seemed to the doctor that he had never started over it
in his life that something was not bearing down. He stopped the
car, and as the train in its heat began to pass in front of him he

saw it to be a doubleheader, a loaded freight this time. It was going right on through Holden.

He cut off his motor. One of the sleepers rocked and complained with every set of wheels that rolled over it. Presently the regular, slow creaking reminded the doctor of an old-fashioned porch swing holding lovers in the dark.

He had been carried a cup tonight that might have been his own mother's china or his wife's mother's—the rim not a perfect round, a thin, porcelain cup his lips and his fingers had recognized. In that house of murder, comfort had been brought to him at his request. After drinking from it he had all but reeled into a flock of dresses stretched wide-sleeved across the porch of that house like a child's drawing of angels.

Faintly rocked by the passing train, he sat bent at the wheel of the car, and the feeling of well-being persisted. It increased, until he had come to the point of tears.

The doctor was the son of a doctor, practicing in his father's office; all the older patients, like Miss Marcia Pope—and like Lucille and Oree—spoke of his father, and some confused the young doctor with the old; but not they. The watch he carried was the gold one that had belonged to his father. Richard had grown up in Holden, married "the prettiest girl in the Delta." Except for his years at the university and then at medical school and during his interneship, he had lived here at home and had carried on the practice—the only practice in town. Now his father and his mother both were dead, his sister had married and moved away, a year ago his child had died. Then, back in the summer, he and his wife had separated, by her wish.

Sylvia had been their only child. Until her death from pneumonia last Christmas, at the age of thirteen, she had never sat up or spoken. He had loved her and mourned her all her life; she had been injured at birth. But Irene had done more; she had dedicated her life to Sylvia, sparing herself nothing, tending her, lifting her, feeding her, everything. What do you do after giving all your devotion to something that cannot be helped, and that has been taken away? You give all your devotion to something else that cannot be helped. But you shun all the terrible reminders, and turn not to a human being but to an idea.

Last June, there had come along a student, one of the civil-rights

workers, calling at his office with a letter of introduction. For
the sake of an old friend, the doctor had taken him home to
dinner. (He had been reminded of him once tonight, already, by
a photograph in the city paper.) He remembered that the young
man had already finished talking about his work. They had just
laughed around the table after Irene had quoted the classic question the governor-before-this-one had asked, after a prison break:
"If you can't trust a trusty, who can you trust?" Then the doctor
had remarked, "Speaking of who can you trust, what's this I read in
your own paper, Philip? It said some of your outfit over in the
next county were forced at gunpoint to go into the fields at
hundred-degree temperature and pick cotton. Well, that didn't
happen—there isn't any cotton in June."

"I asked myself the same question you do. But I told myself,
'Well, they won't know the difference where the paper is read,'"
said the young man.

"It's lying, though."

"We are dramatizing your hostility," the young bearded man
had corrected him. "It's a way of reaching people. Don't forget—
what they *might* have done to us is even worse."

"Still—you're not justified in putting a false front on things, in
my opinion," Dr. Strickland had said. "Even for a good cause."

"*You* won't tell Herman Fairbrothers what's the matter with
him," said his wife, and she jumped up from the table.

Later, as a result of this entertainment, he supposed, broken
glass had been spread the length and breadth of his driveway. He
hadn't seen in time what it wouldn't have occurred to him to look
for, and Irene, standing in the door, had suddenly broken into
laughter. . . .

He had eventually agreed that she have her wish and withdraw
herself for as long as she liked. She was back now where she
came from, where, he'd heard, they were all giving parties for
her. He had offered to be the one to leave. "Leave Holden without its Dr. Strickland? You wouldn't to save your soul, would
you?" she had replied. But as yet it was not divorce.

He thought he had been patient, but patience had made him
tired. He was so increasingly tired, so sick and even bored with
the bitterness, intractability that divided everybody and everything.

And suddenly, tonight, things had seemed just the way they used to seem. He had felt as though someone had stopped him on the street and offered to carry his load for a while—had insisted on it—some old, trusted, half-forgotten family friend that he has lost sight of since youth. Was it the sensation, now returning, that there was still allowed to everybody on earth a *self*—savage, death-defying, private? The pounding of his heart was like the assault of hope, throwing itself against him without a stop, merciless.

It seemed a long time that he had sat there, but the cars were still going by. Here came the caboose. He had counted them without knowing it—seventy-two cars. The grass fire at the edge of town came back in sight.

The doctor's feeling gradually ebbed away, like nausea put down. He started up the car and drove across the track and on up the hill.

Candles, some of them in dining-room candelabra, burned clear across the upstairs windows in the Fairbrothers' house. His own house, next door, was of course dark, and while he was wondering where Irene kept candles for emergencies he had driven on past his driveway for the second time that night. But the last place he wanted to go now was back to the club. He'd only tried it anyway to please his sister Annie. Now that he'd got by Miss Marcia Pope's dark window, he smelled her sweet-olive tree, solid as the bank building.

Here stood the bank, with its doorway onto the stairs to Drs. Strickland & Strickland, their names in black and gilt on three windows. He passed it. The haze and the moonlight were one over the square, over the row of storefronts opposite with the line of poles thin as matchsticks rising to prop the one long strip of tin over the sidewalk, the drygoods store with its ornamental top that looked like opened paper fans held up by acrobats. He slowly started around the square. Behind its iron railings, the courthouse-and-jail stood barely emerging from its black cave of trees and only the slicked iron steps of the stile caught the moon. He drove on, past the shut-down movie house with all the light bulbs unscrewed from the sign that spelled out in empty sockets "BROADWAY." In front of the new post office the flagpole looked feathery, like the track of a jet that is already gone from the sky. From in front of the fire station, the fire chief's old Buick had gone home.

What was there, who was there, to keep him from going home? The doctor drove on slowly around. From the center of the deserted pavement, where cars and wagons stood parked helter-skelter by day, rose the water tank, pale as a balloon that might be only tethered here. A clanking came out of it, for the water supply too had been a source of trouble this summer—a hollow, irregular knocking now and then from inside, but the doctor no longer heard it. In turning his car, he saw a man lying prone and colorless in the arena of moonlight.

The lights of the car fastened on him and his clothes turned golden yellow. The man looked as if he had been sleeping all day in a bed of flowers and rolled in their pollen and were sleeping there still, with his face buried. He was covered his length in cottonseed meal.

Dr. Strickland stopped the car short and got out. His footsteps made the only sound in town. The man raised up on his hands and looked at him like a seal. Blood laced his head like a net through which he had broken. His wide tongue hung down out of his mouth. But the doctor knew the face.

"So you're alive, Dove, you're still alive?"

Slowly, hardly moving his tongue, Dove said: "Hide me." Then he hemorrhaged through the mouth.

Through the other half of the night, the doctor's calls came to him over the telephone—all chronic cases. Eva Duckett Fairbrothers telephoned at daylight.

"Feels low in his mind? Of course he feels low in his mind," he had finally shouted at her. "If I had what Herman has, I'd go down in the back yard and shoot myself!"

The *Sentinel,* owned and edited by Horatio Duckett, came out on Tuesdays. The next week's back-page headline read, "TWO DEAD, ONE ICEPICK. FREAK EPISODE AT NEGRO CHURCH." The subhead read, "No Racial Content Espied."

The doctor sat at the table in his dining room, finishing breakfast as he looked it over.

An employee of the Fairbrothers Cotton Seed Oil Mill and a Holden maid, both Negroes, were stabbed with a sharp instrument judged to be an icepick in a crowded churchyard here Saturday night. Both later expired. The incident was not believed by Mayor Herman Fairbrothers to carry racial significance.

"It warrants no stir," the Mayor declared.

The mishap boosted Holden's weekend death toll to 3. Billy Lee Warrum Jr. died Sunday before reaching a hospital in Jackson where he was rushed after being thrown from his new motorcycle while on his way there. He was the oldest son of Mrs. Billy Lee Warrum, Rt. 1. Reputedly en route to see his fiance he was pronounced dead on arrival. Multiple injuries was listed as the cause, the motorcycle having speeded into an interstate truck loaded to capacity with holiday turkeys. (See eye-witness account, page 1.)

As Holden marshal Curtis "Cowboy" Stubblefield reconstructed the earlier mishap, Ruby Gaddy, 21, was stabbed in full view of the departing congregation of the Holy Gospel Tabernacle as she attempted to leave the church when services were concluded at approximately 9:30 P.M. Saturday.

Witnesses said Dave Collins, 25, appeared outside the church as early as 9:15 P.M. having come directly from his shift at the mill where he had been employed since 1959. On being invited to come in and be seated he joked and said he preferred to wait outdoors as he was only wearing work clothes until the Gaddy woman, said to be his common-law wife, came outside the frame structure.

In the ensuing struggle at the conclusion of the services, the woman, who was a member of the choir, is believed to have received fatal icepick injuries to a vital organ, then to have wrested the weapon from her assailant and paid him back in kind. The Gaddy woman then walked to her mother's house but later collapsed.

Members of the congregation said they chased Collins 13 or 14 yds. in the direction of Snake Creek on the South side of the church then he fell to the ground and rolled approximately ten feet down the bank, rolling over six or seven times. Those present believed him to have succumbed since it was said the pick while in the woman's hand had been seen to drive in and pierce either his ear or his eye, either of which, is in close approximation to the brain. However, Collins later managed to crawl unseen from the creek and to make his way undetected up Railroad Avenue and to the Main St. door of an office occupied by Richard Strickland, M.D., above the Citizens Bank & Trust.

Witnesses were divided on which of the Negroes struck the first blow. Percy McAtee, pastor of the church, would not take sides but declared on being questioned by Marshal Stubblefield he was satisfied no outside agitators were involved and no arrests were made.

Collins was discovered on his own doorstep by Dr. Strickland who had been spending the evening at the Country Club. Collins is reported by Dr. Strickland to have expired shortly following his discovery, alleging his death to chest wounds.

"He offered no statement," Dr. Strickland said in response to a query.

Interviewed at home where he is recuperating from an ailment, Mayor Fairbrothers stated that he had not heard of there being trouble of any description at the Mill. "We are not trying to ruin our good reputation by inviting any, either," he said. "If the weatherman stays on our side we expect to attain capacity production in the latter part of next month," he stated. Saturday had been pay day as usual.

When Collins' body was searched by officers the pockets were empty however.

An icepick, reportedly the property of the Holy Gospel Tabernacle, was later found by Deacon Gaddy, 8, brother of Ruby Gaddy, covered with blood and carried it to Marshal Stubblefield. Stubblefield said it had been found in the grounds of the new $100,000.00 Negro school. It is believed to have served as the instrument in the twin slayings, the victims thus virtually succeeding in killing each other.

"Well, I'm surprised didn't more of them get hurt," said Rev. Alonzo Duckett, pastor of the Holden First Baptist Church. "And yet they expect to be seated in our churches." County Sheriff Vince Lasseter, reached fishing at Lake Bourne, said: "That's one they can't pin the blame on us for. That's how they treat their own kind. Please take note our conscience is clear."

Members of the Negro congregation said they could not account for Collins having left Snake Creek at the unspecified time. "We stood there a while and flipped some bottle caps down at him and threw his cap down after him right over his face and didn't get a stir out of him," stated an official of the congregation. "The way he acted, we figured he was dead. We would not have gone off and left him if we had known he was able to subsequently crawl up the hill." They stated Collins was not in the habit of worshipping at Holy Gospel Tabernacle.

The Gaddy woman died later this morning, also from chest wounds. No cause was cited for the fracas.

The cook had refilled his cup without his noticing. The doctor dropped the paper and carried his coffee out onto the little porch; it was still his morning habit.

The porch was at the back of the house, screened on three sides. Sylvia's daybed used to stand here; it put her in the garden. No other houses were in sight; the gin could not be heard or even the traffic whining on the highway up off the bypass.

The roses were done for, the perennials too. But the surrounding crapemyrtle tree, the redbud, the dogwood, the Chinese tallow tree, and the pomegranate bush were bright as toys. The ailing pear tree had shed its leaves ahead of the rest. Past a falling wall of Michaelmas daisies that had not been tied up, a pair of flickers were rifling the grass, the cock in one part of the garden, the hen in another, picking at the devastation right through the bright leaves that appeared to have been left lying there just for them, probing and feeding. They stayed year round, he supposed, but it was only in the fall of the year that he ever noticed them. He was pretty sure that Sylvia had known the birds were there. Her eyes would follow birds when they flew across the garden. As he watched, the cock spread one wing, showy as a zebra's hide, and with a turn of his head showed his red seal.

Dr. Strickland swallowed the coffee and picked up his bag. It was all going to be just about as hard as seeing Herman and Eva Fairbrothers through. He thought that in all Holden, as of now, only Miss Marcia Pope was still quite able to take care of herself —or such was her own opinion.

E. M. BRONER is the author of a verse play, *Summer is a Foreign Land* and is working on a novel and an historical drama. *Journal Nocturnal,* a novella and stories, will be published this year. Her stories have appeared in *Epoch, North American Review, New Campus Writing ⅏3,* and other magazines. Mrs. Broner is a member of the English Department of Wayne State University in Detroit, Michigan. She and her husband, the artist Robert Broner, have two daughters and twin sons.

The New Nobility

FIVE BOYS and a girl sat in the booth of a bar, holding their quarters for tap.

"How do you rate Eleanor Roosevelt among the living and near living?" Thomas asked, testing.

"The world's Baba," Rube said and slid down to let his stomach rest on the wooden table.

Thomas, who had taught Plato in Freshman English, was socratic in his methods.

"Was Eleanor Roosevelt noble?" Thomas asked. "Would she be the new nobility?"

There was unanimous agreement. No.

"Nor would Schweitzer have been," said Edward, a Negro. "Come to me, my little African children."

In a corner Bernard's stomach growled. "The Beats didn't make it," Bernard said, to cover the sound. "They drove to the West Coast to go wading."

"Was it Stevenson?" a passing, romantic girl asked, attracted to the politician's blue-eyed eloquence.

"The great American nebbish," Ruben said. "The American failure."

"The New Nobility" – E. M. Broner, *Epoch,* Copyright © 1967 by Cornell University.

"He was not," said the girl, seating herself next to Bernard. "He once spent two weeks vacation on Archibald MacLeish's farm."

Rube was also informed. "The late Dorothy Kilgallen said the late Stevenson ran off to see a French starlet."

"Either way I loved him," said the girl, unperturbed.

Bernard watched her out of the corner of his eye and sloshed beer on his fingers. He wished either way she loved him too.

The talk of the cemetery ended.

"Humility," said Thomas, a former seminary student, "that is, freedom from pride and arrogance."

"No," Rube objected, with Jewish pride. "Glory, not humble pie."

"Ah," said Thomas, speaking in his thin voice. "Humility the way Auden said to Spender, 'Art is born in humiliation. You are so infinitely capable of being humiliated.'"

"Old Master Jackson Pollock," Glenn, an artist, said, using a swizzle stick from the bar to dip in beer and drip on the table. "Beautiful, beautiful, the way he controlled his drip technique. And the Ops. And the Pops. And the Electricians. That's nobility."

Too much. Bernard's hand shook as it rested on his head. He had been up drinking here the night before, then to a friend's house where he had fallen asleep on the couch. He was still in the same clothes. The romantic girl next to him shifted away.

Bernard lay his head on the table, then raised it. The table was damp and his sinuses began to ache.

"Kenneth Tynan," Thomas said, condensing a 50-minute lecture. "Osborne in England and Pinter. That's the new nobility. Durrenmatt in Switzerland. Gelber and Albee in New York. Brecht, Weiss from Germany."

"Why would the absurd be noble?" asked the oldest member of the group, Celia.

"King," said Thomas. "Martin Luther King. That's the nobleman today."

"Maybe once," said Edward, "not after *Time* magazine cover. Then he's the man of the week, along with General Westmoreland, man of the year."

Above the objections of Edward and Rube it was established,

while Bernard dozed or scratched, that the nobility arose from
no ethnic past. Swinging clear.

"They don't make them like they used to," Rube said, trying to
exorcise the nostalgia that anything Yiddish evoked in him. "They
sunk Ellis Island and drowned the old ladies from the old country."

It was the part of Rube the others objected to. He was parochial,
but doing better.

"Where's your catholicity?" Thomas asked Rube.

Rube brought back another beer from the bar, ignoring the
waitress. "Where are the old ladies?" he asked. "Where's Mother
Nature?"

"Buried with the Transcendentalists," answered Thomas, the
nineteenth century expert in the group.

It was also established, and this time Bernard heard, for his
mind was suddenly *poing, poing* wired, intense from no sleep,
coffee and beer, that the new nobility could fail in everything but
one facet. No more Renaissance man. One did not have to die
as Addison (or was it Steele?), still setting an example.

"Bravery," said Edward. "*A* brave thing."

"Originality," said Thomas. "That is, close to the origins of."

Celia, a woman among the boys and girls, had her own dimension of sadness.

"Mobility is nobility," she said. "Be there, where the action is,
like Clancy Sigal's *Going Away*." Celia, too, was going away. Her
frame of reference dated back. "If it's in Spain," she said, "be
there." But nobody wanted to be there anymore.

"What's the matter with stability?" asked the girl who had
liked Stevenson.

"Nothing," said Celia, "except it's not nobility."

"Keeping the dream green," said the artist Glenn. "The struggle
is noble."

"If you're a writer," Bernard added, "you throw a character
far out and follow him. You don't have to do anything else so
long as that character is out enough.

"If you're a musician," Bernard continued, his transistor radio
always tuned in to a Canadian cultural station, "you swing. You
don't have to be a happily married. You only have to be a
noble musician."

"Does the nobility have to show?" Celia asked.

"No thorn marks," said Rube.

"Who's for Isadora Duncan?" asked the barkeeper's wife, a blond with eyes that protruded, from a thyroid condition. "The noblest of them. My idol!" She wiped the counter with the hem of her blouse. "Who's for Isadora Duncan?"

But, alas for her, all the votes were in and counted, including Puerto Rico and Hawaii.

Bernard touched the arm of the girl next to him. Someone was holding the front door open and let daylight in. Bernard's eyes were touched with light, his face unexpectedly happy. The visiting girl, forgetting who he was, looked at him and enjoyed him.

"Let's go to my place," he said.

She considered.

"Cruelty," Thomas continued from the other conversation. "The new nobility needs impersonality and spiny edges to ward off the public."

Bernard rested his chin on the girl's shoulder and his hand on the inside of her elbow. She saw his cracked nails and skin abrasions.

"No," she told him.

Dismissed, he left the table and the bar, Bernard Applebaum, the new nobility.

I. St. Bernard (Close to the Origins of)

Bernard made the fourth dimension of nobility, the dimension after vision, narrowness of purpose and spinyness. He was of the dimension that shed unnecessaries. In that way Bernard was the greatest peer of his time, the noblest nobleman of them all.

Thomas, Rube, Edward, Glenn, and Celia had nominated Norman Mailer, Staughton Lynd, Chaddi Jaggen, Stokeley Carmichael, Malamud, Nkrumah, and Saul Bellow. But none of the nominees had given up what Bernard Applebaum had given up. He even gave up the possibility of applause.

"He ate his meat walking," they said of Jonathan Swift, that old nobleman, who, when fierce indignities smote his heart, walked, his thin, tall frame having become the bones of his sorrow. He never sat at his table. So it was with Bernard.

When indignities smote Bernard he walked, all day, late at

night, all night. He quit his job to walk. He quit eating to walk. He quit drinking and walked until his lips cracked, and he would find himself near a public drinking fountain, fishy with bubble-gum.

His ears, like a blind man's, became acute, his sense of poetry accurate. He became the recorder of life, close to the source, in a notebook. Let not a word escape the chronicler. He became so intense about accuracy, so concerned about not missing a single word that he wrote until his forearm ached, and the faster he wrote, the more rapidly the people around him talked.

He had a pile of children's speckled notebooks in his room, on the metal guard of the radiator. He was waiting for the right moment to make organization, to revise, for he had to keep record-ing while the record was playing.

Bernard gave up reading, not to distract himself. He heard so much that he thought he read a great deal.

He overheard Thomas talking about Saul Bellow. "The writer must live in the gutter, says Bellow," and Bernard took the motto for his own. He knew no one up on the curb was with it.

Systematically he gave up. He gave up cleanliness, for clean-liness was next to phonyness. His apartment developed lice. Lice, he decided, were victims of social prejudice. The same with the bedbug he saw when he made up his studio couch. He kept cigarettes. He didn't give up cigarettes. More easily than ciga-rettes he gave up family; mother, brother, lawyer father and small town. His old dog too he gave up. His family, to his annoyance, never gave him up and sent tokens of matching coffee cups and saucers for four, knitted sweaters, the transistor radio, socks, and once, after Bernard had been home for a visit to collect his blankets, underwear.

He gave up friends. Married friends first, for it was like they lived uptown, beyond the subways, in this subway-less town. Hometown friends, of course, and cousins his own age. In order to do the latter, he had to give up the telephone, which was more painful than leaving people. Some things gave themselves up. The transistor in its plastic case fell in his bathroom and gave up.

He didn't intend to give up love, but without a telephone, without cleanliness, with lice in his apartment, it gave itself up. Slowly.

A girl admired his mother's knitted sweater and had a sudden urge to knit him together, too. He loved her in the bar. Once, extravagantly, he bought her beer and chips, then ripped the package of chips in the middle, a cornucopia for her. But bar is just that, a line drawn, an obstruction against daylight and responsibility. When she made a kind of housekeeping in the bar, expecting him a certain time every day, always to sit at her booth, it was monogamous, and he couldn't hear enough that way. Besides, he had filled his notebook with her already.

When Thomas saw him writing in his notebook, his knit sweater loose in the wrists where he had lost weight, Thomas asked, "How many hours credit you getting for that?"

The others never mentioned it, something sensitive, unless one contributed to it.

"Bernard," said Rube, who shared circumcision with him, "I have something for your notebook." Bernard listened while Rube told the conversation, then Bernard would go off by himself and write furiously, his tongue between his lips.

"Let me tell you something for your notebook," the bar owner's wife said. "A personal experience with Isadora Duncan." Only the story came out of Shaw.

Castro was added to the New Nobility, as blind, foolish, hairy and noble as Samson.

"Larry Rivers," said Glenn, but these were literary minded people and ignorant of art. "King of the organs. Great nude oils of his mother-in-law are astonishing. That's brave."

They looked blank. He tried again.

"Nevelson," said Glenn, "and her little black boxes." But they had never heard of the sculptor. She hadn't been part of the curriculum.

To Bernard the list began to include more than it excluded. Thomas tried again to please Edward. His Martin Luther King had been rejected. "The two King Jameses," he said, to put them off the track, "James Baldwin and James Meredith."

Old hat. "Leroi," said Edward. "The King, Leroi Jones."

The time came when Bernard had used up his speckled notebooks and the dime store where he bought them ordered no more, nor expected any further orders. That made the first difficulty in carrying out his noble purpose. Plain paper got mixed and

lost. He had never owned a stapler or paper clips. Spiral sheets
tore out, as did loose leaf. It wasn't the same.

He found himself, in his distress, walking and talking. Indeed,
that day he had stopped at an old brick wall and written on the
side of it with a piece of loose brick. He was not the type to
write in bathrooms, nor make mustaches on bus signs, but he had
to accommodate himself to the new medium. Scratching on side-
walks, marking brick walls, the stoop of his old rooming house.

"I've read it! I've read it!" he shouted at the bar to Thomas
about a book not yet published.

"I've heard it! I've heard it all!" he said to Rube, refusing a
new story.

Bernard walked more at night now, sleeping exhaustedly in
the daytime. He walked and moved his shoes slowly, his feet
sockless. He sometimes found that he could manage a block or two
before he sank to his knees. Sometimes he would walk a block on
his knees. He ripped his pants.

Then Bernard, the new nobility, erected himself, off his knees,
onto his feet. With purpose, even lightly and quickly, he entered
the bar. The first time in a month. He issued an invitation—his
notebooks, at his room.

People are loathe to leave bars for any purpose, but he persuaded Thomas, who hoped for little, and Rube, who was compassionate, and Edward, because Bernard had supported Stokeley,
and Glenn, who respected literary people for their spelling.

They went to Bernie's house, slowly, following him, noticing
marks on the walls along the way. Marks on the stoop, the banis-
ters, the wall paper, even scratched with something into glass. In
his hallway Bernard flung the door open and invited them in.
They, less than twelve, less than disciples, crowded the one couch,
the one chair, and waited for the notebooks.

Bernard, his coat still on, removed them from the radiator,
counted them, shuffled them into chronological order.

Thomas opened the book first, to read The Word. He saw lines
of scribbles, dashes, wavy lines, page after page, never missing a
page, often missing a line.

Bernard was tuned in to the wave length of the world. He was
close to the origin of it, heard it all, felt it all. And he, only he,
had the copyrights to it.

11. The Story of Rube (Bravery, A Brave Thing)

Rube was a success at hatred. During Brotherhood Week Rube was NOT convinced by the bus posters. It was never the season for love. Each holiday was an ascetic experience. On Yom Kippur he re-examined his soul but could not ask his victims' pardon; they were anonymous.

Rube hated all things German. His father pronounced it, "Chermann," and had objected when Rube studied it in college. In Rube's family this hatred was acceptable. Indeed, Rube limited his hatred, for his family's, like pouring light, ran over all things Gentile or Colored.

Rube's early reading was a Belsen Black Book. Rube, a good Jewish eater, lost weight then. In his sleep his nightmares were Nazis in the closet. He took to leaving on a bedroom lamp and his closet door ajar. When newsreels came out, Rube went in search of his hatred. He carried forever, in his extra stomach, an army blanket of bones. He had seen liberating soldiers carrying the breathing bones of people between them in an army blanket.

At Passover, always a good son, he participated strongly, reserving for himself the right to open the door and see, as it was written, if anyone were listening outside.

"And they slew the blameless and pure, men and women and little ones, with vapors of poison and burned them with fire." Rube's hatred was most intense when he prayed, in the new Martyr's Passover prayer, for the incinerated. In bakery shops and shoe stores of his neighborhood he saw posters commemorating the Warsaw ghetto uprising, the letters leaping, burnt stick fingers.

Rube longed to punch people in bars for saying kike; it bugged him that no one said kike anymore. Where the slogan of the early 40's had been, "Boycott Japan," the slogan of the 50's and 60's was "Buy German." Rube held out against Telefunken and the Volkswagen ("Just plain volks," he told himself), the Voitland, and, at his bar, Lowenbrau.

"They're just plain volks," he repeated to Thomas, trying to explain his hatred, but Thomas was too impatient to have abiding hatreds.

Those around him had a world view, so he kept his parochialism to himself, but documented it. He centered on Wernher von

Braun, beginning with a *New Yorker* profile on the hero. He kept articles on Von Braun in a dresser drawer until his socks and shorts were crowded out; then he moved the growing file to a metal cabinet under his desk. It became a scholarly job, a curatorship that he tended.

There were fillers on the bottom of page one. Von Braun, at his Alabama home, hating to tend grass and pouring green concrete over his lawn. Von Braun addressing striking atomic plant workers, reminding them of their patriotic duties. The Huntsville citizens greeting Von Braun's family from Germany moving into new homes. On a back page Rube found an addendum. A short, thin-faced, heavily spectacled New York theater director revealed that his father, a noted Rabbi, had perished as a slave laborer for Von Braun.

Rube brought newspapers into the bar each day, not consciously looking for Von Braun, but reading carefully. It was Thomas, over his shoulder, who pointed out the lecture in the suburb, Von Braun the guest speaker.

"Your hero is coming next Friday," said Thomas. "Where will you be? Wernher Von Braun's coming to town," he chanted.

"Forget your hatred," said friend Edward. "If I can, you can. 'Love your enemies,' says the Reverend King. 'You can't hate them,' says James Baldwin."

"It is a sin to forget," said Rube, rabbinical for a moment. Against his chest he pressed his palms. His overly wide tie hung in front of his wrists. The tie was fashionable now, despite him. "Evil is not fashionable. Why is it not evil now and it was then? It was evil in the Middle Ages."

Rube's nose began to run a little, as it did when he drank sometimes.

"I'm angry from the Middle Ages, from York, from France and Germany. From the time of yellow caps and stars on chests. EVIL. EV-il."

"Yfel," said Thomas, "a good Anglo-Saxon word, one of the few four letter words left. Let us recognize the need for evil." Thomas turned on his non-turning bar stool. "That was the trouble with Emerson, actually. He never recognized evil."

"I personally came out of Egypt," mumbled Rube. He stud-

ied the newspaper article. His cheeks flushed. To have one's
enemy nearby is like unexpectedly encountering one's beloved.
"I can't go," he said, shy, a wallflower. "It's the second night
of Passover. I have to help make the seder."

Thomas and Glenn cut him out. The girl Celia entered, overheard the last of it and moved from the bar to the booth. Rube
had been ignoble.

The first night's seder Rube, in a new dark suit, clean white
shirt, wedding white satin yarmelke, read of the power of his
Lord: "What ails thee, O sea, that thou didst flee; Jordan, that
thou turnest back?" During the ceremony Rube spilled three
drops of sweet red wine into his white dish, and read, "Blood,
Fire, Pillars of Smoke."

He studied the seder plate and told the time of his life from
the placement of the objects. The shank bone was at 1 o'clock.
(It sorrowed him that his mother never used a lamb's shank anymore. "A chicken shank," she comforted him.) At 4 o'clock
on the plate was haroseth, at 8 o'clock the parsley, at 10 o'clock
the egg of rebirth, and off 12, the bitter herbs. The shank bone
had once bloodied the doors to warn off the angel of death. The
haroseth was a wine-nut-apple mixture like the mortar of bricks
the slave laborers made in Egypt. Rube stopped and thought
again, with the bitter herbs, of Von Braun.

The second night of the seder, Rube, in the same costume, new
black suit, starched white shirt, satin, shiny yarmelke, seated
himself in the audience of the lecture hall. Von Braun's brother,
a missile expert for an automotive firm, sat on the platform,
along with the chairman. Rube had entered late and the audience
was already laughing. Von Braun was making anecdotes.

"I was asked what kind of people I expected to find once we
landed on another planet, and I answered that the nuts are
here, not there," Herr von Braun said.

"An old woman asked me once, 'Why do we have to do all
these things, try to get to the moon? Why can't we just sit back
and watch TV and do the things that God intended?'" The
audience laughed at her unsophistication, but not Rube. She of
the story was his ally, one in that hall, but then not in the room.

Von Braun concluded the lecture, reminding the audience that

this was their battle, morally and financially, and their support
was necessary to build greater thrusting power.

Von Braun had charmed his audience. They trusted him.

"Idolatry," Rube thought, and, from the Psalms of Praise,
"Like them are those who make them, and those who trust in
them."

At this moment of Germanic hubris, Rube arose, perspiry,
unlovely even in his good suit. He looked around at the suburban
audience which was avoiding his eyes, his skull cap.

"Here I am," said Rube to the local chairman calling on the
questioners. "I would like to ask one main question and sub-
divide it into four parts."

The chairman, intimidated into democracy, nodded.

"The main question is," Rube said, flushing, hoarse voiced,
"Why is this night different from all other nights? On all other
nights. . . ." Rube went on unhurriedly to ask the meaning of
the bread of affliction, of the bitter herbs, of the dipping of those
herbs, and the seder position of the free man—leaning against a
pillow.

That night Rube, the youngest son, asked the questions innocence has asked of its elders for thousands of years, questions that
have had to be asked and answered, and yet again asked and
answered.

III. The Flying Young Glenn

If Rube asked public questions, I, the artist, ask private ones.
I would swing out, come back free, no nets, no one to catch. I'm
not afraid of the act.

I read, last year, where a circus family fell from grace. From
the high wire they fell, from the trapeze. This year, a Wallenda
walked up the slanting wire to the globe under the top of the tent.
She swayed that globe, slowly, to one side and back, the other
way, and back. Then she slid off. I would rather sway the
world and fall off than give up the climb.

I see the world in what Francis gave up since he and Ingeborg
married. We visit, while she nurses their huge baby, under swords
of Ethiopia, puppets of Milano, South Pacific daggers, American
Indian headdresses, Sicilian tambourines and carnival masks,
North African sheep skins. Francis has grown a mustache to

make up for what he lost. He paints in the dining room, strong
colors, strange fantasies, of the travels he once took. When he
uses up his memories, will he turn to pastels of mothers and
children?

"I hear," says Francis, pulling on his mustache, "that each
child is one hour painting time less a day. I guess if I count the
overtime at work I have put in now, it's more than that."

I took my girl over there once and Francis pressed gifts on us
as we departed. He even wanted to give us an oil painting, a circus scene in Italy. I finally took his only print of an etching,
pale but beautiful of a man with airforce insignia on his out-
stretched arms, flying around the world. I'm going that way too!

I'm ensnared but in honorable struggle. No wives, however
quiet, not any babies with sucking mouths, whose fists clench and
toes stiffen when they eat. Nothing personal, I told my girl, to
break it off—and I've been trying ever since. But:

She puts Vigoro into our memories.

"Make it a fine, brave ending," I told her at our last meeting.
She keeps tending the plot.

"Be good to my memory," she had said, smiling with sorrow
as I kissed the top of her head in a final, public kiss.

And then I forgot her. But she called and calls yet, to hang
up after four rings. I wait for that fourth ring before I answer
the phone. In my little apartment the ring is too loud. I can't
crap without being lifted off the seat by the sound of it. I can
reach the phone from everywhere in my apartment, practically,
from the table, the bed, the sink, the one window. When she
rings and I don't answer, the furniture is still vibrating with the
call.

Two Sundays ago I picked up the phone, my mouth full of
supper.

"I'm in pain," she said.

I wasn't ready for it. After all, what can you do about someone's pain when your mouth is filled with food?

"No," I told her and hung up. I haven't spoken to her since,
but the furniture and I are waiting.

She bugged me; she was on my back. A thing can't get that
way. I didn't look at her (with my artist's eye); she looked at me.
Her eyes followed my hand movements. I'm a chain smoker. She

watched me smoke until the pleasure went out of it. My arms
became stiff and webbed with smoke.

It was clean and crisp at first, sharp lines between us, but then
our relationship became smeared charcoal from overhandling.

I am a temperate fellow by nature, if not by habit. I do many
things to excess, but not relationships. I am a once a week date,
and I read, paint, even work for money when I must. She is
someone of daily wants. She phones before a date in anticipa-
tion; afterwards, in summation.

I would take her once in my room and be fulfilled. I would
tell her so, subtly, my finger on her forehead, on her nose. Then
I'd dress to get on with other business. But she lies there cuddling
the memory of it. If I'm not next to her she bends the pillow
around her, the blanket or her coat.

"Get off my back," I said, and she did, loving me uncritically,
and, therefore, not enough.

"Put yourself in my place," I told her. She did, for a moment,
surprised, but then she forgot.

We parted on a crisp spring day when she talked, and, out
of the corner of my eye, I watched a sparrow drinking drops
from a public faucet.

We had loved each other for the first time on a slushy winter
day. I drove out to the lake where we watched the grey.

"We'll put the color in the day," she said, and I grabbed her.

The first time I missed. Everything wrong. I wasn't new at it,
but each girl is a different way. She waited me out, until, when
I was swinging, I didn't want to take her out anywhere again,
no movie, no drive, no restaurant. I only wanted her in.

She liked my work, *enthusiastically*. She liked each stage of a
thing until it was completed. I mean, each unfinished stage. I had
a small portrait I was working out, on a linen-covered panel. I
treated the Negro head solidly, brightly, realistically, at first. She
loved it. Then I blurred it, criss-crossed the flat face, muddied the
color. After a while she came around to my way of seeing it
and loved it. But I was ahead of her and had the third stage
ready to blot out the second. She argued for the second stage as
if it were her own, but when she saw the third, that I had
completed largely with palette knife since her last visit, she nar-

rowed her eyes and nodded her head. I could do no wrong, and how could that be? The responsibility of it!

On the phone she knew, at the other end of the line, when my eyes were averted, looking at my own work on the easel. She could pause in the middle of a sentence, insisting on attention. If I loved her in bed and saw my work on the wall at the same time, I'd keep two things going in my head at once. Her eyes would make me choose between her body, which was becoming familiar, and the painting, which was always new.

When we were ending the love between us, beautiful, perfect things happened to confuse us. A clear winter day we went for a drive, looking for trees, and found a wooded cemetery. A group was finishing its business, quietly as snow, and dispersed when we started walking hand in hand. Near a stone wall we built the perfect angel of death, a snowman, with twig arms from the cemetery trees. We put Canadian pennies in for eyes and a rag someone must have dragged from an auto became his scarf. My love embraced that snowman, indenting his body on one side with her coat buttons, and on the other with the pressure of her bare fingers. We left him silent, mouthless, at home.

A plane passed, writing in the sky, snow in the sky, and we embraced in the cemetery against a tree until a caretaker came out of the little house, limping badly, using a cane, to see who we were. We beat him out of that place, and he shouted puffs of breath at us.

Another time, when the weather warmed, we walked from my place through a vacant lot. She took off her jacket and pressed her torso against the trunk of an old, rough elm, her breasts rounded like knots of the tree. I was the dog, sniffing her out.

I turn my face, just as I can, with some ease, avert my eyes. One does not dwell on a thing, regret, or long for interference. I'm packing for the world.

"I love you," she cried. "All the time."

"No one can love all the time," I said fiercely, and learned that I can be cruel to women. It isn't even unpleasant. I loved, the few times left, with cruelty, watching her face until she said, "Boss! Boss!" Then moving away separate, not talking, complete unto myself.

Then, as our present ended, she gave us a past. She talked

like a virgin, of our first kiss, how my fingers played with her face, her mouth, into her opened mouth, eensie, weensie spider. She spoke, and chilled me, of seeing my sleeves rolled up and paint on my shirt.

She had us loving each other that first time smoothly. The Thin Man and his wife, William Powell and Myrna Loy, with cigarette holders.

"Stop it," I said. "You're distorting the picture. Leave it bad, don't pretty it up."

She reworked all those original times, piling fresh dirt around them to make them grow, giving them a fragrance, a lifelessness.

"You're killing me," I said one day, trying to cry but unhappily clear-eyed. "You're leaving me out of the past."

"If there's no present," she said, emerging as a housewife, "tend the past."

And she wanted me to tell her how she looked when I first spotted her at a party, how it was love at first sight.

I, the pilot, would soar. She would have me a snowman with twig arms, a heavy-bodied, domesticated fowl. Or a sparrow drinking from a public foundation, on that day in early spring.

The earth has thawed. I whir my arms to keep the dirt from around my face and over my chest. If I don't keep moving, my eyelids will be heavy with it. I move, away from the present, and the false past, away from the keening song of the cemetery.

IV. Edward, Keep the Dream Green

"I had a dream last night," the Reverend King's voice was broadcast from the auditorium to the throng that couldn't get inside. "I had a dream last night," and the Reverend dreamt of black man and white man together, not affectionately but respectfully.

Edward squirmed on the grass along the waterfront. The river was despoiled by industries but whistles of excursion boats still gave an illusion of river.

"I had a dream last night," Reverend King shouted, while the audience applauded. And the Reverend dreamt of all people voting, being housed and schooled together.

The speech had come when Edward was weary. There had been a long fund-raising campaign. The Dexter Bethlehem

Church had given. The Mayflower Baptist had given. The state highway commissioner had contributed. The chairman of the state fair had stood up to the call. There were two hours of giving. The people outside the auditorium were passed among with jingling canteens. Something kept Edward from giving. He couldn't give to NAACP, to CORE, to SNCC, to Evers' fatherless children. He couldn't put his coin into a canteen.

The day was hot, the refreshment stand cruelly far off.

Edward had not marched. He came to march, then lowered his posters and stood to one side, apart from it, watching the Negro and white motorcycle cops (like matched horses, he thought) who led the parade. He saw the mayor, a defeated governor, a police commissioner march. King led the parade for a token block, then was taken in a limousine to the auditorium on the riverfront.

The fund raising had embarrassed Edward. What will the white people think? A woman near Edward shouted the song, "We Shall Overcome," like she was at a slum church meeting and Edward cringed again.

He had enjoyed the walk last week. The group had met and marched into Grosse Pointe. Edward had never had occasion to go there. He smelled the lake, saw the art theater and dress shops in the business section, the modern local library with its donated collection of art books.

In Edward's four-family-flat neighborhood the ancient elms had kept the streets 10 degrees cooler than here, but there the grass was often untended—disagreement between landlord and four separate tenants—turning to sand or dirt that spilled on the driveway and sidewalk. The houses needed painting. The screened-in porches had holes. The garages were unsafe, bricks or roof beams falling and often catching fire. Edward only listed these things with his eye, though, not so much with his heart. His neighborhood was dark, the old elms having grown over the street lights, and the city had taken its good time cutting the branches that lay on the lights or had overgrown electric wires. Children played in the alleys, but garbage disposal was infrequent in his section of town. Nor did the city street cleaners go through, early in the morning, with their water tanks and flagella.

In Edward's neighborhood the shopping area had changed

rapidly, so that there were still kosher butchers, whose customers came to them from the suburbs, around the spare rib houses. Ladies dress shops had moved out, leaving dissembled parts of a mannequin, where no other business moved in. The dime store was self-service now, with cheap dresses.

"Where have they all gone?" Edward thought, seeing, on warm summer nights like this, his people promenading in the Southern manner. "Where have those other people gone?"

Edward didn't want a checkerboard of faces, just recognition some place by others.

Yet when it happened it was an unexpected thing.

Edward had left his friends at the bar one night to go to the music booths of the Main Library. Outside the Library Edward met a white girl, someone not from the bar, certainly not his neighborhood. Someone who had sat next to him years ago in an undergraduate course. She was back again, Edward saw, carrying blue examination books for the week of Finals, and a new brief-case. Her initials in gold on the briefcase were unfamiliar to Edward. Married, Edward thought, probably getting her education certificate. Edward thought all this while nodding hello, not too broadly, for he had been trained by his mama to caution. He catalogued her faster than a library science major. She had been all right sitting next to him, shy and uncomfortable, but trying friendship.

On the day of their final in that class he and she had finished at the same moment, handed in their blue books, walked outdoors and continued walking. They walked the few miles downtown to see "The Jolson Story." Edward squirmed while the actor played in blackface. "Boo," said his new friend next to him suddenly at the screen. "BOOOOOOOOOooo." They laughed, parted later. He phoned her once or twice. She was hesitant, and they hadn't seen each other (surely it was planned; if meetings are fateful then maybe separations are too) since about 1946.

"I'm back again," she said, lifting her briefcase.

"So I see," said Edward, the man.

("We don't want to marry your daughters," James Baldwin had said. "But where have all the flowers gone?" sang Edward's mind, a folk song, or was it a Thurber fable of a man, a woman, and a flower—all white, all colorless?)

Without a word Edward carried her briefcase for her inside the revolving door where the library funneled all patrons. Edward felt like a porter, leading her, lifting the case over obstacles. He wished he could return the case. There were benches on the first landing, surrounding a wall map. Edward placed the briefcase on a bench.

"I'm going to a music room," he declared, a little too strongly.

"I've never been there," she said, unthinking.

Then, as a Southern-trained gentleman, he had to issue the invitation.

"Would you care to join me?" he asked, but this time let her lift her own briefcase.

"I'm studying for Finals," she said.

"It's quiet there," he meant not to persuade.

She, an indefinite person, was always making resolutions. She resolved to go with Edward. They mounted the wide, marble stairs. Edward, seeing the names chiseled on a band near the ceiling, quoted Mr. Dooley to her: "A library is architecture, not literature. . . . The most celebrated dead authors will be honored havin' their names painted on th' wall . . . The live authors will stand outside an' wish they were dead."

She had never heard of Mr. Dooley, and this was another thing that separated them.

"How is your poetry?" she asked, remembering suddenly.

"It's too late," he said. Last fall he had published a Rimbaud-type of poem in a little review magazine, but it had come after too much sending, too long waiting for the return of manuscripts (the smaller the magazine, the longer the time lapse until the rejection). He was printed and it was his epitaph.

He felt his skin warming; he had once sent her a poem. It was a harmless poem, but people are nervous about poems.

In the sound-proofed music room there was scarcely room for her briefcase. The door shut fast on tight springs. They sat knee to knee, the area so small they could count the holes in the soundproofing, irregularly little and big, spaced like code.

Edward pressed his palms together, with no supplication in mind. His eyes were beautiful, ascendant, under Gothic brows.

"How does one talk to you," he wanted to know.

"There's nothing to tell," she started, and said overmuch giving him the benefit of her last twenty years.

He had only meant, How do people who have been close for a moment touch each other again, without Auld Lang Syne?

His eyes became glazed donuts, held wide open with sleepiness. His hands dropped from their oriental pose, and he, seeing her thighs, touched her legs with three fingers of each hand, in butter-fly kisses.

Her leg kicked forward. He, only reacting to woman, sat in the stiff-backed chair, unable to lean away.

"A knee-jerking liberal," one of his friends had called her. That hit it. That hit it.

"Don't hate them," Baldwin had said. "Love them, not with affection, but in the deeper sense," the Reverend King had preached.

She opened her briefcase on her lap, making a school desk there. She hunted in her purse for her glasses; they were not there, nor in her briefcase. She debated going back to class, but, in vanity, wore no glasses in class.

"Everyday another bit of me is missing," she said. "It's 'When Johnny Comes Marching Home Again,' without all his parts, only these are detached parts that I lose."

He was suddenly interested.

"I lost the screw on my glasses," she said, "and an ear piece fell off. Another time I lost the chrome design, but only on one side, so my face became an irregular design. Periodically I lose my glasses. Always during vacations they disappear so I won't read. But this is the first time during finals that I've lost my glasses. The last time I had misplaced them for so long that a draft came into my good eye and it chilled whenever I read."

She was telling him something, but this was the high priced puzzle with 250 pieces.

"I lose everything," she said, and her eyes without glasses moistened. "I lose coat buttons and don't bother to sew them on. I had a flowered raincoat with a green velvet collar and buttons. A green velvet button came off, gathered dust on my dresser, slipped behind the dresser, right against the wall, and now it's gone, along with the discarded coat.

"I have a girlfriend who loses things when it comes time to

depart so every departure is prolonged with hunting for her. But no one loses their glasses or their vision for as long as I do."

He watched her talk, her mouth and tongue dark in her face, while his mouth and tongue lightened his face. She was emptying lint from her purse now.

"Into the kitchen cabinet I'd put my glasses," she said, "into bill drawers, between pages of our Webster's Unabridged, on top of the TV, and, finally, where I last recall seeing them, in the breadbox."

Now she said it, said the original hesitancy twenty years ago. "To keep track I have to marshal the whole family on glasses hunts, the children in the upstairs drawers, my husband retracing my steps from the ironing board to the glove compartment of the car. It takes all of us to keep track of me. And," a tear escaped and fell to wrinkle her examination book, "when they aren't all with me, when I must keep track alone, I lose bits of myself. I unravel."

She was pleading for pity, for a controlled environment. She wanted minute commitment and aid. She wanted coin in the canteen.

"Ah," said Edward to himself, his dream was still green. "I know where all of them have gone. Inside themselves. That's where they've been."

And he could carry his placard, Open Housing, down their streets, and stop at their houses. They were hiding inside. They had long been there.

V. Man in his Mind is Drying

Celia was a woman among the boys and girls. She had married twenty years ago, too young and nervous to dance at her own wedding. She had borne children in various stylish ways, from natural childbirth, where she saw her daughter's hair reflected in the mirror above the delivery table, to twilight sleep, where she knew nothing of the delivery, only realizing later it was she, undisciplined, screaming in the distance. Being wife and mother separated her from the group at the bar, that still spoke of mother resentfully. More than this, Celia was of the 1950's, they of the '60's.

"Celia," Bernard had asked her, before he became so rattled, "Do you *feel* different?"

"No, honey," she told him, annoyed, "I was just at a party you weren't invited to."

Celia taught in the adult education program of the university where her husband held an instructorship. He baby-sat on the two days that she went down early to research her lecture, teach and loosen up in the bar afterwards.

One day, during the summer session, after a long drought, while the children suffered from prickly heat, Celia walked down a path where the sun was merciless. A veterans' mall, in honor of students killed in World War II, had been torn up to make room for classroom buildings. The buildings shone white, pre-cast concrete, like more sidewalk. Along the path the university had planted geraniums.

"There is perversity in the university," an old woman said suddenly to Celia. The woman leaned on a cane. Her shoes were white straw, baby doll. "Perversity in the richest nation on earth." she said. She had a faint, slavic accent. "No rain is not good. Those flowers are dry."

The geraniums were thin but not yet dying.

"Everything is dying. The farmers know it."

On her jacket was an unravelling paper flower.

"The vegetables in the ground are not getting enough water. The fruit of the trees is dying also." The old woman lifted her cane and touched her head with the handle. "And man, in his mind, is drying."

Celia told Ruben, Bernard, Thomas, Edward and Glenn that man in his mind was drying. Rube was reading his newspaper, looking for Wernher Von Braun. He found no Wernher but Von Braun's brother was being named correspondent in an English divorce case. Rube was pleased, then dismissed the material as too rarefied for his collection.

"If man's mind is drying, his body's not," said Rube and showed the group pictures of the Miss Universe contest.

"Here's Miss Free Cuba," said Rube. "That's a new contestant."

"Who will be there at that contest," asked Celia, "with Miss Free Cuba? Miss Nationalist China? Miss South Vietnam, Miss

South Korea and Miss West Germany." Celia leaned back and
drank her beer. "There's perversity in the university," she said,
"in the Miss University."

But Celia had left the world in 1951. Her mind, like a microfilm machine, had rolled the pages of 1951, turning slower, slower,
more horrified, to stop with the type illuminated and enlarged.

In 1951 Celia saw the Kefauver crimes investigation committee on her television set in Manhattan. Costello said, "I am begging you to treat me as a human being." And Senator Tobey
said, "But solution there is none, Save in the rule of Christ alone."
Came the end of the Hiss case in 1951, with Hiss handcuffed to a
mail thief. The thief hid his face in a black hat, but Hiss,
manacled, walked unblinking into the flashbulb light. His tweed
coat was open, his vest respectable, his fingers long and veined,
his mouth soft, as he went to serve his five-year sentence.

In 1951 Celia found she lived near Ethel Rosenberg's mother,
in an apartment building on the Harlem River. Ethel and Julius
were convicted, he looking at her through a locked wire door, she,
solemn faced, with a cloth coat and small Persian lamb collar.
They sang, in adjoining cells, to each other, she, Puccini's "One
Fine Day," and he "The Battle Hymn of the Republic." *Time*
called him "sallow Julius Rosenberg," but Celia read where Judge
Kaufman called them more: "Plain, deliberate, contemplated murder is dwarfed in magnitude by comparison with the crime you
have committed . . . I believe your conduct in putting into the
hands of the Russians the A-bomb . . . has already caused the
Communist aggression in Korea."

Judge Kaufman, inaccurate in fact, stared at Celia from the
newspaper. She became an anti-Semite, looking at the mama boy
face, the pudgy features, the oblique glance, in that era of disloyal
Jews and the one terribly loyal judge. The list was added to for
her with David Greenglass, fingering his sister and brother-in-law,
Harry Gold, the courier, and Morton Sobell.

Celia moved with her husband from New York to the Midwest,
but she never left the 38th parallel, the Yalu River or 1300
casualties a week. And she ceased casting her ballot.

Once everything had appealed to Celia. She giggled with sentiment.

"Celia, oh Celia," sang Thomas L. Thomas and Jessica Dragonette through her childhood radio cabinet. Celia dreamt of romance or a homeland to come. Even later, during her courting days, Musack, in its piped, wordless songs, brought tears to her eyes and set California palms to growing in her heart.

"Come, my Celia," her husband used Ben Jonson to encourage her in "the sports of love."

Celia loved immediately and befriended warmly. But, "Be mobile," said her husband, signing a new one-year contract. "Leave unintelligible traces, wave the sand."

Celia had made stability of colonial signs, colonial furniture, a bestiary, or adopted distant cousins in Los Angeles and even eastern Alabama.

"Who owns us?" her husband would ask, piling cartons of books into the station wagon. He took the cat to the humane society but retained its carrying case for the next city. "Do we own the furniture or does it own us?" he wanted to know, thinner and taller than the customers who came for the baby dressers, cribs, refrigerator and marred desk, from his ad in the Negro weekly.

Friendships that had become dear to Celia were hosed down with departure and neglected before the farewell.

"Why lay up treasures which moth and rust will corrupt and thieves break through and steal?" asked her husband, citing an older nobility.

With the lack of voter registration, Celia also stopped bidding farewell. She found duplication everywhere, a drug store country with toothpaste and hair tonic, an A & P country, the land of Sears and J. C. Penney.

"Where's the action?" Celia suddenly asked the group. Surprisingly she pleaded. "Tell me where the action is and I'll go there." She rose.

Glenn entered the bar then. Behind him, through the opened door, Celia glimpsed the old woman of the drought limping by. Celia sat down again wildly. "Erosion," she shouted, "what holds it together?" She panted, then wept, remembering the red earth of Alabama. "The roots are too thin."

Thomas, rarely moved, never sensual, turned to Celia, who was one of three on his side of the booth. One arm, unused to embrace, went behind her neck and knocked her hair comb loose. Thomas' other hand rested on Celia's womanly stomach.

"This is celiac," said Thomas, "and this is Celia, of the stomach of life. Here's where the action is."

What a surprise of love there was then. Rube, on the other side of the booth, pressed Celia's left hand and lifted it to kiss. No one had ever kissed her hand, with its thinning, inexpensive gold band.

"You're mobile," said Bernard, warming for Celia's own embarrassment, "like Ruth."

"Dear God," said Celia astonished and her mouth opened, while small water therein leaked out unheeded, as it did from her baby's mouth when his thumb slipped out during the nap.

Edward, not comfortable enough with white people to kiss them, smiled and smiled at Celia. "Lucky husband," he said, "to have all that action."

Celia leaned back, crowded in the booth as she was in her bed every morning, when the children and cat climbed in, one by one, come dawn, to dislodge her from her pillow, to make her shoulder ache with turning sideways. Her husband, always sleeping on the outside, shut off all alarm every morning, while the baby, the youngest, snapped the shade on the new day.

Celia could vote again. She left the bar for her night class, the tincture of sunset, pale red, medicinal.

VI. Look Not at the Sun with a Naked Eye

Edward, Celia, Bernard, Rube and Glenn sat up during the wake of Thomas. Their wake was at the bar. They bought bottled beer, not tap, in honor. Rube wore his Passover suit. Celia hired a baby sitter and came with her husband. Some of them wept, Edward did and Rube, but Celia first, for, in the parade of tears, a woman is majorette.

Rube became pompous and ritualistic, his voice accented: "Wherein is the nobility in the descent through sin? Orpheus descending didn't make it, with the best of intentions, nor, in a way, did Thomas."

The parable that unfolded of Thomas was spoken in the chronologically reversed order of mourning. It was established that Thomas was 33, the age of crucifixion, a coincidence which had disturbed him.

"When he was 30," Edward said, "he started gathering disciples."

Thomas had spent more time at student interviews. That year, also mourning his youth, he had accelerated his research, rising at 5 A.M. to write in his parents' quiet house. He stayed at the library after his lectures to avoid duties as eldest son, those of driving his mother to the doctor, seeing about the taxes, picking up nephews and nieces.

Celia sorrowed. She knew from experience that grief lasts about three months. "He was worried about his own spiritual death," she said, "when he tested our nobility."

"He wrote me off for lust," said Glenn, there alone without the girl.

Bernard raised a finger to recite. "Sloth," he said.

"Gluttony," said Rube. "And he said that I committed the capital sin of anger with Wernher von Braun."

In the seminary Thomas attended for three years he had measured himself again the cardinal virtues and capital sins, remaining ascetic in everything but excessive in height. He was underweight permanently, under-colored, his eyes a pale blue, his hair colorless, and straight, and the teeth in that long, thin face had grown jammed together, forming a prehistoric double row.

Rube was thoughtful, "Thomas was conqueror, but the Prize conquered him."

Rube was speaking of Thomas the prudent and temperate, Thomas the just, Thomas filled with untried fortitude until he was selected by Pulitzer Prize for his biography. Thomas wrote of the Nineteenth Century Catholics, Orestes Brownson and the Paulist Father Isaac Hecker, both of Brook Farm.

"Then," said Edward, "he was the Ziegfield boy, walking down a set of stairs with Dennis Morgan singing. He was Mr. Universe. He was of the world of the stage, the silver screen and radio."

"More precisely," said Celia, "the world of the carpeted lecture hall and educational TV."

"And parties," said Edward.

Thomas never did get to go home to his parents' quiet house, nor did he take time to pay the taxes, paint the woodwork and take nephews and nieces on excursion boats.

"What was he first?" asked Rube. "Glutton. That came first."

Thomas' stomach stretched and pushed his belt forward, while the rest of him, not used to it, stayed thin. The Business Bureau, thinking him a city attraction, catered to him at the Yacht Club. He was given a medal by the Irish mayor of the city and an amity award from the Jewish Community Council. He had steak at the Yacht Club, whiskey with the mayor, and stuffed derma at the Kosher Rainbow Terrace.

"The talk was of food," Rube said. "I'd ask 'Thomas, how did the lecture trip go?' And he'd say food. 'Massachusetts has steaks that cut like butter.' "

"He committed a worse sin than gluttony," said Edward, out of sympathy with Thomas. "He became a tourist. Without living here, he thought we had the same address."

This had happened one day at the bar when Celia was talking about selling her house and moving away again with the coming school year, in search of tenure. She had sold to Negro clients, the first on her block.

"All the colored buyers," Celia told Edward, Rube, Glenn and Bernard, "had one child, just one child, usually one grown child. They were like Depression couples. And when they went out to see the backyard the women got on the swings and their husbands pushed them."

Thomas looked down at the group in the booth from his stool at the bar. He exhibited pride, the expert now in all things besides the American Nineteenth Century.

"Edward," Thomas called.

Edward had to work his way out of the booth.

"Edward," Thomas said, "do you know how realtors designate Negro clients?"

"With cryptograms," said Edward, disentangling himself from Pulitzer Prize affection.

"Double X," Thomas informed Edward and the group, denied entrance to no world now. "Negroes are Double X clients. And do you know what white clients are?"

"What?" asked Edward, not really part of the game.

"Just clients," said Thomas, and turned back to the bar. Edward, dismissed, returned to the booth.

Thomas turned again. He had thought of something. "Edward,"

he called, "my sources tell me that Danville, Virginia, was the worst place for your freedom marchers. Is that right?"

"Thirty-two cops and the judge, all wearing guns," said Edward, SNCC now; "Nobody allowed in the courtroom and sandbags all around the city hall."

"Gre-at!" said Thomas, not grimly. "Take me with you next time."

Bernard was listening at the wake, taking no notes. He had graduated from the state mental institution to weekly appointments with a psychiatrist. Bernard no longer had to record conversations; he lived for the moment, in fragility.

"Lust came next," said Glenn, "and he didn't struggle."

With gluttony Thomas had entered the age of greed. Lust, like the stretching belt on his stomach, grew within his body. His girl students in Nineteenth Century began carrying the new Catholic bible, *The Holy Bible,* recently translated from the Hebrew and Greek by Ronald Knox. His best Protestant students attended meetings of the Newman Club.

"Where did he have all those girls?" Bernard wondered. "I mean *where* did he sin?"

"In his office," said Glenn, "on his summer lounge chairs."

It was not planned. It never had to be. On warm days the air conditioner made a wind tunnel of the hall, slamming his door during a student appointment or when a female teaching fellow was visiting. If Thomas had the energy he left the door shut, having been given his own private office along with the Prize. If the light poured in, reflected off white marble campus buildings, Thomas pulled down the metal blinds, along with his pants.

The girls left notes in his faculty mailbox. "Dear Doctor," they began, before making the proposal. Thomas tried to be careful at first with girls under 21, but then he told Glenn, "If they have their own apartments, they must know what they're doing."

"It was never seasonal fruit," said Glenn.

"He actually became a much warmer person," Celia told them, while they laughed and her husband frowned. "I mean, he was touched at last. He was exposed to people."

The laughter became ribald and Celia angered. She had noted physical change in Thomas too. She remembered vaguely her own

body having grown to fit her husband's hands, and saw the same
in the subtle reshaping of Thomas' lips, in the curve of his palm.

"He wasn't built for lust," said Rube. "His stomach was always upset and he had to carry medicine for diarrhea."

Drinking had kept Thomas awake long after the drinking had
stopped. He would stare, in the early morning light when he had
previously arisen to work, at the giant elm outside his windows
shadowing his bedroom, and wonder who was gaining on him.

"Envy," observed Bernard, "was next."

A second-rate expert in the Nineteenth Century was hired by
the English Department. The Department was making it easier
for Thomas to accept outside speaking engagements to spread the
name of the university. The second-rate expert came out, fairly
rapidly, in a group of first-rate journals. Thomas' classes were dismissed earlier, his research dated.

At the meeting of the Policy Committee, Thomas, in envy,
voted against an assistant professorship for his colleague, thereby
lessening that man's chances for tenure.

"Anger," said Rube, "only, with Thomas, it was not displeasure
or rage."

Celia's eyes moistened. It was an academic discussion, but
she had private memories with skin and bones.

"He had a dictionary with him one day here," said Celia.
"He opened it, without speaking, and creased a line with his
fingernail under '*Anger*. Old Norse, affliction, sorrow.' 'What do
you think of that, Celia?' he asked.

"'What are you angry about, Thomas?' I asked him. "What
could it have been?" she asked them now at the bar.

It was the girls, first. No privacy. No damned time. A satia-
tion, beyond exhaustion. At night, sleeping on his back, the
muscles in his palms twitched and ached as if pressed with
sharp instruments. He couldn't belong to them all, to the ladies,
the gentlemen adult students, the buyers of tickets to his lectures,
his relatives, or his colleagues. So he belonged to none, withdrawing first from the girls as rapidly as the act was over.
Withdrawing, lying alone—once in a while remembering to give
a one-armed embrace. With the end of lust, the sounds in his
throat became hoarse. He, mounted, was animal, guttural, il-
literate.

"He wasn't always angry," said Celia's husband. "My feeling was that often he was placid."

His anger having been spent, he was strangely placid when others invaded his privacy, people with even less reason than the girls.

"I was in his office once," said Bernard, "when two teaching fellows working on their Essays under Thomas came into his office." The new Bernard was shaved, conventional. "These guys both came from New York, had curly hair and were growing new beards. It was an invasion of Talmudic scholars. I knew Thomas felt priggish. But he said nothing. The bigger guy leaned against his filing cabinet and knocked folders off the top, which he picked up. The smaller guy opened up a giant bottle of shaving lotion that he had won at a campus auction. He just wanted the Expert to have a smell."

Ah, this was something to listen to, and don't worry—Edward, Celia, Celia's husband, Rube and Glenn were listening.

"The damned thing leaked on the floor," said Bernard, giving a hiccup laugh. "That cheap shaving lotion leaked all over Thomas' floor, oily on the floor, rainbow on the office tile. These guys, picture these guys—they were not ashamed. They only wanted the Expert to love the smell of them. They left—he didn't throw them out, and he closed the door—not slammed it—afterwards."

With helpless things Thomas could sometimes be careful. But not with the women from the Lecture Series, still flappers and flapping.

"Next he coveted," said Rube. "He got himself a little Nazi car."

"Eh," said the others, dismissing Rube.

"But wait. Listen. He was given things," Rube said. "Everybody wanted to give him things. He got a jacket from a jacket manufacturer in California and space shoes from a New York shoe chain to advertise the product. Then he said to me, 'Why should we with the brains work so hard, give so much of ourselves—from our blood,'—he said, that's what he said, "blood" —'reading, lecturing, researching, when *they,* the businessmen, no brains, no virtue, live like kings?'"

"That," said Glenn, "made sloth easy."

It was harder to work for Thomas' returns were meager, compared to his dentist friends, acquaintances in real estate, the furniture business, the gas station business.

"I liked him better descending than in the ascent," said Celia.
"He was more human. The ascent was Thomas with everybody
else, but he came down alone, all the way."

"Yet he was an innocent," said Glenn. "It was all new to
him."

"Innocence is a sin," Edward told them, much sterner these
days, "along with tourism. It's the guy who goes too slow on the
Expressway and smashes everybody else up. That's innocence."

Celia's husband shook his head. He was still shocked, having
heard from Celia about one of Thomas' girls, Joan. Celia had
described to him how the girl came into the bar hunting for
Thomas. She was badly buttoned, not especially pretty but all
body.

Joan saw Thomas at his stool and tried to knock him off it,
while he grabbed the counter. "I lost it," she cried. "A stunted
seed. That's what you gave me. I lost it. You're not a man.
You're a short prick."

Thomas sat there, taking the full nine counts, while Glenn,
Bernard, Edward and Rube helped the girl out of the bar.

She wasn't the only one to come looking for him. His brother
came once. They talked quietly. Thomas did not leave the bar.

"You're killing the folks, you know," said Thomas' brother.
"You're killing them. Pa was in the hospital twice with coronaries.
Ma spends all her time crying on the phone to me and my wife.
You think you can live alone in this world?" His brother tried
once more. "Thomas," he said, "you're part of the congregation."

As Thomas sat in the bar, neglecting his family, he became
extremely accessible to others. Students found him first and took
up his time with their papers, and occasionally, poetry. Faculty
members, seeing compassion, made him confidante of their affairs, borrowed his car and even his apartment.

Thomas sinned the other way from pride. He sinned into
humility, sitting with people who devoured his time, his energy.
Once Celia saw him with the fanatic old woman she had met
on campus, who was worried about the drought. He took great
pains to help her across the street, at the precise traffic light

she wanted. Thomas saw Celia watching him when he crossed
to the bar.

"Celia," he said, "I helped an old lady across the street and
when I got there, I felt good about it. Celia, I have sinned."

But this he did not, in so many words, say to his priests.

Said the priest from his Catholic university, who had pried:
"Are you sure you've told me everything? Search in your innermost heart. You'll find the thing which you think is so horrible
and which you think you can't tell me. But you can tell me."

He tried again, his parish priest, sent by his parents. "O.K.,
so you're a sinner," had been the attitude of his childhood confes-
sor, not in those words, nor in these: "What makes you so different from anybody else? Don't tell me a big story."

The campus chaplain wore his purple stole, but did not "My
Son" Thomas, nor use a screen.

"AAAaah," said Thomas, in the fading scream of Tarzan's
victims falling off cliffs to raging jungle rivers. And he clutched
the edge of the chaplain's desk, which, suddenly, with its crucifix,
its arched legs, became an altar.

"I'm baited, Father," said Thomas, "like a minnow with the
hook through the eye. Where will I be thrown? What will eat
me? Why am I there, the temptor, the dying temptor?"

But the chaplain dismissed Thomas as not a true penitent—he
was too emotional.

Then Thomas unrelieved was hung up on the pains of the
world. He clipped articles from the *New York Times* that he
bought for fifteen cents in the faculty lounge. He wasn't tourist,
nor participant, only emphatic reader and feeler. ERROR! ER-
ROR! cried Thomas, whose judgments had hitherto been reserved for theme faults.

He wept easily now, not even personally, and it rendered him
so weak that he was incapable of lust. Stain-faced Thomas sat at
the bar, hollowed over his beer, having lost the gluttonous stomach. From excessive appetite, Thomas went to hunger fasts. In
the morning he ate nothing. For lunch he peeled a sweet orange,
let it wet his fingertips and licked them with each segment. His
tears had become salty, citric like the orange.

The parks, where he had watched frazzle-feathered damp
pigeons and looked at alley-like hibiscus, became places of evil

to him. He saw the police stopping Negro children with new bicycles to question them, to harass them, until the boys rode skiddingly out of the park.

Where was the pleasure if not in excess and not in deficit?

"That was the worst," said Rube. "He was just a bundle of nerves. He was a tooth-ache, and the world was drilling. After that, the nerve had to be extracted or deadened."

What could Thomas do? He couldn't release souls from hell. He couldn't soften the Fall. He couldn't be a lion, and he was only a foolish lamb. So he challenged Nature. He challenged God. He jumped off the top of pride and looked at the sun with a naked eye.

"What did he do that for?" asked Glenn, always careful of his artist's eyes. "Looking at the corona during the eclipse. What a stupid thing. What a waste!"

"He didn't even pretend about it," said Edward, "No darkened glass or filter on a telescope or sunglasses. Not even an inadequate defense. He went out there, while the moon made a lima bean out of the sun, and he turned and looked right into the eye of the eclipse."

"His father came for him," Celia told her husband. "His father was a sick old man, but he came for Thomas. The parish priest was with him, shaking his head, shaking Thomas. And the nurse, with the bandages for Thomas' eyes. They all came to take care of Thomas."

And they mourned the waste of Thomas, now not a blind Homer or Milton, only a blind Thomas, the last of the nobility.

SHLOMO KATZ'S stories have appeared in a number of periodicals and anthologies. He is the editor of *Midstream* magazine.

My Redeemer Cometh . . .

I

THE ARGUMENTS went on a long time, acrimonious arguments that almost invariably ended with old Mrs. Fein crying softly, and her son Herbert pacing back and forth before her in silent wrath. And as he stopped to say good-by, she would cringe in her chair like a child expecting to be punished. "I don't want anything from you," she would plead. "I don't want a thing. I can take care of myself. Just don't make me do that."

"But, Mother," Herb would try to keep his voice calm and controlled, "but Mother, be reasonable, please; you aren't a baby after all . . . Don't you understand? It's for your own good. We are much concerned about you."

Mrs. Fein would then hunch her shoulders to control their twitching and pat her eyes with her handkerchief to soak up the tears. "I know, I know. But you needn't worry about me. I can take care of myself. I can take care of myself perfectly."

And feeling that the danger had passed for the moment, she would suppress her sobs and regain her composure somewhat. Frustrated, desperate, helpless, Herb would dutifully touch his lips to his mother's wrinkled old forehead and bid her good-by, but not before having his final say, like the last rumble of a passing thunderstorm that hints of an early return, "Mother, you are being unreasonable. You just can't go on living like this all alone at your age. Something must be done about it before any-

"My Redeemer Cometh . . ." – Shlomo Katz, *Midstream*, Copyright © 1967 by Theodor Herzl Foundation, Inc.

thing happens to you. All right, all right, we'll talk about it next time, more calmly. Good-by, Mom."

"Yes, Herbie; yes, son; next time, of course, of course," she would smile approvingly like a child dismissed from school for whom the misery of next day is infinitely remote. "Good-by, and come to see me again soon, soon, and bring the family next time."

In the beginning there was not much rancor. The idea first came up when Mrs. Fein was in her middle seventies and her husband had died. Herbert then suggested with apparent warmth that she come to live with him. He argued with conviction and what he believed was sincerity. But his face flushed with guilty shame when he felt decidedly relieved that she rejected his suggestion. The offer was repeated a few times more, but now it was little more than a formality, both mother and son sharing the secret knowledge that the offer was not genuine and that it would be a severe breach of etiquette between them were she to take it literally. Since Mrs. Fein really did not want to go to live with her son and daughter-in-law, these polite exchanges were soon dropped.

But about one year later Mrs. Fein fell ill and needed an operation. When she returned from the hospital, Herbert made no mention of her coming to live with him. A home-maker was engaged to help her during her convalescence. As soon as she fully recovered, Mrs. Fein discharged the home-maker, and it was then that Herbert first suggested that, in view of her age and condition, it would be a sensible idea that she should seek admission to a Home for the Aged.

"Go on, I'm not that old," she tried to make light of the suggestion.

"Mother, you are wonderful," Herb complimented her. "I always knew that. Of course you're not old. There are times when I feel older than you. You know, a person feels as old as he . . ."

But the look of suspicion on his mother's face cut short his banalities, and he blushed at the betrayal he was plotting.

She had caught him in a lie and was moved to pity and forgiveness, as often she had been when he was a boy and she caught him in some mischief. "Don't kid me," she said, and there

COLLEGE OF THE SEQUOIAS
LIBRARY

was the suggestion of a wink in her eye as she tried to make
a joke of the matter and to assert her maternal authority. "I
know I am old." (Mama knows best.) "But let's not talk
about it now." (Attend to your own affairs and be sure to do
your homework.) "Let me make a cup of coffee." (Mother,
protector and source of nourishment, is not to be sent away to
a Home for the Aged.)

Thus the first conversation on the subject ended with Herb's
defeat, and for months the matter was not brought up again.
Mrs. Fein continued as before. She overcame the shock of her
husband's death, and the loneliness turned out to be not unbearable. She talked to herself much, and to the invisible presence
of her husband, and found it comforting. Life seemingly could
go on like this indefinitely and peacefully, making her bed in
the morning, doing the bit of shopping for her modest needs, cooking a simple meal for herself, washing the couple of dishes,
glancing through a paper, visiting with an old neighbor, occasionally entertaining a friend and listening to gossip, and, of
course, the daily telephone conversation with her son and her
daughter-in-law and her two grandchildren. Good-by, grandma,
call again.

In talk with neighbors, the Home for the Aged came up now
and then, but always concerning others. Not she. No. Not she.
It was really a wonderful place for those who needed it, and
it should be helped, and it did provide a wonderful service for
the community.

She had visited it once years before together with her late
husband, on some social occasion, a fund raising meeting or
something like that in the Home auditorium. So terribly long
ago. The Director had showed them around the place. "Two
to a room," he had pointed out proudly, "and every two rooms
have a joint bathroom." They looked into one of the rooms.
Two beds neatly hugged the walls, a window faced on a lawn,
two dressers on each side of the window were cluttered with
bric-a-brac and many photographs of children and grandchildren,
all young and vital and always being graduated from something.
Then they were shown down the length of the hall to a wide

lounge furnished with sofas and soft chairs and a television set. They were taken to the dining room where the tables stood in military order.

"May we see the second floor?" someone in the party had asked.

"Oh, the second floor," the Director had sounded embarrassed, "why, of course, but there is really nothing special to see there; the arrangement is pretty much the same as on the ground floor. You see," he smiled self-consciously, "we do everything we can to make the old folks happy, but the second floor of course, you understand, we mostly assign the older ones there, I mean the ones who are not ambulatory, or who are sick or senile maybe. And we really don't have much time now . . ."

But some in the party insisted, and they were taken to the second floor.

As they turned on the landing they were assailed by a pro-longed, thin scream and they looked at each other and at the Director in alarm. He tried to reassure them. It was not someone in pain. "No one is being tortured," he smiled wryly. Just an old man who for some reason expressed himself thus.

But now their equanimity and sense of pride in the Home had been shaken. They huddled in a bunch at the top of the stairs, vaguely afraid to venture down the length of the corridor. An ancient woman was feeling her way along the wall with the help of a cane; another stood in the doorway to her room, her face blank, her mouth wide open, and stared at them with incomprehension. In the distance an attendant was pushing an old man in a wheel chair and his lifeless fingers dangled over the side of the chair like dry and twisted sticks. And over all hung the piercing scream of the unseen old man, terrifying, creating its own nightmare, that was ignored by the other inmates. An old woman stood near the hall telephone holding the receiver to her ear, and in a loud and querulous voice demanded: "I want to talk to my daughter, Syl; I want to talk to Syl; hello, I want to talk to. . . ." Yet somehow it seemed certain that she had not dialed any number.

Quickly the Director led them down the length of the hall and herded them into the unusually spacious elevator. They too were anxious to get back as fast as possible to the ground floor, to be among the living again. But the doors of the elevator remained open for what seemed an eternity, until at last they eerily glided toward each other, slowly, as if closing upon them forever, and finally they touched with a click of finality, like the closing of the lid of a coffin, and the elevator began smoothly groping its way down, moving in time, without a destination, toward eternity.

"The elevator is specially adjusted," the Director explained. "Old people are afraid, and many of those on the second floor move very slowly and must have lots of time to get in and out of the elevator."

Mrs. Fein later recalled: It had felt like a reprieve to be on the ground floor again; it was school letting out; it was the doctor smiling and saying: You're all right, everything is in order, you can go home and just take it easy. It was forgiveness. It was a gift.

That was long ago. And now the months passed and Mrs. Fein had recurring minor ailments, not serious ones, to be sure, but grave enough to confine her to the house for days at a time when neighbors dropped in to help her, and Herb visited more frequently, more anxious than before, more irritable. And the subject was broached again. But now in a different tone, for now it was: "Mother, you must. . . . It is dangerous to go on as you do."

And indeed there was no denying any longer that it was not sensible to continue as before, nor even that it was dangerous, for anything could happen, and who would hear the whimper of an old woman in the night? Therefore the attack was now mounted ever more frequently from a different angle by the son, the strategist, who sensed his advantage. And thus it was no longer, "It is best for you," or even, "You must," but, "You have no right to do this to us, mother," against which assault old Mrs. Fein had no defenses and could only resist with tears, and arguments which did not convince even herself, for she pleaded, "Don't worry about me," and, "I want nothing from you," and at the same time knew that the staff of authority had passed from her hands into her son's, and that when he was a child and sick and pleaded not to be given medicine, not to be taken to the doctor, or not to be taken to nursery school, she had disregarded his pleas, and she had done all these things to him, and now the wheel had come around full circle, and it was his turn to do them to her.

Therefore she knew that there was no hope, that in the end she would have to submit, that unless sudden death intervened, a release which she felt would not be forthcoming, it was merely a matter of time, and of little time at that—for the son's urgency was growing daily, and, indeed, how could she do that to him?

And so, "All right," she said one day, "I'll go. You can start making arrangements and I will sign the application when you bring it."

Yet when the son, good, loyal Herbie, showed himself fore-armed and already had all the necessary papers with him for her to sign, the sense of hopelessness and betrayal overcame her and she wept copiously and silently, for now she knew that the end had come indeed, that she was no longer free, that even her consent was now a mere formality which she was expected to give graciously, lady that she was, and that withholding it would not in any way change the course of events. For thus people condemned to death are led to execution, and if they are brave, they walk of their own accord to the gallows, but guards go at their side anyway, in case they refuse to walk of their own free will, and so, what did it really matter, and, might as well be gracious about it, and with trembling hand she signed, in triplicate, and handed the papers to the son, who took them all too eagerly, seized them almost, and put them in his vest pocket quickly—and smiled. . . .

"Mother, I forgot to mention it, but you are coming with me to the house, for dinner, you are expected, the kids are expecting you, and Jean too." But in his immense relief that responsibility was now being lifted from his shoulders, that Mother would be taken care of and looked after by others—like handing a patient over to a hospital, let the doctor look after him, the doctor knows how, and, relieved, one can oneself retire to the waiting room to await the verdict and meanwhile think all kinds of thoughts and even read a paper or do a crossword puzzle or make a business call from the pay station in the lobby—in his great relief Herb had become confused and forgot one mo-

ment what he had said the moment before and picked up the
receiver and called his home and, "Hello. I'm bringing Mother
over for dinner. Yes. What? Oh! No, I am bringing her. Out?
That's out of the question. Well, do what you can. Yes, I must.
Good-by."

While old Mrs. Fein slowly shook her head and understood
and, "Herbie, some other time, please; I am tired," she whispered.
"I see Jean isn't prepared." And Herbie, flustered, dared con-
tradict the obvious, and offered alibis: "Kids, scatterbrains, forgot all about it and made a date with some friends. It's all
right. They'll cancel it."

And so she shook her head and said no more, for this was
already part of the new life, and there was no turning back,
and pretenses could no longer be scrutinized—they had to be
accepted.

And she went.

II

WHEN MOVING DAY CAME it was a day of snow and wind, a day
chill as death, a day known and expected, yet, when it came, it
was a dreaded surprise. Mrs. Fein had prepared for it, indeed
she had. She had been packing and repacking for days. What
should she keep? What discard? And this she had thrown out,
and that. And each was a wrench and a burial. What a load
of history one accumulates in the course of a lifetime! Objects
and more objects. A piece of paper, and a letter, and a scrap
of cloth, and an old garment and many, many other things.
And she said to herself: This is the final moving and things
of this world have to be discarded—so she discarded and set
aside and eliminated and condemned. Until, at last, there were
only two suitcases and a handbag full of essentials—and a secret
hope of resurrection in her heart, for this, after all, could not
be the final end, now could it?

And then Herb came, cheerful, flushed, rubbing his hands.
"Mom, it sure is cold, what I mean *cold*. Must be ten below.
You ready? Wow, what a day!" She understood, and smiled, and

said, "Yes, I'm ready. It certainly is a cold day; haven't seen one like it in a long time."

He helped her with her coat, then took the two suitcases and went out to the car, while she gave the place a final check to see that no light was left turned on, that the closets were indeed empty, that nothing essential had been left behind, and when Herb came in again and picked up the handbag, she was ready to follow him to the door, and as they walked out she turned the key in the lock and handed it to him.

He hesitated a second, then took it and slipped it into his pocket.

The car turned into the main thoroughfare on the way to the Home and Herb kept up a constant bubbling of small talk about his children and the weather and how he had nearly skidded into a tree the previous day, now and then interjecting a little item of information that concerned Mrs. Fein, and the Home, and the arrangements he had made. He had been to the Home office a day or two before, he said, and they had shown him the room she was assigned, a corner room, he hastened to point out, as if this was very important. And she would share it with a very fine partner, a woman not really old, who didn't have to live in the Home at all—she had chosen to do so for convenience, because she preferred to have company, otherwise there was no need for her to live in the Home at all, he repeated, as she was healthy and active.

He saw the question in his mother's eyes and tried to avoid it so he stepped on the brake unnecessarily and the car skidded on the hard snow until he maneuvered it to a halt at the traffic light and cursed under his breath, and muttered something about things of this world, such as snow tires that are guaranteed to grip but skid instead, and only then did he remark in a casual tone: "The room is on the second floor, yes, a corner room though, and therefore quiet; no traffic in the hall before it, really comfortable."

What he did not tell her was how he had haggled and bargained with the admissions committee pleading for a room on the ground floor, and was turned down because there were other applicants, wealthier ones, whose children undertook to contribute regularly and substantially to the Home in addition to the flat sum paid at the time of admission, whereas he could undertake no such obligation, until the committee members flatly told him to decide quickly whether the arrangement on the second floor was acceptable to him, for there were other deserving applicants waiting for that room too, and it was indeed a great favor they were extending to him and to his mother only because she had been well and favorably known in the community for many years, and because his father before that had been a respected member of the community, for otherwise, God help us, there are so many deserving sick old people, and it was such a struggle to keep up the Home, and some of the other applicants, why, it was positively heartrending the state they were in.

So without consulting his mother and without further discussion he had said, Yes, the arrangement was agreeable, and he was properly appreciative and all that. But he did not then inform his mother, and only told her about it now as his car crunched through the dry snow and labored its rutted way to the outskirts of the city where the houses were small and surrounded by lawns, now under a thick layer of snow, and in the distance they could already see the Home, a stately two-story red brick building floating on a rise in the midst of an expanse of snow broken by rows of bare trees now swaying dark branches in the dismal grey of the icy late afternoon.

One other thing was on old Mrs. Fein's mind: Who had been before her in the room she was about to occupy? What had happened to her predecessor? How old had she been? Of what had she died?

But this she could only speculate about, and meanwhile they drew up to the Home and she noted with surprise that Herb was not driving up to the front entrance but carefully maneuvered the car through the deep ruts in the snow to the rear. So that when he stopped before the delivery entrance she remained in her seat wondering why he had done so, until he announced cheerily: "Well, here we are, Mother. Come. Let's go inside. It's miserably cold."

She gripped her handbag and remained standing at the door as Herb opened the trunk and took out the two suitcases and then she followed him inside and an attendant led them to a large room off the corridor. "Mrs. Brown will be here soon," the attendant said and left.

"Mrs. Brown, that's the manager," Herb told his mother. "A wonderful woman. You'll love her."

Old Mrs. Fein sat down on the edge of a chair. With pretended cheeriness Herb paced back and forth, occasionally rubbing his chilled hands.

There were three chairs along one wall. Several hampers stood along the opposite wall, and a desk and a chair occupied one corner. A cluster of unshielded lamps shed a harsh light. They waited, Mrs. Fein with trepidation, Herb impatiently. The winter evening set in quickly and the glaring yellow light became more depressing by the moment, yet the door remained shut, so that for an instant Mrs. Fein was about to say, Come, Herb, let us go back; Mrs. Brown can't receive us today—and just as quickly realized where she was and that there was no going back, that all that remained for her to do now was to wait.

And Herb, too, found the waiting oppressive and began to tell something intended to break the gloom, something about what one of his children had said or done, and he did not really care what he was saying, or whether his mother was listening, and then Mrs. Brown entered.

She looked flustered and harassed, for it was late afternoon, and dinner had to be served soon, and something had gone amiss in the kitchen, yet here were these two to be attended to, so that when Herb said, "Mrs. Brown, this is my mother, Mrs. Fein," and old Mrs. Fein rose and timidly extended her hand, Mrs. Brown merely looked at her and vaguely said, "Yes," and, "You'll have to open the suitcases so that we can go through the things," and only then, as Mrs. Fein lowered her hand and her lip began to tremble, and Herb bent down to the suitcases, did Mrs. Brown recall her duty and she smiled faintly and said, "Haven't we met before, Mrs. Fein? I am sure we met somewhere."

But the tardy gesture of friendliness lasted a mere instant, for Mrs. Brown was distraught, and as Herbert opened the suitcases and Mrs. Fein bent over them as if to help him, Mrs. Brown said rather brusquely, "Take out all the things, put them on the chair there."

One by one the various articles were taken out of the suitcases and placed on the chair while Mrs. Brown watched the proceedings, and one item or another she ordered put aside. "This you can't keep; we must maintain a minimum of uniformity in the Home." And of some others she said: "These will have to be laundered. Put them in that hamper." But seeing the tears gather in old Mrs. Fein's eyes, she explained: "I know, dear, I know. Of course they are clean. But these are the rules of the house; for purposes of disinfection, you understand. And now you can put all the rest back in the suitcases and I'll have someone show you to your room. And yes," she added to Mrs. Fein, "please remember, there is to be no laundering of any kind in the room, nothing at all, not even handkerchiefs. If we were to permit it, every room would become a laundry."

Herb replaced his mother's possessions in the suitcases and snapped them shut. Mrs. Brown stepped outside into the hall and called to someone. A young woman attendant came in. "Show Mrs. Fein to room 24," she ordered her. And then to Herb: "When you deposit the suitcases you will please take your mother down to the office so that she can be properly registered." And as they walked out, she called to Herb: "Mr. Fein, by the time you are through at the office dinner will be served. Take your mother to the dining room, and you too be our guest for dinner tonight."

They followed the attendant down the hall to the big elevator, then slowly floated upward and emerged in the corridor on the second floor. They turned right and walked the length of the hall. Some old people wandered about. One or two turned to look at them inquiringly, and someone remarked, "That's the new one, for 24, where Mrs. Sylvan used to be," and paid them no more attention. When they reached room 24, the attendant merely nodded, "This is it; the bed on the right," and left them. The doorway to room 24 was blocked by a tall, gaunt woman in a flowered apron. She looked Mrs. Fein over critically and made no move. Herb, who had met her before when he was shown the room being assigned to his mother, did the honors. "Mrs. Harris, I want you to meet my mother, Mrs. Fein. She will be your roommate." Mrs. Harris still made no move and continued her critical survey of the two. "She will share the room with you," Herb added foolishly.

Mrs. Harris said Hello and stepped into the room where she sat down on her bed and continued scrutinizing them. Mrs. Fein and her son entered and Herb began fussing around, first placing the suitcases in the corner, then moving them elsewhere, until he suddenly realized that his mother was still standing in her overcoat in the overheated room and he turned to her, "Mom, take your coat off; here, let me hang it up for you," and when he had done so, and Mrs. Harris still stared at them without saying a word, he took his mother to the window and pointed out, "See? What did I tell you? A corner location. You can see two streets from here." But the gloomy winter twilight had already darkened into early evening and all that could be seen was the expanse of greying snow.

With a curt "I'll see you later," Mrs. Harris rose and walked out. Casual small noises came from the hall. Herb went to the doorway, looked down the hall, and seeing no one nearby, he shut the door. Mother and son were now alone. Mrs. Fein sat down on her bed, thought of the unknown woman who had occupied it so recently, jumped up, then sat down again with a barely audible sigh which could have signified resignation or simply tiredness, and invited Herb to sit on the chair nearby. She glanced for a moment at the other half of the room, at Mrs. Harris' neatly made bed, at her dresser with its load of photographs, at the open clothes closet that was full, at the waste basket with its fruit skins and wrapping paper, and then for an instant she surveyed her own side of the room, still so empty and untenanted, apparently so easy to walk away from, but was again aware of the impossibility of it and gained control of herself, and cheerfully said, "Well, this is it." Herb seized on the chance offered him. "Yes, yes, Mother, you will be comfortable. Just wait and see." And then to the business at hand.

"You have the money with you?" he asked.

"I have it, a bank check, for one thousand dollars."

"Well, let us go down to the office and give it to them. I still say you should have kept some of it out—never mind the rules. But anyway, don't worry, anytime you need anything, you know, I am right here."

They walked down the hall to the stairway. This time some
people stopped to talk to them briefly. "You the new roomer?
In 24? This your son? Glad to know you." And sensing Mrs.
Fein's mood, or remembering the day of their own arrival, one
or two added: "You'll be fine here. This is a good Home."

There was more activity and motion in the hall on the ground
floor. Groups of old people clustered here and there talking while
waiting for the dinner bell. From a few rooms came the sound
of radios. On one side of the hall they passed a chapel, and
then a large room that served as recreation hall and library. A
bulletin board at the entrance announced a variety of activities
and entertainments for the week. A folk singer was scheduled
to perform that evening and an acrobat later. The Ladies' Auxiliary of the Home was scheduled to hold a meeting. Residents
too sick or old to write their own letters were informed that
a special committee of volunteer women would come on a certain
afternoon to write their letters for them. Another announcement
listed new books borrowed from the municipal library that were
now available, and requested the return of others. There was
also a schedule of religious services.

They entered the office. A large executive desk near the
window was unoccupied. At a smaller desk a secretary was
talking on the phone. They patiently waited till she finished and
turned to them.

"Yes?"

"This is my mother, Mrs. Fein," Herb said, and seeing the
blank stare on the secretary's face, he added, "She just moved
in, room 24."

The secretary opened a filing cabinet, withdrew some papers
and glanced through them. "Did you bring the money? You were
supposed to bring it here before you moved in."

Mrs. Fein took an envelope from her pocketbook and handed
it to the young woman, who glanced at it briefly, clipped it to the
other papers and put them in one of the desk drawers. "It's
almost five-thirty," she said. "Come in tomorrow morning and
we will fill out the necessary forms."

And she turned away.

Again they were out in the hall. Now the commotion was

greater still as nearly everybody was out of his room waiting for the call to dinner. They went into the library and looked around briefly, then they glanced into the chapel, and then the dinner bell rang.

The dining room was in the basement. They followed the throng down the stairs while others waited for the elevator. It was a large, long room with windows at ground level and now banked with snow. There were three long rows of pale yellow formica-topped tables seating four each and now set for the meal. As they stood confused not knowing whether to take any available seat or whether seats were permanently assigned, Mrs. Brown, who supervised the serving, noticed their forlornness and led them to a table. "You can sit here," she said, "or any place you like. There is no permanent seating in the dining room." And she was off to her duties. Another man and a woman sat down at the table and greeted them with a nod. The man was very old. With trembling hands he took a soft roll from the plate in the center of the table and began tearing it into small pieces. He looked at Mrs. Fein, and then at Herb. "You are too young to be here," he said to Herb. "I have a son older than you; he is in business, furniture."

The other woman showed some interest.

"He is my son," Mrs. Fein said. "He is only visiting."

"Oh," the old man said. "A guest, good, good, a guest. Nice to see you, young man," and his mind wandered off.

Attendants wheeling carts served the food. There was thin soup, and when Herb tasted it, he automatically reached for a salt shaker, for it was bland, but there was no salt shaker on the table. He was prepared to overlook the matter, but the woman across the table had noticed his gesture and now shouted to one of the waitresses: "Girl! You! Bring some salt here, for the young man." And to Herb she explained: "They put no salt on the tables unless you ask for it. And they put little of it in the food. Lots of people here have high blood pressure." And again she shouted: "Girl! You! Bring the salt." Until finally someone did bring a salt shaker. And then there was well cooked meat and mashed potatoes and finally crumbly cookies and very pale tea and milk with which to dilute it still further. Mrs.

Fein picked at her food dispiritedly. Herb pretended to eat with gusto, frequently urging his mother on.

As the tea was served, the atmosphere in the dining room relaxed and from here and there, over the hubbub of conversation and an occasional sigh or belch, there were heard complaints about the tea. And even as the old people added large quantities of milk to the pale liquid, they protested against its weakness and recalled far off days, at home, when they brewed their own tea which was strong and aromatic and young even as they had been then. But the clatter of the dishes being picked up from the tables grew louder as the waitresses hurried to finish their work, and the old people began to rise and wander slowly to the stairs and to the elevator. They were fed and content for the moment, and there was a long evening ahead with little to do, and few if any visitors could be expected on such a cold night to break the monotony. The folk singer, to be sure, was scheduled for this evening, but that was later, at eight, and meantime there was nothing except satiety and resting and perhaps a bit of gossiping in the corridors.

Mrs. Fein and her son rose and went up to her room. Mrs. Harris was already there and seemed to be waiting for them. "Well? How did you like the dinner?" she greeted them. "Dishwater! Slops! That's what it is. Won't give a person a decent meal! Something got to be done about it." But finding no response she got up and walked out.

Herb unpacked the suitcases and helped his mother distribute their contents in the dresser and closet. Finished with this he suggested that he stay and later take her to the concert downstairs. But Mrs. Fein would not hear of it, and pleading tiredness asked him not to stay. He all too readily agreed and kissed her lightly on the forehead and went out promising to call her the very next morning.

III

"I AM REALLY BEGINNING TO LIKE IT HERE," Mrs. Fein said one month later when Herb and Jean and their children were visiting her—not for the first time of course, for Herb had been coming almost every day the first two weeks that his mother was in the Home, and Jean too had visited Mrs. Fein before. "I'm really beginning to like it here," Mrs. Fein repeated this phrase which she had said several times before during the first month of her residence. But now she had agreed with herself while all the other times she had only tried to reassure her son.

Indeed, it hadn't turned out to be so bad, after the first night that is, for then, as soon as Herb had gone, Mrs. Harris returned to the room, sat down on her bed and without any preliminaries, announced: "She died of cancer; Mrs. Sylvan, the woman who had your bed before you."

"Oh! I am so sorry to hear that," Mrs. Fein said and frantically searched her mind, exhausted after the experiences of the day, for some other subject of conversation. But before she could think of anything else to say, Mrs. Harris resumed: "She was old all right, said she was eighty-three, but I knew better—must have been closer to ninety. Oh well. How old are you?" she asked, and smoothed some folds in her flowered apron as she stared critically at Mrs. Fein.

"I am seventy-eight," Mrs. Fein replied, uncomfortable at the tone of interrogation.

"And this young man, your son, is he your only son?"

"Yes."

"I have two daughters," Mrs. Harris declared. "I am eighty-one and my daughters live on the West Coast."

"How nice."

"What's nice about it?" Mrs. Harris frowned. "They come to see me only once a year. They won't come again till next July."

"Oh," Mrs. Fein was apologetic.

"But they send me lots of things; I get packages every month."

"Indeed," Mrs. Fein said neutrally, fearing to offend again.

Mrs. Harris got up and looked suspiciously down the hall, then returned and whispered ominously. "But most of it gets stolen. You are new here; be careful. There are a lot of thieves on this floor. They steal things right out of your closet. See what I mean?"

"Indeed? It's unbelievable."

"It's true," Mrs. Harris straightened rigidly and stared sharply at Mrs. Fein. "It's true, and you must be careful. They come

prowling around at night. I hear them opening my dresser and
closet. I pretend to be asleep, or they might kill me. If you hear
any prowlers in the room at night, you too keep still, or they
might kill you."

"Indeed I will," Mrs. Fein said, now thoroughly upset, and rose
from her bed. She edged to the door, smiled painfully at Mrs.
Harris, and quickly walked toward the stairs and down to the
ground floor. She went into the recreation hall where a handful
of people milled around and only casually glanced at her. She
found a newspaper lying on a table, picked it up and tried to
read it, but her eyes filmed over with tears of fear and abandon-
ment, and thus she sat not knowing how long, turning over wild
plans in her mind, and one moment she almost decided to go to
the hall telephone and call Herb and implore him to come out
at once and take her to his home, to plead with him, to cry, to
threaten a scandal if necessary; and the next moment she realized
that were she to do so Herb would indeed come out but under
no circumstances would he take her to his home, but would
only talk to her and try to calm her and maybe go to the
office, if it was still open, or to Mrs. Brown, or to the resident
nurse and describe her plight to them and ask their help, have
them talk to her or maybe give her a tranquillizer, and one of
them would come and disapprovingly, gracelessly, almost cruelly,
try to talk sense to her, try to calm her as quickly as possible, for
it was evening now and their day's work was over and they too
were entitled to some hours of rest by themselves, and at best,
with an impatient shrug of the shoulders they would take her to
the infirmary and give her two, instead of one, tranquillizing pills,
then take her to her room, room 24 shared with Mrs. Harris, who
was still there awake and about. And many people would notice
and see and look at her and ask questions, Who is this? What is
the matter with her? themselves fearful that something serious
was happening to an old woman and they were all old men and
women and it could happen to them, whatever it was—only to
be informed that, It is nothing, just the new roomer in 24, you
know, where Mrs. Sylvan used to be, it's her first night here
and she's nervous—and they would relax, and smile knowingly
and condescendingly, for they had been through this and had

survived it, so it was now a laughing matter, and they could afford to feel superior; or someone might say, Oh, Mrs. Harris' roommate, no wonder. But only she, old Mrs. Fein, would be the focus of their ridicule.

And then it seemed to her that if she were to put on her coat and go out, for it was still quite early in the evening, and call a taxi, and then, and then, well, she could say, To whom?, to a policeman, that she had lost the key to her apartment and they would come and pry the door open for her because she was a nice old lady who had lost her keys on a cold winter day when they fell out of her chilled old hands and sank into the snow, or something like that, or she had dropped them somewhere not remembering where, only that, when they had opened the door and with the strong beam of their flashlight found the light switch and turned it on and seen that the apartment was empty and no longer tenanted, why that wouldn't do at all, of course, and they would quickly get her story and bring her back to the Home, and it would be still worse, for everyone would stare and ask questions and she would be interrogated and pacified and put to bed and people would ask, What is the matter with her? Not in her right mind, that new woman in 24, some might say. But why the police? Had she done anything? And Mrs. Harris, gaunt and towering in her flowered apron, pointing an accusing finger: It's she! She stole my dress, the one my daughter just sent me! She stole it and cut it up into pieces! I know! I saw her do it!

Then what was she to do? Perhaps just stay where she was and then the hall would fill with people and the singer would give his concert, and when he had finished they would all retire to their rooms, but she could stay in the hall, huddle in some corner so that no one would notice her until finally the lights would be turned out and she would be left alone. But that would not do either, for someone was bound to discover her. So what was she to do?

But meanwhile the hall began to fill slowly, and without knowing it, bowed figure of grief that she was, she did attract the close attention of one, a certain Mrs. Godin, who noticed her, discreetly inquired who she was, and at once understood and went up and introduced herself, and just as quickly called over two or three others, and introduced them, so that Mrs. Fein had to raise her head and be courteous, as was her nature to be, and Mrs. Godin suggested that since the concert would not start for a while yet, why shouldn't they go to her room which was almost directly across the hall, and as she had an electric plate and some dishes and all other things required, she would make some tea and they would visit. And the thunderhead of terror in Mrs. Fein's mind began to break up and dissolve, leaving only a thin haze of apprehension, and when they sat down in Mrs. Godin's room, which was bright with extra floor lamps, the last mist of unease disappeared and they talked of children, and of life, and of snow that was white instead of grey. When the concert was about to begin, they all entered the hall in a group and sat together and the folk songs which the singer sang were a solace.

And later, when Mrs. Godin escorted old Mrs. Fein to her room on the second floor, even Mrs. Harris, who was already there and grumbling about something, had lost much of her terror.

Thus it was that a month after entering the Home, Mrs. Fein could say to her son and daughter-in-law that she was beginning to like her situation, but still she only half agreed with her own words, and what she really meant was that she was partly becoming reconciled to her new way of life; but what she did not herself understand or even distinctly know was that a hope had been born within her of a life after this life.

IV

SPRING BROUGHT MANY CHANGES and improvements. As the snow melted and the lawns turned green, a new spirit of animation came over the Home. The healthy residents now became more mobile as walking outside became safe and no longer presented perpetual danger of slipping on the ice and falling and breaking a bone. It was also easier to go by themselves to other parts of town to do light shopping or simply to visit. The prospect of waiting for a bus in zero weather had kept almost all of them, even the youngest, indoors during the winter. Now the world opened up before them. It was pleasant merely to sit in the sun on a bench on the lawn. The corridors inside the Home were now frequently entirely abandoned as even the wheelchair cases were taken outside for a sunning. Only the very oldest, the sick and senile remained in their rooms. Sons and daughters and in-laws now drove up on weekends not merely to visit with the old folks, but to take them in their cars to their own homes or to picnics.

That spring also brought a change in administration and a new young Director who was full of ideas for the greater happiness of the old people. Occupational therapy was the thing needed, he insisted when addressing a meeting of the Board of Directors of the Home, emphasizing his points by rhythmically tapping his pencil on the table. You can't make old people young, some of the Board members objected. But you can make them healthier and happier, the Director beamed. And he was given his way.

An annex of the basement was transformed into a laundry room for those who cared to use it, equipped with sinks, washing machines, dryers and drying racks. Ironing boards and irons were provided. And a big sign proclaimed: "All laundering must be done in the laundry room only." A corner of the extensive lawn was plowed up and divided into small plots and old men were encouraged to plant vegetables and flowers and to tend them. A number of young fruit trees were planted and their care was assigned to volunteers.

And as the days were both long and warm, most of the people swarmed outside also after the evening meal and indoor enter-tainment was reduced to a minimum.

Almost, it seemed to Mrs. Fein, like living on one's own, and even better in some ways, for Mrs. Godin, though much younger than herself, had become both friend and mentor, and she had also established friendly relations with a number of other old people. Company was now at hand and did not have to be sought, as was the case when she lived alone after her husband died. Late afternoons, when she awoke from her nap, all she had to do was go outside and there were people she knew and could talk to. Some, to be sure, had to be avoided, like her roommate, Mrs. Harris, who now protested loudly to everyone that enemies were throwing dirt or dye into the sink where she did her laundry, or the unpleasant old man from the first floor who moved from one bench to another, sidling up to aged women, and with lewd and knowing smirks suggested indecent doings, past or current. But the lawn was huge and the benches numerous and scattered about, so that it was easy to avoid those who were unpleasant. And fears and sorrows seemed to dissolve or at least to thin out in the open air, once they were taken out of the confining rooms and restricting corridors. The moaning of the sick woman in her bed, the loose babble of the senile man standing at the head of the stairs, the secretive whisper of another seeking to impart some dread information about his calamitous condition receded to the privacy of their owners. They aroused sympathy, but did not impose their burden of painful knowledge on all others.

Herb and Jean and their children now paid regular visits to Mrs. Fein on weekends and these were usually pleasant, not as during the cold weather when the visiting had to be done in the lounge, and many stiff old fingers reached out to caress smooth young flesh—Come here, little boy, come here, I'll give you a penny—seeking impossible rejuvenation from contact with the young, caressing a frightened cheek or head that tried to flee the terrifying, ravenous love, only to be met with cantankerous senile complaints from others, already too deep in their twilight and resenting its violation—Go away, you bad boy; don't make so much noise—finally rebounding to Herb and Jean: Let's go home, ma; I don't want to stay here, Let's go home now. For now even the children enjoyed the visits, romping about the lawn, examining the vegetable beds and sampling their immature growths, and if some old man felt outraged by what he regarded as vandalism to his particular plot, to his estate, his anger was dissipated under the endless blue sky and the children only ran to play somewhere else.

And for a brief moment there was even the illusion of youth and of romance, for one day a messenger delivered a bouquet for Mrs. Godin bearing a card "From Your Secret Admirer," and, as could have been expected, word of the tribute spread rapidly from one bench to another and there was much speculation about the identity of the swain, and the younger residents joked about the possibility of marriage and wedded bliss, the first ever to happen within the Home. Curiosity and gossip mounted when the first bouquet was followed by another and still another at approximately weekly intervals, all bearing the same cryptic message. The bus stop near the Home was watched, especially by the old man who was in the habit of making prurient suggestions about other residents. Who from the Home was making regular trips downtown? Suspicion fell first on one and then on another, but when the bouquets stopped coming after a while, and the summer wore on into August, the matter was forgotten.

The mood of animation subsided. The season began to exert a depressing effect. In the heat of August the residents of the Home began to shun the scorching outdoors. The vegetable plots were ripening quickly and required no more attention. Now and then some old man, who had proudly tended his few square feet in June, would pull up a bunch of carrots or of beets, look at them approvingly, but having no use for them himself would give them to the kitchen. The spurt of life of early summer was quietly ebbing away. Sons and daughters who lived far away had already paid their annual visits and the flurry of excitement was at an end, not to be repeated until another autumn, long winter and spring had been survived, and vague apprehension set in in the Home. Who would survive till the following summer? This was bound to be the last summer for many. Who were they? Could they still, before the cold rains and first snow flurries set in, escape from this place where their fate was sealed?

It was on an afternoon late in August that Mrs. Harris appeared before a group sitting quietly, some lightly dozing, on the benches on the lawn. As usual she wore a flowered apron and her face was grim as she announced: "I saw it, I saw it with my own eyes. She was beating her."

"Who? What?" There was more surprise than curiosity, for Mrs. Harris' standard complaint had to do with alleged thieving on the premises.

"I saw it with my own eyes," Mrs. Harris was rigid with indignation. "The attendant, the freckled one, she was beating Mrs. Goodman, on the second floor."

"Why was she beating her?" someone asked.

"Mrs. Goodman spilled some medicine she was giving her, so

she beat her, slapped her face, then knocked her down, told her
not to get out of bed till dinner."

"Why didn't she go to complain to the office?"

"Complain? Complain?" Mrs. Harris shrieked. "To those
thieves in the office? The attendant would kill her for it." And
she stalked off.

"Crazy, that woman," someone remarked without conviction.
But others wondered.

For summer was over, and they were older than in the spring;
soon the Home floating on its knoll would suck them in from the
lawn and swallow them for the winter, handing them out one by
one as they died.

V

IN OCTOBER THE COLD RAINS BEGAN and quickly turned to sleet.
Mornings the slush lay on the still green grass under a lowering
sky. Raw winds tossed the branches violently, ripping off the
remaining oak leaves. The residents of the Home stayed indoors.
Some of the women occupied themselves with a new project
started by the Director—knitting. Mostly they knitted pot holders;
a few younger or more ambitious ones knitted scarves. These
were later sold by the Ladies Auxiliary at its annual bazaar and
the proceeds were used to finance a party or two around New
Year time. The old men, with nothing to occupy them, slept
much during the days, wandered about the corridors and frequently engaged in pointless arguments with each other, and when
they tired of these they sat in the lounges repeating to each
other ancient incidents from their lives which they embellished
and modified with each telling, until they created fragmentary
new biographies for themselves.

The season of ailments was at hand, and one after another
came down with respiratory diseases. Old Dr. Sloan was kept
busy prescribing antibiotics, administering injections and ordering
rest and more rest, while his patients fretted, fearing that this
might be their last ailment. Harried by their additional duties
the attendants became ever more irritable and impatient with
their old charges.

"There now, be a good boy, up we go," and a shrivelled old man's body would be propped to a sitting position. A couple of pills and a sip of water, and then his pillow fluffed, and he would be given a quick pat and sink back into a stupor as the tranquillizers took effect. Or, "How are we this morning, dearie? Come now, sit up and we'll put nice fresh sheets on this bed. My, but you look grand today, a real beauty, couldn't have looked better on your wedding day." And with quick and sometimes rough motions the old woman would be moved deftly this way and that, the old sheet taken down, a new one spread, and the patient given her medicine, more often than not merely a tranquillizer, and put back to bed. For in the infirmary, as he wrote out his prescriptions, entered notations on the charts and gave instructions to the resident nurse, Dr. Sloan shrugged his shoulders with resignation. Peace was what they needed, for they were old, and much individual care could not be given them. Always short of help and with a great turnover of staff, the Home could do only what was essential and the dreads of the old patients could not be indulged, for they were often unreasonable, for what they wanted most was constant reassurance that this was not it yet. Therefore sleep was best for them in every way, until they would be roused at meal time, fed, and quickly nudged into sleep once more.

And those whose illnesses were serious were taken to the municipal hospital, while the healthy ones, sitting in their lounges and looking outside, would see the ambulance pull up before the entrance now and again, take its horizontal load on a stretcher and drive off. Then heads would nod fearfully. And sometimes the patients returned after some days, or even after a week or two, and other times they would not return. And those who returned came back almost as newcomers, for frequently they were forgotten almost as soon as they were taken away, and they had tales to tell and were listened to eagerly as after a fearful adventure.

It was at this time that Mrs. Fein suffered a stroke which paralyzed her right side. Well after midnight she suddenly awoke in great terror. She felt no pain but it seemed to her that someone or something was heavily pressing the right side of her body against the mattress. She struggled against this pressure, to sit up, or at least to turn, but could not. She wanted to cry out for help but her shriek died in her mouth and only a suppressed gurgle rattled in her throat as she squirmed helplessly. In her terror she soon gave up her attempts to move, afraid that the crushing weight would descend all over her, and thus she lay till morning and heard her roommate, Mrs. Harris, awake with her usual complaint: "They were here again, the thieves: I heard them. Didn't you hear them at all?" she turned to Mrs. Fein. And getting no answer she stalked into the bathroom and slammed the door after her.

Mrs. Fein's condition was only discovered later, when an attendant came to clean the room and saw her plight and, herself frightened, ran to inform the nurse in the infirmary. Dr. Sloan was called urgently to come to examine her, and when she failed to respond to the measures he applied, Herb was called and arrangements were made to have her taken to the hospital. Her son and Mrs. Godin went with her in the ambulance, and stayed with her as long as they were permitted and tried to comfort her, but she could not respond and showed her terror by the spasmodic movements of her left arm and by pleading looks.

She recovered to a considerable extent and returned to the Home three weeks later, but now she could not walk without much assistance, nor sit upright unaided, and the attendant would, when she had time, put her in a soft chair and strap her to it so that she would not fall out of it and injure herself, and thus she would sit, sometimes abandoned for a long time, until someone was free to unfasten her and help her back to bed. She was fed on a little table that was moved close to her bed, and, left alone, her head often slumped to the table, crumbs getting into her hair, and she was unable to lift it herself.

Herb now came to visit her more frequently, on evenings during the week, and also on weekends. But not the children who after a visit or two began to dread this apparition of a grandmother, so that rather than force them to a duty they resented, Herb and Jean decided not to bring them to the Home.

And indeed it would have served no purpose to force the children to visit, for Mrs. Fein had undergone a profound change and entered a condition in which grandchildren no longer belonged. She often shed soundless tears when her son was with her and looked pleadingly at him, for she could talk with difficulty only, and once, as he patted her shoulder reassuringly, she moved his hand to her lips and kissed it imploringly.

"What are you doing, Mother?" he sharply pulled his hand away.

"Herb, Herbie, you always were a good son," was all she said.

And he guessed what she wished to say, and one moment he thought, My God! My God! and the next, What can I do?

But it was not till some weeks later, as he was about to bid her good-by, that unexpectedly and in an earnest tone she articulated with difficulty: "Herbie, take me home with you."

"What are you saying, Mother. You know you are ill. Now, when you get well . . ."

She stared at him and seemed to forget her request. And he left.

VI

ONE NIGHT A SHORT TIME LATER old Mrs. Fein had a strange dream. There were many people, there was music—it was a wedding. The music woke her into her dream, and it was her wedding. Yet in the crowd of guests she was alone and looking for someone, for her groom, of course, and she could not find him. With growing exasperation quickly turning to frenzied fear she shoved her way forward until at last she saw him some distance away. But it was not the man who had been her husband all her married life; instead it was a resident of the Home who lived on the ground floor. She was not at all surprised at this. It was the man who had sent bouquets during the summer. "I knew all along it was you," she said. "I am so glad I found you at last." "Where have you been?" he asked. "Everybody has been looking for you. The ceremony is about to start." "I was in the hospital," she said. He took her by the arm and unbearable happiness surged through her. But the gladness that filled her quickly dissolved and gave way to a great anxiety. The wedding party melted away. She was alone and terribly worried. Her son—not Herbie, but another boy who was somehow her son—had gone out from the house and lost his way. She could visualize him clearly, though she could not see his face, standing on a street corner and crying, for he was only a boy of eight, and many people passed by him yet nobody took compassion on the crying child to ask what his trouble was and to bring him home, and she was tormented by the thought, Why doesn't someone do something about the lost boy? And then this, too, faded and gave way to quiet assurance. The boy would find his way after all; her son would come back. And she slept peacefully.

The following day, when Mrs. Godin came to visit her as usual, Mrs. Fein was in a more cheerful mood than she had been for some time, and even her articulation was noticeably improved. Altogether she looked like a person who had heard some good news. And when Mrs. Godin expressed her admiration for Mrs. Fein's great improvement and assured her of a complete and early recovery, Mrs. Fein asked to be helped into her chair.

"I want to ask a great favor of you," she began.

"Of course, dear, of course. What is it you want?"

"I want you to write a letter for me," Mrs. Fein said. "To my son," she added in a confidential tone.

"To Herbie?" Mrs. Godin wondered. "Why, I will call him for you and he will come. Or I can wheel you to the phone and you can talk to him."

"No, not Herbie, my other son, the younger one."

"Oh," Mrs. Godin was perplexed.

"I have another son. You didn't know; I married again; I have a younger son. Herbie is a good boy. But I want to write to my younger son."

"Why this is wonderful, you never told me about it. Where is your younger son?"

Old Mrs. Fein's face clouded with a strained expression. She appeared to be trying to recall something that eluded her, and she said: "He has been away a long time. He doesn't know I am here."

"Where does he live?"

"Where he lives?" the strain on Mrs. Fein's face became more pronounced. "He lives, well, you know, on the coast. You write this letter for me. He will come and take me out of here. He will take me to live with him."

"Do you have his address?"

"Address?" she looked bewildered. "He lives on the coast." And then, confidentially, "He is a doctor, a very famous doctor. He cures everybody. You know," she added in a whisper, "when he was a boy he once got lost, couldn't find his way home."

"Oh!"

"You write this letter for me. Yes? He will come and take me with him."

CALVIN KENTFIELD was born in Keokuk, Iowa and worked for some years as a merchant seaman. He is the author of two novels, two collections of short stories, and two novels not yet published. Mr. Kentfield has contributed to *The New Yorker, Harper's Bazaar, Holiday,* the *New York Times* and other magazines.

Near the Line

> . . . he is like unto a man beholding
> his natural face in a glass:
>   For he beholdeth himself, and goeth
> his way and straightway forgetteth
> what manner of man he was.
>   James 1:23–24

HARRY CAME ABOARD in the middle of the night, the last man. It was June. Over Manhattan starry queens and dragons calligraphed the sky; the air was languid and full of salt. The ship did not stop for him, he came aboard from a moving launch at Rosebank where the anchor lights of silent vessels reflected down deep into the Narrows.

"The Jacob's ladder, pull it up behind you," the Mate said, speaking down to Harry from the bridge. "Then give the lookout a spell for coffee—"

"When I get my gear, thanks, if you don't mind," Harry said under his breath as he touched the deck. He found a line and tossed it to the launch below, swearing to himself because no man was there to help him.

"You walked right into a watch," the Mate said.

"Near the Line" – Calvin Kentfield, *Texas Quarterly,* Copyright © 1966 by The University of Texas.

Harry hauled up his seabag, his portable radio, his brown-paper parcel of Chinese-laundered shirts, carefully setting them one by one on a tank top which was certain to be cleaner than the deck, then he drew up the ladder. The launch revved up and pulled away with one eye red and one eye green, heading back for Staten Island.

"You walked right into a watch," the Mate said.

"That's not all I walked into, Dumbo," Harry remarked under his breath. He mounted the catwalk and strode to the bow, leaving his belongings where they lay.

The lookout, an ordinary seaman who fancied the name of The Rock—because he suspected some lode of steadfastness lay concealed in his untested character, perhaps, or simply because his real name was Drury Orestes Tyler—had been keeping watch all the hours of darkness down the Hudson without a single cup of coffee because the watch he stood had been short a man. He was a recent orphan, this Tyler, from the West. He had never known a mother, and when his father died he was left footloose and prey of the winds and, like a seed, he had drifted to sea.

"Get your coffee, son," Harry said when he reached the fo'c'slehead. "And take your time." He belched roughly into the sensitive night, slapping his iron stomach with the flat of his hand. "Name's Harry, what's yours?"

"The Rock," said the ordinary as he walked away.

Harry laughed, disrespectfully, and belched again, turning his attention to the departing shore. "Look at 'em," he said aloud. *"Listen* at 'em."

A hum like a generator or like a distant litany of prayers repeated crept over the water from the parkway that described the island with a current of headlights and taillights. "In the middle of the lousy night," said Harry, "going to Brooklyn and coming back. I'm glad I'm where I am."

He unleashed another laugh that roughly handled the tender silence of the night and brought a megaphoned word from the bridge, "No talking up there, you disturb the pilot."

"No talking," Harry muttered to himself. "No smoking, no open lights, no visitors. Shhh—that's a tanker life." Again he laughed, but quietly. "Pilot!" he exclaimed under his breath. "I could run this harbor with a bucket on my head."

This, of course, was untrue, but he believed it when he said it as much as he believed he was glad to be there. At a booth in Bukie's he had sat for three hours being shanghaied by relentless Seven-Highs and flattery. As he was an heroic drinker, the bourbon pleased him but did not sway him, but the flattery, on his heroic vanity, had an insidious effect.

"Hairy, wur not beggin' you to go, Hairy, don't get us wrong, we don't squat down for no man, but we ast you to consider the *Union*. She's got turis' for a *crew*, Hairy. There ain't a sing'l *sailor* inna deck depotment. They're all right wit *brooms;* come up wit innage er outtage er ullage an' wur back in kindegarden. Hairy, we *know*—" They, two up-and-coming patrolmen in the Union, knew he had just come from a year in the Persian Gulf and had money in all his pockets, but what with shipping the way it was that month, they had plenty of itchy kids, but experienced *men* with AB tickets and guts enough to turn right around and go back—"Look Hairy, we *need* you. She's comin' down tonight from Rensaleer, goin' to Texas to load high-octane for Limeyland, and we know *you* ain't scared a high-octane. They're *babies,* Hairy. We coun't tellem they was goin' to the Guff afta, but we don't hide nuttin from you, Hairy, wur on the up and up wit you." Harry nodded. The blunt end of an index finger punched his shoulder. "It'll take a *big man,* Hairy, to keep the babies straight."

The Rock, one of the babies, returned to the fo'c'slehead with his coffee.

"How long you been going to sea?" Harry asked. The neon tube of the Brooklyn shore was backing steadily around to the left. The ocean was before them. The Rock replied, "Since my Daddy died last year. I've got sea time for seven months and seventeen days."

"You going to sea all your life?"

The Rock shrugged.

"See that light?" Harry said. "You know what that is?"

"I've been here before," The Rock replied. "That's Ambrose."

"Ring it up," Harry said. "Bye bye New York."

At four o'clock in the light of their fo'c'sle, The Rock introduced Harry to their other watchmate who had been on the wheel. His name was Bob and he had gained his AB ticket from time spent in the Navy as a yeoman.

"Oh Christ!" cried Harry. "Another one. How old are *you?* Twelve?"

"Twenty-two," said Bob.

"You an AB? Oh Christ!"

Harry began to unpack his gear which was tidy and spotless in Scandinavian fashion saying, as he laid the predominantly white, carefully folded articles on the shelves of his locker, that neatness and cleanliness were a sailor's greatest virtues next to strength. Each piece of work clothing that he precisely stowed away was marked, stenciled HARRY on a seat or a collar or across the shoulders of a T shirt. He peeled off his jumper, slid off his slacks, then stepped into the washroom next door for a double quick shower. Almost instantly he returned, dripping wet, and began drying himself in the middle of the fo'c'sle taking care to point out his enormous shoulders and to thump his steel chest. He puffed himself up as he swiped the towel across his back, working and flexing his ponderous arms in a nonchalant way. "You know how old I am? I'm forty-two." Actually, he was thirty-seven. "You'd never believe it, would you?"

Bob moaned. "Oh man oh man, of all the guys I could get me, I got to get a mister. Hey mister, who was you, Mister Yorkville or something? You a Kraut?"

Harry froze; and Bob, who was short and broad and from the city, stared at him impertinently with black eyes that were softly enormous at the same time that they were quick and knowing. After a long intimate look at Harry, up and down, he snickered, then left the fo'c'sle for the washroom. Harry at once laid a huge grendel hand upon The Rock's shoulder and leaned toward his ear. "He's a Jew?" And held a forefinger to his lips for silence.

"He ain't no Jew," The Rock corrected. "He's Italian. His name's Martini."

Harry smiled and tapped his lips with his finger. Still smiling, he withdrew a pair of red-embroidered Arab slippers from his locker and set them carefully beside his bunk in case he should have to rise in the night. Then he slipped himself in just as carefully between the fresh sheets and chuckled himself to sleep.

During their next watch in the bright clear afternoon while the ship, with Bob at the wheel, made a fine speed down the coast, The Rock and Harry worked together on deck in a place secure from the eyes of officers. Harry spent more time talking than working. "Never trust anybody that's little and dark," he told The Rock. "No dark little people of any kind." He explained that all Italians were Jews disguised as Italians and were not to be trusted. They never made good companions, neither Italians nor Jews. The Rock was about to say What are you, nuts or something? but he was painfully conscious of being young and ignorant, and he wanted to learn, so he said, "How come?"

"Listen," Harry began, leaning confidently toward his young pupil. "You ever hear of the Lost Tribe of Is*reel?* Well, twelve thousand years ago there was the biggest fight ever fought amongst the Christians and the Jews, and it was led by a Christian name of Armand Gideon, and all the Jews was killed or taken prisoner by Armand Gideon except for one wandering Jew name of Roamus, and his uncle, Remus, and they wandered all around until they come to It'ly and that's how come."

"That's how come what?"

"How come all Eye'ties are Jews in disguise—because they don't want it spread around that they're the lost tribe, see, because once they got going again, calling themselves *Roamins,* see, they started to toss Christians to the hungry lions."

"How could they start up again if there was only this guy and his uncle? Who you trying to kid?"

"Don't believe me, son, believe the Bible."

At Port Arthur, the ship sucked up to its brim the touchy cargo and headed out, back across the Gulf and along the keys, close in, deep in the water, flying like a fish on the powerful Gulf Stream. Harry, on the fantail, waved at the pink-and-white hotels that lined the shore, shouting across the narrow tarponed sea, "Bye bye Miami." By now he had a band of listeners that gathered on the fantail each evening for purposes of enlightenment. This little deck, opening out from the messroom, with a ladder leading to the boat deck, was the crew's back porch. There, between watches and after supper, the men leaned upon the windlass or the taffrail, took conversational seats on facing

bitts, or moved out chairs or boxes from the galley to sit around
and smoke and say what they had to say, and to listen in
return. When Harry talked, everybody listened, not just those
gathered for that purpose but even those who sat inside the
messroom playing casino or rummy. To them his voice came
through the open door in clear snatches sanctioned by the heartbeat of the vessel's screw, seeming, thus, to be the true voice of
sea experience. It took their minds off their games. Of course,
those aqueous starry evenings were open sessions, but the babies,
empty of knowledge and full of respect, said nothing; and the
others, mostly stewards or members of the black gang, who were
more seasoned, could not compete with Harry's compelling style,
so they sat alone without disciples pretending to read or play
solitaire but listening, listening.

With the sun setting behind him, Harry perched on the taffrail
secured by a scarlet Mohammedan-slippered foot hooked around
a stanchion. His only clothing was a pair of boiled khaki shorts.
His hair, bleached by the sun and the salt air and parted in the
middle, poured straight as rain down both sides of his head. His
deep little eyes were a Husky's eyes; and on his naked sand-
colored chest of prodigious breadth hung a polished shark's tooth
on a cord. He wore it, he said, to keep off evil airs, to put lead in
his pencil, and to keep his complexion clear. It was also
valuable, he explained, as an anecdote against the influence of
certain stars, particularly Venice, the cause of all unfaithfulness in
women.

The Rock, in spite of himself, was a regular listener. "Who
you trying to kid?" he said.

"All right, son," Harry said, shrugging his shoulders. "You
don't have to believe me. Only let me warn you. Watch out.
Because they'll get you in the end. See up there?" Harry pointed
to the sky now dark enough to show its strongest bodies. "Follow
my finger. There. There's Vegas . . . and Sinus . . . and Altar
. . . and there, over there, that's Venice, the worst of them all,
like I said, it watches out for love. I bet you got a girl."

"Sure, I got a girl in Coos Bay, she's a telephone operator,
she says number please and I got your number—" he laughed.
"We're going to get married when I'm twenty-four."

"You're a smart kid, Rock. Only—you're nineteen now? Think she'll wait?"

"Sure. She *said.*"

"You're a smart kid, Drury, only you don't know much of anything about *women.*" Harry laughed, and all The Rock's contemporaries joined in as if they knew all there was to know. "You don't have to believe me, but if you want her to be there when you get back, you should of hung a tooth on her before you left."

"Aw, shee-ut," The Rock said, turning away from Harry's grin. "Who you trying to kid?" He stepped into the messroom and threw himself moodily into a chair opposite Bob who was playing twenty-one with himself.

"So why'd you listen to the lousy squarehead?" Bob asked.

"Some of what he says is inneresting," The Rock replied.

"What? Like I'm a Jew and his lousy teeth? And Venice? Who's he trying to kid. I used to be inna Navy, and it's *Venus,* not Venice. My old man come from Venice, he didn't come from no Venus; and it's not a star, it's a planetoid."

"Tell *him* that."

"Shh—" Bob shrugged. "Voluntarily I should be dis*mem*bered?"

Near Hatteras the ship veered off to cross the ocean. Four pale-blue evenings of ingenuous summer passed and, during the fourth night, a fog appeared ahead of the ship, rising from the sea like the moonlit ramparts of some alcazar. It proved to be Harry's realm. Day after day the sun rolled dully as a pewter plate across the sky. The ship dead-reckoned, feeling its way through ship-infested seas, its whistle blowing a persistent and monotonous warning, its sailors harried by the cries of unseen birds whose voices swarmed about their ears like the tweets and squeals of spirits. Those were very fishy seas, and the birds dove to feed then rose and soared into a world of light and air that opened wondrously not fifty yards above the captain's head as he stood his gloomy bridge. His vessel had no radar. Human vigilance was his only protection against collision. Back aft, Harry sat on his perch each evening. The house lights cast a prodigious shadow of him on the fog, and he told his listeners of a murder that had been done on board a ship of his acquaintance in a foggy stretch of lonesome sea. "You couldn't see your hand before your face, so no one could see who done it. It could of been anyone among them, anyone at all." He told them of the fate of a man should he be so hapless as to fall overside in a heavy fog. "Even if you heard him yell, heard him holler his guts out, you'd never find him, you'd pass on, just pass on and leave him there."

After a few of such accounts, with the fog showing no signs of clearing, Harry's audience diminished, but The Rock and three or four others stayed on to hear the story of the *Naxos* disaster, the *Øresund* disaster, and the recent disaster of the *Temple* and *John Paul Jones*. These last, two high-octane carrying tankers, one empty bearing the perilous fumes, had done no more than brush together lightly in the fog off Cape Charles and only two charred human fragments out of eighty able men had been found with the odorous smoke of life in them. Harry claimed to have seen the collision though he didn't explain how since it had taken place ten miles out in fog as opaque as a limestone wall, but he described enthusiastically the appalling scream of the tortured sea when assaulted by cataracts of molten steel.

"And *both* of *them* had *radar,*" he added. "We don't have *shit!*"

Bob, who, together with many others, had overheard the story from the messroom, walked out and confronted Harry, saying:

"Whyn't you shut up."

Harry slid off the rail and rose up over his watchmate like the genie over the fisherman. Bob stepped back. "Whatsa good of talkin' like that," he said. "Man, we're all in this together."

"That's right," Harry said. "If I was you, son, I'd watch your step in this fog. Say, Rock, did you know that Hitler was a Jew, and that Joe Stallion, he's a Jew, and that Winsome Churchill, too, they're all in cahoots. That whole war wasn't nothing but Jew business. And the True Man, himself, he was a Jew just like your little Dago friend here."

"Whyn't you shut up?" Bob said, angrily, doubling his fists. Harry just turned away and faced the fog that held them all together like the walls of a room. He threw back his head and began to shake with villainous laughter, slapping his hard bare stomach the while with the flat of his hand as though he were attempting to control some kind of seizure.

Next morning the ship left the region of fog, exiting on the stroke of ten as though by the postern gate. The sun remained partially confused by fragment webs of high clouds, but, for that hour, the horizon was unnaturally clear and the first noon position in seven days was subsequently obtained. The captain, finding he was coming up, roughly, on Fastnet trimmed his course accordingly for Bishop's Rock. Another three and a half days of perfect weather and he was pumping out his skittish cargo at Jarrow on the greasy Tyne just down the hill from the ancient remains of the abbey of the Venerable Bede. The mail came aboard, but there was little for anyone and none for The Rock who was expecting something, a letter or a post card, from Coos Bay.

Harry naturally made a point of saying I told you so, repeating his belief of the power of a shark's tooth on a woman's virtue. He promised The Rock he'd catch a shark for him as soon as they reached infested waters. He was by all standards and by any method, he explained, the most expert shark catcher around. Some experts went about it one way, some another, but his way was the best. He used entrails instead of flesh for bait. He used a good gantline except for the big babies which took wire and the steam winch to haul in. The Rock replied that he didn't need any charms because just because he didn't get a letter didn't mean that she wasn't waiting just as faithful as could be.

By that time everyone knew that they were heading for the Persian Gulf, and in twelve days they were halfway there, anchored in the bay at Suez waiting for the fuel barge to come out from Port Tewfik. The clear waters bristled with ravenous sharks. The mail came aboard and this time The Rock did receive a letter from Coos Bay, Oregon. When the mail came, The Rock and Bob were playing casino in the messroom while Harry, true to his promise and his passion, was angling for a shark off the fantail. He lowered a heaving line with a bloody piece of bait on a billy hook and almost instantly a glowing blue creature was shuttling the salty anchorage with the hoop in its maw. Several crewmen were watching and shouting suggestions, but Harry ignored them all and steadily pulled the creature in with his bare hands exhibiting a strength so prodigious that the evil fish, without hope of escape, gained the spectators' sympathy. It was a smallish shark, no more than five feet long, and Harry was clearly disappointed. He dashed it to the deck where it instantly lost its sheen and lay dull, quiet and alive, its eyes wide open at the feet of its captor. Harry then took the maul he had at hand, raised it with one arm alone and brought it down, bashing the creature's head. Quickly then, efficiently, with fire axe and clasp knife, he began hacking away at the shark's bony jaw, digging with his knife to extract a tooth. As he worked, the deck began to smell barbarically of fishy blood and sea water, bringing complaints from the cook. Harry wiped the bloody tooth on the cuff of his shorts and scraped the carcass overside. Wiping the gore from his hands on the seat of his pants, and holding the tooth like a gift before him, he entered the messroom where The Rock was reading aloud to Bob the following short intelligence from Coos Bay:

Rock, boy, I don't know what you've heard, but in case you've got any ideas, it wasn't me. I don't know who it was. I don't know where she's gone neither probably up to Seattle where she can get it fixed. I just wanted to tell you that it wasn't me, that's all. Have a good trip. Your good buddy, Bucky D.

"Here, Rock, good buddy, I brought you a tooth," Harry said with a wide wicked grin. He had heard the message. He tossed the tooth on the table in front of The Rock who turned blistering red.

"Whyn't you go 'way," said Bob.

"I used to know a girl, once," Harry said, "who was telephone operator in Newark."

"They got dials in Newark," Bob said savagely. "Man, whyn't—"

"She was Long Distance," Harry calmly pursued, explaining in his deliberately inhuman style how he had met her and what she had done the very first time. By the time he had finished he had proven, by is own logic at least, that telephone operators were the same thing as call girls.

The Rock, furious, hurt, and blazing red sprang from his chair. Tears were starting in his eyes as he rushed toward the door.

Harry reached out and jerked him to a halt with one arm, saying, "Don't forget your tooth, good buddy."

"*I don't want no crazy tooth!* What d'you think I am, a *can*aball or somethin', you a *can*aball or somethin'? Whoever said you was so smart?"

Harry smiled indulgently and released the boy. He shrugged his shoulders as The Rock stormed out. Bob made a move to follow but Harry's monster hand restrained him. "Let go of my body," Bob said.

"You mind, Jewboy, what you say about me to your buddy," Harry warned.

"You thickass squarehead, can't you see he don't want nothin' to do with you. Take your stinking hand off my body."

"And keep your shadow off my path," Harry said, letting go.

The watch that night was an anchor watch. At the end of the first part The Rock relieved Bob and was in turn relieved by Harry. Harry spoke to him, but he did not reply. He went aft and mounted the ladder to the boat deck which had become in the hot climate an open dormitory of canvas cots. His cot was next to Bob's who had already retired. "You asleep," The Rock asked. There was a long pause while The Rock sat down on the wooden edge of his bed and took off his shoes.

"His time'll come," Bob said.

The Rock stripped to his skin and lay down on his back and, to keep off the thousands of flies that would awaken at dawn, he drew up the sheet from the foot of his cot until it covered him to the bridge of his nose. "His time'll come all right," he said. Like Bob, he pillowed his head on his arms, and like Bob, he let his gaze search deep and then deeper into the black Egyptian sky until it became entrapped in the intricate calligraphy of the stars. There, Antares, the fierce pink eye of the Scorpion, found them out, and they fell asleep, dreaming revenge.

And Harry, before going to bed, let down his heavy line again. Sometime during the dark hours the bait was taken, but whatever creature had come and eaten had escaped the hook.

By noon the next day the fuel barge still had not come and the twelve-to-four went on anchor watch again—working on deck, keeping to the shade. Over the anchorage in the enormous air, there was not a bird nor a cloud nor a touch of wind. The bay, transfixed in midday slumber, stretched out to the East to the pink hills of Sinai which stood against the cerulean sky like pyramids; and to the West fingertips of still water touched the golden line of the great drowsy desert. Near the town at the head of the bay, against the deep green of the date groves, a few white sails stood out but, like the hands of a clock, they would not move if they were being watched. Nothing moved until four o'clock when a prodigious creature, a shark, slipped out of the shade of the vessel's hull and slowly, slowly began to swim toward the stern.

Harry, just relieved of his labors on deck, spotted it at once. He judged it to be twenty feet long though in truth it was closer to fourteen. It was light blue-grey and seemingly eyeless with a tail as curved and keen as a sickle. Indeed it seemed to scythe the water as it swam, back and forth and forth and back, foraging, apparently, or harvesting, and revealing from time to time, as it rolled slightly on its side, a glimpse of its milk-white belly.

As Harry watched from the rail, others gathered including Bob and The Rock who saw their watchmate's usually scornful, rather stony, expression change. His little eyes withdrew into the bony outcroppings of his skull as the feelers of certain insects withdraw in time of danger. He smiled to himself in a way that neither of them had seen him smile before. Leading the group, he moved aft along the rail, speaking to the shark as it moved along the stern, "Come here, baby, come over here," he said. His thick, limber, tremendously powerful arm reached out over the water, beckoning, and revealing between its own restrained, deliberate coaxing and the motion of the fish, a sinister consanguinity. "Come over here, baby, come over here," he cooed.

The monster, however, kept on its way, and when it neared the point of the taffrail where Harry's line slackly hung, it sounded out of sight.

"That's the baby took my bait," Harry said. "You just watch me get him. He won't bite before sundown, but you just watch me get him." He knew their habits well, he said, and he'd bet his life this one was laying just easy under the stern waiting for dark. "And he'll come the other side from where he sounded, too," he said. He drew up his line, baited it again, and dropped it from the other side of the fantail, the port side, taking care before doing so to sharpen the billy hook with a file and to secure the mess of entrails with seizing. Then he went below to clean up for supper. He took a salt-water shower to cool off, then a cool freshwater shower to wash off the salt. Only then did he begin to wash in earnest. With soap and hot water and a small stiff brush he scrubbed his body like a Dutch housewife scrubbing her kitchen floor, and when he had finished lathering from head to toenails, he rinsed off and started again, working from the roots of his hair down.

While this was going on, Bob stepped into the next shower which had a porthole. He turned on the water and made a lot of puffing noises while he reached out of the porthole for Harry's fishing line. The showers were on the starboard side one deck down from the fantail; and The Rock, knowing Harry's habits as well as Harry knew his shark's, as soon as Harry had gone below, drew up the hook, cut off the guts, and led the end of the line around the fantail to the other side, letting it loop deeply under the stern. He dangled the hook in front of the shower room porthole and Bob reached out, caught it, and brought it inside. As long as Harry stayed in his shower, Bob remained in the next stall, standing in front of the porthole, bathing assiduously until Harry finished and returned to the fo'c'sle. Bob, then, slipped the prong of the hook over the hot water pipe, dried himself off, concealed the hook with the damp towel, dressed, and went back up on deck. Harry, he knew, would take another thirty minutes rubbing himself with oil, shaving, patting his cheeks and neck and granite chin with sweet shaving lotion, picking at his face in the fo'c'sle mirror, and plastering his amber-colored hair to his temples with apple-blossom pomade. When Bob joined The Rock on the fantail, they both inspected the line and agreed that there was nothing suspicious about it, dropping, as it had done before, easily into the water.

Several of the crew waiting for supper had watched The Rock rig Harry's line and had instantly recognized an old trick. They quietly passed the word around that the big man was in for a big surprise.

At half-past five, cleansed and purified as a Moslem before prayer, his faded buttonless armless dinner shirt softly laundered and showing the grey remains of HARRY across the shoulders and hastily tied by its tails around his middle, his lean tan chest ostentatiously exposed, bearing the tooth and glowing with soft oil like the burnished breastplate of a Roman centurion, Harry stepped into the messroom; and Bob, who had finished his supper, slipped out. The Rock quickly swallowed his dessert and followed him.

The sun had declined considerably, the bay was busy now with feluccas and bumboats, and the cooler air was drawing scents and vapors from the shadowed groves ashore. In Port Tewfik near the mosque which was reflected now in the green-glass bay, automobiles, horse carriages, and long-robed inhabitants could be seen moving along the sea wall and the boulevard. Gradually, the messroom emptied. Those of the diners who had heard of the trick collected on the fantail smoking and waiting and watching the bay while Harry, who always ate the menu through, finished up his second dish of stewed fruit and fourth piece of chocolate cake, wiped his mouth carefully on three successive paper napkins, and reached for the largest, reddest apple he could see in the bowl before him. As he was polishing the fruit with the soft spotless tail of his old chambray shirt, he heard The Rock, in a voice that was cold and absurdly indifferent, call in to him saying, "Hey, Harry, looks like something's after your guts."

The others around The Rock giggled, but Harry did not move except to stretch his neck a little to see out the porthole. He could see the sun was far from down, and he was absolutely certain his victim would not take the bait until the sun was under the horizon.

"Maybe he's nibbling," he said, "but he won't bite."

"*Oh yeah?*" cried The Rock. "He's *got* it! HE'S GOT IT!"

Down in the shower room on the other side, Bob gave a great pull on the line to make it shudder and then he began to reel it through the porthole onto the shower deck while every man on the fantail shouted and crowded toward the rail.

"Look at 'im go, look at 'im go," someone cried. "He's that big bastard, *I* bet."

Harry rose, still polishing the apple, and stepped inquisitively out of the messroom.

"Hey Harry," The Rock said. "Thought you was so smart, thought you said he wouldn't bite till sundown."

"Man, man, MAN! Look at 'im antelope!" one of the ordinaries shouted as the line whizzed over the taffrail.

"Take a turn! Take a turn, somebody," The Rock said. He reached toward the running line.

"NO!" cried Harry, "leave him slack."

The Rock did not obey; he grabbed the line and threw a quick turn on the bit and brought the line up short. Harry, as The Rock knew he would, tossed his apple overside, and, swelling with fury, seized The Rock by the shoulder and gave him a shove into the crowd. "This is *my* devil!" Harry exclaimed. "So do what I tell you," he said, threateningly. He quickly unsnubbed the line that now, slowly by its own weight, slipped over the rail.

"Sure, sure," The Rock said, "if that's the way you want it, you don't have to get rough about it." He stepped aside then as Harry let the line run free for a few more feet.

"Now's the time to snub it," he said, doing so. *"Now,* we got him *hooked."*

Feigning indifference, The Rock, barely able to contain his laughter, turned from Harry to the others and cautioned them to silence. The noise and commotion had brought several others to the stern including an officer or two from the saloon; and quickly, surreptitiously, the simple news of the joke went around.

Harry began to organize the bystanders, seizing, of course, upon his usual prey, the babies of the crew. His line was nearly out so he sent one ordinary after an inch-and-a-half gantline. Another he sent for a maul and an axe, and he sent The Rock below to get his clasp knife from their fo'c'sle. Each man obeyed without question, and as The Rock passed the shower room, he gave Bob news of their progress. They dissolved in laughter; then, pulling themselves together, decided upon a way to end it.

"Stand back," Harry said. "Everybody stand back." The ordinary with the gantline approached. "Here, stupid, bend those lines together," he ordered. Then he let out a little more line that Bob reeled into the shower.

The other ordinary returned puffing under his burden of an axe and a huge maul. Harry told him to stand by.

"I'm sure glad ole Harry knows his beans," one of the bystanders said. "I sure wouldn't know how to catch me a shark, I mean, a big ole shark like that, I mean."

"Yeah, I'm glad too, sure is a tricky business all right," said another. There were a few muffled giggles from the crowd, but Harry didn't hear them. In fact, he scarcely heard any of the remarks so intent was he now upon his killing.

"Run that gantline outboard there," he ordered The Rock, who had returned with the knife. "And lead it through the after chock and around the fairlead, then stand by to give me a hand, we're going to pull him in."

Now the sun was low over the desert, and a long, long shadow of the ship and its men along the rail lay across the surface of the deep bay. A sluggish felucca traversed that shadow as Harry said to The Rock, "Take holt, now, and . . . PULL!"

The two of them heaved on the line which Bob, with a turn around the pipe, let out with a tolerable strain upon it. After a bit though, he tied it off, so that in a matter of seconds the two men were pulling against the ship's plumbing.

"This kid here's weak as Sally," Harry said with extreme irritation. "Come here some of you punks, let me see how much men you are."

The other two ordinaries took the line and pretended to pull, but, accomplishing nothing, they let go while Harry continued to pull with all of his incredible strength. The muscles of his arms and shoulders grew turgid and red, his feet braced against the bitt and his mammoth thighs and thick calves strained. With sweat on his brow and tears in his eyes, he threw back his head to the crowd and cried in the agony of passionate exertion: "STEAM ON DECK! Somebody get me STEAM ON DECK!"

"Now wait a minute," said the Mate who had been watching from the rear of the group. He was of a serious turn of mind and he feared there might be trouble when Harry, having gone so far in his blind commitment, found out he was being fooled. He didn't dare expose the joke, but he thought he had better give some kind of warning. He stepped up and told Harry that it looked like he'd just hooked the screw or the rudder post.

"No no no," cried Harry in desperation. "Can't you see he's there. He's a monster, he's a devil. I need the winch. I need STEAM ON DECK!"

The line gave a little and Harry staggered, then it gave way altogether landing Harry on the deck, flopping on his back, his color changing from red to pale as his blood drained away. As if he were the shark, his eyes were open, looking up at all those who had crowded around to see him fall.

"You're too strong, Harry," The Rock said, coldly, looking down. "You broke the line. Looks like he got away."

The crowd chuckled nervously as Harry got to his feet and, unable to believe what was obvious to all the rest, began to pull in the limp line. His audience then burst into outright laughter, but Harry didn't see. He continued doggedly, assiduously, and with increasing despair, to reel in the wet flaccid line. The others pushed in around him, laughing, burying their faces in their arms, in each others shoulders, the babies roaring and dancing and hugging each other, egging him on:

"Come on, come on, Harry, let's see whatcha caught."

And Harry still did not see, still pulled in the line, taking care, as he did so, to let it drop to the deck in the neat practiced coils of good seamanship. When he reached the bitter end, he found in his giant heroic hand his carefully sharpened billy hook on whose prong was impaled a pair of his shorts neatly stenciled HARRY across the seat.

The laughter ceased for the full half-minute that he contemplated his marked garment. When, finally, finally, he saw what had been done to him, he looked up; the sun had died in the desert, and across the water from the town came the voice of the muezzin, over his public address system, calling the faithful to prayer.

When he saw Harry's face, The Rock's steadfastness shook a little, not so much because he was afraid of what Harry might do to him, rather because he had never seen on a human face such desolation and loneliness, such mortification and dismay. These together came to The Rock as a single expression of profoundly childlike hurt. He was very young, The Rock, and he had never deliberately hurt a man before. He was like a boy playing crooks and cowboys with another and discovering by the horrible blast and the bloody head that his gun was loaded; but he was man enough to enjoy his victory, too. He suppressed an impulse to say, I'm sorry I didn't mean it, I didn't mean to play so rough; though he possessed no equipment that could tell him how complete his victory was.

Unable to speak, avoiding eyes, clutching his dripping shorts, Harry went below to his room, hanging his head. A long time later when The Rock and Bob came into the sweltering fo'c'sle to get bedding for their cots on deck, Harry, still dressed and saturated with sweat, lay on his bunk with his face to the wall. He neither moved nor spoke, but he was awake because Bob, leaning quietly over him, peered boldly into his eyes and saw that they were open.

Just before midnight, the ship was ready to proceed. Harry stood his watch that morning, took his trick at the wheel, kept his lookout, and spoke to no one except to shout to the officer of the watch, Lights Are Bright! when he struck the time on the fo'c'slehead. He ate neither breakfast nor lunch, nor did he take up his station on the fantail after supper, in fact, he seemed to fade altogether from the society of his shipmates.

With a constant following wind the ship sped easily down the long finger of the Red Sea, through the Strait of Bab el Mandeb, and around the rocky, sere Arabian coast to the Gulf of Persia. In Mena al Ahmedi Harry, complaining of his stomach, asked the captain if he could see a doctor. The captain assented, but the doctor in a hasty examination could descry no malady. The ship returned through the Suez, deflected through the troubled strait of Messina, passed the monstrous Liparis that seemed to be burning slowly to death in the night, and discharged its crude cargo in the Ligurian port of La Spezia. Again Harry requested medical attention, but the Italian company doctor found him well-made and fully sound.

The ship, whose orders had been changed, instead of returning to Kuwait, made out for South America passing through the Gates of Hercules into the full Atlantic. Though Harry never spoke a word to The Rock or to Bob outside of passing on the course at the change of the wheel or other requirements of simple duty, it became apparent to them by his gauntness and loss of weight, by his sleeplessness and his smell that he was drinking. The captain freely issued beer, but Harry was drinking the brandy he had bought with cigarettes from the bumboats during the bunker stop at Gibraltar. On the far side of the

Canaries that supply ran out and, as the ship traversed the sullen Sargasso Sea yellow with weed, the twelve-to-four fo'c'sle began to reek of a sickening mixture of Harry's sweet shaving lotion and vomit.

One evening then, in the doldrum latitudes near the Line, Harry called upon the captain in his room. He said he was in pain. In the hard confined light of that little space he looked like Death or a harbinger of Hell—his glazed eyes ringed with red and purple, his skin blotched and pallid, his person unkempt and unclean. The captain, who had had one man die on him before, sent him instantly to the infirmary, then began to scan those empty seas for a doctor. The clouded sky hung close upon the breathless water, the air was hot and vaporous; and through the night while the signals went out from the radio shack, Harry, clutching his stomach, writhed and howled with pain; and those who came to view him through the open door saw the marks of bestial suffering graven on his face. Towards morning, a black-hulled vessel, answering, hove upon the thick horizon. The two ships drew together, a boat was lowered, the captain and the doctor conferred, and Harry was removed.

The black-hulled vessel took him away, and from the taffrail where Harry had been so wont to stand to fascinate and terrorize, The Rock watched him go. He watched him go without remorse. It was not light enough for him to see what the vessel was, not its name or nationality. Its stern light, reflecting on the glassy surface of that grey, dispirited sea, slowly diminished into the sultry dawn, then it vanished altogether. The Rock watched it go without remorse; and the moment the horizon took it, it took Harry from his mind; for he was young, very young, and like to a man who beholds his natural face in a glass, and goes his way, and straightaway forgets what manner of man he was.

NANCY HALE is the author of fourteen books, including novels, nonfiction, a collection of short stories, and one of essays. She was a portraitist before becoming a writer. Miss Hale has lectured on fiction at various institutions, especially at Bread Loaf Writers Conference where she has often been a member of the staff. She lives in Charlottesville, Virginia where her husband, Fredson T. Bowers is head of the English department at the University of Virginia.

The Most Elegant Drawing Room in Europe

"THE CONTESSA doesn't seem entirely real, she's so exquisite," wrote Emily Knapp to her friend and fellow-librarian Ruth Patterson, at home in Worcester, Massachusetts. "I wish you too might have seen her in her tiny jewel box of a palazzo yesterday, as we did! She'd lent us her gondola for the afternoon. (I can't tell you how super-elegant we felt, or how much attention we attracted on the Grand Canal.) Persis Woodson, the artist I wrote you about meeting on the Cristoforo Colombo coming over, remarked that all over America next winter people will be showing home movies with us prominent in them, pointing us out as aristocratic Venetians lolling in our private gondola!

"It is Persis that Mother and I have to thank for this wonderful opportunity—this unique experience. Her older brother, Tim Woodson, who was American consul here after the war, wrote to the Contessa about her. The Contessa can't seem to do enough for Persis, and even for us as Persis's friends. Do I sniff a romance in the dear dead days? We ended the afternoon

"The Most Elegant Drawing Room in Europe" – Nancy Hale, *The New Yorker,* Copyright © 1966 The New Yorker Magazine, Inc. Originally published in *The New Yorker.*

having cocktails at the palazzo. Never in my wildest dreams did
I think I'd catch a glimpse of quite such high life! Strange
to relate, Persis seems more irritated than charmed by the Contessa. But Art is all Persis lives for, and besides, through her
brother she is more accustomed to such grandeurs than we."

Emily paused and looked around, taking conscious pleasure
in her surroundings. She was sitting at a table in the grape arbor
at the end of the terrace of the *pensione,* where she was sheltered
from a hot September sun. Through interstices of the grapevines
there was a view of a short stretch of the Grand Canal, framed
by two tall palazzos, one pink, one yellow. Up the little San
Trovaso Canal moved coal or garbage barges, ponderously putt-
putting; more rapid launches; and an occasional, palpitatingly
leashed-in speedboat. As each boat passed by, waves were
created that slapped for a moment against the marble steps to
the *pensione,* then subsided. Wooden planks, nailed together,
leaned against the stone entrance post, ready for use as a bridge
to arriving boats. On the main, flagged terrace the sun still struck
robustly at five o'clock in the afternoon; between the terrace and
the shade of the arbor, monstrous big dahlias raised flaming
faces to the sun. Everything was very quiet right now. Older
people were resting. The servants were busy in the kitchen.
Persis Woodson was off seeing a Bellini Madonna at the Church
of San Zaccaria. Emily was saving her strength for the concert
tonight. She felt a little nervous about venturing out at night
in Venice; but Persis, whose judgment she deeply respected,
told her that was nonsense.

Suddenly a launch backfired, out in the San Trovaso Canal,
and Emily leaned forward to see. A young Italian was tinkering
with his trouble-making engine, very handsome in profile, his
neck round and brown and strong. In a moment more he got
his engine going and was moving out toward the opening into the
Grand Canal; in another moment he was gone.

Once more all was quiet. All of Venice seemed to subside
into its omnipresent waters, to be a mere illusion of iridescent
bubbles that floated on the bosom of an ageless, maternal sea.

"The Contessa's gondola was a marvel to behold," Emily resumed. "All the *pensione* help dropped their work and dashed
out to have a look at it. It was enamelled black, with brightly

polished brass sea horses and dolphins. And not one but two magnificent gondoliers, all in white, with broad red sashes. As we boarded it, the *signorina* who runs the place said to us, 'That is a most beautiful gondola. There are not many such left in this day of launches.' You could see her opinion of us soar!

"To help one, the younger gondolier standing on the steps offered a positively rocklike elbow to put one's hand on—instead of grasping one's arm the way the public gondoliers do. From inside the craft the older, fat gondolier supported one with a proffered elbow equally rocklike.

"Inside, instead of the worn black leather seats the public gondolas have, they were slipcovered in white linen, piped with red and yellow, the Contessa's colors. Even Mother was impressed!"

Emily paused again. Her mother—small, indomitable, highly critical of what she didn't like—was never abashed by her surroundings, never ashamed to say she preferred Massachusetts to Italy. She had, Emily reflected, twice her daughter's character. At the memory of the disgraceful way she had behaved to her mother that morning, she licked her lips and tried to close them over her teeth. Her awful teeth. . . .

"Everybody on the Grand Canal stared as we made our progress down toward the Rialto Bridge on our way to view the Church of Santi Giovanni e Paolo (in Venetian dialect, San Zanipolo)," she continued, turning with relief to the pleasure of writing the letter. "The passengers on the vaporetto all rushed to our side, and people even came out on the balconies of palaces to take a look!

"Persis, who knows more about Venice than I, having paid a visit to her brother here when she was a young girl, said the public gondoliers would recognize our gondola by its colors, and by the coat of arms on the gondoliers' silver arm brassards. Isn't that impressive?

"One young gondolier yelled something at us, and Persis, who knows some Italian, said he said, 'You got American *miliardi* there?' And our man said, 'Oh, sure, sure.' So while we may have deceived the tourists, you can be sure we did not deceive the professional gondoliers into thinking us Venetian aristocrats!

Still, I did enjoy lolling back like a lady. Loll is what you do, in a gondola."

Emily thought of her mother again. Mother hadn't lolled! Mother was, perhaps, incapable of lolling. She'd sat upright in the reclining seat, looking about her with calm curiosity as they turned off the Grand Canal into a very narrow one. Up this they had slowly progressed, squeezing past barges moored along the *fondamenti*. The marble water steps here were moss-grown and slimy. The overhanging houses and decayed palaces could not have changed to any extent in four hundred years. Emily turned to smile up at the gondolier behind her—the young, slim one—to show her appreciation. When he saw her looking at him, he smiled back. She turned around in her seat again, as always aware as soon as her eyes met another's of how her teeth looked.

"Hoh!" the old gondolier shouted as they slid up to an inter-section, hesitated, and swung into an even smaller, more obscure canal. Black tidal waters lapped against moldering palace por-tals and underneath the sills of square windows, crossbarred like those of the prison. They passed a tiny baroque church standing in a little stone-paved campo. Medieval stone arches and crooked *calli* led back on either hand into the secret inner places of Venice. "Unsanitary? I hope to tell you," Mother remarked.

"We drew up before marble steps the full width of the campo," Emily wrote. "They call them campos in Venice, not piazzas as in the rest of Italy. It was so thrilling! Because there right in front of us stood the Verrocchio statue of Colleoni! The Scuola San Marco with its marvellous Renaissance façade was on our left, and the church was straight ahead across the campo."

Emily paused again. She did not intend to tell Ruth the way she'd felt inside the Church of San Zanipolo. It was the way she so often felt inside these Italian churches: almost in tears. She, who'd gone to a Unitarian Sunday school, to nothing at all since she grew up! She had the feeling she would give anything to share whatever all those kneeling figures with ker-chiefed heads were experiencing.

"We did San Zanipolo—doges' tombs, and a notable Bellini and a Veronese. Then we started back, to wind up at the Contessa's for cocktails. The gondoliers had been consorting in a nearby café, and came bounding across the campo to assist us into the gondola. A whole crowd of people were assembled on the steps to watch us embark. We slid off, and made our tortuous way back to the Grand Canal. The Contessa lives up near the mouth of the Canal.

"Such swank! The Contessa's butler came out to the water steps to receive us, dressed in a tail coat and batwing collar. He led us into a little walled courtyard with black-and-white marble paving, said something in Italian, and disappeared. Persis told us we were to go up to the balcony, via the marble outside stairs. After we got up there, we felt in a bit of a quandary as to where to go next—whether to stay on the balcony or go into a drawing room we could see through open French doors. It all seemed very European and intimidating, at least to me.

"We were tentatively approaching the drawing room when our hostess put in an appearance, looking absolutely stunning. What is it women of fashion *do* to make them look so different? The Contessa simply has everything!

"*She* made the drinks, not the butler. He only brought out the plates of things to eat. I'd thought of course he'd make the drinks, but somehow it seemed even more sophisticated her doing it. Mother and I sat down, and Persis walked round peering at the Old Masters that hang on the Contessa's walls, looking stony-faced. Mother, of course, was perfectly at ease. Far more so than poor me! You can't faze Mother.

"The drawing room had an air even the grandest rooms in America don't have. There were little armless, satin-upholstered chairs and sofas; little tables with, set out on them, the Contessa's chairs and sofas; little tables with, set out on them, the Contessa's collection of jade. The Contessa herself sat draped at one end of a sofa. She kept urging us to take the food the butler had brought in and left on the tables. There were hot cheese things over a flame, and tiny hardboiled eggs. I asked what they were, and the Contessa said they were quail's eggs! She didn't hop up and hand things the way you or I would. Just sat there waving a hand and saying, 'But doo . . . You must . . . Please . . .' I've written you what I remember, but I can't catch what that extraordinary air of hers is. I guess one just can't understand someone like that. She's too different.

"Her hair, like everything else about her didn't seem real. It formed an enormous aureole around her head. I got my nerve up at one point and asked her to recommend a hairdresser in Venice. The Contessa said, as nearly as I can reproduce it, 'For your hair go to Carlo, darling. He is the best hairdresser in all Italy.' I can't explain how foreign and sophisticated it sounded. I glanced at Persis, but she just looked black, as she does when things become sophisticated. I couldn't help feeling maybe the Contessa rather took to me, although I know people like that say 'darling' to everybody.

"She had on a good deal of makeup; she has some skin trouble that has pitted her skin. She wore a brilliant yellow-and-orange flowered silk shift—you have no idea how fashionable! And wonderful little delicate slippers of yellow lizard! I couldn't help exclaiming—you know me, always gushing—'What a beautiful dress! Isn't it, Mother?' Dearest Mother, who is nothing if not frank, said, 'A nice dress for the morning.' I happen to know she doesn't approve of shifts—I shouldn't have asked her. But the Contessa, of course, could handle it. She said, 'I'd hardly wear it in the morning,' but with the most charming laugh. It's all so obvious that she's always at ease and has been everywhere and speaks quantities of languages and knows everybody and is rich and does exactly as she pleases!

"While we were there, she answered the telephone that stood by her sofa, and had a conversation with someone in Italian. You could tell it was a man. Her face got all eager and her voice softened and you could tell she was using pet names. She seemed almost pleading, but, of course, I didn't understand a word. When she hung up, her face came back to its chic, hard composure, and she said to Persis, 'Now, tell me more about Tim, and darling beloved Monica.' What I'm trying to say, Ruth, is that that kind of utter perfection *defeats* me. It's hard to believe that I belong to the same race as the Contessa, she's so exquisite.

"She said goodbye to us on the balcony; the butler saw us to the boat landing. This time we were helped into the launch. The Contessa told us she only keeps the gondola out of sentiment (quite an expensive sentiment, I feel sure!) and that she goes everywhere in the launch. 'Where?' I asked, and she said, 'Oh, to the Lido, darling, in the morning, for my swim and lunch in my cabaña, and to parties, and to friends. . . . And to things like tomorrow night.' I had a glimpse of her life, like an exquisitely designed work of Venetian glass art.

"The launch was as smart as the gondola, with white linen slipcovers in the cabin, also piped in red and yellow. How do you suppose it feels to have your own colors? The Contessa told us about tonight's concert at the famous Scuola San Rocco, decorated by Tintoretto. We would never have known about it otherwise. It will be an all-Vivaldi program by the Virtuosi di Roma. She said she'd take us home in her launch afterward. Doesn't it all sound like a movie? Not a bit what I expected when Mother and I boarded the Cristoforo Colombo!

"I tell Persis she is a perfect angel to ring us in on all this, but Persis says she wouldn't have gone at all if she'd had to go alone. In the launch, as we sped home, I said, 'The Contessa certainly couldn't do more for us,' and Persis said, 'I know. But in another way, she doesn't know we're alive.' 'But that's sort of fascinating,' I said, and then, because dear Mother gets offended when she is left out of the conversation, I said, 'Didn't you think the Contessa was fascinating, dear?'

"You know Mother! She said, 'I thought her hair looked like an African bushman.' All I could do was hope the man running the launch didn't understand English. . . ."

"*Well!*"

The voice was Persis's; she had entered the arbor, broad-brimmed hat in hand. Instantly Emily's being, which had been flowing into her letter, shrank back into an awareness of herself. She had an abrupt picture of how she looked, bending over the table, teeth hanging down like a silly fringe. She looked up and, helplessly, smiled at Persis, knowing that whatever she did, anywhere, her teeth always preceded her—splayed, jutting out, a fool's teeth—while around them she smiled and smiled merrily. "Did you enjoy the Bellini?" she inquired.

"Yes, it was a superb one," Persis said. She stood leaning against the post of the grape arbor, fanning herself with her hat—a bulky, jolly-looking woman in her late thirties, like Emily. Her gray hair was clipped short. "There was an Andrea del

Castagno in a side chapel. They have to light it for you. Afterward I went back to the Doges' Palace for another look at that Bellini, to compare them. I came back on the traghetto. Do you realize the fare is less to be ferried over if you stand up than if you sit down?"

They laughed together, with the pleasure they took in local detail and in laughing. Persis sat down.

"I had a *caffè cappuccino* at Florian's," Persis went on. "To comfort myself after having looked across from the Doges' Palace at the prison again. I agree, the terror still clings to it. Sitting at Florian's, I found this in Morris." She flipped open a guidebook she carried and read aloud, " 'Sometimes the stranger, passing by the Doges' Palace, would find a pair of anonymous conspirators hanging, mangled, from a gibbet, or hear a whisper of appalling torture in the dungeons of the Ten. Once, the Venetians awoke to discover three convicted traitors buried alive, head downward, among the flagstones of the Piazzetta, their feet protruding among the pillars.' "

"Oh dear!" Emily said. "Right where we were *standing!*"

They stared, half pleasurably aghast, at one another.

"Was it wonderful in the Piazza?" Emily asked.

"It was all right enough. Too many Germans, as usual. But at least it's no longer the absolute sink of high society it was in my youth! If Florian's would just lower its prices, it might belong to the people some day."

"But all those grand dukes," Emily couldn't forbear saying. "And Cole Porter and everybody. . . . It must have been awfully glamorous."

"Glamorous enough," Persis said. She smiled indulgently at her little friend. "You never actually saw it, as I did when I was young. The young sense so much, they know everything— But I don't need to tell you about being sensitive! The trouble was, Venice was wasted on those people. They just came to look at each other. They'd just as soon be in Palm Beach. They don't care about the true Venice."

"Didn't you think the Contessa's pictures were good?"

"Certainly," Persis said indifferently. "She probably got Perseoni to select them for her. In fact, I think Tim said Perseoni did select them. Anybody who's rich enough can get good pictures."

"You were so angelic to ring us in on the Contessa," Emily began once more. She couldn't seem to help saying it over and over.

Persis smiled and didn't reply. She would never have gone to that ghastly woman's at all except for the treat she knew it would be for the New England Knapps. She was attracted by little Emily Knapp, and was sorry for her—so pretty and gentle and sweet, crushed by that old tyrant of a mother. The morning when the *valet de chambre* had called her downstairs to the *pensione* telephone, where the Contessa was holding on, she had taken a positive satisfaction in saying that she was travelling with friends. She said "old" friends. She said she couldn't leave them. Might she bring them, she asked briskly. There was a moment's silence. Then the Contessa said, in that husky voice, "But of course." Although, while she was standing at the telephone in the *pensione* lobby, Persis hadn't yet met the Contessa, she knew just how she would look. And sure enough, she looked exactly that way.

Here, in the grape arbor, Persis was visited by a fleeting memory of herself, long ago, on that visit to Tim in Venice. She giggled now. "Remember I told you Italian men seem to have changed since the old days? Because they don't pinch one and call out '*Bella signorina!*' the way they used to do?"

Emily nodded, all receptiveness.

"Well, at Florian's it came to me why. It's not that *they've* changed. *We've* changed!"

Emily began to giggle, too. They looked at each other and laughed some more. It was the kind of joke that drew them together—a joke on their own old-maid state. Together they scampered companionably over the bridges of Venice, in and out of galleries, through the vast rooms of palaces, like girls together whispering and giggling.

Emily began to put her writing things away. "I must go and help Mother get ready for dinner," she said. "If we leave for the concert about eight-thirty, it's time enough, don't you think?"

"How is your mother this afternoon?" Persis asked politely.

"She's very well," Emily replied, politely.

But when she got upstairs to the large room the Knapps shared, Mother was still looking for that wretched comb.

"Darling. *Please* let me buy you another," Emily said.

The bedroom had a chandelier of inferior Venetian glass, each spoke forming a different-colored flower, three tall French windows that opened on a narrow balcony over the San Trovaso Canal, and an odd little closet that had been converted into a lavatory. The toilet was down the hall. There were twin beds, and on one of them Mrs. Knapp sat holding in her lap the overnight bag in which she kept her curlers. She had been going through its contents yet once more. Now she paused in her search to regard her daughter.

"What's the use of that," she said, "when it has to be somewhere in this room? I'm not in the habit of taking my comb around with me in my pocket, the way I know you young people think it's smart to do."

Emily tried to close her lips over her teeth. What her mother *was* in the habit of doing, she wanted to retort, was using her daughter's things when she mislaid her own. She mislaid them with increasing frequency. But Emily was determined she would not disgrace herself as she had done this morning, when, opening her eyes, she had found her mother sitting before the mirror combing her hair with Emily's comb. The most awful rage had leapt up in her and she'd cried, "Why must you use my things? I loathe sharing my things!"

Mrs. Knapp had turned full around in her chair. "Well! Now we know," she said.

Eight hours later—all this time since—the anger was still there. "I never mind sharing my things when there is some reason for it," Emily said very gently, going right on with the morning, "but all I would have to do is go round the corner to the *farmacia* and buy a comb. There isn't any reason why we have to use the same comb."

"A waste of good money," her mother pronounced. She went back to rummaging around in the overnight bag. "It has to be somewhere right in this room."

Emily sighed. "Time to dress," she said.

"Dress for what?"

"Well, for dinner, dear. And we're going to this wonderful

Vivaldi concert at the Scuola San Rocco that the Contessa told us about."

"You can count me out," Mrs. Knapp said. "I have to find my comb."

"But it's such an opportunity! And we're coming home in the Contessa's launch. Think how exciting *that* will be! Didn't you enjoy yourself yesterday?"

"It was all right," Mrs. Knapp said. "Your Contessa seems to deny herself nothing. But I can't spend my whole life in pleasure, the way you seem to do."

It was so unjust! "Darling. We only came to Europe to enjoy ourselves," Emily said.

"Pleasure doesn't have to cost so much money," Mrs. Knapp bore on, licking her lips easily. "Take soft drinks. You young people think you have to have soft drinks all the time. When *I* was young, we might make a pitcher of lemonade and carry it under the walnut tree and sit and drink it, after the chores were done. But we didn't think we had to drink soft drinks all day long."

It was so unreasonable! "I planned our trip just in order to give you pleasure," Emily said softly. "And we haven't had any soft drinks since we left home—"

"Hah!" Mrs. Knapp said. "I never wanted to come—you know that. I said so enough times."

Emily took a firm grip on herself. "But you didn't mean it, dear," she said. "All my life I've heard you say you wished you could see Europe and its treasures. That's what you really want. I'm only thinking of *you*—"

She broke off, for her mother had whirled around on the bed and was sticking out her tongue at Emily. *"'Only thinking of you!'"* she mocked, like an antique little girl. "Always perfect, aren't you?"

Emily's mind seemed to explode. Fragments of outrage came drifting down from above. Her teeth, her teeth . . . So far from perfect; so always in the wrong . . . unbearable, unbearable. In the end, as ever, the debris of Emily's thoughts settled down as into a smoking ash heap, soft, growing cooler. The only thing to do was bear it. Sometimes she had the feeling that her whole life was spent waiting for her mother just once to say she was sorry that she had not had Emily's teeth fixed when Emily was a little girl. But it would have to come from her. The accusation was too appalling to be made, and grew more so.

"You have to realize that from now on your mother's bound to fail," Persis said soothingly, as during the concert intermission they stood together downstairs in the Scuola San Rocco, smoking cigarettes, two women wearing hats and carrying the raincoats they hadn't dared leave in their seats. "She *is* getting like a child. But of course she still has flashes of great wisdom," she added politely.

"It just makes me feel guilty, not to be kinder," Emily explained. "She can't help it if her memory is failing."

She had told Persis enough of the scene in the bedroom to make her see what it was like, dealing with Mother about things like the comb—not enough, she trusted, to disgrace her parent. She hadn't mentioned the sticking out of the tongue, for instance, or her own violent reactions.

"It is true, she *didn't* want to come, once we'd made up our minds," she went on. "I suppose the truth is I made her come. Perhaps I did the wrong thing. Perhaps I was selfish. Maybe I should have let her—oh dear!"

"You did the right thing," Persis told her firmly. "You're giving your mother a wonderful trip, and don't ever forget it, no matter what happens." They gazed into each other's eyes, thinking of death. "Let's go back, shall we? . . . Aren't the Tintorettos superb?" she said as they began climbing the flights of broad, shallow steps, looking up to either side and ahead at the pictures.

"Have you spotted the Contessa yet?" Emily asked when they had regained their original seats along the side of the enormous chamber that was lined, walls and ceiling, with the huge, dark Tintorettos. They stuffed their raincoats behind them to make the pewlike seats more comfortable.

It had been raining, although not hard, when they took the vaporetto down the Canal after dinner. They scampered through the drizzle from the *pensione* to the Accademia, bought their shoddy paper *biglietti,* and nipped onto the waterborne covered waiting room, which had a central rail to separate those embarking from those coming ashore. In a moment a vaporetto crashed up to the waiting room with, as usual, a stupendous bump. It had been fun sailing down the Canal, seeing the lights of the palaces through a blur of rain. Disembarking at the Frari stop, they scampered up through dark *calli* and over little bridges with a sense of adventure, at last gaining the Campo San Rocco, with its lighted Scuola and the people streaming in for the concert. There was no question but that it would have been most unwise for Mrs. Knapp to come out in such weather. In Venice, there was no way to escape rain.

"No, I haven't seen her," Persis replied to her friend. She looked about the hall, which was filling up with a seemingly all-Venetian, or at least all-Italian, audience. The only light was furnished by huge striated Venetian-glass lanterns, standing along three sides of the room. This flickering and glancing radiance fell on handsome, archaic faces—old, proudly beak-nosed men and beautiful red-haired women like those in Titians. One such Venetian beauty sat just in front of them with her blond little girl, who rested a lovely, oddly mature face against her mother's shoulder.

"There she is. Look," Persis said, poking Emily and nodding across the hall. "Over on the far side, this row, talking with an old gentleman with white hair. See?"

"Do you suppose he's her lover?" Emily whispered.

"I don't think so," Persis said.

"I do so appreciate your giving me this opportunity to see so many wonderful—" Emily began once more.

"It's a pleasure to me to do something that will give you pleasure," Persis declared. Then, for the violins were tuning up, "Sh-h-h!"

After the concert, feeling bemused with Vivaldi, the two women moved slowly down the great stairway with the push of the crowd. At the bottom they took up a stand facing the stairs, to await the Contessa.

She was an unconscionable time coming. At last, after almost everyone had descended, she appeared at the top of the lowest flight of steps, talking to a man with sleek black hair, her huge, *cotonata* head tipping one way as she spoke to him, tipping the other as she turned away to take another deliberate step down.

She wore another silk shift like the one she had had on the day before—this time a purple-and-blue flowered print with a long blue silk stole she held wrapped tightly around her shoulders as she continued to descend the stairs one step at a time, stopping entirely now and then to reply to the man or to free one hand and gesticulate. She spied the two women waiting and tossed up her chin in recognition. "Ah!" she said, coming up to them. "You are here. You have enjoyed the concert?"

"It was wonderful," Emily said. "I was simply carried away."

"Yes," the Contessa said. "I have told you I will take you home. We go this way. My man is at the campo steps with the launch. Follow me." Her vivid, erect form swept forward, the ends of the silk stole floating behind. At the main door of the Scuola, some young Italians seemed to be waiting for her; she held out her hands to them, then swept them into her entourage so that they, too, were following. She did not introduce Emily and Persis, who stood awkwardly waiting while she spoke to the young people. By now the Contessa's companion of the stair-case had disappeared.

Her group of guests followed her through steadily falling rain across the campo to steps that led down to a narrow canal. The launchman of the day before, now in oilskins, helped the Contessa first into her boat. Then the young Italians got in—two men and a girl. Last of all, Persis and Emily were helped aboard.

"I love your white slipcovers," Emily chattered nervously as she took her seat inside the cabin. "Isn't this snug here, out of the rain?" The launch had started up, and was moving very slowly along the dark canal, which was clogged with moored boats.

"Yes, very," the Contessa replied. "Have you all met? Countess Lieto, Count Morosini, Prince Fenna, Miss Woodson, Miss Mmmm. . . . All these young people live on the Giudecca, where the launch will take them after it has dropped us off."

With that the Contessa fell silent. The young people talked to each other in Italian, laughing and exclaiming with extreme gaiety. The launch, which had moved so very slowly, now turned into the Grand Canal and picked up speed.

Persis, no doubt, could feel at ease, Emily thought, but for herself she felt most uncomfortable with no one speaking to her.

She peered out through rain-streaked cabin windows at a Canal like black velvet. Only a few lights were left burning in the palaces they passed. Emily held her wristwatch up to the faint glow from outside and saw that it was now twelve-fifteen. The launch drove steadily, strongly, through the midnight waters.

"Why, there's our canal! That's where we live!" she exclaimed, pointing, to the Contessa, who sat in the shadows wrapped in her stole.

"Yes," the Contessa said.

Emily looked toward Persis, but Persis was peering out of the window beside her. Everything must be all right. The Contessa could hardly be abducting them! She spoke such good English she must have understood just now. Perhaps they were to be asked into the palace for a nightcap.

Past the black bulk of the Accademia, past the still lighted-up grand hotels they swept, and at last made the turn into the Contessa's canal. At the landing the launchman jumped ashore and stood holding the boat to the water steps, extending one crooked elbow to support the ladies as they got out.

"Here is where we leave our young people," the Contessa observed, going ashore.

"*Arrivederci!*" cried all the lively young Italians, not stirring. "*Arrivederci, Leonora! Arrivederci, signore!*"

"Goodbye, my darlings," the Contessa replied, and stood waiting for the two women at the top of the steps, under the faint light shed from the windows of her palace.

They followed her into the paved courtyard. The Contessa opened a door underneath the balcony and led the two women into a dining room, all white, through which she passed to a square white hall ringed with short columns on which stood the busts of doges. Then the Contessa opened another door onto the night.

"Here is the street," she said in her husky voice. "Your way leads straight ahead. You need only keep going in a direct line and you will arrive at your *pensione.*"

"Good night," Emily heard herself say as she stepped out into the rain.

She heard Persis, too, saying, "Good night."

"Good night," said the Contessa, and closed the door.

In the street they stared into each other's eyes.

"Well!" Persis began.

Suddenly the rain began to descend very much harder.

"Come on, we have to dash," Persis continued. "Fortunately, I know this part of Venice well. Not that she knew that."

It was thundering massively out over the Grand Canal. Flashes of jagged lightning revealed pitch-black alleys opening on either hand and the oily waters of the small canals they crossed over humpbacked bridges. All around, inscrutable dark façades looked down.

"This is scary!" Emily panted, hurrying along.

"Nothing bad seems to happen in Venice nowadays," Persis threw back over her shoulder. "Small thanks to the Contessa."

"I don't know how people ever dared live at all, in the old days!" Emily cried. Not a soul was visible abroad on the streets, but every turning, every archway suggested an assassin.

They had just entered a deserted campo when the sky all at once burst and rain came down in a deluge. The two women shrank back as far as possible into the doorway of a church facing into the campo. Emily kept hoping that the church door they backed up against would not suddenly, horribly, open.

"Never," Persis began. "Never! In all my life! Have I ever imagined anything so unspeakable, so insufferable! I told you people like that are appalling, but this is the worst. I never dreamed anyone could *do* such a thing! And those damned young Italians being taken all the way home."

"Why would she do such a thing?" Emily asked. "Why would she want to?"

An earsplitting crash broke overhead, silencing them. Each wondered, as she huddled back into the comparative shelter, what she had done to deserve being treated so at the hands of the Contessa. It seemed to each imperative that there be a reason for tonight, and that she should discover it.

"I am very angry," Persis announced when she could once more be heard. "I never want to hear of that woman again."

"I'm afraid it was I who let you in for this. You said you wouldn't have gone—" Emily began.

"Don't be absurd," Persis said. "It's not *your* fault she's a monster. I shall certainly write Tim about this—every word of what happened."

"Maybe that's what she wants you to do," Emily said, coming up with one of her solutions. "Maybe she used to be madly in love with your brother and he jilted her. Maybe this is her way of getting even—doing this to you."

"I doubt it," Persis said. She smiled grimly into the rain. She was fairly sure the reason for this outrageous performance was that the Contessa hadn't liked having the little Knapps brought along yesterday. Well, let her not like it! Persis didn't for one moment regret bringing them.

As suddenly as it had increased, the rain now decreased in volume. The two women ventured forth, and scurried the rest of the way home in silence. Downstairs in the *pensione* the light was on, and the *signorina's* brother lay on the sofa in the entrance hall, asleep. Yawning, he rose politely as they came squelching past him in their soaked shoes, their saturated raincoats. They could hear him putting out lights behind them.

"Mother'll be so upset," Emily whispered as they climbed the stairs to the bedroom floor. "She can never get to sleep till I come in."

"Just tell her what was done to us," Persis whispered back.

"Oh dear," Emily sighed, beginning to rehearse it all. They crept down the corridor, past closed bedroom doors, past the door marked "Toilette," to the turn in the corridor which separated their rooms.

"Good night," Persis whispered. "Dry yourself off thoroughly."

"You, too. Good night. . . ."

Emily opened the door upon a dark room where a breeze stirred, and tiptoed in. She was astonished to realize, from a faint snore, that her mother was fast asleep. Rather than risk awakening her by turning on a lamp, she tiptoed to the converted closet and, closing its door softly after her, switched on the light inside. She had begun to run water in the basin when Mrs. Knapp called, "Emily? That you?"

"Yes, dear." She opened the door again. "I hope you haven't been too worried."

"Worried? Why should I be worried?" Mrs. Knapp, aroused, sat up in bed. "You were with that friend of yours, weren't you? Miss What's-Her-Name, Miss Woodson. The bully."

"Well, dear, you do worry at night, you know," Emily began, but it was too late to engage in argument. She turned back to the basin. "We got wet," she said. "It's been raining hard."

"I thought your Contessa was bringing you home."

"Well, that's it, she was, but . . . I'll tell you about it tomorrow," Emily said, too tired to face the explanation. "It's very late."

"How late?" the old lady demanded.

Emily looked at her watch; it was half past one. "After midnight," she said.

"Mercy!" said old Mrs. Knapp. "I thought it was about ten. I found my comb!" she announced, triumphantly. "Guess where it was."

"Where?" Emily asked faintly.

"Right here in my bedside table!"

"Oh, good," Emily said.

There was silence. When at last Emily jumped into bed, she said softly, in case her mother had fallen asleep, "Good night."

"I hope you enjoyed your evening of pleasure," her mother said.

It was too much. Emily's body—as though even an instant's rest had refreshed it—seemed to rally. "I'll tell you all about what happened," she said. "It wasn't pleasure at all, not a bit." She swallowed indignantly, and began her tale. "Wouldn't you think anyone as fortunate as the Contessa—with as many gifts from the gods," she went on, "would be above base motives and acts? After all, surrounded as she is by a life like a work of art—"

"Poor thing. Face all pitted," Mrs. Knapp said. "I don't see what's such a gift of God about acne."

"But I barely noticed her acne!" Emily exclaimed.

She hesitated, contemplating the idea of the Contessa with a complex. But it was impossible. In all the blazing crown of the Contessa's perfections there was only that one tiny flaw. Emily brooded. Suddenly she was struck by the implications of the compassion her mother had expressed, and sat up straight in bed, furious.

But a snore informed her that her mother had already lost interest.

GWEN GRATION, who died in 1962, spent her childhood in Illinois and also lived in Canada and England. She had just started to write at the time of her death. This is her first published short story; it was published post-humously.

Teacher

"I HAD ONCE a tall big pup—like this one," said Mr. Shaw.

"We have a cat, too. Would you like to see our pussy-cat?" shrieked young Charlie. "She's called Kitty Fisher, Mister Shaw, Dad says she's of the fur-line tribe."

"Oh, ay—'Lucy Locket lost her pocket, Kitty Fisher found it—'" The old man absently stroked the collie pup. "And what did I do now with my big pooch? Well, I put him in a sack and I drop a stone in with him. And I throw him in the pond."

"Mister Shaw!" Ma shuddered, and young Charlie and Wendy stared horror stricken, and even the dog sought cover under the couch.

"Mister Shaw, that wasn't right," Aunt Bird chimed in.

"Needn't be telling me, Ma'ams, that I did a mean thing, and needn't be thinking that I haven't paid in full." Mr. Shaw blew his nose. "But you see, Ma'ams, a dog that kills chickens can't be trusted, and no farmer can keep him. Already a neighbor said my dog had caught his duckling, and I stick up for him against my neighbor. Then that night and with my own eyes I see him snatch my hen, and I was so—so—frothy angry that I just put him in a gunnysack and pitch him in the pond."

Aunt Bird clucked loudly, like the hen the erring dog had caught. "It's only nature."

"Teacher" – Gwen Gration, *Four Quarters,* Copyright © 1967 by La Salle College.

"I was punished," Mr. Shaw said decidedly. "It was in no other pond, Ma'ams, they found my Sally—ten years later. And what could my girl be doing dead in that same pond, only nineteen she was, and carefully watched over like an uncommon flower and never had an unhappy day. And after her engagement, it was always parties, showers, joy. And that very night a Do, a big Do, and all in her honor, with caterers and a paid orchestra. So much happiness she had; her wedding dress all sewn and her marriage three weeks off." His face darkened. "Did something beckon her from way down the pond? I have often wondered."

"My dog beckons me, with his tail," said young Charlie.

"Hush, Charlie." Ma was watching the children with troubled eyes. "Mister Shaw, don't torment yourself. That dog had nothing to do with Sally's drowning, nothing. Perhaps someday, we'll know how it was. It's such a shock, and all so fresh now. But time, Mister Shaw, time will—" Ma paused and looked at Wendy. "Time won't heal, but maybe soften it. And now, you two children—"

"I was her helper; she always let me pass the chalk," young Charlie bellowed. "I was janitor. Teacher said, she said, 'Charlie, you wash blackboards blacker than anyone.'"

"Charlie, please—" Ma pleaded.

"Much obleeged, young nipper, much obleeged. She loved the children, always said she'd have eight of her own. She just *loved* the children—but 'To bed, to bed, mine curly head, and rise up in the morning,'" shouted Mister Shaw as he left, laughing, as if to make good his outbreak.

"But where is that there dog?" Wendy whispered excitedly to Charlie, and Aunt Bird reassured Ma the children didn't understand.

"Poor old devil, he can't comprehend," said Dad. "Now it's guilt. Last week something else. And even a dog has to get in on the blame. But better a dog, though. Poor Albert Armitage can't hold his head up."

"Ned—the children," said Ma, as mothers do. "Now, kids, off to Blanket Market. Quick, quick. See which one of you can get there first."

"I think Albert Armitage wants locking up." The children had stopped on their way to Blanket Market and were listening in the stairwell to Aunt Bird. "His wife has left him. You knew that, didn't you, Lily?"

"Oh, but Oriole," said Ma, "that Shaw girl was tied to her mother's apron strings."

"Not tight enough," Aunt Bird said grimly.

"Oh, Oriole, she—"

"Albert Armitage's wife has gone to her mother's with the children," Aunt Bird cut Ma short. "And he was always seen with this Sally Shaw."

"Not always," said Ma. "He took his children to school and picked their teacher up if she happened along at the corner after she'd cut across the pond. Charlie idolized Sally Shaw. He doesn't do well since she— And he calls Miss Penny 'crabapple.' Miss Penny is the teacher now for first grade."

"It's some obsession he has about Sally Shaw," Dad said. "Things go deep with that kid."

"He must lead poor old Miss Penny a dance," clucked Aunt Bird. "He passes our Silvester's class on his way to the principal's office for punishment. She can't handle him."

"People expect too much of a big kid." Dad's voice sounded angry. "The shrimps get away with murder."

"I shouldn't have kept Charlie home that year," Ma said worriedly.

"A bally shame, Lily." Dad's voice was still harsh.

"But, Ned, I was afraid of the highway, and I wanted our two to start school together. You know, Ned, neither of us thought he'd be so big for his age."

"And in addition a year older than the others. Doesn't matter that he's unusually intelligent—he's head and shoulders taller, and all the class hoot at him, 'Charlie Longshanks.' "

"He was all right with Sally Shaw. She gave him duties and made him feel important. Her biggest pupil, her helper." Ma sighed.

"You should have heard him purr," said Dad.

"Teacher's pet!" said Aunt Bird. "Fancy."

"Sally Shaw knew every child's need. It was a quality in her." Dad's voice hadn't gone soft yet.

"I was her helper," bawled young Charlie from their lurking

place in the stairwell. "We got pussywillows by the pond. Me and Teacher. After school. We got them for the little kids."

"My word! If you two don't go to bed," called Ma.

Yet Aunt Bird's voice still floated up to them. "Old couple . . . it goes to show . . . drowned in a pond she'd crossed over every day of her life . . . so wrapped up in her . . . lolly-dollied her . . . you never can tell."

"I'm scared of that there dog." Wendy shivered.

"I ain't, 'cause how could a dog?" Charlie said, but wavered.

Their world was full and full of mysteries—

The man in the moon.

By digging and digging, you come to China.

How only the birds and Mr. Shaw knew the exact day the sweet cherries were ripe.

If you put out your tongue or made a face at anyone, and the wind changed, you would be stuck with that face for life.

The rainbow—God's promise He would never again destroy the world by water.

By eating crusts and carrots, you could acquire beautiful curls.

When hens took a drink, they raised their heads and thanked God.

Teacher tied to her mother's apron strings.

Teacher—the day Ma registered them at school and ever since, they had loved Sally Shaw. Teacher—her curly hair, her soft voice, her sweet smell, her blue eyes, and the way she laughed with them instead of her mouth.

"Sometimes," Charlie glowed, "she wears a hard dress" (he didn't know about starch), "and sometimes she wears a soft dress." And yesterday in a game he had "tccked hold of her hand."

Even though Elaine and Emily Armitage were twins, they were lesser lights compared with Teacher, although one was dark and one was fair and they could sing duets.

And this was another mystery: dark people sang alto, and fair people sang soprano.

Then one day Ma told them Teacher had gone to live with Jesus and had added in the same choky breath, "Now, you two, try to be good friends to Elaine and Emily Armitage. Never let anyone say anything against them."

But that was only another mystery, like the mystery of God being able to see them any time—even when they were in bed and under the clothes.

"Elaine and Emily don't have birthdays like other people do," Charlie told Ma the next week.

"That's because they are twins," Ma answered. But Charlie scratched his head. No—it wasn't because they were twins.

Instead of a party and kissings, and their mother crying that she was losing her babies, their father left their birthday presents in the principal's office at school.

"Maybe he hid the presents there like Mama hides the jelly beans," said Wendy; but it wasn't that, because when the twins arrived home, their mother got blazing mad and went to the phone and asked the Salvation Army to pick up some children's toys.

Elaine cried over her doll. To have had it, and then to lose it. And the Salvation Army representative said, hoping to console the wailing child, "A little girl called Louisa, whom Santa forgot, will have *this,* and you can be happy thinking of her and her joy."

"Why did Santa be forgetting of her?" Wendy asked avidly.

"Maybe she spit." Charlie remembered the most heinous sin of all—but it was another of those mysteries.

That night when Charlie said his prayers, he added after the God-bless-all-the-orphans clause: "But don't bless Weeda." An orphan named Louisa had got Elaine's doll—

"Miss Penny is always putting her finger to her lips and shaking her head at me when I sing, but Miss Penny can't sing," Charlie complained. "She sings funny. She sings high. 'Pip-pip-pip-pip—'" he mimicked in a falsetto.

Teacher had taught them to say *America*—like a prayer—and *My Country,* and then they must pause and think of their country. Charlie and Wendy always thought of peach and cherry blossoms, instead of woods and templed hills. They lived in a fruit belt— a land of color, a land of sky—with the girls and boys like gay and rare birds in their reds, yellows, and blues to make them visible on the highway. Every year, reporters came from the city with cameras to take pictures of the blossoms, and this year they had stripped off their coats and sat in Thorpe's ditch bemused. Ma had sent the children with water and ice cubes, thinking maybe the newsmen were faint, and the reporters had murmured something about the "never-never land."

But that was another mystery.

One Sunday of each year, city folk drove out in buses and cars, craning their necks and pointing to this and that orchard all along the marked route. The children, proud as punch, watched the traffic pass, and Ma invariably said, "Well, well, it should have been 'Blossom Wednesday' instead of 'Blossom Sunday,' although the sours are very lovely."

"It's a good land. My people came here as pioneers," Mr. Shaw would tell sightseers who stopped at his fruit farm. "My ancestors followed the trail of the black walnut. You could grow walking sticks even in this soil." The same joke did for these city slickers year after year.

Throughout cultivation, the children helped Mr. Shaw by sitting on a trailer in back of his tractor. Mr. Shaw needed weight, he said, and thus the boys and girls supplied his need and earned a bumpy ride. The children knew the fruit was ripe when bangers fired off from early morning until twilight and scared off the flocks of birds, and all the farmers drove their trucks to Stop 20 on the highway and hired waiting men and women as pickers. Then once more the children played a part; when Mr. Shaw hauled the loaded baskets through the orchards, they again supplied the weight.

In blackflytime they would beg or steal lacy curtains from their mothers and jog along in back of Mr. Shaw like so many small ghosts. It was on one of these hazy May days that Elaine and Emily Armitage stood silently by Mr. Shaw's tractor, waiting to gain the rough ride. But there was no welcome for them in the old man's disconsolate face.

"But why?" Wendy asked Charlie, as the twins went off, their baby faces stricken. Charlie had a mind to bring them back, but the chugging tractor won over his intended act of kindness, and he put the curtain over his head against the flies.

"Don't they know we be going through the farm?" asked Wendy. Charlie shrugged his shrouded shoulders.

It was only another mystery. Such as the mystery of the bazaar when they had collected everybody's stuff, and Mrs. Donald (to get even, Ma said) had given them three dozen of Mr. Donald's books on his own life, written and published by himself (the girt fool, Mrs. Donald said), entitled, *The Life of James Gordon Donald—Atheist.* Their lemonade had gone begging, and the neighbors had flocked to buy those dry old books without pictures.

In season when the orchards were forbidden, they played in the cemetery. "Land where my fathers died," Teacher had taught them.

"Greater love hath no man." The small fingers would go in and out of the engraved characters on the Soldiers' Monument.

There were gravestones showing gates. "The Gates of Heaven," Charlie said with authority, as they stood in awe.

There were two little concrete lambs: "In innocence they lived and in innocence they died." Wendy and Charlie remembered every word on those stones they loved the best.

And now this *new stone*—quaint—with the picture of Teacher glassed in. They kissed the sweet lips still smiling at them. "Sarah Shaw Dearly Loved."

And somehow or other they never connected *her* with the dead. *Teacher had gone to Heaven.*

Yet Charlie nattered Ma and Dad. "What if the world ends and everyone dies but me?"

"Mixed-up kid," Dad said. "Only Sally Shaw seemed able to give him a sense of security."

"Hush, Ned," said Ma, as mothers do. "Charlie, fetch me a drink, and make the tap run a long time."

"My teacher she said, 'Charlie, when you get water, it has a chocolate malted flavor,'" Charlie said proudly, as he brought water slopping over the side of the tumbler.

"My word, Charlie," said Ma, as she mopped her dress.

"When I spilled water on Teacher, she said, 'Charlie, you have a generous nature,'" said Charlie.

"People like Sally Shaw never die, it seems," said Dad.

"Wendy, Charlie, you mustn't go to that pond alone, *ever,*" Ma said one day, as the tall young pup came dancing up to her.

"The dog." Charlie wagged his head sagely.

"The children will get weird," Aunt Bird warned. "And, Lily, I would enjoy a walk over to the pond where that young teacher was murdered. And the man who drowned her—I could fair hamper him."

"But, Oriole. They don't even know if—"

"I know."

"But, Oriole—"

"I would have tried him. I would have proven him guilty. I would *that*. And so would his wife."

"Oriole, I declare! Come and look. And you, too, Charlie and Wendy. Hurry and see this herring we're going to have for tea. See Christ's thumb and forefinger. I've never seen His prints so distinctly," said Ma, as she held up the fish.

Yet by listening and acting daft and pretending they weren't listening, the children got the story. They got much from Aunt Bird; they got more from Aunt Bird's son, Silvester. And even some from Ma and Dad. These "little pitchers with the big ears" found it out, piece by piece and every piece. They added what they wanted. Took away what they didn't understand.

The evening that Teacher was drowned, Albert Armitage and she were seen together at the corner leading to the shortcut over the pond. He had never been able to explain. Never been able to clear himself. He had been questioned. Never tried. Yet never exonerated.

"I was with Teacher," said Wendy. "All day. Didn't I?"

"Me too," added Charlie. "Me too."

It was just another mystery. So many, many mysteries. Mrs. Green telling Ma she had left her teeth at the dentist's. "Now how could she have done that?" they wondered aloud, pulling at their own.

Their world was chock-full of mysteries.

There was something romantic and heartbreaking even to young children when Teacher's own sweetheart came to live with her parents and became a son to them. But to live so close and be able to see her grave any time—and the holly wreath when Christmas would come.

"He believes in her still," said the neighborhood, as Nicky Wade carefully clipped the grass on her grave.

"Poor soul, the mother has more trouble than she can bear," Ma was always saying, and Dad was always answering, "No, Lily, no. God puts His hand underneath the burden." And Aunt

Bird would add pointedly, "I'd hamper the one who killed her."
And then Dad would answer quietly but with deep anger, "No
one had a perfect alibi, Oriole, and the men at the canning plant,
the men who know Albert Armitage best, don't think he's capable
of it."

And neither did Charlie or Wendy.

They had seen Albert Armitage again. He had come in Mr.
Bean's candy store. Mr. Bean's face was growing redder with
rage, as the kids scanned and re-scanned the trays of caramels,
toffees, spice drops, sour balls, lollipops, and bubble gum. They
were just asking Mr. Bean to change their dime into ten pennies
when Mr. Armitage said, "Give them *all* some of everything,"
and so ended their terrible problem of decision.

That night Charlie said to Ma, "I imagine God looks like
Elaine's father—clean and sad."

"Charlie, dear, now listen. Miss Penny is Teacher now. You
must try and love her like—But why *don't* you be kind to Miss
Penny?" wheedled Ma, as the quarterly black-balling note came
attached to the report card.

"Old Miss Penny, stick-stick-stenny.

"He-legger, hi-legger, bowlegged Penny!" Charlie hooted
fiercely.

Ma's face was red with shame in front of Aunt Bird's disapproving glance. "But surely, Charlie, Miss Penny doesn't let you
cheek her like that."

"Oh, she can't hear. I say it when I'm in bed," Charlie said
craftily.

"He's always in the wrong. Now it's his dusty shoes," said Ma.
"They have some sort of shoe drill. He never passes."

"Shame," clucked Aunt Bird, crossing her two fingers back
and forth. "When I was a girl, my shoes were always bright, and
I was a right good scholar, too."

"Teacher—I mean *my* Teacher—she said, 'Charlie, I can see
your shoes a long way off down the highway, shining like traffic
lights,'" Charlie said proudly.

"He adored Sally Shaw. Just worshipped her. He used to work
and work on his shoes. Kept them on the dresser in case the floor
would soil them, and I couldn't keep a clean towel for his polishing." Ma's voice was floating after him as he ran to join Elaine

and Emily Armitage. "I've got to thinking, Oriole, that Sally Shaw killed *herself*." Charlie stopped in his tracks.

"No, never. Fancy a girl like *that* killing herself. And her marriage three weeks off," Aunt Bird said. He held his breath and waited for more. There was some buzzing and inconsequential chatter about Teacher's sweetheart, Nick Wade, and how the Shaws had always waited up when Sally was out at night; and how she was the child of their age and was tied to her mother's apron strings. Charlie scratched his head. Then he heard Aunt Bird's voice again. "Whatever do those Armitage children believe?" He shrugged.

All the children discussed freely what they believed. There were Gypsies, Santa Claus, the Devil, and the Weather Man to believe in. They wondered if any or all of them were true.

Charlie decided he believed in Santa Claus. They all felt they *must,* as he might get even by refusing to believe in *them.* All determined the Weather Man was something of a "stork." And the Devil they thought was in the same class; but when they got scared at night, they would all play safe and repeat: "At the name of Jesus, Satan's host doth flee." Gypsies, they all concluded, must be a made-up affair. And with the supercilious authority with which people dismiss superstitions, they dismissed the Weather Man and Gypsies as ignorant folklore.

"Miss Penny she said, 'Charles Graham, *please,* you throw everyone off tune,'" Charlie had sobbed to Ma the day the children sang at the Town's auditorium, and he and a few other grunting boys were left out. "But *my* Teacher said, 'Charlie, sing with your feet.' *My* Teacher said the little kids couldn't sing right if I didn't keep time with my feet."

It was Charlie's off-day. Simply because he was embittered about the singing, when the three little girls came home, he took them to the pond to prove he wasn't afraid of the dog. Aunt Bird's boy, Silvester, was there too, catching frogs, and Charlie, still indignant at Miss Penny, threw rocks and spoiled Silvester's frogging. Things went from bad to worse, and it all ended by Silvester shouting that Elaine and Emily's father was a murderer.

"Gizzard!" Charlie, impotent with rage, yelled at Silvester.

"What's the matter with *you?*" the older boy asked coldly.

"Gizzard!" Charlie fired back, knowing no other word as ade-

quate and stinging. "Gizzard! Gizzard!" He would have liked to
bite Silvester, only his biting days were past.

"Gizzard, gizzard, gizzard!" Charlie hooted Silvester all the
way from the pond and down the highway.

"My word—and what is it now? What are you saying?" asked
Ma, as he burst in the door, weeping bitterly.

"Sticks and stones will break my bones
  But names can never hurt me.
  When you're dead and in your grave,
  You'll suffer what you've called me."

Silvester was chanting righteously from the other side of the road.

"Gizzard!" shouted Charlie through his sobs.

It was an eventful day all around. Mrs. Armitage paid them
her first call. She seemed flustered and excited. "I came to tell
you I'm sending my girls to their aunt at the weekend—just for
awhile." Ma got Mrs. Armitage out of one chair and into another,
and Dad left his paper and fussed about the lights in the living
room.

"Now, Charlie and Wendy, Elaine and Emily's mother would
like to see Kitty Fisher," said Ma. "Go find her. I think she's in
the farthest orchard."

"You've been kind to my girls—" Mrs. Armitage hesitated.
"And I want to ask a favor. Tomorrow I've a noon appointment
I can't very well postpone, and my mother is away—and—would
you give them lunch?" Mrs. Armitage was making a great effort to
make the situation normal and usual, but before Ma had time
to say she'd be very glad to have the girls to lunch, Mr. Shaw
had opened the back door and was walking in as always. "Ma'am,"
he said, "I've brought you some of my celery, celery as breaks
like an icicle, Ma'am." He was yelling as he hunted Ma through
the kitchen, dining room, and into the living room, where they
were sitting.

Mrs. Armitage was staring at the celery held in front of Mr.
Shaw. She looked ashen and ill, and her shaky hands had gone
to her head. "She's dizzy," Charlie whispered to Wendy. They
both crouched in their lurking place behind the door.

Charlie left Wendy and was in the living room with a glass
of water. It was filled full and slopping over. He handed it to Mrs.
Armitage, "For you," he said.

"Charlie—why, Charlie—how could you know?" Mrs. Armitage murmured, paying no attention to her drenched condition.

"Teacher—I mean my *own* Teacher—let me get her water the day she was dizzy," he explained proudly. "That was the day she was drowned."

"Boy! What are you saying, boy?" Mr. Shaw's celery had fallen on Ma's new living-room rug.

"Teacher she said, 'Charlie, any water you get has a chocolate malted flavor.'" He waited, flushed, well pleased with himself.

"Go on, lad, tell me all," Mr. Shaw said slowly. "Think carefully."

All the kids had sung at the Auditorium excepting him and two other grunters, and now it was *his* turn. He puffed with importance as he saw the interest in all the grown-up faces around him. He was smart and could tell a straighter tale than anyone. Dad was always sticking up for him. He pushed the day's humiliations behind and expanded.

"Teacher said to me, 'I feel dizzy today, and all the room is going round, and I can see hundreds and hundreds of Charlies.'" He stopped.

"My daughter was ill, and she never told us," said Mr. Shaw.

"Nah, she wasn't ill. She was dizzy," Charlie said dogmatically. "And Teacher said not to tell anyone, because she'd be all right for the party anyhow; and if her ma and pa knew, they'd put her to bed—like me when I had the measles. But I was the biggest and her helper, and I got her drinks all day." Charlie had done himself proud and now stopped for breath.

No one was talking now. Mrs. Armitage was sobbing, and Mr. Shaw was blowing his nose loudly. "Much obleeged, young nipper. Much obleeged, Mister Charles," he finally said.

But Charlie hung his head. He was a Judas. Teacher had trusted him, and he had told on her. The dog who couldn't be trusted had been put in a sack and pitched in the pond. He burst into tears. But Ma and Dad, and even Aunt Bird, who had silently entered the house, were kissing him, instead of— He felt embarrassed. He, Charlie Longshanks, the biggest kid in class, slobbered over like this. *She* had said he was so tall, he might grow up like Abraham Lincoln. Abraham Lincoln? He wailed again and loudly, as he thought of Teacher and then of his treason.

"Why?" It was Wendy's voice that bore the normal and familiar note. "But why do they?" she started again. He felt comforted, and he looked at Wendy and shrugged. Wendy repeated, "But why are they all a-kissing of you?" And Charlie shrugged again.

It was just another mystery.

F. K. FRANKLIN has written three novels and a book for children, as well as articles, book reviews and short stories. She has lived in Europe and Alaska and served almost four years in army field and evacuation hospitals during World War II. Miss Franklin now lives in Bucks County, Pennsylvania with "two horses, five cats, three dogs, two children and a husband."

Nigger Horse

THE AUGUST DAY began sleepily. By eight o'clock, the sun was already hot, and humidity hung like a thick blanket of steam across the pine forests and drought-stricken fields of western Louisiana. Highway 171, a cracked and beaten ribbon of concrete stretching south of Many toward Lake Charles and the Gulf, lay comparatively quiet beneath the quickening glare. An hour earlier, empty log trucks, coming north with slack chains clanking on their bouncing trailers, had met and passed empty oil trucks booming southward to the refineries of Lake Charles. Soldiers, living in whatever they could rent along the highway, had long since gone down to Fort Polk, and there were no school buses to take up the slack between the other men coming to town to their jobs and the housewives driving in later to the stores.

Mrs. Findley led her daughter's small dun horse around the corner of the house. Stooping, she tied his halter rope into the swivel of the picket pin she'd screwed into the baked ground the day before. "There's not much to eat, old fellow," she murmured, straightening to survey the sparse lawn, aware in a kind of passive relief of the transitory peace on the highway. The horse lowered his head, blew dust with his soft breath, then drew back his lips to nibble at the seared grass with the edges of his teeth.

"Nigger Horse" – F. K. Franklin, *Southwest Review,* Copyright © 1967 by Southern Methodist University Press.

Mrs. Findley sighed and stretched a little, thinking of her second cup of coffee warming on the stove. For the next hour or more, the shade of the tulip tree would be across the back porch. The breeze rising from the meadows would still hold the night's coolness. I'll put out the crayons and paper, she thought; the children can draw while I drink my coffee. It's going to be another breathless, blazing day.

She sighed again. Her gaze wandered, following the white ribbon of the highway to its vanishing point among the green-gold cottonwoods that separated the piney forests from the cow pastures that ringed the town. Dreamily she raised her hand to push back the short bangs clinging damply to her tanned forehead. The gesture brought a sense of life to her languid body and a momentary pleasure. To be young was the great thing. To be young . . . And regretfully she remembered that Cart wouldn't be home for another five nights.

"One more damn battalion exercise to test what we learned on the first one," he'd said. "I think myself it's a general's nightmare put to practice. God, I tell you, Katty, love, it's hot out there in those woods!"

Poor Cart . . . Well . . .

With a last glance for the knot she'd tied on the picket ring—knot-tying being with her an uncertain skill—she turned back toward the house, just in time to see her year-old toddler pivot near the edge of the raised and unrailed carport as he gravely mimicked the whirling dance of his five-year-old sister.

"Mikey!" She ran toward him, mentally hearing the thud of his small, defenseless head against concrete and the anguished wail that would follow, but imagined disaster and her own abrupt movement were suddenly and bewilderingly effaced by the whine of overheated rubber, the squeal of brakes, the blare of a horn, and a frantic drumbeat of hooves upon pavement.

The horse!

She swung around wildly, sure that he'd broken from a careless knot to run to certain doom upon the highway, but he was where she'd left him, his small head raised, ears pricked, compact body swinging on his haunches to face the racket just beyond the hedge screening the edge of the lawn. A great bay horse came pounding down the center of the highway. Black mane and tail flying, head up, he veered in terror as brakes shrieked again, a horn blared its raucous cry, and an empty oil truck clattered around him. Trumpeting his panic, the horse galloped past, and Mrs. Findley saw his eyes roll wild with fear. Suddenly he wheeled, steel shoes sliding, air grunting from his big barrel. For a second he hesitated, head high, snorting, then came charging diagonally back across the highway to slide down the steep embankment onto the Findley's lawn, where he made a wide circle around the excited dun, who, whirling to meet him, threw the weight of his body against the picket rope with audible stress.

The scene remained frozen. The horses stood nose to nose blowing in soft recognition of their kinship; the highway was once more empty; the two children remained mute and round-eyed at the edge of the carport; Katherine Findley, still entranced by the tranquility of the hour and the image of a second cup of coffee, stood rooted in surprise and confusion—until the moment exploded as a large van truck applied air brakes for the long curve and hill toward town. Sssssssst! The bay whirled back on his haunches, terror renewed, while the dun, caught up in the contagion of his fear, lunged forward, teeth bared. The creak of his strained tether shook loose the vestiges of Mrs. Findley's morning dream.

She ran back toward the horse, sure that at any moment he would break away to join the bay now rushing down the lawn toward the highway again. She grabbed the picket rope, heaving her weight against that of the plunging dun, and somehow won enough slack to get the knot untied, the rope free of the pin. Her fingers rubbed raw, she half pulled, half ran with the excited horse toward the corner of the house and the fenced lot beyond.

"Watch Mikey!" she screamed over her shoulder, but was drowned out by a sudden melee of trumpeting animals, for the bay, seeing them go, had swung back from the highway to come racing after them. Neighing shrilly, he circled them with long-legged bounds that set the dun to wheeling and lunging. In the confusion Mrs. Findley heard the baby's distant wail, but she could not stop. On she plunged, half pulled, half directing the dun toward the safety of the lot. As they raced through the open gate, the big bay shot in behind them to circle the fence with ringing bugle calls, his long legs skimming the dusty ground, his lean body stretched, neck extended, head turning this way and that. With her last ounce of strength, Mrs. Findley jerked rope and halter from the excited dun, then jumped back as he tore off in the stranger's erratic wake. Affected by each other's terror, the two horses dashed around the lot, charging in close upon each other, the bay with his bounding strides, the dun belly close to the ground, short legs driving.

My God, they'll go through the fence! she thought, a little frightened and wholly awed by their unleashed power. Mesmerized, she stood and watched them careen around and around the dusty lot, gradually exchanging panic for pleasure. They began to buck and lash out at each other with teeth and heels. At the far corner of the lot, they wheeled, reared, feinted at each other's quarters, then broke away in a drumming gallop again. Their intoxication was infectious, and in spite of the heat Mrs. Findley felt, herself, a powerful urge to run and leap. God, I used to run and run, she thought, remembering the feel of cool damp earth beneath her bare feet as she ran down a rustling lane of cornstalks, or the feel of grass cropped smooth and close as velvet down the pasture slope, or the soft dust of the road and the small clouds she sent puffing from under her racing sneakers. I ran, she thought. I ran and ran, and I'm glad I still remember the feeling.

"Mommie!"

Dimly she heard the baby's howls and the older child calling. Ah now . . . ah now, and she turned, running, to the shed where she filled the oat can quickly and banged it hard against the door until the dun slowed, turning his head in her direction. He came to an abrupt, stiff-legged halt, them ambled over.

"Chowhound!" she said to him, scattering the oats in the big washtub under the cottonwood that was shedding its fuzzy bark like a winter coat into the dust. "And lucky for me that you are," she added, for the bay was still making his rushes along the fence. As she fastened the gate behind her, she saw him come to a halt finally, then turn toward the shed, puzzled. He nickered softly and started toward the dun at an easy, swinging trot, his ears pricked, nostrils widening to the scent of the sweet grain. She couldn't wait, though, and tense with awareness of her deserted children, she ran toward the house.

"Ah, Mikey, Mikey, what's the matter?" She gathered the
toddler against her breasts and swept the two children into the
house. "Did he fall, Jeannie? Are you hurt, honey?"

"No, he didn't fall or anything. He's just kind of scared. He
thought the horses ran over you, I guess." Jeannie wrinkled her
golden round brow in disdain.

"Well, there's nothing to be afraid of. Somebody just lost their
horse, and isn't that an odd thing to lose?" She brushed the little
boy's forelock back from his damp forehead and was acutely
conscious of the yearning of love she willed through her fingers.
As though a touch could make safe, she thought. Or hold back
terror.

Jeannie giggled. "How could anybody lose a horse, Mommie?"

She looked up and smiled into the wide blue eyes. "I don't
know, but he certainly looks lost."

"Can I go see it, Mommie? Can I?"

"Yes, after awhile. We'll all go down, but right now let's let the
poor fellow calm down. He got pretty frightened out there on the
road with all those trucks. I wonder how on earth I go about
finding . . ." Through the screen door, she saw an elderly car
slide to a stop before their mailbox. Oh, maybe the mailman would
know. "Run out on the back porch, Jeannie, and get your crayons," she said. Swinging the baby to her hip, she hurried through
the front door and up the drive, calling, "Mr. Enders! Oh, Mr.
Enders!"

He waited, and, panting, she bent to talk through the open
window, the sun like fire upon her back, the baby dragging at
her arm. He nodded wisely at her question and considered. Old,
dry-boned, his every movement so slow it seemed a series of
separated jerks, he fumbled forth a single letter for her.

"Yep. Saw that horse, I reckon. Saw him back toward town
maybe half an hour ago. Like to have got hisself killed. Big
truck dern near run him down. Nope, don't have any idea in the
world who owns him. Ganted like he is, reckon he's a nigger
horse. That there's all you got today, Missus Carter." He added
the last in a tone that took some satisfaction in the meagerness of
her mail. With a vague jerk of bony fingers, he let out the clutch
and moved slowly away as she stepped back on the highway
shoulder.

Nigger horse? What did that mean?

Sticking the letter between her teeth, she juggled the baby to a firmer seat over her left hip, then moved slowly down the drive. One hand freed, she turned the letter over. Damn! Someone had opened it. Across the stained front "MISSENT" was scrawled in pencil and the flap, rudely torn, had been pasted back down with a ragged piece of scotch tape. Irritation shook her. Four times in one month! Couldn't that old man read? Surely there wasn't another Major and Mrs. Carter Findley on Route 1, Many, Louisiana! And, she thought, touched by surprise, we've lived here almost a year!

She stared at the ugly, penciled word, her privacy invaded. Who was this mysterious reader of their mail, this presumptuous person who tore open their letters so crudely and so crudely tossed them back? In anger she visualized a fat woman in a shapeless dress stained down the front, a regular country woman obsessed with the private life of her neighbors, so meager was her own. Why woman, though? she wondered, stopping short in the drive. Why not some dried-out husk of a man given to spending his days on his front porch the better to watch the comings and goings of his neighbors? No, the woman was there to stay, fat, not wholly clean, with a broad moon face and narrow lips pursed in perpetual disapproval. Pale, freckled skin, thin hair, pale eyes . . .

Ugh! She almost dropped the letter in revulsion. Really, this time I'll put in a complaint at the Post Office. I should have done it long ago!

"Hey, there, boy," she murmured aloud as Mikey nuzzled his warm face and cool, button nose into her neck. She put him down in the drive and bent over him in the sun as he immediately squatted to explore a bright pebble with chubby fingers. No, she thought with un uneasy mental shrug, I can't make trouble for that old man. I suppose it's enough to be working at all at his age and frail as he seems. Perhaps, as they say, if someone took his job away he'd lie down and die. Vaguely, she felt that she'd stepped close to cruelty, that she'd been indulging in a certain city-bred smugness. What a struggle it was to be tolerant, especially for a Yankee before what seemed so much nonsense in southern ways.

She patted Mikey's cropped head and stooped to catch one small hand. "Come on, chum, or you and I'll come down with sunstroke."

"Hey, lady!"

She straightened and turned, startled, bringing Mikey to his feet. Except for the occasional passing car or truck, she'd felt herself alone in the hot, bright morning, but there was a man not ten feet away at the head of the drive grinning amiably, his reddened eyes bold. He was almost as old as the mail carrier, but where the years had withered the carrier's flesh they had bloated the body of this man, encasing his large bones in yellowing fat. Soiled khaki pants, beltless, strained to meet a filthy white shirt over the protuberance of his belly. A greasy stetson, wide brim curled on each side, sat far back on his sweating head.

"Seen you catch that there horse, lady," he drawled, moving down the drive toward her, his gaze roaming her bare brown legs with relish. He bent to touch Mikey under the chin. The small boy clutched Mrs. Findley's leg, trying to hide behind her sunburned calf. Hastily she stuck her letter in the back pocket of her shorts and stooped to lift him again into her arms.

"Seen you from yonder," the man continued unperturbed. "Waiting for a ride to Lake Charles and seen that truck all but hit the critter. Ain't yours, is he?"

"No. Oh no. I don't know whose . . ." She shook her head helplessly. Where on earth had he been standing that she hadn't seen him? She glanced along the highway, deserted now except for the distant glitter of an oncoming car. The skin along her backbone prickled. Strange people and so much she didn't understand about them . . . Sometimes, no, often, she felt a sense of threat, a kind of obscure violence. Especially when she answered the reiterated question, "Where you from, Missus?" and then watched the cold suspicion move into their eyes. "Up North, eh?"

"Keep the Negro thing out of your talk, honey," Cart had warned her. "It's like waving a bloody shirt at a bull. Oh, sure, if you get pinned down, tell 'em you think this race thing is all wrong, but don't go looking for trouble. You'd not have far to look, I'm afraid."

For his sake, and hers too, because they had to live here and she did not want to live afraid, she'd ridden herd upon her in-

clination to protest, to denounce; yet even so, there was still
suspicion, half-smothered, and her own sense of unspoken threat.
Why? She wasn't altogether sure.

"Naw, never laid eyes on that one before. Ain't a bad-lookin'
animal, huh? Skinny as all get out, but he's got real classy action,
don't he?" the man was saying, his gaze wandering from her face
to her legs and back again.

"Yes. He's too good a horse to be running up and down the
highway like that. I wonder what I ought to do." Mikey was
heavy in her arms. She shifted him to her other hip. "I don't
have any idea how to go about finding his owner. I don't know
many people in town, and then my husband . . ." She stopped,
letting it drift away, remembering her isolation in this house from
weekend to weekend, and Cart's stern instructions never to mention to anyone that he was gone so much.

"It gives me the heeby-jeebies to think someone might notice
that I'm not around," he'd said. "If it weren't for the damn
battalion hours, I could at least get back a couple of nights a
week."

"I've the dog and the pistol," she'd reminded him. "Who needs
you?" Often, though, in the dark hours she'd not found it so merry
to be alone with two small children with the nearest neighbor out
of sight across a meadow and beyond a small wood. Drunken
voices sometimes sounded on the highway and hitchhikers shouted
curses after the cars that did not stop. Sometimes obscene cries
sprayed the night and whiskey bottles clattered on the gravel
shoulder. One night she'd been awakened by the frantic barking
of the dog and the sound of someone moving about on the carport, but the dog's fierce yapping had sent whoever it was back
into the night. After that, when the dog was aroused, she prowled
the house, the loaded pistol in her hand, all the dire stories
of rape and murder she'd ever read crowding her courage.

"Whyn't you call Rod Jones?" the old man suggested lazily.
"Being town marshal like he is, chances are he'd know all about
that horse. Or, anyways, figure something to do with him. And
when it comes to liking horses, he don't take second place to
nobody in this here parish!"

"Rod Jones? Oh, thank you." Relieved, she shifted the baby

once more and started down the drive. That rheumy, red stare
upon her bare legs made her flesh creep.

" 'Course, if it's some nigger horse, likely he can't help you
none," he called after her.

She nodded and went on thoughtfully to the house. Nigger
horse? There it was again. Once inside the house, she carefully
latched the screen door and deposited Mikey with his sister amid
the reams of paper and the crayons, broken and whole, on the
back porch. She poured her long-delayed second mug of coffee
and went to stand by the back door. In the lot, the two horses
were standing quietly now, head to head, in the shade of the
shed. Nigger horse, whatever it meant. Funny that they never
said whiteman's horse, or whiteman's shack. Coffee mug in hand,
she turned and went back through the kitchen to the hall and
here searched through the thin phone directory until she found
Jones, Rod. What must it be like to be characterized in one
great lump like that, she mused, listening to the dial tone change
to an intermittent buzzing. Two rings, two rings, two rings . . .
It's all part and parcel of forbidding a natural human dignity. It's
akin to never addressing them as Mr. or Mrs. or Miss. But why
do people . . . ?

"Jones speaking."

The drawling voice stopped abruptly, leaving silence in her
ear. Confused, she gasped and rushed into the breach. "Oh, Mr.
Jones, this is Mrs. Findley, Mrs. Carter Findley out on the Lake
Charles highway. I was told that perhaps you could help me . . ."
She went on to explain, too effusively, too incoherently, with no
sound from him on the other end of the wire. Good grief, she
thought, when she had finished, is he there? She cleared her
throat. "Ah, Mr. . . . ?" but the slow voice cut in lazily, "Bay,
you say, Ma'am? Seventeen hands or more, huh? Big fellow,
ain't he? I reckon, though, it's a new one for me. Wasn't sweated
much, you say? Can't have come far then. Nope, can't think
whose horse it might be, less it belongs to some nigger close in
to town. Tell you what, Missus Findley, if anybody calls wanting
word of a lost horse, I'll send 'em right on over to your place,
okay? You can keep him in your lot awhile, can't you? Good.
If don't nobody claim him by nightfall, why then I'll come over
and fetch him to the Fairground and get him outten your way.

You just give me another buzz around five o'clock, okay? Fine."
His voice was friendly, reassuring. It came over the line to her
like a fatherly pat on the shoulder.

She hung up bemused. There might be a thousand people up
and down the highway and in the town of Many itself, and among
them perhaps forty horses and mules, most of which she already
knew on sight, for she, like Marshal Jones, had a fondness for
horses, and she would run to the window at the first clatter of
hoof on highway to watch the cow pony or walking horse go
by. Like a child, she thought. Just like a child. Still, they had
a fascination. There was the thin, white walker whose rider favored black—black stetson, black shirt, black pants, black boots
—and sang nasal cowboy laments at the top of his voice as he
paced through town. There was the old brown plow horse that
came by every Saturday morning with two boys on his broad
and sagging back. The only Negro she'd seen with horses was
an old, very dark man, bent and worn, who drove a rail-thin
team, always with a plow in the wagonbed and a woman, his
wife she'd presumed, as white as herself, sitting erect and with
a painful dignity on the seat beside him. She'd spent many an
unquiet moment wondering about this couple.

If this was a . . . if this horse did belong to a Negro, might
he have had to keep him hidden because he was so plainly a
good horse, far too classy for a Negro to own?

Oh Lord, she thought, would they begrudge him even this?

Still, she held back, knowing herself prone to find this thing,
knowing she'd brought it with her to the deep South, that she'd
come with her Yankee mind convinced of the evil, the bigotry,
the cruelty of this land. That was a year ago, though, she thought,
and now I'm only confused. Oh, there was no honor to the South
in the dingy café entrances marked colored that opened from
dismal, trash-laden alleys; the waiting rooms, Colored, always
dirty, shabby, hopelessly overcrowded; the separate and inferior
sections of movie theaters; the branded ads in phone directories
and newspapers; the long unpainted and unrepaired firetraps
that were the Negro schools; and last and perhaps worst, the one-
room shacks and tiny shotgun houses with yards that served as
gardens, chicken pens, cow lots, child's play yard, family privy,

and dump with everywhere, inside and out, the smell of poverty, humility, indignity.

No honor, no honor here for any race or region; little enough compassion for a man, a woman, or a child if the skin was black . . . yet, she'd found no human fiends, no country dolts, no southern Jukes. In the cold light of honesty she would have to admit that these people, their neighbors, had treated her and Cart with great friendliness, great generosity. Everyone they'd had dealings with had been unfailingly courteous, eager to help the strangers in their midst, eager to oblige, quick to stop with a word and a smile. Why is it they aren't collapsed by guilt? she wondered. Are they perhaps like pit donkeys that are slowly blinded in their daily darkness until they forget the sun?

"It isn't easy to be righteous any more," she said aloud and walked to the front door to stare out at the glittering morning.

"We go back to the Bible for our way of life," Mrs. Justin Bayard, their neighbor across the meadow, had told her once, and it was the first time anyone had mentioned the subject to her though they'd been in Many almost half a year. "It's Noah's curse on the seed of Ham because he dared to laugh, he dared to think evil of his father. Their skin and their souls will be black until God chooses to lift that curse, you know. Until then it is destined that they must be set apart. Oh yes," she said softly, smiling upon her visitor, her face still pretty though wreathed in soft wrinkles, "all this was decreed a long time ago."

"Oh?" Mrs. Findley had murmured, bewildered.

"That's why, you see," Mrs. Bayard went on calmly, fluffing out her graying hair. "If the Church should ever reinterpret the Bible, why then, I suppose we might . . . well, there would be change. Justin says there might have to be . . ."

But I didn't even bring it up, Katherine Findley thought. I only mentioned that in Pennsylvania we'd not have green grass and flowers so early. Do I touch a nerve every time?

Her relief had been great when Mrs. Bayard suddenly clapped her hands and raised her soft voice in a shrill cry toward the clink of china and silverware in the kitchen. "Nancy! Bring Missus Findley coffee, hear?" then went on to describe the beauty of azalea gardens in New Orleans. She neither interrupted herself nor glanced up when a large sullen Negro woman, neat and clean,

came slip-slopping into the room to set a heavy silver tray of
coffee things before her, then, relieved of the burden, grunted
and turned her white sneakers, slit to accommodate every bunion
and corn, toward the kitchen.

"Oh my!" Mrs. Bayard had looked after her then, sighing
lightly. "Do you take cream or sugar, my dear? If you do, I'm
afraid she's forgotten . . ."

"No, I really prefer it black," Mrs. Findley had replied hastily.
Louisana coffee, dark and bitter.

Somewhere in the back of the house a thin voice had wavered
like a slice of bright sky in a broken puddle. "Here chick, chick,
chicky! Come chick, chick, chicky!"

"My mother," Mrs. Bayard had explained, rising. "She's eighty-
two and her blood pressure is very high. On some days even
the tranquilizers don't help very much. Will you excuse me?"

"Of course."

When Mrs. Bayard returned, her smile was both affectionate
and rueful. "Poor Mama, it worries her so that she hasn't fed
the chickens or that maybe we aren't all in for the night. There
were nine of us, you see, and when her blood pressure's up she
calls us all night by name wanting to know if we're home and
the doors are locked. She must go back thirty years in time, poor
thing, to do all her fretting over again. It's a little strange sometimes to hear her call, because my oldest brother died years ago
and one of my sisters passed away just last fall . . . She had a
hard life, Mama did."

And Mrs. Findley had left remembering the wry affection and
the morose Negro woman who carried the curse of Ham's children
on her shoulders. How do you make anything of that? Where
was evil clear-cut and defined? Mrs. Bayard who'd sent Nancy
over to care for the children during the siege of doctor's treat-
ments for her infected chigger bites, or Mrs. Wilson across the
road who showered them with washed, crisp produce from her
garden, or Mr. Hainey at the store who was kindness itself when
she ran short of funds the month Cart was gone to Texas on a pro-
longed maneuver . . . how could she find evil among them? And
yet . . . wouldn't they, all of them, deny a Negro dreamer his
dream of being a knight of sorts mounted upon a big bay charger?

Wouldn't they call him biggety for riding a free-walking horse, a gaited horse?

God knows, she thought, the pride-saving dreams of such dreamers are sometimes manifested in bizarre and childish ways —old cars streaked with clashing colors and loaded down with cheap chrome ornaments, unnecessary lights and mirrors and horns, raccoon tails flapping from every jutting surface; gaudy parasols and costume jewelry; bright, sleazy dresses or shirts— all like this horse, impractical and bankrupting. A man can buttress a meager livelihood with a mule, but this horse can only eat. He's far too high-strung, too leggy for wagon or plow. A silly thing to own. A Negro dreamer must surely know . . .

Oh, she told herself sternly, I've work to do!

Slowly, the shade retreated from the house. The children grew hot and fretful as the sun invaded every corner. Mrs. Findley moved more and more lethargically about her tasks, washing both dishes and clothes, dusting a little, sweeping, trying to entertain the restless children, bedding Mikey at last for his nap and settling Jeannie before the phonograph with a stack of her favorite records. She returned to the kitchen to give thought to supper, but, worn by the heat, went instead to stand in the doorway, hoping against hope that a wandering breeze would drift out of the late afternoon. Nothing stirred. Not a leaf, not a long weed, not even a fly. In the dusty lot, the two horses stood motionless, head to head, in the shade of the cottonwoods.

Can I survive the summer? she wondered, then saw abruptly that the dreamer had arrived. He came, a bridle in his hand, in a group of four Negro men who walked diffidently along the hedge, skirting the edge of the lawn. Irresolutely, she moved across the porch and opened the screen door to call across the yard, "Are you looking for a horse?"

They halted, clumping. All four turned their heads toward her, and she was not even sure which one replied, "Yes, Ma'am, we's looking for a hoss."

Hurrying down the steps, she moved toward them. "He came down the highway this morning. Oh, quite early. It's really a miracle he wasn't hit by a truck or a car. He saw my horse. I had him staked out front, you know, and he saw him and came into the yard. He followed me into the lot when I took my horse

in and I didn't know what to do. I didn't know how to find out
whose . . . then someone told me to call the Marshal, Marshal
Jones, and he . . . I suppose he told you where he was." Discon-
certed, she paused, conscious that she was chattering, painfully
conscious of their impassive stares and wanting only to be easy
and natural, wanting them to be easy and natural in return and
hating with all her heart the whine of apology she heard in her
voice. Nervously, she stooped to pick a piece of paper from the
ground.

"Yes, Ma'am. Can we get him outten there now?"

"Oh, yes, yes, of course. Just go on through the gate. Here, I'll
help. I'll keep my horse back. They've gotten kind of chummy."
Ah, Lord, why this shrillness, this overemphasis, why anything
at all?

They waited, letting her precede them into the lot, their faces
unchanging. Once inside, though, the dreamer moved away from
his companions toward the horse. "Heah, Big Boy, heah, son.
C'mon now, hear?"

"He's an awfully fine horse!" Mrs. Findley exclaimed, overrid-
ing that soft entreaty. "He's certainly a good-looking animal!"

No one spoke. They merely glanced sideways at her from the
corners of their eyes. Young men, all in their early twenties, they
were dressed as though they'd come straight from their work.
Their faded overalls were sweaty and stained, their T-shirts dusty.
Cutting trees, she thought, or working at the lumber mill.

"He got on just fine with our horse," she went on compulsively.
"They've been playing like . . . a couple of kids. You know, running and kicking up. I fed them . . . him. I hope you don't
mind . . . ?"

"No, Ma'am."

Again, whose murmur?

"Heah, Big Boy," the dreamer said, extending his hand palm
up. Recognition pricking his ears, the bay turned his head, then
came lazily toward him. The dun followed, loath to lose his new
friend.

"Hey, Big Boy. Hey now." The bay stretched his long, slender
neck to nibble and blow softly into the open hand. Man and
horse stood a moment, then the man moved the reins over the
thin neck and slipped the bit swiftly between the even teeth. He

turned and led the bay from the lot. His mute companions followed. Mrs. Findley had her hands full keeping back the disappointed dun and getting the gate closed between the two animals.
By the time she had it fastened, the men and horse were halfway
to the highway. Defeated, she moved slowly off at a tangent
toward the house. Nigger horse! she thought, watching the bay's
long, springy strides, the arch of his neck. Ah, my God, it isn't
my fault! It isn't the way I feel! Can't they tell? Can't they understand that I didn't do this to them, that I never would? Never!
I cannot help that my skin is white . . .

Startled, she caught herself up. How many times must they
have said that to themselves—I cannot help that my skin is . . .
Ah, how terrible and how stupid! All one's life, for no reason . . .

Aching for forgiveness, for absolution, she raised her head and
saw that the men had stopped at the edge of the highway, still
closely clumped, the horse a part of that clump now. The dreamer
had half turned back, the reins in his hand. Oh, she thought,
stabbed anew, he's certain to think I'll tell. He'll be sure I'll
destroy his dream. And she hurried toward them, crying, "I won't
mention . . . I'll not tell the Marshal whose horse . . ."

The others turned back also, then exchanged glances.

I'll promise, she thought desperately, still hurrying toward them.
He must understand that I'm not one of them, that I'll not help
them. He must not be allowed to worry . . .

"I won't say you came. I'll not tell them. It'll be quite all
right . . ."

They stared at her blankly.

Sweating, panting a little, she heard herself babbling and fal-
tered, overcome by futility. I can't ever climb that wall, she
thought sadly. I can't even find the words. I've tried. And I've
only made myself ridiculous . . .

But unable to give up, she cried, "I like horses. I . . . I hate
to see them . . . suffer just because . . . when it's not fair. . . ."

Three of the men laughed harshly, turned their backs, and
walked on out upon the highway. The dreamer paused a moment
more. "Thank you, Ma'am, for catching him up. I'm obliged,"
he called across the intervening space, his gaze direct.

She smiled, vastly relieved, for it seemed to her that his voice was normal, even sincere, and that their eyes met upon a human plane. Then he cleared his throat, spat toward her into the grass, and turned to run after his friends, the bay trotting gracefully behind him.

NORMA KLEIN was born in New York City and has lived there all her life. She began publishing short stories during her sophomore year at Barnard, where she won the Elizabeth Janeway Prize for Prose Fiction in 1959 and again in 1960. Since that time she has published stories in many magazines. Miss Klein has just completed a novel. She is married to a biochemist and they have one daughter.

Magic

"LOOK AT THIS: 'Marilyn Monroe Dead,'" Hermione said to her son Grant's fiancée, holding up *The New York Times*. "Can you imagine!" She was standing near the window in a purple oriental dressing gown and her face, as Melissa walked in, was half lit up from the sunlight. Her wild, unruly cascade of gray hair made her look like a benign, if eccentric, lioness.

"How terrible!" Melissa said, frowning and glancing down at the paper.

Hermione gave a brief, mirthless laugh. "Well, she had enough in her short life, didn't she? Four husbands . . ."

"Three," Melissa said steadily, looking right at her.

"Was it three? These women—they're like children, blundering from one man to another. They never learn, it seems." She smiled at Melissa. "Well, it's funny, but in this photo she looks quite a lot like you, my dear. It's amazing."

Melissa looked at the photo of a smiling blond girl in a tight, print blouse. She laughed nervously, trying to balance irony and politeness in her voice. "Why, how can you say that, Hermione?" she said tensely. "It doesn't look at all like me."

"Magic" – Norma Klein, *Mademoiselle*, Copyright © 1967 by The Condé Nast Publications Inc.

But Hermione just patted her arm and smiled slyly. "Oh, it does, it does. Her smile, her hair—"

"Well, we're both blondes, if that's what you mean," Melissa said, still frowning, somewhat hurt. She felt an obscure insult to herself in this. It seemed to her another of Hermione's ways—not always so subtle—of voicing her disapproval of her son's engagement, a disapproval not so much of Melissa herself as of the idea that one of her sons should be leaving her. "Look, Mother's just like that," Grant had said after a similar incident a few days earlier. "You've got to understand. All her life she's been the only woman in the family—a husband, two sons, even teaching all these years at an all boys' school. She's used to being the center of attention herself. She doesn't like sharing it. . . . God, I hate to imagine the treatment she'd give a fiancée of Paul's! This is mild in comparison."

Melissa was glad that her upbringing had trained her so well in the art of concealment. She was able to meet all of Hermione's remarks with seeming detachment. Anyway, the ordeal was only for ten days, six of which were already over. It was to be, as Grant had put it, an unofficial vacation, an introduction of Melissa to the small Pennsylvania town in which he had been brought up, until Andover and then Harvard had made him almost a stranger to it. When they returned to New York in mid-August, Grant would start work at the law firm he had entered and Melissa would return to her secretarial job at a publishing house for art books. The marriage was planned for Thanksgiving when Grant's father, who was in Europe for an academic convention, would return home.

Grant wanted Melissa to quit her job after their marriage. "So it's $110 a week," he said when he heard. "It's insane! Your father's got money. I've got some. What's the point in it?" Melissa had tried to explain that, although she knew her father could well afford it, she hated the idea of taking money from him. She had resisted asking him to pay for her two night courses in Chinese—she was working toward an M.A. in Oriental Civilizations at N.Y.U.—because she had known he would protest and feel the money better spent on a mink coat. As for being psychoanalyzed, he would never have given a penny toward that, if the psychoanalyst father of one of Melissa's friends had not called up and yelled at him over the phone for half an hour. But on that point

Grant agreed with him. "What the hell do you need to be analyzed for?" he had said when he heard. "Of all people!"

Melissa knew Grant was right about the job. It was dull, tiring; she came home each day worn out and simply fell asleep on her studio-couch bed, without taking off her clothes. But somehow, it was still better than having endless days stretching before her in which to sit around and be depressed. "Why be depressed?" Grant had said in bewilderment when she had tried to explain how she felt. "I don't know. I just would be," was all that Melissa could reply.

As for Dr. Kaufman, Melissa's analyst, he didn't like the idea of Grant any more than Grant liked the idea of him. "This man knows nothing about you," the doctor had said. "You've said this yourself. He's made a snap judgment based on a few superficial things. To him, you're just a conventional, poised, attractive young lady, evidently just what he wants in a wife. But you know, yourself, that's only a deception. That's not the real you. The real you spends half the day depressed, indecisive, drifting along through life without knowing where you're going, feeling a failure for some reason we still don't know. I'm not saying he'll fall out of love with you. I'm saying you don't know yourself well enough at this point to know *who* you could love. There's a side of yourself you're not taking into consideration at all."

But I *hate* that side of me, Melissa thought to herself. Her hope was that by marrying Grant she would in time become like his image of her. She felt certain he truly was all the things people commonly assumed to be true of her—conventional, poised, attractive. Together they would lead a life like a couple out of a *New Yorker* ad, comfortably well off, relaxed, secure, playing chess in the evening—she in her hostess gown before the fireplace, sipping cream sherry, and he sipping Scotch. What a tempting image! Rather than stay and defend these ideas to Dr. Kaufman, however, she abandoned the analysis.

"You've made a good decision," Grant had said when he heard. "You won't regret it for a minute." Whether he was referring to her stopping the analysis or to her deciding to marry him, Melissa was not absolutely certain. But even if she felt she could not share his firm sense of conviction, she nonetheless wanted to convince Grant's mother, Hermione, and his older brother, Paul, that she would make Grant a good wife. If she had deceived Grant (though perhaps deception was too strong a word), why not them?

There was a sound of typing from out on the porch and, through the window, Melissa could see Paul, his back bent, his face scowling.

"Paul and I were going over his dissertation last night," Hermione said. "It has some interesting ideas, but they need to be worked on. And did he tell you about the controversy he's gotten into with that lady don at Oxford? Oh, I wish he'd withdraw the whole thing. He'll just get into trouble."

"No," Melissa said. "Grant mentioned it, though." She turned and sat down at the breakfast table.

"It would be good if Grant would talk to him about this controversy thing," Hermione said, idly stirring a cup of coffee. "Paul respects his opinions so much. It's as though Grant were the older." She smiled at Melissa encouragingly. "Or you could say something to him yourself, dear. It's your field too, isn't it?"

Melissa looked embarrassed. "Well, not my field, really," she said. "I mean, I'm just taking these two courses."

"Still," Hermione persisted. "You're working toward a degree, aren't you? An M.A.? And it *is* odd, isn't it, an odd coincidence, both you and Paul being in such an unusual field. There can't be that many people in it. . . . What made you pick that particular field?"

"Well, I don't know," Melissa said, choosing her words carefully. "I've always liked Chinese poetry, and I'd like to go to China one day, to visit or study or . . ." She stopped, remembering that when she married, these hopes were hardly likely to be fulfilled.

But Hermione was too distracted to listen. Looking out at Paul again, she said, "I think now that Paul's passed his orals, he's gotten over the big hurdle, you know? I think that was the great divide, in a way. . . . It's just that I wish he would see *people* more, take out a girl now and then."

"At our engagement party, he brought this one girl," Melissa said, glad to convey one bit of good news. "She seemed very nice. She's the secretary in his department at Columbia. . . . But then suddenly he stopped seeing her. I guess it never amounted to anything."

"No, his relations with girls never do. I think he scares them off, somehow. And yet he's quite shy, really." Hermione's face usually so determinedly cheerful and bright, clouded over slightly. "He'll never marry," she said. "I don't even expect that any more. I just thought perhaps . . ."

But she left her thought unfinished. Grant must be such a relief to her, Melissa reflected, being a success in everything—carrying everything off so easily, a well-paying job, his cheerful, open disposition, so much like Hermione's own, his fiancée—yes, even she, Melissa, was part of his success, taken not so much as a person, but as a thing composed of a double strand of cultured pearls, a pair of black alligator heels, a bouffant hairdo, and a faint smell of Chanel No. 5. Paul stood outside of this. Even though he had partly recovered now, the nervous breakdown he had had eight years earlier, when he was 24, had left its mark on him. "You should have seen him before," Grant had said. "He was always full of the devil, playing tricks, kidding around. I was so proud of him. He was my idol practically."

It was hard for Melissa to relate this image of the fun-loving, good-natured Paul to the person he was now. At this point he led a solitary life, rarely ever went to plays or movies, studied all day by himself, ate heartily, and only showed his eccentricities in his mannerisms and in the occasional off-color jokes that he would tell and then burst into loud, nervous laughter. Melissa could not feel at ease with him. It was awkward trying to think of congenial things to say, yet underneath, a secret, silent, but barely acknowledged current of sympathy extended from her to him. He was like her, she thought; they were a pair, separated by some fine but clear-cut line from Grant and Hermione who also, in her mind, stood grouped together, like characters about to begin a dance.

". . . be coming to the magic show tonight?" Melissa, breaking out of her reverie, heard Hermione say. She looked up and found Hermione's bright, curious eyes resting upon her hands. Without realizing it, she had been shredding the napkin into little pieces. She laughed, embarrassed, and scooped them all together. "I didn't know there was one," she said.

"Yes, it's an annual thing with the summer school, giving a show

at the end of the term. And Paul's always helped out by donating
his services for a magic show. He's very good, you know. He
always liked to give home magic shows when he was little. Grant
used to help him. Where *is* Grant, anyway? That boy! Isn't he
up yet?"

"I imagine not," Melissa said. "He would have come down."

"Well, yes, he needs the rest. He's so pale and run down,"
Hermione said. "He worked so hard on his bar exams." She
reached over and patted Melissa's hand. "And you, too," she said.
"I want the two of you to have a nice rest and do just whatever
you please."

Grant lay in bed, half-asleep, wondering if he should get up.
Groping for his watch on the bed table, he saw it was past
eleven. He had a vague feeling he had dreamt something, and he
couldn't remember what it was. Well, the hell with it. Melissa was
always telling him that if he wrote down his dreams and then
wrote down whatever came to his head about each thing in the
dream, he would see something important about himself. Sometimes, for fun, or to make up to her for teasing her about her
analyst, he'd do it. He even kept a little pad near his bed for that
purpose; but nine times out of ten, in the rush to get to work on
time, and to walk Melissa's poodle (since the engagement they
had been living together, and he had acquired that chore), he
forgot, and by the time he thought of it again, the dream had vanished. Well, this was vacation. Down with dreams. He stretched
and lay back again.

The door opened. It was Melissa, who quickly closed the door
behind her. She was in her blue robe, her light hair falling loose
and slightly messed up on her shoulders, giving her a sexy,
languid look that he liked.

"Sloth," she said, smiling. "It's eleven."

"I know."

She came over and stood by the bed. Reaching up, he pulled
her down next to him and smiled. She frowned, nervously sweeping back her hair. "What if your mother . . ."

"Oh, Mother, schmother! Let her worry about it. Anyway, it'll
give her a vicarious thrill if she does come in. She and Dad have
slept in separate bedrooms for so long. . . ."

Melissa laughed. "Have they really? How funny!"

His face kept the same amused, half-teasing expression. "You know. She likes to sleep with the windows open, he likes them closed, things like that."

But Melissa's face looked worried again. "What about Paul?"

"Oh, he'll be working all morning."

"He could stop early."

"It's possible."

Melissa crossed the room and lay down on the other bed. Paul's. Grant watched her. Part of his impulse had died from her lack of response. But even this did not take away his good humor and sense of well-being. There would be other times. "Sleep well?" he asked.

"Umm hmm. . . . You?"

"I *always* sleep well," he said, smiling.

"That's right. I always forget."

They lay there in silence. Through the half-drawn Venetian blinds a stream of sunlight fell on the wooden floor.

"Marilyn Monroe died," Melissa said.

"Did she?"

"Yes, it was in the paper. She took an overdose of sleeping pills."

"Hmm."

"I felt sad about it, somehow. . . . I don't know why."

"It *is* a sad thing. She was fairly young, wasn't she?"

"Thirty-eight or something. I don't know. I can't explain it, but I felt badly."

Grant looked at her sorrowful face. He had only seen Marilyn Monroe once in a movie and hadn't been struck by her, but it was typical of Melissa to react to something like that. She never read the newspapers thoroughly, yet always found some obscure notice about an animal that was becoming extinct or a play that had been forced to close which would make her brood all day.

"It's funny sleeping alone," said Grant, to change the subject.

Melissa reached over and pressed his hand. "For me, too. But it's only four days more."

"No, I know. I can wait."

If only Melissa had something to do, Grant thought. That was the trouble with this visit, something he hadn't foreseen. He had

COLLEGE OF THE SEQUOIAS
LIBRARY

a whole stack of briefs to study. He could relax part of the day—
swimming, playing tennis—but the rest of the time he had to
work in the library. That left Melissa with no other company than
Paul, who was certainly not much fun, and Hermione, who, Grant
well knew, was inclined to be chattery and nerve-racking, even
in her desire to be nice.

"Why don't you try some sketching today?" Grant suggested.
"You said you'd like to."

"Well, I'll see."

Grant swung his legs out of bed and gave her a perfunctory kiss.
"That's the spirit," he said.

"Don't let me disturb you," Hermione said, tiptoeing through
the porch. "I brought you that article, though, in case you want
to look at it."

"Oh, thanks, Mother," Paul said. He had sensed rather than
seen her hovering around in the kitchen, ostensibly making prepa-
rations for lunch but actually watching him; he could tell. It had
made him so uncomfortable that he wasn't concentrating. He had
just gone over her corrections on the outline for his dissertation,
rereading her remarks, but unable to look at them objectively. He
hated it when she felt it necessary to help him as though he were
still a schoolboy, and hated himself for accepting the help. And
somehow the whole morning had drifted by. Incredible!

"You just go right on working," Hermione said. "You can see
it later."

"No, I'm about ready to quit now," Paul said abruptly. He
tilted his chair back, balancing on two legs, something he knew
made Hermione nervous.

"Did you work at all on that point we were discussing last
night?" Hermione asked, peering over his shoulder.

Deliberately he shuffled the papers together and turned them
face down. "No, I did something else."

Paul could see the conflict in Hermione's face about whether or
not she should pursue it. After a moment she said, "Well, maybe
just for now it would be best if you stuck to the outline, don't
you think? I mean, so you can get it done on time for Professor
Herman?"

He looked outside, as though he hadn't heard her. "Melissa and Grant up?" he asked.

"Melissa was just here a moment ago. I don't know about Grant."

"We were going to play some tennis today."

"You and Grant? How nice!"

He fiddled with the scissors. "Of course, I'm not a 'champion' like Grant, but I thought it might be good to get some exercise."

"Yes, I heartily agree with that," Hermione said. "It'll be good for both of you." She turned to go inside. "That film star, Marilyn Monroe, died, you know. Melissa was very upset about it."

The sky had clouded over. Melissa went inside to get a sweater, then came out again. Grant had gone over to the library, saying he'd be back at one. Hermione was preparing her class for the following day. Melissa had promised to gather some raspberries in back of the house, and she began slowly, bending down so all that she saw were the dusty bushes in front of her.

"You won't find too many," Paul said.

Melissa stood up, her face flushed from stooping over. "I didn't hear you come up," she said.

"Cat's feet," he said, pointing to his sneakers. "Grant at the library?"

"He has some briefs to go over," Melissa said, trying to sound noncommittal.

"Yes, he always does, doesn't he? Well, it's just as well. There's not much else to do in this town."

Melissa tried to smile. "Yes, you must have had a dull summer."

"It isn't the Riviera. . . . Oh, well, there are such startling compensations as tea with Miss Landy and picking raspberries. I say, you won't find many because I went over them just last Wednesday."

"Your mother mentioned something about a controversy you're in," Melissa said lightly, trying to win him over.

He smiled sardonically. "Yes, of all things, a lady don, Millicent Tushingham, has taken it upon herself to disagree with a defense I wrote of one of her articles. She's been writing some rather amazing letters to me."

"I'd like to see them."

"Would you?" He looked at her suspiciously. "You haven't read the article so you wouldn't understand it," he said.

"I know the gist of it."

Convinced, he brought a whole sheaf of papers out on the lawn. "I want to read you the whole thing," he said.

Melissa propped herself against a tree to listen to him. At first, she tried to follow the essence of his dispute with the lady don. But it was an intricate, scholarly point, involving the meaning of two words from a Lady Murasaki story, and she soon gave up. Why did he get involved in these entanglements? To put such energy and interest in it! If it had been a more wide-ranging, creative essay, it would have been one thing. Yet she sensed somehow that the narrowness of the topic was deliberate on his part, as though he only wanted to look straight ahead at a single point, like a horse with blinders on. He has nothing else in his life, she argued to herself. What else can he do?

If only he had someone, some girl friend. But who would accept him with his strange mannerisms and peculiarities, his sarcasm, his abrupt sense of humor? Paul's eyes were lowered to read and, taking advantage of this, Melissa looked at him closely, studying him, as though to find the clue to his character. He was a large, muscularly built man with an unusual, powerful face, quite unlike the typical, bespectacled image of a scholar she had expected. Yes, he would be attractive to women, she thought, but who? Perhaps some nurse, some strong, capable woman who could be a source of security for him as Grant was for her. The strong with the weak: that was the only way things could work out.

". . . do you think?" he was saying.

Melissa came back to reality with a jump. Daydreaming again— the second time that morning. She realized she hadn't heard a thing he had said for the last ten minutes.

"Woolgathering?" he said. "I admit, it isn't the most fascinating of topics."

She blushed, embarrassed. "No, it was terribly interesting, really. . . . I know that story, actually. I once did a paper on it. . . . Yes, I think you're right. You should stick to what you've said."

"Mother doesn't. She thinks it can only lead to trouble."

"Well, that's silly, you've a right to your opinions."

"Mother says you feel badly about the death of Marilyn Monroe," he said, pronouncing the name in an odd way, as though he had never heard it before.

"Yes, I do," Melissa said, thinking: Why does she have to tell everything?

"Suicide is a sin," he said flatly, still staring at her in his rude, abrupt way.

"I feel differently about it," Melissa said very quietly.

"Do you?" He smiled in a strange way. "Is that Grant's opinion or yours?"

Her face reddened. "It's mine. Why should I take up his opinions?"

"I thought you were one in everything."

"You know that's not true. Why do you say it?" Despite herself, she had done precisely what she had intended not to do: she had lost her temper with him. She looked down and was silent. Damn him.

"Perhaps you ought to go back to your raspberries," he said.

"I will," Melissa said. "That's a good idea."

And she did. But he was right; there were hardly any, just a handful or two, and those already brown from the heat.

"What's the score?" Paul said. He was standing at the net, having just bent down to retrieve the ball while Grant strolled back to the base line. "Your ad, isn't it?"

"I thought it was deuce," Grant said, squinting into the sun. "I might be wrong, though."

He was wrong; he knew it himself, and most likely these small devices on his part to give Paul a point now and then did more harm than good. But there was no way out of it. If he played his best, it would be slaughter. And right now, as it happened, he was in good form, whereas Paul's game had deteriorated since the last time they'd played, probably from lack of practice. Now Paul either threw games away, in anger at himself, or deliberately played his worst so as to negate any advantages Grant tried to give him. The best way was to forget about it and play normally, with good, steady strokes, no curves or short shots.

"I'm pretty sure it was your ad," Paul said, still standing there. "Don't you remember? I hit that return of yours out before."

"Did you?" Grant said. "Yes, that's right. I forgot. O.K. My ad, then." He smiled. "It's getting pretty hot, don't you think? Maybe we should quit after this game—or soon, anyway."

"Whatever you want."

"Well, I mean, I can go on, if *you* want to. I just thought . . ."

"Look, if you want to play, I'm perfectly willing. It's up to you."

"I am a little beat." Grant grinned again, but Paul's straight stare with his usual hint of sarcasm took whatever good humor there might have been out of his remark. Caught lying again. Well, the hell with it.

Paul's net serve came just over the net, veering slightly to one side. Grant rushed in and hit a long, smooth shot into the back court. He moved back to get in position for the return, but Paul, rushing forward too quickly, tripped on the white tape. He fell forward, his racket flying out of his hand.

"Hey, are you O.K.?" Grant jumped over the net. Paul was examining his knee. The skin had been broken and there was some blood, but it was not a severe cut.

"It's nothing much," Paul said.

"Well, still, we'd better wash it off."

"Maybe we should finish the point."

"Oh, it's not worth it," Grant said.

This remark hung in the air between them for several moments before Paul said in a low voice, "That's right. It was your game anyway, wasn't it, with that last point."

"You can't count the last point," Grant said heartily.

They gathered up the scattered balls and walked across the court toward the car. Grant felt in a good mood. Grinning, he put his arm loosely over his brother's shoulder. "Your serve is a lot better," he said. "You know that? If you could just get it in more consistently, your game would improve 100 per cent. . . . If you'd let me, we could come out and practice. I'll show you a few things. I think it would make a big difference."

But Paul said nothing, and they drove home in silence.

"Isn't Melissa's hair nice?" Hermione said as they all got into the car to drive down to the lake. "How do you get it so high up? It's just like a little hat on top of your head."

"I just put it up," Melissa said, getting into the back seat next to Grant. Paul was driving and Hermione sat beside him.

"You don't do that thing—what is it called—teasing? That's very bad for your hair, evidently. There was an article on it somewhere."

"No, I don't tease it," Melissa said.

"Melissa hates to be teased," said Paul. He drove down the driveway and turned left. "Miss Landy, who as you know was kind enough to invite me to tea several times this summer, told me that a woman in town got a beehive hairdo and a bee got into it and stung her. She went into the beauty parlor all dripping with blood and the next day she died."

For a moment no one said anything. Then Hermione said, "Well, really, that's ridiculous. I've never *heard* anything so foolish."

"It's the gospel truth, as Miss Landy herself will tell you," Paul said.

Hermione made a disgusted face. "Oh you just like to carry on," she said, huffily.

"He's just pulling your leg, Mother," Grant said, putting his arm around Melissa.

"I suppose he is," Hermione said.

"Just pulling one of your beautiful gams, Mother," Paul said. "Watch out one doesn't get longer than the other." And, tilting back his head, he began singing a song that went, "Those beautiful gams, oh my, what beautiful gams, as white as lambs, oh where, oh where did you get those beautiful gams?"

"What song is that?" Melissa said.

"That is a song of my own creation," Paul said. "Do you like it, Melissa?"

"It has a nice tune," Melissa said softly.

"Mother, did you say Williams Hall for you?" Paul asked, slowing up.

"Right here is all right," Hermione said. "Well, I'll tell you, why don't you drop Grant and Melissa off now, as long as we're so near the dock, and then you drive me around, if that's all right."

As Grant and Melissa walked hand in hand down to the lake, Hermione turned to look at them once more. "I wonder if that's

Melissa's only suit," she said, frowning. "I don't mind, myself. I'm sure it's very comfortable. One must get so much more sun that way. But I just thought if some of the neighbors were down there. . . . Well, of course, it is a pretty little suit, though, isn't it? And you can't tell Melissa what to do. If I live to be a hundred, I'll never understand what goes on in that little head of hers—I mean, not that I expect or even want to live to be a hundred," she added.

Paul drove up in front of the big, redbrick building. "The expression is usually used figuratively, I believe," he said.

Floating out on the lake, Paul closed his eyes and gave himself up to the enjoyment of the sun. It was nice to be this far out where the yells of the kids jumping off the dock could hardly be heard, where the sounds of cars passing on the road nearby were almost inaudible. The water right on top was warm. It was only when he dangled his feet farther down, treading water and breathing through his nose, that he touched the cold bottom.

A plane was passing overhead. Odd, the sense of dread he still felt at the sound of planes. The mental hospital had been near an airport, and his earliest memories of the place were of planes flying over. At the time, he had gotten them confused with planes in war movies he had seen, and their droning, as he had lain on his back in the dark for an endless stretch of time, had awakened in him a feeling of terror that even now had not entirely vanished.

Lifting his head slightly, he could see the red spot of color that was Melissa's bikini and the blue that was Grant. Lying in the sun, talking. Grant holding forth on one of his theories. Wasn't she bored? Or did she want that? Maybe she did. Boredom equals security. Even Melissa was willing to accept boredom in preference to fear.

He had read her diary once, gone into her room, or rather his father's room, which she now occupied, and found the diary face down in the drawer. Scattered phrases, drawings. "I have nothing to talk about with Hermione. . . . Up at eight, went in to see Grant. Can't get through to him. We talk about trifles. Why do I feel so detached with him? It doesn't do any good to condemn oneself for it, yet I can't help feeling guilty about it. . . . Wish

I knew how to drive so I could go off by myself during the day. . . ." Nothing about him, though! His vanity had been offended. Not even a slighting or nasty word: Paul is being difficult again. If only Paul would leave us alone. Nothing. And yet when she looked at him, when she had brushed past him this morning in the raspberry patch, wasn't there some feeling there? Or was he just foisting his own longings onto her?

Slowly, with firm, sure strokes, Paul began swimming back to shore. As he climbed onto the sand, he heard Grant saying to Melissa, "I just hate guys like that."

"Like what?" Paul asked, reaching for a towel.

"Oh, I was just telling Melissa about these lawyers at the firm —you know, the kind that will only take on a 'perfect' case, nothing involving any element of risk. Christ, it makes you think the whole profession is just a bunch of pompous bastards."

"But *you're* not a pompous bastard," Paul said. A second later, he added in a low voice, "At least I don't *think* you are."

Melissa broke up at this. She began laughing so hard, tears streamed down her face. Grant looked at her, puzzled, but Paul, catching her infectious laughter, began to laugh himself. For nearly five minutes the two of them sat there, gasping, clutching their sides, until Melissa managed to compose herself. "I'm sorry," she said to Grant. "It just struck me as so funny."

Grant eyed her suspiciously. "I didn't even hear what the joke was," he said. And, getting up, he folded the three wet towels neatly into the straw basket.

"You said nothing about a magic show, Mother!" Grant looked annoyed. "Why didn't you say so before?"

"Didn't I? I thought I did. Perhaps it was to Melissa." Hermione looked flustered. "It's nothing so much, really. The faculty of the summer school always puts on these little skits every year, and I thought, why not have Paul do a little something? It was just an idea, but I mentioned it to him a few weeks ago and he was glad. You know, he always liked doing tricks. Why, he even went to a magicians' convention at Rochester to get some pointers."

Grant gave a snort of laughter. "Are there magicians' conventions? How crazy! What do they do, go around pulling rabbits out of each other's hats?" He drummed impatiently with his fingers on the desk. "No, the point is, I wish you'd let us know earlier. We have plans for the evening."

"Well, dear . . ." Hermione looked at him helplessly. "He'd be so pleased if you'd come."

"Yes, I'm sure, but that's not the point. . . ."

"Melissa can forego a little evening's entertainment," Hermione said. "You've been out almost every night."

"Well, aside from that not being true, it's not Melissa, it's me, too. . . . Look, we'll see what we can do. That's the most I can say."

There was a "No Trespassing" sign in front of the fence. "That doesn't matter," Grant said. "It's just old land. No one'll see us."

"Are you sure?" Melissa stood uncertainly and did not move. It was just barely dark out, that instant of twilight before darkness falls.

"I'll help you over the fence," Grant said. "Give me your hand. You won't fall."

Clutching him, Melissa jumped, and fell, not hurting herself, in a pile of leaves.

They wandered through the forest. It was cooler than it had been walking along the road, since here the sun had been shut out all day. Grant walked ahead of Melissa, holding back the branches so she could proceed. He, too, was silent now. When they had set out, it had been on his mind that he wanted to make love to her. All day he had been distracted by the thought: when she had lain beside him on the beach, when she had come into the bedroom in the morning. The tentative abstinence he had planned for these weeks—sublimate everything into sports! —had suddenly seemed impossible. He felt that he could literally not survive this stay, which was awkward enough anyway, without making love to her.

When the road was no longer visible, he stopped, pulled her down beside him on the ground, and began kissing her. He had intended to be gentle, to soothe her into the proper mood with tender endearments, but as the kisses lasted longer, all that blanked out of his mind. He drew her dress over her head.

"It's so hot," she said, drawing away from him.

Grant smiled at her. "Why don't we, Lissy? It's so lovely here."

"There are too many mosquitoes," Melissa said, laughing nervously. "We're too near the road."

"We can go farther in."

He walked ahead again and she followed, nude except for her thong sandals, her dress draped over her arm. Within a few minutes they were deep into the forest. Once again they lay down. Grant spread out his shorts and shirt for Melissa to lie down on.

Above her, Melissa watched the trees that arched together, blocking out the sky. Up until this moment she had felt she wanted him also. But now, suddenly, a feeling of loneliness assaulted her. She thought: this is how he thinks of me—a sexy blonde, to sleep with in the woods. What does he care what I feel? And yet, even this mood passed, as quickly and mysteriously as it had come. He made love to her slowly, and half without her will a feeling of passion overcame her; she forgot everything else.

Afterward, she dozed off and had a dream: she was lying next to Paul and he was kissing her, but these kisses were extraordinarily sweet, sweeter than any real kisses. He was leaning over her and saying, "You pretended not to be interested in me, but I could tell you were." Then, suddenly, the dream changed. He had cancer and would die in two years, and if she loved him, she would catch the cancer from him and die also. And with that, the sweetness of the dream vanished, for she knew she loved him and would die.

"Honey," Grant said. "Are you sleeping? Do you want to go?" He bent over her and grazed his lips against her neck.

Melissa awoke and looked up, startled to see Grant. His touch on her, his kiss, seemed crude and flat compared to the kisses in the dream.

"That was nice, wasn't it?" Grant said.

"Umm," Melissa said, afraid he would realize what she was feeling.

"We always wanted to do it out-of-doors, remember?" he said. "I'm glad we did. . . . It's strange, but nice—to escape like this. . . ."

". . . go back to a primitive state," Melissa said, trying to joke.

"There's something beautiful in just being here, in nature," Grant said.

Melissa smiled.

"It *is* a beautiful forest," she agreed, turning her head. "But these damn mosquitoes—there are never mosquitoes in D. H. Lawrence."

Grant laughed. "You'll never be a romantic," he said.

"Are you?" The dream still possessed her, and she could not help looking at him as though he were a stranger.

"Maybe more of one," he said, grinning. "I don't know."

It was hard to sleep. Downstairs, the faucet in the kitchen was dripping, and she found herself lying awake to listen to it. Ping . . . ping. . . . Where was it she had read of someone dying who had heard the sounds: pitti pitti. Someone was dying—who was it? Marilyn Monroe. Why had that been haunting her all day? A silly blonde, a movie star. Someone trapped by a false image of herself, which she could not escape. And yet it was her fault! She preserved the image willfully! Her fault! She killed herself because of it! No, that was no good. She'd never get to sleep that way. Melissa sat up, hugging her arms around her legs. Well, it was silly to get all upset. She would not be a suicide, certainly—there was something too melodramatic about it.

She got out of bed and quietly tiptoed downstairs. There was no carpet on the stairs, and the wood felt cold and slippery under her feet. Hugging her bathrobe around her, she walked into the kitchen. Everything was still, and the furniture sat silently, like props on a deserted stage. What was that! A tapping on the window startled her and, whirling around, Melissa saw Paul outside on the lawn, leaning toward the window, his face near to the glass. She opened the window and found herself face to face with him. He had left on the makeup from the magic show. His skin was unnaturally pale, and a dark moustache had been corked on his upper lip. He was wearing a cape tied around his neck.

"How did it go?" Melissa said, feeling guilty about their not having shown up.

"Didn't you hear?" He said mockingly.

"What? We just got back a little while ago." She looked at him gravely. "Wasn't it held?"

"No, it was held." He put out his hand to her. "Why don't you come outside?" he said. "It's beautiful out."

Melissa hesitated only a moment. "O.K."

When she came outside, he was standing on the back lawn looking up at the stars. "There's another one," he said.

"What?" Melissa looked with him. The sky was black with a haze of stars, so many that they made the sky oddly radiant. Standing there in the darkness beside him, she felt peaceful for the first time all day.

"Shooting stars. Look, there's another." He grabbed her arm and pointed.

"Where? I don't see." Melissa looked back and forth. The sudden, abrupt touch of his hand on her arm stirred her profoundly.

"It's over." His voice became flat and uninterested again. He turned to her. "There're a lot of them this time of year. I've counted 50 in one night."

"So many," Melissa said softly.

They were silent a moment.

"You didn't see Mother when you got back?" Paul said.

Melissa shook her head. "I think she was asleep."

"That's right. She would have been." He put his hands together lightly, as though he were praying. "Well, you missed something," he said in his former, ironical voice.

"Did the tricks go over well?" Melissa asked.

"Oh, the tricks were fine." He smiled, and reaching into his pocket, pulled out a red silk scarf which he draped over his hand and whipped back a moment later to reveal a bunch of flowers. Melissa smiled.

"But at the end," he said, "there was something in the nature of a fiasco, you might say." He paused, but Melissa said nothing. "I was going to do a prophetic trick," he continued, "you know, the old one of picking someone in the audience and getting him to help you guess certain things. So I took out this crystal ball I use and said, 'You may not see anything so unusual about this. You may think all magicians have crystal balls.'" He looked at her, waiting for a reaction. "You don't think that's funny? Well, senses of humor differ. Anyhow, it broke up the show. They roared. They sat there for five minutes, roaring. It was just one

of those things that you couldn't stop once it got started. I just
stood there, tried to start over. They wouldn't let me. They
whistled, screamed. Finally I walked off the stage and went home,
which, so I hear, upset everyone because they were waiting for
the rest of the act." He dug his heel into the ground and moved
it back and forth. "I thought I'd given them enough entertainment for one night," he said. "Don't you agree?"

The pain in his voice was just barely concealed by the irony.
Melissa stared at him, deeply touched. For that one instant he
seemed incredibly close to her, someone she could love in a way
she had never loved Grant or anyone before.

"What do you think, Melissa?" he said, using her name for the
first time and giving the word undue emphasis. "Do you think
some people always make *mistakes* like that, always spoil what
they want once it's within their reach?"

"I don't know," Melissa said uneasily. The change in his voice
frightened her.

"Do you *want* Grant?" he said, continuing in the same way.
"Is that your goal in life? Well, it's an interesting goal, a worthy
one. . . . It's a mistake, though, to leave your diary around.
One might assume from a perusal of it that your feelings weren't
so simple, and that would be a mistake, wouldn't it?" He reached
out to touch her, his hand on her shoulder, near her neck. Melissa,
looking at him for an instant, saw a flicker of fear cross his eyes
and it was this, as much as the touch of his hand, that made her
pull back.

"I don't know," she said in a whisper, almost pleading. She
began backing away toward the house.

"What do you think?" Paul cried after her. "Tell me, Melissa,
tell me what you think? Am I a failure? Tell me!" His voice,
trembling, followed her as she fumbled with the door.

"Yes," she flung at him, her voice rising. She turned a second
to see him standing there on the lawn with the dark cape hanging lopsided off one shoulder. "Yes! You are!" Melissa whispered.

Going into the house, she nearly bumped into Hermione.

"Oh, dear, I just happened to be passing your room," Hermione
said, "and I saw the door open and your bed empty. I wondered. . . . A pity you couldn't make it to the magic show

tonight." She stood near Melissa, her face large and pale in the darkness.

"Yes, yes, it was," Melissa said, hearing nothing, dazed.

"Paul did so well," she said, "so well till the very end—and then it was just this little thing that upset it all. He's so hyper-sensitive, you know. Just a little joke. But where did you and Grant go? I thought—"

"Please, I'm terribly tired," Melissa said, trying to brush past, her whole body trembling uncontrollably.

"Always sneaking off—you two—like lovebirds." Her voice suddenly turned reproachful. "But, you know, it's just as well you weren't there in a way. It would just have made him feel worse, knowing you saw everything."

"Please, stop it, stop it!" Melissa heard her own voice burst out in a terrible scream. For a moment she was not even aware of who had screamed, but wondered who was making so much noise so late at night.

"My God, Mother, what's going on?" Grant appeared in the doorway, dressed in his pajama bottoms. He went over to Melissa, and took her in his arms. "Darling, what's wrong? What hap-pened?"

Melissa tried to speak and couldn't; the tears poured out of her.

"What—have you and Paul been pestering her again? Christ, I'm sick of the two of you! I bring her home and all week it's the same business—innuendos, gossip, everyone picking away at everyone. Look, this girl is going to be my wife!"

"No one's denying that," Paul said dryly. He had come in so quietly no one heard him. "The case is conceded."

"Oh, hell! Why don't you cut out all that stuff? 'The case is conceded,'" Grant mimicked. "Can't you say something straight out? All this damn Chinese courtesy!"

Paul raised his eyebrows and bowed slightly. "Honorable sir," he said, drawling his r's in an oriental way.

"It's not that," Melissa said. "It's not that."

"Well, what is it, then?" Grant said angrily. "What's all the commotion about?"

"I was just showing Melissa a few of the magic tricks I did in the show," Paul said, exquisitely polite. "And one of them scared her. She isn't *used* to magic tricks."

Grant looked suspicious. "Were you?" he said belligerently. "What tricks?"

Paul smiled, sleepily. "Oh, nothing unusual really, making things appear and disappear, a few transformation tricks, the old routine."

"You remember? You and Paul used to do them together once," Hermione said, looking anxiously from one to the other. "That summer you both put on that act, remember? You cut Mademoiselle Bijou, the French teacher, in half."

Grant relaxed. "Yes, I *do* remember," he said. "Whatever happened to her?"

"She got false teeth and married a dentist from Duluth," Paul said. "They have eight children."

"Eight! Good God!" Grant said. He shook his head. By now he was almost in a good humor.

"Yes, and she's a weak woman," Hermione said, grasping at this straw. "I said to your father more than once, 'Mademoiselle Bijou is a weak woman.' She had liver trouble. She had diabetes. Why, do you know that that last semester she was so tired she had to teach sitting down! She came to me especially one afternoon. 'Mrs. Fordyce, I have to teach sitting down. I just don't have the energy to stand.' That's what she said. And yet she had all those children!"

"Maybe she had *them* sitting down," Paul said.

Grant laughed and even Melissa smiled.

Later Grant came into Melissa's room to put her to bed. She was tired and drained of feeling, almost light-headed. Grant sat on the edge of the bed, holding her hand. The lights were off and the house still again.

"Listen, if Paul acted funny tonight," Grant said, "you've got to understand. He still isn't really all . . ."

"No, I understand," Melissa said quickly.

"It's too bad Dad isn't here," Grant said. "Things always get out of hand when he's away. He's terrific. You'll love him. He has a great sense of humor. And he plays a damn good game of tennis for a man his age. He keeps himself in shape. . . . You'll see at our wedding."

"Yes, I'm looking forward to meeting him," Melissa said formally, knowing now, for the first time, that there would be no wedding.

He kissed her lightly before he left. "I'm glad we didn't go to the magic show, actually." He smiled intimately at her.

She smiled too and lay there, the smile remaining on her face almost by inertia. Listening, she heard his footsteps retreating down the hall into his room. Several moments later Hermione passed by and closed her door with a sharp click. And last of all came Paul, his step slow and light, as light, it seemed to Melissa, as the gesture he had made when he had flipped back the red silk scarf, revealing the three perfect rosebuds underneath.

BROCK BROWER grew up in New Jersey and attended Dartmouth College and Merton College, Oxford as a Rhodes Scholar. Since returning from England he has written articles for *Esquire, Life, Holiday* and other magazines and his stories have appeared in *New World Writing* and other quarterlies. Mr. Brower's first novel, *Debris,* was published in 1967. He has also worked as an assistant editor of *Esquire,* an associate editor of *Transatlantic Review* and taught for several summers at the Breadloaf Writers Conference. With his wife and four children, Mr. Brower lives in Princeton, New Jersey.

Storm Still

IT WAS SOMETIME WINTRY, probably in 1608, at Bankside, and he was clearly at the Globe, among the groundlings, chinned up against the front stage by the pushing of the farrier's apprentice behind him, and the garlic-breathed orangegirl on his right. Robert Armin was playing the Fool. That was why he had come. To see Armin in his motley, coxcomb, and huge ass's ears, the bladder rioting in his lunatic hand. But then Richard Burbage was also acting that afternoon. He was playing Lear. Brilliantly, he thought. "Take heed, sirrah; the whip." The steely core of kingly authority. Lear not yet mad, still regal. He suddenly wanted to tell somebody, anybody how fine an actor Burbage was. He turned smiling to the orangegirl. She smiled back coquettishly. He started to open his mouth to utter some critical *bon mot,* but closed it quickly around her wild kiss. Then she was clinging to him like a daughter. "I cannot heave my heart into my mouth," she cried. "I cannot heave my heart into my mouth, I cannot heave my heart into my mouth, I cannot heave my . . ."

"Storm Still" – Brock Brower, *Tri-Quarterly,* Copyright © 1967 by Northwestern University.

Then everything turned on a great, dizzy wheel, wrenching his attention around to the stage again, away from Cordelia, the orangegirl. He was horrified. Lear *was* whipping the Fool, beating him mercilessly to the cruel, cheek-cracking tune of the thunder. The cannonball rolled back and forth behind the stage, and Armin sang to the beating of the whip.

> *He that hath but a tiny little wit,*
> *With hey, ho, the wind and the rain,*
> *Must make content with his fortunes fit,*
> *Though the rain it raineth every day.*

The Fool jigged, and the whip cut.

He tried to shout out. The Fool should not be whipped, it wasn't in the play. He started to climb onto the stage. First it grew higher and higher, forcing him down and down as he climbed. Then it collapsed under him. From the three balconies around the octagonal Globe they laughed at him. "But the Fool is *not whipped,*" he shouted at them, almost defensively. "Lear must never do such a thing. Never, never, never, never, never." Then they began to disappear, laughing, behind the rising flames. He saw why the stage had collapsed. It was on fire. The great Globe itself was on fire, burning like a wooden bucket. But that was wrong too. The Globe fire was in 1613. "Stop, stop!" he cried at the flames. "You're too early. Don't burn. Don't whip the Fool. Don't burn. Don't whip the Fool." Then he woke up.

Immediately he felt his old fumbling sense of panic. He'd slipped again in some matter of the play. There was a reference he carelessly hadn't checked all the way back—some date or alternate reading he must look up this very instant, or they were going to catch him out. He knew it was something terribly minor. Some question about the colophon on the Pide Bull Quarto, or a line he'd wrongly attributed to the source play *Leir* or to Holinshed, or even some stupid quibble over the spelling of Cordelia's name. Really that picayune. It didn't affect his main argument in the slightest. But they would crucify him for it, put his whole scholarship in doubt at next spring's meeting, if he didn't find it now and burn it out like a tiny plague spot in his critical acumen.

He knew all this was nonsense, yet he still began shuffling

furtively through the papers on his desk to see if he hadn't possibly made a note somewhere, perhaps in the margins of his Spenser. It was one of those involuntary things that had finally become quite voluntary. He needed something to clear his mind when he napped off, and this seemed to do the trick. One of these days, he suspected, he was going to nap off altogether. His mind would simply fail to clear. Last scene of all that ends this strange, eventful history. Second childishness and mere oblivion. But somehow that would be all right too, because, look, he was only here picking over his papers after an insignificant reference. There was nothing really important to get back to. . . .

But he was awake enough now to hear the knock. It was hard to tell whether he was hearing it now, actually at the door, or whether memory was echoing it for him. Such distinctions were becoming difficult for him to make at times. Or just not worth making.

"Yes?" he asked peevishly. He wondered if he wheezed at all. Manly voice, turning to childish treble.

His study door opened part way, and a bearded face cocked around at him, its smile still back in the door's shadow. "Busy?"

This was young Nelson's way of asking permission to come in out of the shadows. For a moment he mused on just leaving him there in the shadows. Forever. Perhaps he would eventually fade into the umbra, pulling his bearded smile in after him, and become a complete shadow, instead of the furtive, diffident half shadow he already was. But oh what silliness, he warned himself, and said pleasantly, "No, no, no. Come in, Nelson. Please."

The young instructor bowed out of the doorway, bringing in a towering pile of corrected blue books. On top of them was the marking book, stretched open to the proper page with a rubber band. Nelson seemed to come bearing them almost like a hecatomb, yet at the same time he managed somehow to be putting them aside—to ask about obviously more important work. "How are you coming along with the old fool?"

He meant Lear, of course. Almost certainly, he meant Lear.

Nelson handed him the pile, which was deceptively heavy. He lifted it the little height onto his desk, straining every chest muscle not to puff.

"All right, my boy," he laughed. "I'm having most of my

trouble with the young fool. If I can settle his hash. . . ." He decided he'd better be hospitable. "Can you stay a minute?"

Nelson nodded and slipped over to the other chair by the cold fireplace. On his way he ran his fingers along the books on one shelf. Too lightly, too quickly. Looking for his poems, the older man knew. Feeling for them, actually. An absurdly thin volume, and from the spine, it really was hard to see. A two-dimensional piece of work. If that. It was silly enough to find a scholarly press going in for that sort of publishing, but it was much sillier to have it inspire a beard. An effeminate beard too, he felt, even though it covered those sallow cheeks blackly. A shadow would grow just such a beard. That plushy. His book and his whiskers had both come out far too soon, and that summed up Nelson precisely as far as he was concerned.

Nelson crossed his legs and all his fingers in one nervous motion. "You know," he said, "sometimes I think Shakespeare himself must've been a jester one time or another."

How he hated that kind of remark. Shakespeare was Marlowe, or Bacon, or the Earl of Essex, or the boy who held the horses, and now a Fool. It threw everything out of balance. *The Tragedy of Lear* by Crazy Will.

"Oh?" he said simply.

"Everything he does—well, it has the fool's wit. I was reading an article the other day, sir. You might look at it if you're working on this theme of Folly." He smiled quickly. "I suppose you've got your material down pat as it is, but this man had something really new—I mean, he puts you up against it on a couple of points. Quite up against it."

Nelson had studied a year at Oxford. It had made him an expert at malicious deference. Maddening.

Nelson mentioned where he might find the article. It was in a publication that had not been in existence before his fiftieth birthday. He'd read a few issues, and thought it all nonsense. Then he was flabbergasted to find that he had to suffer a certain amount of condescension for thinking it all nonsense. He kept silent about it nowadays, but he would certainly not read the article.

"Have you been doing anything on *Lear* yourself?" he suddenly thought to ask.

The instructor bowed low before the challenge. "No. Not at all. Nothing on *Lear* itself. I just thought you might like to hear about this man's work. Are those exams all right then?"

"Must be, my boy, if you've done them. You ought to be thanked, of course. It's very pleasant to be left free—"

"Not at all."

Gratitude was the very cup of bitterness sometimes, he thought. But he was too old to be much surprised by the taste. That same taste crept into so many things that were supposed to be ennobling.

"But I'm afraid, sir. . . ."

"You must run along. That it?"

"Yes, I'm afraid."

"Of course. Mustn't keep you. I know better. Thank you again, Nelson. Won't keep you. Must work myself." Sometimes, he calculated, a properly self-effacing old man can lick the pants off any youth for modest demeanor.

Nelson went out, closing the door without a sound, almost as if he didn't want to wake somebody. Maddening.

He leaned back heavily in his chair, lifting the front legs about an inch off the floor, and patted his girth. His Phi Beta Kappa key, comically oversized, topped the hillock like a small tablet of laws. A back leg of the chair suddenly hobbled on its uncertain shank and brought the chair down sharply onto all fours again. The slip shook him for a moment.

So it is all happening to me, he thought. I can't even stay steady in my own chair. I shall simply have to toss up this *Lear* business and seek level ground. Unburthen'd crawl toward death.

That was why he's asked for young Nelson. Actually asked for him, absurd as that seemed now. So he could gather his thoughts in peace and produce them in final form. Which he hadn't done before, because of the pressure of . . . now, of course, with young Nelson, he'd be able . . . able now, with young Nelson.

Calling him Nelson, that was his first blunder. He'd meant to keep him kindly at a distance by using his last name without the Mister. It would've been just right. Mr. Nelson was too formal, but the last name alone, that set up just the correct balance of friendliness and seniority. Only his name wasn't Thomas R. Nelson. It was R. Nelson Thomas. He must've seen it somewhere on a list as Thomas, R. Nelson, and simply slipped the comma. Bad textual error. Trapped into familiarity. But then he seemed to recall vaguely hearing students call him Mr. Nelson. At least he assumed they were using the Mister. My God, he thought, what has happened to Degree. Take but Degree away and . . . and you get familiarity, and familiarity breeds contempt. He shook his head ruefully. Could he do no better than that innocuous cliché?

He hauled himself out of his chair, away from these thoughts—away from all thinking, in fact—and stood in front of his long, narrow Queen Anne window. Somebody else would have this window all to himself soon, and he'd be outside it. His study was on the first floor of the Library, and the campus was framed before him, cut into neat, rectangular cards by the panes. He'd be out there somewhere. Mostly bare elms, stark in the winter gloom. A five o'clock January gloom. He looked at his watch, a little loose on his wrist now. He should be hearing the Library bells, somewhere in the tower above him, ringing a knell in the gloom. Lights were already dotting on in the buildings behind the elms. The wind was coming up, bringing in the snow again.

Yes, of course, there was snow on the ground. How could he stand there and not think of the snow first thing? The white, even stretch of winter over the earth. Fresh and flocculent yesterday. Old and icy today. The hoary, arthritic, fallen snow. A crust.

Tom's a-cold, he mused. Prithee, Nuncle, be contented; 'tis a naughty night to swim in.

Then he noticed somebody running across the campus towards him, struggling hopelessly with the deep, crusted snow that broke under him at every step. Tom's a-cold, he mused again, looking out at the battling figure. Tom's adrift.

Quite suddenly, he felt himself adrift. His eyes watered and wanted to blink, only ever so slowly. He fought to keep his attention on the figure struggling in the snow, and a sensation of steepness, all about him, grew until he felt he was once again climbing onto the stage in the burning Globe to rescue the Fool. Don't whip the Fool. The whip cut, and the Fool jigged, raising the powdery underdown of snow about him like a rich mist.

He had come nearer the window now. He leaped and pirouetted and somersaulted, playing with the snow as if it were a partner.

Bells jingled. He ran to an elm tree, even nearer the window, and passionately kicked it. Immediately he was remorseful and threw his arms around the tree. A long kiss on the icy bark. Then he kicked it and laughed. The bells on his cap trembled. He looked about him inquisitively and discovered the window.

He rushed towards it and pressed his nose moistly against a pane of glass, bordered in frost. His face cocked and bobbed on his nose like the ticking moon in an ancient clock. He grinned and brayed through the glass. He shook his bells, and banged the head of the marotte that he carried against the window. And then his own head. The bells rang. The five o'clock knell rolled through the gloom.

Soberly the old man shook himself, and a certain richness of sensation deserted him. He did blink finally and reassured himself that there was no nose mark on the window pane. Outside, only the gloom. It was the first time in his life he had dozed off still on his feet. Mortifying. He forced himself back to his desk. Work.

I suppose that's really what old age is, he thought. Getting fuzzy about whether you're awake or asleep. When is Lear mad, and when is he sane? He wants to sing like a bird in a cage when he and Cordelia go off to prison. That's mad as much as it is sane. On the heath he wants the storm to strike flat the thick rotundity of the world. That's sane as much as it is mad. What's the difference?

He took the trouble to jot these ideas down in a creaky scrawl, and stuffed the paper in the corner of his blotter. After supper, he'd come back and reread them. He hadn't yet kept his promise to himself to work after supper, but tonight he would.

But already he knew what he really thought of his jottings. If he'd found them in a freshman paper, he'd have put an encouraging remark in the margin, something like, "An interesting approach, but don't rest on it. Sh. certainly intended L.'s madness and sanity to have a distinction. Same with Ham. What is it?" And in a senior thesis, he'd expect a carefully argued answer.

But *was* there an answer? Could any distinction be made between madness and sanity, wisdom and folly, sleeping and waking? He stared at the clutter of papers, the underlined books, the closed Quarto interleaved with ragged notecards, the mere ink-

blots before him. The impulse to plunge his head into his hands
and groan helplessly tugged at his dignity like the impish pluck
at the king's sleeve by the court imbecile. What were the lines?
"O, let me not be mad, not mad, sweet heaven! Come in," he
almost moaned. "Come in, come in, come in."

Then he realized he was saying it, and tried to remember hearing a knock. Yes, most certainly. He could distinctly remember
hearing a knock. At his door. So things were back in order again,
and he must immediately do the next thing. He reached out to
open the door. But his hand bumped the knob long before his
grasp closed, and the door moved away from him, a good foot,
swinging shut.

For a long moment he did not move his hand. He frowned at
the knob, trying to remember many more things, and their proper
order. Time ran back and forth in his mind, but he still could
put nothing between the last two closings of the study door. It was
like that discrepancy in exits he'd once discovered in a bad
Jacobean quarto, which forced an important extra character on
stage and opened up a wholly new interpretation of the entire
scene. That had made his reputation. But this shocked him. It
suddenly seemed such a wretched business, trying to think things
through, and he decided not to think, only listen. He heard the
tunnel echo of his own strained silence, and then deep within it,
bells, softened by cap and curled toes, jingling almost in a whisper, and then unmistakably, laughter. Inane laughter.

He whirled around in his chair—too quickly for his age—and a
small dizziness seized him, so that the riot of color, the gro-
tesquery, the motley patches of things possible over the chimerical
fabric, all assailed his sight at once. Then he was at last able to
blink again, and the cowl, braided over with a red coxcomb,
dipped toward him in a mocking bow, and the bells on the comb's
points shifted. Their fleeting tinkle struck at him, and his old,
uncompromising body gave way before the onrush of a deep
shudder.

The Fool had his motley feet drawn up in the chair. He was
grinning much as he had through the window. With great, friendly
inanity. Everything in the room seemed instantly to delight him.
His head lolled about on his neck, an imbecile motion exaggerated
by the huge ass's ears that flopped from his cowl. When he saw

something that had any brightness to it, he pointed his marotte's puppet face toward it, and pretended to whisper violently in the marotte's ear.

The old man's first thought was to rush at the coxcomb and beat him from the room. Never in his life had he felt such savagery rise within him, and he sensed it was all about to burst from him with a leaping howl at the Fool's throat.

But, the Fool abruptly stopped his meandering and rounded his grin on the old man. The grin was even more imbecile. Stupidly loyal, it seemed. The Fool was waiting. Then suddenly he kicked his motley legs with a great mocking jangle of bells, and teased at the old man with groping fingers, daring him to come ahead. Then one finger only, crooking at him blackly, like the dead wick in the lamp of reason.

It would kill me. He saw that one fact, and then began to catch hold altogether. Oblivion was smirking at him through a Fool's grin, but he was not going to let loose from the holds of logic and age and certainty. Not yet.

His first thought—his first self-possessed thought—was whether anybody had heard or seen anything. Whether anybody anywhere in the world had heard or seen anything. That he had very nearly attacked the Fool—*admitted him*—filled him with terror. Thoughts carried. Even the silence of the mind was suspicious.

Deliberately he turned back to his desk. He picked up the Pide Bull Quarto and set painfully to work on the storm scene. He courted his powers of concentration, and counted upon them to shut out any other presence that might be—that was how he must think of it, *might be*—near him. Gradually they did. The rollings of the bells and the little chuckles merged with the rising storm outside, and together, close to either side of his window, they passed away, out of his ken.

II

He ate his supper in the upper hall of the undergraduate Commons. He frequently did this for the sake of a change from his quiet widower's meal, served up uneventfully by the bad-tempered housekeeper who had outlived his wife's patience with her. But tonight he wanted something else from the dining hall. Something almost tribal.

He listened gratefully to the tumult of undergraduate cutlery. The meal was eaten out of various triangular, oblong, and serpentine depressions in uniform aluminum trays, collected from a cafeteria line, and the din reminded him of nothing so much as the Roman legionaries going into battle, beating their shields. On top of this, there was the babble of at least two hundred youths, all talking at once, none of them yet sure how his voice should really sound. Bedlam, Jericho. Or a thousand twangling instruments.

It all had a strangely reassuring effect upon him. The noise and liveliness argued against the Fool. When he got back to work, there would only be frost at his window. In a few days he might be able to talk confidently about hallucination, or tricks of the dozing eye, the dream-fondled ear. He tidied his wrinkled mouth with a napkin, took advantage of his age to leave the tray on the table rather than face the confusing actions of the dishwasher's chute, and left the Commons, mantled in an overcoat.

The walk back to his study followed shoveled canyons through the old snow. Within the last hour, they had begun to fill up again with a new undergrowth of flakes. A good way to put it, he thought. It stings your face like nettles, it clings to your clothes like burrs, so why shouldn't it be considered some kind of uncontrollable, prickly weed? The false logic of it pleased him. It kept him warm during the rest of the cold, devious walk, barriered him against the increasing storm that whipped at him devilishly. No matter which way he bent his head, it seemed to strike him on his unprotected side.

He reached the Library. Inside, he stamped his boots in the dark corridor—managed to kick one off, but had to stoop over for the other. He walked briskly down the corridor, congratulating himself on his desire to work after supper. Even if it might be false desire. He unlocked his study door and pushed it open, but it moved too lightly ahead of him, and he caught enough glimpse of haste in the Fool to know he'd just skipped back to the fireplace chair in time.

Disappointed, he told himself. Not surprised. Not afraid. Just disappointed.

He sat down at his desk with his back again to the other chair. He would have to do a little work, make a little progress before he could safely turn around. He did not know where the feeling came from, but he was certain that to work well was his only hope against the Fool's inane grin, his seductive, will-o'-the-wisp bells. The stir of the outside world—the noisy community of the dining hall—he realized now, were useless.

He decided to give up the Pide Bull Quarto for the evening, in fact, to turn away from *Lear* itself altogether and read *The Tragecall historie of Kinge Leir and his Three Daughters*. Over the years he'd read the source play in patches, little snippets for his lectures, but he'd never sat down to read the whole play through for itself. He suspected it would be dull, wretchedly jangling, and stupid. In only a few pages he was convinced he was right. But he refused to give in to boredom, to let his mind slip out of its set task. The Fool was seated too near him for that.

The verse trotted along like an old dray. He had to stop reading line by line, and rushed ahead for the sense alone. The play dragged on preposterously. Leir was arrogant, lachrymose, and stupid. Truly stupid.

His patience began to wear. He tried to stifle his irritation, but it grew into a repressed anger. Finally, he yielded to a loss of temper he could hardly understand himself, and flung the book down on his desk. The old fool, he snapped to himself. Yes, precisely. The old fool, because there is no fool worse than Lear without his Fool. And that was Leir.

Suddenly he had the feeling of tottering on the verge of some immeasurably deep but opulent unknown. It was like that quibble that always touched the unsettled edge of his waking, only he felt he was much nearer the instance this time, that it *was* important after all. Terribly important. They were right to catch him up on it. It was a reference he needed to make. Properly. He had to refer back . . . and just as he seemed to have it, something frightened him away from the very thought, and his tottering was all nonsense again.

Behind him, the Fool tittered, and in a rage the old man turned on him. Through the waves of his vision, so tired now, he saw the Fool had taken up a new attitude.

He was sitting straight up in the chair, studiously attending upon a large book in his lap. He was turning the pages as fast as he could with the dexterity of one finger, and keeping time to the flipping of the pages by bobbing his cowled head up and down like a mechanical sage. Yes. Certainly. Quite. True. Most. Likely. Yes. Indeed. Why. Of Course. He was very soon through the book. Immediately he stuffed it back into its place on the shelf, took down another one right next to it, and began the whole burlesque again.

Ignore it, he warned himself. But he watched the bobbing head and the passing pages with utter fascination. He was horrified, but somehow the horror did not reach, could not break in upon the rhythm of the mockery itself. The Fool increased his tempo. The pages beat by as if the book had been blown open, and a shifting wind were leafing through it. The Fool began turning pages either way now, in sharp little gusts of mindlessness. It struck him suddenly that the Fool had probably been hunched over a book, clowning an intelligence this way, all the time he'd been reading *Leir*.

He got to his feet, trembling. But the Fool, the moment he rose, stopped turning the pages and slowly, patiently took up his grin again. The horror at last broke through. For the first time, he really looked into the Fool's face. It was like looking not into a mask, but out of one. He was not in front of the Fool's face at all. He was behind it, staring out of its vacant eyes and teething its ruthless, dumb, ecstatic grin.

Hastily he piled his papers, closed his books. When he took his overcoat from the hook behind the door, he leaned against the door for just a moment, not realizing that a full minute passed before he pushed away from it again. He left the office, locking it behind him. Then he hurried out of the Library, forgetting his boots in the dark corridor. Once outside, he noticed he'd also forgotten the light in his study. Unless it had been turned on again. He went back for his boots, but decided to leave the light. It would go out when it wanted to.

III

The next afternoon his retirement was announced at the faculty meeting. He came in late, and heard the announcement almost as a surprise, having forgotten that it was to be made.

He looked around at his colleagues, who were clapping tenderly and avoiding his eye. Good night, old prince, he mused foolishly, may flights of angels help you up the stairs. He was amazed at himself. For the past few months, he had been planning how to suppress uncontrollable anger at this inevitable insult to dignity, professionally disguised as a tribute. But listening to the mannerly, almost withdrawn applause around him, he wasn't at all angry. There were so many other furies in his bosom now that he was actually relieved. Good, he thought, they haven't caught me out. They don't know. Then he realized exactly what it was they did not know. That he was suddenly unburdened of them. He had begun an existence which simply did not include them among its cares. Even as he stood among them, reaching for their kind hands, he felt he was setting them aside for good and all.

Nelson was among the first to rush up to him. No longer maddening.

"Congratulations," said Nelson. "Forty-three years. That's a long time."

So it is, he thought. Or said. He wasn't sure which. And forty-three on top of twenty-four makes sixty-seven years' presence of mind, and now I've chucked it all. Don't need it. Wish I'd never had it. Wish I'd never been bothered with it.

He looked carefully at Nelson's face to see if he was possibly saying these things too, not just thinking them. But Nelson's face didn't seem to know either.

"Thank you, Nelson," he made sure to say, not think.

"I wanted to mention to you," Nelson went on, "the light was on in your study this morning. I tried to get in to turn it off, but your door was locked, and I couldn't find the janitor."

It occurred to him that Nelson too said all this without thinking. Or at least without thinking of any of the rich and enchanting possibilities. The scene if they had forced the door and found the Fool asleep at his desk, sprawled out in a garish parody of the pedant adoze over his dry books. The great blot of ink on the end of the Fool's nose, making him look like a broken nib. The marotte stuck into the Variorum like a bookmark, grinning over the binding in a frozen mime of the Contents. For all this, no thought. Of course, Nelson did not have *his* knowledge to go on. But somehow that came off as only another very distinct limitation in Nelson himself. He found it easy to fault him for it and set him aside.

Why, there was even snoring. Great hawking at a burbling lip. A grand jest. The Fool curled up in exactly his own napping posture, when he opened the door that morning, pretending the noise of entering had troubled his sleep, bestirring himself with a loud carillon from his cap. He'd really almost laughed out loud, but suddenly sensed the open door behind him. He fell back against it, listening hard for any approaching sound outside in the corridor. God's spies, he thought, it's broad daylight. The Fool chuckled, beaming at him over that great noseblot with blank, uncanny eyes, bright with false sleep, and he felt himself pulled another small tug away from the order of things into the clutter of that merry-andrew gaze.

Perhaps he really ought to tip Nelson off. Perhaps it would be better, even now, if he simply leaned over and whispered, "Look, there's a pest of a fellow in my office. Will you run over and tell him I won't be by today?" Only he knew he would be by, and alone, and all he could bring himself to say was, "Thank you again. Stupid of me. Getting a little careless lately. Need to be watched, don't I?"

An older friend in the English department came up to him then and had the good sense not to congratulate him.

"Working on anything now?" he asked simply.

"Yes. *Lear.* Cleaning up, really. Talked about it enough in my lifetime, haven't I? Never make a book. But a little—a little *opusculum* would do, wouldn't it? For 'A poor, infirm, weak, and despised old man'?"

"Utter nonsense," replied his friend, staring at the floor. "You'd better save a little room in the pasture when they put you out there next spring. I'm afraid they won't give me those extra few years of grace they gave you. I'm not that tough."

"Plenty of room." He wondered if Nelson could see how graciously his friend had turned the compliment. Probably not. But then it really made no difference. They were both foolish even to try. Eptly or ineptly, they stayed nothing by it. They were only tarrying here, all three of them.

"What is it you're trying to do with *Lear?*" his friend asked, bringing back the subject.

"Oh, I'm taking up Folly. Much the same way Erasmus does. Though he's quite wrong about her, you know. She isn't a goddess at all. Only a fool."

"I'm not surprised."

"You would be. I've been spending most of my time lately on the Fool. If you stay with him long enough, he becomes a sort of familiar. A goddess is only a conception. The fool's much more than that." He said all this lightly, edging as near as he dared to his own peccant sense of the matter. The risk was titillating. "I'm really trying to decide just what his existence amounts to."

His friend frowned in a way he quite understood, but Nelson smiled in a way that escaped him. What bit of dried fungi had he managed to fire in that tinderbox this time?

Nelson seemed for a moment to want to hold it all in, but he couldn't resist. "I suppose you might even call him," he said nervously, "the existential fool."

So. That poppycock. When was he going to learn to watch every single word he used in front of this young Holofernes? He felt a wild urge to reach out with grand punctilio and pluck Nelson's velvety beard, but the deepening of his friend's frown kept him off.

"You suppose whatever you wish to suppose, young man," his friend snorted at the instructor, "but remember it's your own tomfoolery." Then he turned back again. "But I must admit I don't quite see what you're driving at either. The Fool's simply a character in the play. His existence is in his role, isn't it?"

And so. More poppycock. This was harder, riskier. "Of course," he agreed affably, "but I'm wondering if that role isn't just a bit wider than you think it is. The Fool is a character in all of sixteenth, seventeenth century life. He has a role even *off*

the stage. We find Queen Elizabeth footing the bill for a huge
wardrobe of motley. Read the list sometime. The fools Robert
Greene, Jack Green, and Mr. Shenstone. An Italian named
Monarcho. A little Blackamoor. Thomasina the Dwarf—oh, I'd
like to have seen her—and Ipolyta the Tartarian. And Clod.
Clod—bless him—Clod is even chided by his Queen for not
criticizing her sharply enough. Royal displeasure at his failure
to play his role. Not quick enough in his hits upon Glorianna,
can you imagine?" He warmed to his own tired lecture style,
feeling how safely he could dissemble under its fey pedantry as
others gathered around him. "The Fool is with us, you see?
With them, I suppose I should say," he added hastily, "but I
mean, abroad. That's important. Abroad. As the Lord of Misrule,
as the Comte de Permission, guilty of 'Fleering and making of
mouths.' He is fed on crow's meat, they say, and monkey flesh.
Or he eats only what the dogs have tasted, and so they serve
the dogs great delicacies for the Fool's sake. An odd, rarified
life, you realize. Terribly indulgent, but at the same time terribly mangy. It says of Will Sommers, for instance, Henry the
Eighth's great fool, that he 'laid himself down among the spaniels
to sleep' after he'd pleased his Harry with a riddle. A silly
riddle at that. Damnably silly. 'What is it that, being borne
without life, head, lip, or eye, yet doth run roaring through
the world till it die?' "

He looked quickly around him, hoping for someone to answer.
It was so easy, but they all seemed to give up. He felt the
silliness take an oddly dreadful hold upon him, and spoke as
lightly as he could.

" 'Why, quoth Will, it is a fart.' "

He knew he was the only one laughing—senselessly—yet all
their faces were bent up in a way that meant they might be
laughing too, if he could only hear them. Desperately he
fought his way out of his own shameful laughter.

"The most ridiculous bawdry. Not funny at all. Just not funny.
Very weak. Very. But you see—I think we can sense in it—
the Fool's familiarity." He wormed loose again. "To an Elizabethan, Jacobean audience. What I mean is, that the Fool might
have more reality for these people than Lear, even though they
did know kings too. They wouldn't expect to go into the narrow

streets at Bankside and find Lear walking abroad. But they could very well expect to find the Fool. That, actually, is how fools were found. They existed, you see. Naturals."

He stopped, hoping he was nearer sense now. "Fascinating idea," his friend said, but he knew that was coddling. He must be more careful, he realized, much more careful, even with friends, and this suddenly enraged him.

"Do you know how to pick a fool?" he burst out. "There was one in Germany named Conrad Pocher—the Count Palatine delighted in him—he was considered ripe for the court's pleasure after he hanged a little boy from a tree. Pocher hanged the little boy because the little boy had scabs. It was a joke that Pocher would hang you if you had scabs too. Beware, all you who are scabrous—"

He felt his friend's hand grip his shoulder, as if to pinch off what he was saying. His friend said to him, "I'm afraid I still don't see what you're getting at, but good luck with it anyhow." The others hastily agreed.

He closed them out and turned abruptly to Nelson. "I'm letting you take all my classes."

The surprise of it dropped his friend's hand from his shoulder. But he couldn't bother to care. He went on to Nelson. "I'd appreciate it if you'd do the exam as well. I'm afraid I'm going to want to be left very much alone."

Now he didn't dare look at his friend. He had as good as abdicated. Nelson was in a fidget of self-effacement. He felt he wouldn't be able to stand that maggoty beard another moment longer. Other friends came up to him. They suggested delicately all the wonderful things he had done in the past, and the long life he had ahead in peace and quiet contemplation. In five more minutes, it was over, and he turned from the scattered gathering, found his coat, and went out across the frozen snow that pitched out flat before him like a white heath.

IV

He worked furiously. Every day he was more exhausted, but he fought fatigue with anger, and anger, he found, could keep him going when all his faculties were otherwise ready to fail.

The storm wore on, running in tatters across the stiff snow, almost following his anger. After a ruthless night, it would seem to be dying away, only to regain its ferocity in the late afternoon, cutting icily against the window, closing away what little light there was in the grey sky. But he didn't mind. It kept him alone. He'd taken his card off the door, and nobody bothered him.

The Fool was always decorous. For the most part, he stayed happily in his chair, and thumbed through the books over and over again, timing his flurries to the storm. There were a few pranks. The old man would glance up from his work to find the marotte nodding methodically over his shoulder like a wizened scholar whose head had been shrunk, the Fool pressed right up against the back of his chair. It made him jump, but no more. Or he would come in to find a paper full of meaningless inkblots, almost like writing, lying among his notes. Yet he could never quite be sure it wasn't a scrap he'd used himself to test his pen. The tricks kept him on edge, but they were nothing beside the threat he felt in the Fool's patience. The Fool seemed somehow able to wait without ever losing a moment. Nothing could exhaust his empty loyalty. He was there forever. Or not. It made no difference to him. Only to those in quest of differences.

But he could admit none of this. Not to himself, certainly not to the Fool. Not even by the fleet tribute of another eyeblink that might drop him into an unguarded sleep.

Instead, he settled into a fixed wakefulness, embarking on what he sensed would be some final test of his scholarship. He had already made a beginning, so it was only a matter of shifting his emphasis. Under the pretense of still pursuing his studies of *Lear*—to whom, he wondered, to whom?—he set out to study the Fool himself. He felt certain that if he could only read up on the Fool, chivvy his motley image through the bramble of source material and first mentions and oblique references and analogues, hunt him down like startled sense at bay behind a faulty and obscure text, he would have him. As simple a thing as fixing the Fool's dates properly might trap him, he was half convinced. He was depending upon his last reliable habit of mind. Somewhere among the disputed readings,

the incunabula, the endless exegesis, he felt he was bound to
come upon the right page. Then, all he would need to do—all
he could ever do to end this jest—was somehow to rip out
that page.

He began working through the literature. Other scholars had
been there before him, but they had no sense of the menace—
he could tell that from the bloodless measure they took in their
writings—the menace that lay within the sweet hollow of folly.
None of them, obviously, had ever kept a fool. Yet any simpleton
writing a pet manual, would at least know his German Shepherd
or his Siamese or his box turtle. He pushed impatiently through
their treacly rationality to the primary sources, testimony from
the great warders who had once kept real fools to fondle like
favored apes.

He searched constantly for a touchstone. He picked finically
even among the original Latinisms in hopes of finding a proper
one. *Stultus. Morio. Fatuus. Sannio.* They all fitted, yet none
quite, really. He set the legends alongside his own Fool for
measure. Til Eulenspiegel, the owl glass, the wise mirror, but
still a brute. At Til's graveside, a cord snapped, and his coffin
tipped upright into the broken earth. "Leave him as he is, he
was strange in this life, he wants to be after his death." So
they buried him standing straight up and stole his estate, which
proved his last mockery, being only a box of stones. His own
Fool could have inherited, yes, easily inherited that owlishness,
that false legacy of stones. But much more his own Fool favored
Marcolf, the jester who watched Solomon dispense justice to
the two women who claimed one child, and as the king calmly
lowered the threatening sword to his side again and judged so
wisely, jeered at him for trusting a woman's tears. Ah, how
that fitted. That exactly, the same jeering laughter that so har-
rowed him, turning his own subtlety of mind suddenly as luggish
as the clapper in a frozen bell.

Yet legend could not satisfy him. Legendary fools were vagrant
in time, and his own Fool carried his days upon his back—a
hunch to his motley shoulders that meant he stooped under the
hour, not under a proverb. He came from a rich period. The
old man relished such labor, and early on, among the many
sotties he dug up, he found Robert Armin's own *Nest of Ninnies*.

The actor-clown's account of the fools of his day. "Simply of themselves without Compound." Just what was wanted—"without Compound"—and reaching into that nest—down among Jemy Camber, the fat fool a yard wide and a nail high, and Jack Oates, eating a hot quince pie while standing in the moat and drinking from it to cool his tongue, and Will Sommers, capping Cardinal Wolsey's rhymes—he felt the quick flutter of his own Fool's ninny soul cross his fingertips.

He reached again, but then drew back quickly from that mock grin, the glissando that ran down the coxcomb bells in chilling welcome.

He pushed deeper into the documents. Account books of royal households, pamphlet Lives of fools, ha' penny street ballads and mock Last Wills & Testaments, extracts from court diaries, an actual letter to James I from his fool away in Spain with Philip II's court. Some of them were on microfilm, and he turned to this newfangled apparatus for momentary escape. He could leave his Fool behind, yet pursue him still, more at his ease, studying the little scrolls as they unrolled beneath the thumbing white light of the scanner. But he soon found this another mockery. The glare of the machine, blowing up the quaint Elizabethan printing into an illusory page pressed without substance against the cold, milky glass, was too much for his weak, old eyes, and somehow for his sense of reality. He could not stand the ghostliness of it. He felt he must be able to turn the actual page, crumble a chip out of its browned edge, smell its acrid, bookish dust, if he were ever going to find it. What was there to tear out here? He hated the skimping artifice that robbed him of the feel of a book, and imagined the scanner as some great Worm that had invested the castle of his learning. Like Spenser's Error, only too uncreatured a thing to spew forth black ink, or disgorge the books it had swallowed. Its only malice, a pale flush of cold light producing an incubus of a page. He knew how ridiculous he was being, possibly senile, and he drove himself to take meticulous notes, as usual. But he only breathed freely again in the staleness of his closed-up study, back within the pied *ambiance* of his Fool.

By then, he had all his facts. He was now thoroughly familiar with, something of an authority on, a good man in the field of. Oh, he understood his own qualifications all too well. It only remained for him to think things through to the entrapment, to perform the sacred rites of abstraction, and in a curious way, he sought to cleanse himself for them. He stripped away his last ragged pretenses to any venerability, all the shoddy of his professorial airs, and bared himself, in all but intellect, for a naked, failing old man.

It ended so many qualms. He could talk to himself freely. He mumbled and muttered as he pleased, and if his mouth grew wet, he wiped it on his sleeve without shame. When he caught the Fool imitating him in some palsied fumble, he hardly cared. Once he watched the Fool's great, dirty tongue loll almost to the floor before he sensed the coldness at his own cheek and brushed away a long, loose string of saliva. Unimportant. All that mattered was the careful tightening of his logic as it closed around the Fool.

"Decide whether natural or artificial," he thought or said or wrote down somewhere. "Could be a mute. Idiot boy sold by a rustic to some great house in exchange for a few acres grazing land free of enclosure. Such happens. But looks brighter than that. Silence too sly. Vacancy too coy. Hidden wits. I see him offering the egg. Like Will Sommers again, asking the King to let him give an egg to every cuckold in England, and permission granted, hands the first egg to Harry himself. What is he here to hand me? What's in his hand? What's in my hand? A page? A page?"

He glanced down at his hand, but there was only the back of it, covered with liver spots, and he realized that the ambuscado, so carefully laid up in his notes, had missed its elusive quarry yet again.

But he started once more, reciting a tale. "Will Sommers loudly broke wind, and glared at the lady by his side. Then he smiled at her and said for all to hear, 'Don't worry. I'll say it was me.' Clever fool. Rich fool. But this is a poor fool. Violent? Often they are insane. No attack yet. But if it comes. . . . Bawdry? A scurrilous fool? Behind that dumbshow, what cess of mind, waiting to pour over me like a chamber pot? Gardyloo!" And then an old man's decrepit giggle, like beans rattling in a bladder, caught him off guard, sucked up from

some grossness he'd suddenly remembered from his long study
of folly. Again and again, he broke away from that giggle, forcing his way back to the needed date or reference that would
repair the break where flatulence and scurrility had escaped
from his thinking.

He even allowed himself little threats now. Never quite to the
Fool's face, but, "Take heed," he would mumble, "the whip. The
whip."

Then suddenly he felt the grip of it in his hand.

Carefully he let go, and gathered up his notecards to give his
hands something else to do. He tried to reshuffle them for the
hundredth time, but found that they were at last, by some
fluke, in a correct order. Irrefutably that order imposed itself
upon him. Sequential, exact, conclusive. This time, all his learning told him, there was no escape. Tapping each card nervously
on his blotter, searching for error, he tried to think how many
days it had been, how many stormy hours had hawked at his
chill window to tumble this sudden, random knowledge upon
him. He counted slowly—days, hours, cards—and imagined the
Fool at his back, counting too, with great pulls at his gross
fingers, unable, like himself, to arrive at any sensible number.

But he did not turn around. He saw that he could corner
the Fool now with a mere glance, that he could positively identify
him beyond any quibble to his colleagues, much more, that he
could whip him, rip him out, do with him as he pleased. He
had all that certainty, but once again it seemed to be forcing
him to the verge of that same opulent unknown over which
he had tottered so often, so perilously. . . .

Only now, at the Fool's warning titter, he deliberately stared
down into its black gulf. He referred back and back, as far
as his mind would take him, and knowledge did not come to
him so much as it physically seized him. The brush of the long
ass's ears around his own cheeks. The plucking up of his whole
spine into a rich, red comb, topped with bells. The whirligig
of his coat plaids turning to lozenges. His grip on the whip
thinning, loosening to a fragile, foolish hold upon the stick of
a marotte. One foot jingled beneath him, and quite suddenly
he could feel just where the whip was going to cut.

He did the one thing possible in the moment left before the

black gulf itself turned over and sat upon his head for a cap.
He jumped into it at last.

"Stay!" he shouted to the Fool. "Stay right here! Right by
my side! Right here with me!"

Then he whirled around and bent over in laughter, jeering
at the suddenly defeated jangling thing in the chair.

"Right?" he whispered. "Right, right?"

The Fool's vacant stare was afire like a bone pit, but his
marotte nodded its eternal grin.

                                    V

He was still laughing when the knock came at his door. Very
cautiously he judged his surprise at it. No, it was no longer
an interruption of his solitude. It was an intrusion upon their
intimacy. The Fool shook both fists as if beating back at the
door, letting loose a rage of bells.

"Who is it?" he asked, smiling at the angry Fool.

"Nelson, sir. Are you all right?"

He and the Fool shrugged at each other, both repressing
laughter this time. He was still a little bit in awe of his own
triumph, the confidence they had so suddenly found in each
other. But then why, he wondered, had it taken so long to see
what the Fool was there for?

"Sir?"

Young Nelson was anxious. He chortled to himself. The
Fool immediately understood him and giggled into his two ass's
ears which he had crossed gleefully over his mouth.

"I heard—well, laughing, sir. I just wondered if everything's
all right. I thought I heard. . . ." Nelson left off.

He hesitated because he wanted to savor this moment, the
superb jest it had finally turned out to be. With this to top it off.

"No, I'm perfectly fine. Excellent fettle." He winked at the
Fool. "Come in, if you've a moment."

The door eased open, just far enough for Nelson to squirm
around it, braving everything with his shadow first. He nodded
from it, smiling, while his eyes flicked nervously around the

room. His stare scurried into every corner, and then he flushed, realizing he had absolutely no excuse.

"No, really. Sit down, sit down."

Nelson gratefully moved over to the chair and plumped down in it. The Fool bounced up just in time. He shook his bells angrily, and scowled. The old man chuckled good-naturedly. Nelson joined him in chuckling, out of deference.

"I'm really sorry, sir." He shifted once, twice in the chair. "Honestly, it sounded like you were in here laughing yourself silly."

"No, no. I was just—" How to put it, how to put it? "I've just finished up my work on *Lear,* you see, and I was having a good laugh over it."

Nelson grew terribly puzzled, but only above the eyebrows. The Fool caught it, and took off this sedate puzzlement with a mock petite frown of his own. An irresistible bit of fleering. Again the old man chuckled, worrying Nelson into joining him again. The frown looked even more ridiculous over the polite chuckle.

"Oh, I must fill you in," he said. "It's just that this whole business with *Lear* has turned out to be, after all—well, a pretty big joke."

"I'm sorry about that," Nelson said elaborately. "Really very sorry."

He looked at the young instructor sharply. He'd caught something, just for a second. Nelson *was* sorry for him, of course. Flamboyantly sorry. Poor old codger. But there was something more, edging in, smacking distinctly of derring-do. He glanced at the Fool, who was leaning with both elbows on the back of Nelson's chair. The Fool poked two saucy fingers up for ears behind Nelson's head, and blew his lips flatulently.

"But I can see how it might come out that way," Nelson went on. *"Lear* is such a difficult play—and . . . *disappointing,* don't you think?"

Had he jumped? He felt sure the Fool had. But the skittishness was not so much in them, he sensed, as in Nelson. Was he about to skip and run for it on his own?

"Perhaps you've found—" Nelson paused at a near stutter and then hurdled, "what *I've* always found." The Fool stared,

and then lifted himself on the chair back, kicking his bells together at the heels in muffled joy. "In the end, it really all
comes to nothing, doesn't it? Dr. Johnson may have been right."

"Then you *have* been. . . ."

He saw instantly that Nelson was going to misinterpret him.
There would now be a painstaking mending of fences, he could
tell, which would only delay the real point. Only the Fool had the
patience for it. His greedy eyes puddled, and that same inane
grin sank down once more into the vapid face like water
crumbling sand.

"No, no," said Nelson, starting in on his fences. "I honestly
haven't. I was leaving that all to you. I touch on the play, yes, but
only with reference to some work I'm trying to do on the older
play. *Leir.*" He leaned forward, and for an awful moment the
old man thought that from the undermining of the grin, the
Fool's face had at last caved in entirely and fallen upon Nelson's
own. But then he saw it was only a great, watery leer. "But if
you *are* giving up on your own work—I mean, if you're leaving
the field free again—and that's the only way I'd want to have it,
frankly—I think I might try to treat the two plays together."

"What *exactly* is it you're going to show?" Besides this abrupt-
ness, this, this. . . .

"It'll be tough sledding, but I'm pretty clear now that *Leir* is
infinitely the better play. At least, in my own mind. You see,
sir. . . ."

Then the flights and dips and swoops and long drifts of a young,
excited mind swept over him. A swift, ignorant, sweet bird beating
its new wings in the heart of an old storm. He listened as carefully as he could, and tried not to look at the Fool. He was afraid
that if he did, he would not be able to account for his tears. Why
was it so irretrievably sad? All that he heard was challenging
and clever and zealous. But it depended upon so many cer-
tainties that weren't really there. The dimness, the vagueness, the
lack of distinction that blurred every final thought, every last, best
guess—he saw that the young man did not even feel their
menace. Perhaps on some midnight balance of his secret fears,
Nelson allowed himself to know he might be wrong, but did he
ever allow himself to know he might not even be that?

The old man's gaze drifted in mute appeal to the Fool. Then it simply drifted, caught up in the aimless wandering of the Fool's vacuous stare. Just in time, he saw his mistake. He looked quickly away before the Fool had a chance to throw his own lugubriousness back at him, and pulled himself together, alert to danger. He cursed his own stupidity. How very much, he realized bitterly, my very own.

"Nelson." He said it for once affectionately, as a first name, not a last. "How sure are you of all these things?" He meant the question to be only cautionary, but he could see it had gone hopelessly wrong. Nelson's face hardened a bit, and the gleeful Fool twirled the marotte over Nelson's head, badgering the old man for—what?—simply an old man, what more? He tried to think of a way to make his words less discouraging, less cantankerous. "I mean, it all sounds very wonderful, but is this to be a whole-hearted plunge into—" Into what? He knew the word he wanted to use, but also what irreparable damage it would do his little contact with the young man. And whose fault is it, he asked himself, the contact is so little? How very much, he thought bitterly again, my very own.

"A plunge into what, sir?"

A plunge into Folly. That's what he wanted to say. There was the Fool behind the chair, with as large a charter as the wind, to blow on whom he pleased. No man could hold him back. *Numerus stultorum est infinitus.*

"Let me put it this way, Nelson. I can't tell you how to do your work. Nobody can." He stopped helplessly. The Fool had turned and lifted one fat buttock at him, dropping the marotte down between his motley legs. The tiny head wigwagged at him like a phallus with an obscene, upsidedown grin. He forced himself ahead. "Do you have any idea what it's really like to work your way to the limits of something?" Limits? Limits of what? "I don't mean just setting out to settle a moot point. I mean plunging in so far that you can't—can never succeed—succeed in getting out again."

He pressed his hands together for steadiness. He saw the Fool imitate him, turning it into a silly prayerful gesture.

"You're alone. But accompanied. It's funny, but your companions are all there to help you feel alone. Because you don't, you mustn't admit they're there." He smiled. "That's the funny part about it. Once you admit—"

The Fool shook like a Sunday morning of church bells.

"Once you admit—" He looked hard at Nelson. There was nothing in his face but sufferance. Deferential sufferance. "Think of Lear of the heath, Nelson. Who are his companions? Who? The boundaries of his loneliness, really. Aren't they?"

He waited now. The burden was on the other.

"I'm pretty sure of my ground, I think, sir. Others have had the same idea about *Leir,* I'm sure you're aware. Tolstoi, for instance, gave it my interpretation. What I should say is, I'm taking up *his.*"

So the harlequinade will go on, he thought helplessly. He did not even look about for his Fool. He tried to keep his weak eyes fixed on a single, groomed tuft of Nelson's beard.

"I appreciate all your advice, and I'd like to come to you for some help, if that's all right with you. But for the moment. . . ."

He didn't hear the rest. They said things near the door, but to him, it was an absolutely wordless parting. He could not be sure, but he thought that something scuttled hastily between his knees as he shut himself in.

He stepped over to his window. It was still snowing, as if forever. Across the flurry he could see Nelson trudging away. A shadow—only a shadow—scurried and scraped about him in the storm with grotesque, unhallowed gestures. With great pain, he admitted they were gestures of fondness. Finally he thought he saw it leap up on the man's back, like a loving thing, and that bowed his own head to the cold window pane.

He knew. Deserted now, even by his own measure of solitude, he knew what he would never know again. Any boundary to his own loneliness. He supposed, since he was still alive, that he must take this to be wisdom.

JAY NEUGEBOREN was born in Brooklyn in 1938. His second novel, *Listen Ruben Fontanez*, will be published this spring. Mr. Neugeboren's stories have been published in *Commentary, Colorado Quarterly* and other magazines and he has also contributed articles to the *New York Times Book Review, The New Republic,* and *Commonweal.* In 1967 he received the *Transatlantic Review* Novella Award.

Ebbets Field

EDDIE GOTTLIEB moved into my neighborhood in the fall of 1955 and I knew right away we were going to become pretty good friends. I was in the eighth grade then, at P.S.92, and Eddie was brought into my official class about two weeks after school had started. At that time I was going through what my parents called one of my "growing periods"—always talking out in class, making some wiseacre remark, or doing something stupid to get attention, and for this I'd been rewarded with a seat right in front of the teacher's desk, with nobody allowed to sit next to me.

There were no other empty seats in the room, so when our teacher Mrs. Demetri told us that we were going to get a new boy in our class, I figured he'd be sitting next to me. Our official class hadn't changed much since first grade and it was always a pretty big event when somebody new came into it. When I saw Eddie walk through the door behind Mr. Weiner, the Assistant Principal, though, my heart really jumped. I could tell right away he was a good ballplayer. He was very tall and lanky— about six-two then—with thick curly hair that reached down into the collar of his shirt. He sort of shuffled into the room, moving very slowly, his body swaying from side to side, his arms swinging

"Ebbets Field"–Jay Neugeboren, *Transatlantic Review,* Copyright © 1967 by Joseph F. McCrindle.

freely. They were really long, coming down just about to his knee-caps. He kept staring at the floor, and when we all started laughing and giggling he must have thought we were laughing at him, because he blushed and fidgeted with his hands and feet a lot; what we were laughing at, though, was not the way Eddie looked, but at the way he looked coming in *behind* Mr. Weiner, and I think Mr. Weiner knew it, because his face got all red and angry. He was only about five-foot-one or two and when he walked he always took these huge steps, almost as if he were goose-stepping. At lunchtime we would always prance around the schoolyard or the lunchroom, mimicking him, and the teachers would never try very hard to make us stop. He was already at Mrs. Demetri's desk, right in front of me, and Eddie was only a couple of steps away from the door, when he whirled around and glared at him.

"What's taking you so long?" he demanded. "Come here!"

Then, I remember, Eddie grinned broadly and in two giant steps he was in front of Mr. Weiner, towering over him, standing at attention, still grinning. We broke into hysterics. Mr. Weiner glared at us and we stopped. "Now, young man," he said to Eddie, "wipe that grin off your face. What are you—some kind of gangling idiot?"

Eddie shrugged. "I don't know," he said.

We laughed again and Mr. Weiner turned on us. "All right then. Who wants to be the first to have a private conference in my office today?" he asked.

We all shut up. Eddie was staring at the floor again. I could tell that he knew he had done something wrong—but it was obvious he didn't know what it was.

"What's that in your pocket?" Mr. Weiner asked him, pointing.

"A baseball."

"Let me see it."

Eddie put his lunchbag on my desk and twisted the ball out of his side-pocket. He showed it to Mr. Weiner. When Mr. Weiner reached for it, though, he pulled his hand away.

"Let me have it," Mr. Weiner demanded.

"No," Eddie said, and he put his hand behind his back, gripping the ball tightly. I could tell from the printing that it was an Official National League ball. It was really beautiful!

"I said let me have it!"

Eddie shook his head sideways. "It's mine," he said. Everybody was perfectly quiet. I glanced across the room at Izzie and Corky and Louie. They were on the edges of their seats.

"Young man, you will let me have it by the time I count three or I will know the reason why!"

"Do you promise you'll give it back?" Eddie asked.

Mr. Weiner blinked. "Do I *what*—?"

Eddie was looking at Mr. Weiner now, intently. "I gotta have it," he said. "I just *gotta!* I never go anywhere without it."

"We do not allow hardball playing in this school."

Eddie grinned then, as if everything was okay, and brought the ball out from behind his back. "I didn't know that," he said. "I'm sorry." He pushed the ball right in front of Mr. Weiner's face. We all gasped and Mrs. Demetri took a step toward them. "See—?" Eddie said, smiling. "It's got Campy's signature on it."

"Who?"

"Campy!" Eddie said.

"Who, may I ask, is Campy?"

"Campy—Roy Campanella—he catches for the Dodgers!" Eddie was excited now. "You know—"

"Of course," Mr. Weiner said. Then he smiled, awkwardly. There was something about Eddie that had him mystified. You could tell. "Well, put that ball away and don't bring it to school again," he said. "This is your first day here, so I'll excuse you. But there are no second chances with me. Remember that."

When he left, Mrs. Demetri introduced Eddie to us. I applauded and most of the guys followed my lead. Mrs. Demetri didn't get too angry at me, though—in fact, after she gave Eddie the seat next to me, she put me in charge of getting him his books and making sure he knew where things were. Maybe she figured I'd be less trouble that way. At any rate, I was glad. The first thing I did was to ask him where he'd gotten the baseball.

"I won it," he said.

"Where?"

"On Happy Felton's Knothole Gang."

"Really?"

Eddie nodded and I nearly exploded out of my seat, wanting to tell all the guys. The Knothole Gang was this show they had on

television then, that came on before all the Dodger games. Three
or four guys who played the same position would get together with
Happy Felton and one of the Dodgers down the right field line
and they'd be tested on different things. Then, at the end, the
Dodger would pick one of the guys as a winner, and give the
reasons he'd picked him.

I asked Eddie a few more questions and then I began telling
him about our baseball team, The Zodiacs. He said he'd read
about us in Jimmy O'Brien's column in the *Brooklyn Eagle*.

"You got that good pitcher, don't you—and that crazy kid
who brings an old victrola to the games and plays the Star-
Spangled Banner on it—right?"

"That's Louie," I said, pointing across the room. "He lives in my
building. But we don't have the pitcher any more. He's in high
school now. Izzie pitches for us most of the time this year."

We talked some more and I asked him if he wanted to play
with us, as long as he was in our class now, and he said he'd love
to, if we'd let him. Then I wrote out a note, telling all the guys that
Eddie had won the baseball on Happy Felton's show and that
he'd agreed to play on our team, and I passed it across the
room to Louie. His face lit up, and he passed it on to Corky. By
the time we got into the yard for lunch that day, Eddie was a
hero, and all the guys crowded around him, asking about what
Campy had said to him and about what team he had played on
before and things like that.

I got to know Eddie pretty well during the next few weeks. He
wasn't very bright—this was pretty obvious the first time Mrs.
Demetri called on him to read something—and he was very
quiet, but he would have done anything for you if you were his
friend. All the guys liked him and we were pretty happy he had
moved into our neighborhood. He was the kind of guy you
wished you had for a brother. His father had died a couple of
years before and until he moved, he'd been living in Boro Park
with his mother. He never talked a lot about her or his home or
what it had been like living in Boro Park, but we all knew the
most important thing—that his family was Orthodox. The first
time one of us said something to him about making the big
leagues some day, he shook his head and said that he didn't
think he ever would because he couldn't play or travel on

Saturdays. When we brought up the names of other Jewish ballplayers who had played—Hank Greenberg, Cal Abrams, Sol
Rogovin, Sid Gordon, Al Rosen—he said that they hadn't come
from families like his. He said it would kill his mother if any of
his relatives ever found out about the things he did on Saturday—
that he could hide most things as long as he wasn't living near
them, but that if he ever got his picture in the papers for doing
something on Saturday, they'd know about it.

Eddie himself wasn't very religious—he played ball with us at
the Parade Grounds on Saturdays—but he was determined not to
hurt his mother, and I guess I could understand why at the time.
I knew she worked to support the two of them, and that Eddie felt
pretty bad toward her about moving from their old neighborhood.
I guess he felt she had moved because of him. At any rate, even
though he may have felt obligated to her in a lot of ways, she
didn't stop him from really wanting to be a big league ballplayer.
That was pretty obvious.

1955 was the year the Dodgers beat the Yankees in the World
Series, and Eddie came over to my house to watch the games on
television. I don't think I've ever seen a guy get more excited
than he did during the last game of that series. The Dodgers had
one of their great teams then—Campy, Furillo, Robinson, Reese,
Snider, Hodges, Newcombe, Erskine—but the heroes of that last
game were two other guys, Sandy Amoros and Johnny Podres.
When Amoros made his famous catch of Yogi Berra's fly ball in
the sixth inning, and without hesitating turned and threw to
Reese who doubled-up McDougald at first base, Eddie went wild.
He couldn't sit down after that. He just kept walking around the
room, pounding guys on the back, shaking our hands, and
repeating again and again: "Did you see that catch? Boy, did you
see that catch?"

We must have relived each inning of that series a hundred
times during the rest of that year. I kept telling Eddie that since
Podres—who had won the third and last games of the series—
was only 23 years old, he'd still have plenty of years to pitch to
Eddie when Eddie got to the Dodgers. Eddie always insisted it
was an impossibility, but then Louie came up with another one
of his bright ideas—if Eddie changed his name and grew a
moustache someday, how would his relatives ever find out? Eddie

liked the idea and that spring, for practice, Eddie used the name of Johnny Campy when he played with our team.

We played in the Ice Cream League at the Parade Grounds and we did pretty well, even though we didn't win the championship. Eddie was fantastic. He batted over .400, was lightning on the bases, only made about two or three errors, threw out ten guys stealing and did the one thing he did in no other place—he talked all the time. He'd be quiet until we got to the field, but the minute he put his shin guards, protector and mask on, his mouth began moving a mile-a-minute, and he'd keep up the chatter the whole game. I loved to listen to him. "C'mon, Izzie babe," he'd yell, crouched behind the plate. "Chuck it here, chuck it here. Plunk it home to Campy, honeybabe. Show 'em how, show 'em how. Plunk it home to Campy! This batter's just posin' for pictures. Let's go babe. Plunk it home to Campy . . ."

He was one of the greatest natural athletes I've ever seen— and not just in baseball, as we soon found out. Until he came to our school I was generally considered the best basketball player of all the guys, but Eddie made me look like an amateur. He was incredible! We were only in the eighth grade then, but when we'd play in the schoolyard on weekends Eddie could hold his own with the high school and college guys.

He was skinny and got banged around a lot under the boards, but he was still the most fantastic leaper I've ever seen. Lots of times, even when he was boxed out, he'd just glide up in the air, over everybody else, and pluck the ball out of the sky with those big hands of his. He could dunk the ball with either hand, too!

My parents knew how much I loved basketball and that summer, for the second straight year, they sent me to Camp Wanatoo, where Abe Goldstein, the Erasmus coach was head counselor. I remember he got pretty upset when I told him that Eddie was supposed to go to Westinghouse—a vocational high school—instead of to Erasmus. Schoolyard reputations spread pretty fast in our neighborhood and he'd already heard about Eddie from a lot of the guys on his team. I explained to him about how Eddie's grades weren't too good, and about his mother and everything.

When I got back from camp and saw Eddie, the first thing he said to me was that he'd decided to go to Erasmus. He said that

Mr. Goldstein had visited him and promised him and his mother that Eddie would get through high school—and that he could get him a scholarship to college. I was really happy. We spent a lot of time that fall playing in the schoolyard together, and Eddie got better and better. He had spent the summer in the city, working as a delivery boy and helper in his uncle's butcher shop in Boro Park, and he had developed a gorgeous fade-away jump shot that was impossible to stop. When we weren't playing, we'd sit by the fence in the schoolyard and talk about the guys on the Erasmus team or about the Dodgers—and we'd have long debates on whether it was better to get a college education and then play pro basketball, or to forget about college and take a big bonus from a major league baseball team.

That winter we played on a basketball team together in the *Daily Mirror* tournament and we probably would have won the championship, only in the big game for the Brooklyn title Eddie didn't show up until the last quarter. He went wild then, putting in shots from crazy angles, rebounding like a madman, stealing the ball and playing his heart out—but we were fifteen points behind when he arrived, and when the clock ran out were still down by four. For weeks afterwards you could hardly talk to him, he was so upset. All of us told him to forget it, that we understood about his mother getting sick and him having to stay with her until the doctor came, but he still felt he had let us down.

His mother got better, spring came, the baseball season started and Eddie stopped coming to school almost completely. Anytime the Dodgers were in town—except for the days our baseball team had a game or the afternoons that he worked as a delivery boy for his uncle—Eddie would be at Ebbets Field. He was always trying to get me to come along with him, but I usually found one excuse or another not to. He kept telling me there was nothing to worry about. He said he knew somebody in the attendance office and that all we had to do was give him our programs and show up for home-room period in the morning—the guy in the office would write in our names as absent on the sheets that went to the teachers whose classes we'd be cutting. He never seemed to get into any trouble and finally, in the middle of June, I told him I'd go with him.

We made up to meet in front of Garfield's Cafeteria, at the

corner of Flatbush and Church, at 10:30, right after second period. Eddie was there ahead of me and we got on the Flatbush Avenue bus and paid our fares. I kept looking around, expecting to see a teacher or a cop.

"Just act normal," Eddie told me. "And if anybody stops us, just put one of these on your head"—he reached into a pocket and pulled out two *yamalkahs*—"and tell whoever asks you it's a Jewish holiday and that we go to Yeshiva. That always works."

When we got off the bus at Empire Boulevard, where the Botanic Gardens begin, we still had a couple of hours until the game started and I asked Eddie what we were going to do until then.

He smiled. "Follow me," he said.

I followed. I saw a few cops along the street, but none of them bothered us. Some old men were getting their boards ready, with buttons and pennants and souvenirs, and when we got to McKeever and Sullivan Place, where the main entrance was, a few guys were selling programs and yearbooks. We walked along Sullivan Place and Eddie stopped about halfway down the block, where the player's entrance was.

A minute later a taxi stopped at the curb and two big guys got out—I recognized them right away as Gil Hodges and Duke Snider. It really surprised me, I remember, to discover that we were as tall as both of them—taller than Snider.

"Any extra tickets?" Eddie asked.

"Sorry—not today, Eddie," the Duke said, and the two of them disappeared into the clubhouse.

I nearly died. "You mean you actually *know* them?" I asked.

"Sure," Eddie said. "Hell—I've been out here like this for three years now." He scratched at his cheek and tried to act nonchalant, but I could tell he was as proud as he could be that a Dodger had called him by name with me there. "I don't think they'll have any extras today, though—Milwaukee has a good team this year and there were probably lots of their friends wanting tickets."

"It's okay," I said, still flabbergasted. "I got a couple of bucks for tickets."

"We won't need 'em, I hope," he said. "If nobody has extras we can try waiting in the gas station on Bedford Avenue. There's always a bunch of kids there, hoping to catch a ball, but they usually hit four or five out in batting practice. If we can get just one the guy at the gate will let us both in—he knows me."

"If not?"

He shrugged. "The bleachers. It's only 75 cents, and after about the second inning you can sneak into the grandstands."

In a few minutes some more Dodgers came by and they all smiled and said hello to Eddie, but none of them had any extra tickets. It didn't bother me! After a while, I just followed Eddie's lead and said hello to the players too, saying things like, "How're you doing, Carl?—We're rooting for you!" to Furillo, or "How're you feeling today, Campy?" and I hardly believed it when some of the players would actually answer me! As I got more confidence I got braver—telling Pee Wee to watch out for guys sliding into second base, telling Karl Spooner that if he pitched he should keep the ball low and outside to Aaron—and after each group of guys would go into the clubhouse, I'd slam Eddie on the back and punch him in the arm. "C'mon," I'd say to him, "pinch me right on the ass, buddy. Then I'll know it's true!" And Eddie, he just kept grinning and telling me how stupid I'd been to wait this long to come to a game with him.

By 11:30, though, we still didn't have any tickets.

"We should of waited by the visiting team's entrance," Eddie said. "They hardly ever use up their passes—"

Then, as we started to walk toward Bedford Avenue, we saw this little guy come trotting up the street toward us. Eddie squinted.

"It's Amoros," he said. "Hey Sandy—any tickets?" he called.

"Oh man, I late today," Amoros said, when he got to us, shaking his head back and forth. He reached into his wallet, handed us two tickets and we wished him luck. Then he continued toward the players' entrance, running.

"Whooppee!" I shouted as soon as he was gone. "Amoros for Most Valuable Player!" I threw my arm around Eddie's shoulder and we ran down the street together, half-dragging each other, until we got to the turnstile entrance. Then we stopped and strutted inside together, handing the guard the tickets as if it was something we did every day of the week. As soon as we were inside Eddie yelled "Let's go!" and we raced under the arcade, laughing and giggling. The instant we saw the field, though, we stopped. The groundskeepers had just finished hosing down the basepaths and the visiting team hadn't come out yet for batting practice. There was hardly anybody in the stands and the sight of the empty ballpark seemed to sober us both up. To this day I don't think there's any sight that's prettier than a ballpark before a game's been played. Watching on television all the time, you forget how green and peaceful the field looks.

We had great seats that day, right over the Dodger dugout. They blasted the Braves, 9-1, with 14 or 15 hits, and we cheered and shouted like mad, especially when Amoros came to bat. I remember everything about the ballpark that day, and I think I remember the things that happened off the field more than I do the actual game. I remember the Dodger Symphony marching around the stands, and Mabel swinging her cowbell, and Gladys Gooding singing the national anthem and playing "Follow the Dodgers" on the organ, and the groundskeepers wheeling the batting cage back out to center field, and the people across Bedford Avenue watching from their roofs. I remember being surprised at how many guys our age—and even younger—had come to the game, and I remember feeling really great when I heard somebody calling my name and I turned around and saw Mr. Hager wave to me. I waved back at him and then told Eddie about him. Mr. Hager was a retired fireman who lived on my block. He went to every Dodger game and when they lost he always wore a black armband. When the Giants beat the Dodgers in the playoff in '51, nobody saw him for weeks afterwards, and then he wore the same black suit day in and day out until they won the pennant back in '52. Everybody in our neighborhood knew him and it was said that he got into at least two or three fights a week at Hugh Casey's bar on Flatbush Avenue. There were a lot of Dodger fans like him in those days.

Most of all, though, I remember how *good* I felt that day—just sitting with Eddie, eating peanuts and cheering and talking baseball. As it turned out, that was the last time I ever got to see a Dodger game. At the end of the season they announced they were moving to Los Angeles.

I went to Camp Wanatoo again that summer and Eddie stayed in the city. His uncle had gotten him a job loading sides of beef into refrigerator cars and this really built up his chest and shoulders and arms. In the fall everybody was predicting he'd be the next great basketball star at Erasmus—maybe even All-City in his sophomore year.

When the time came for varsity try-outs, though, he didn't show up. Nobody could figure it out. Two days later he stopped by my house at night and asked if I wanted to go for a walk. He looked terrible—his face was long and he seemed to have lost a lot of weight. At first I figured it had something to do with his mother, but when I asked him he shook his head.

"Nah," he said, when we were downstairs. He sighed. "I guess you were wondering why I didn't try out for the team, huh?"

"Everybody was—" I said.

"I know. Mr. Goldstein called my house tonight and I had to tell him—that's why I came by your house. I wanted you to know before the other guys. Maybe you could tell them so I don't have to keep repeating the story."

"Sure," I said. "What is it?"

"It's my damn heart," he said. I looked at him and he was biting the corner of his lower lip, I remember. Then he shook his head back and forth and cursed. "I can't play anymore," he said. "The doctor said so." He stopped. "Jesus, Howie, what am I gonna do? What am I gonna do?" he pleaded. I didn't know what to say. "Shit," he said. "Just shit!" Then his body seemed to go limp. "C'mon, let's walk."

"How'd you find out?" I asked.

"Ah, since the summer I've had this pain in my chest and when it didn't go away I went to our family doctor. My mother telephoned him about a week ago and he told her. It's only a murmur—nothing really dangerous—but it means no varsity."

"Can't you play at all?"

"Oh yeah—as long as I take it easy. I just have to get a lot of sleep, and whenever I feel any of this pressure building up in my chest I have to be sure to stop."

We walked for a long time that night—up Bedford Avenue all the way past Ebbets Field to Eastern Parkway, then back home along Flatbush Avenue, and most of the time neither of us said anything. What could you say?

I made the varsity that year and Eddie came to all the games, home and away. He worked five afternoons a week at his uncle's

butcher shop now, but on Saturdays, when it was closed, he'd
come down to the schoolyard and play a few games. He kidded
around a lot, telling everybody to take it easy against him because
of his heart, but he was still tremendous. I was already about an
inch taller than he was, and a pretty good jumper, but he'd go up
over me as if I had lead in my sneakers.

In about the middle of our junior year he quit school and
went to work full-time as an assistant to his uncle. He kept
coming to all the Friday night games, though, and sometimes
when I didn't have a date, we'd go to Garfield's afterwards and
then walk home together.

Eddie and I lost touch with each other during my first two
years of college—I don't think I even saw him once—but when
I was home for spring vacation during my junior year my mother
told me he'd bought a half-interest in Mr. Klein's kosher butcher
shop on Rogers Avenue. I went over to see him the next morning
and there he was, behind the counter. I stood outside for a while,
watching him wait on customers, and then when the store was
empty, I went inside.

"Hey, Campy—!" I called. He was at the far end of the
counter, cutting up some meat.

He turned around. "Jesus—Howie!" He wiped his hands on his
apron and then we shook hands and pounded each other on the
back for a while. "Boy, it's good to see you—how've you been?"

"Pretty good," I said. "When did all this happen?" I asked,
motioning around the store.

"C'mon next door to the candy store," he said, taking off his
apron. "I'll get you a Coke—boy, it's been a long time!"

He got Mr. Klein out of the big walk-in freezer in the back and
then we went next door and Eddie told me about how he had
saved up money while he was working for his uncle—with that
and some insurance money his mother had put away after his
father's death, he was able to buy a half-interest from Mr. Klein,
who was getting old and wanted to retire soon. By then Eddie
could buy out the other half and the store would be his.

"How about you?" he asked. "How do you like college?"

"It's okay," I said.

"What're you studying?"

"Liberal arts."

"Oh yeah?—What subjects?"

I laughed. "You don't have to sound interested," I said.

He shrugged, embarrassed. "Anyway I follow your team in the papers all the time—the *Times* always prints box scores of your games. You did real well this year—second high scorer on your team, weren't you?" When I didn't answer, he punched me in the arm. "Ah, don't be modest—you're a good ballplayer, Howie. Bet you got all those pretty girls running after you, too—"

"We'll be playing in the Garden against N.Y.U. next year," I said. "I'll get you some tickets—you can bring a girl and maybe we'll double after or something—"

"Sure," he said. "I'm going with a girl now—real nice, you'd like her." He shrugged, then grinned. "I'll probably be a married man by this time next year—"

When we played in the Garden the next year I sent him two passes, but I had to leave right after the game in order to get the bus that was taking us back to school that night. I got an invitation to his wedding right after that. It was scheduled for Christmas week but I couldn't go because of a holiday tournament our team was playing in at Evansville, Indiana. I called him when I came in for spring vacation and told him how sorry I was that I hadn't been there.

"Jesus, Howie," he said. "Forget it. How could you have been? You were in that tournament in Indiana. I followed the whole thing." He laughed. "My wife nearly slammed me because on the first day of our honeymoon I rushed out in the morning to get the papers to see how many points you'd scored."

We talked some more and then he asked me over to dinner. I accepted the invitation, but I felt kind of funny about it. I suppose I was afraid we wouldn't have anything to talk about—or, what seemed worse, that we'd spend the entire evening reminiscing about things we'd done when we were thirteen or fourteen.

I was partially right—we did spend a lot of time reminiscing, but I didn't mind at all. Eddie and I filled each other in on what had happened to guys we'd grown up with—who was getting married, who had finished college, who had moved out of the neighborhood—and I had a good time. Susie was, as Eddie had promised, a terrific cook. She had graduated from high school and was in her last year of nurse's training—perfect for Eddie, I thought. After supper, while she did the dishes, Eddie and I sat in the living room and talked. I told him how much I liked her and he smiled.

"She's good for me," he said, nodding. "I'll tell you something —because of her I'm even thinking of going back to high school evenings to finish up."

"Does she want you to?"

"She'd never say so, even if she did—she lets me make up my own mind. But I think she'd like it."

"Sounds like a good idea," I offered.

"Yeah—but when do I have time? Running the store by myself now there's a lot of work—books—I have to bring home, and then I'm so tired after being on my feet all day, about all I can do in the evening is turn on the TV and watch the Yanks or the Mets." He sighed. "But we'll see. I'd like to finish up."

"How's your health been?" I asked.

"Fine," he said, shrugging. Then his eyes opened wide. "Jesus!" he exclaimed. "You don't know, do you?"

"Know what?"

"About my heart—" I must have looked scared then, because he started laughing at me. "Thank God Kennedy put through that draft-exemption for married men," he said, "otherwise I'd be carrying a rifle—"

"I don't understand. I thought—"

"It's a long story," he said, "but the short of it is there was never anything wrong with my heart." He stood up and paced around the room. "When I went for my Army physical about a year and a half ago, they didn't find anything wrong with me. That's how I found out."

"But what about—?"

"Ah, that was just a thing my mother told me that the family doctor went along with," he said, stopping my question. "He was religious or something I guess. I don't know. What's the difference now? Thinking back, I guess he *himself* never really told me outright I had a murmur—"

Susie came back into the room and I could tell she knew what Eddie had been telling me. She put her arms around his waist and hugged him.

"My God!" I exclaimed. "How could she—?"

He was about to say something, but then Susie looked at him and he changed his mind. "That's the way the ball bounces, I guess," he said, shrugging his shoulders, and I could tell that he had used the same expression before in similar situations. He kissed Susie on the forehead and held her close to him. "Anyway," he laughed, "if you're in pro ball you got to be away from your wife and kids half the year."

"But Christ, Eddie," I began; Susie glared at me and I stopped. Eddie sat down and nobody said anything for a while— then suddenly, he started talking. "You know something," he said. "My business is pretty good. I mean, I'm making a good living and at least I'm not working for somebody else—but you know what I'd *really* like to do?" He leaned forward and rubbed his hands together. He looked at Susie and she smiled. "I'd like to coach kids. No kidding."

"He's terrific with them, Howie," Susie said. "Really terrific."

"I love it—I help out at the center sometimes, and with this team of kids from our block. Guess what they call themselves?— The Zodiacs!" We both laughed. "It's something how these things get passed down—"

We began reminiscing again and soon we were both telling Susie about the day we'd played hooky together and gone to Ebbets Field.

"Have you seen it since it's torn down?" Eddie asked. "They got these big apartment houses—"

"I've been there," I said.

"I have a girlfriend who lives in right field," Susie said. I glanced at her, puzzled. "The people all give their section of the development names according to the way the field used to be laid out," she explained. Then she laughed, but the laugh was forced and we all knew it. Eddie and I tried to get up a conversation about the old ballplayers and what they were doing then— Hodges managing the Senators, the Duke still hanging on as a pinch hitter, poor Campy in a wheel chair since his crash, conducting interviews on TV between Yankee doubleheaders—but our hearts weren't in it anymore and there were a lot of big silences. After a while I said I had to get up early the next morning for an interview. It wasn't even midnight. I thanked them for the dinner and I said I'd be in touch when I got back from school in June. Then, when I was at the door, Eddie put his arm around my shoulder.

"I been thinking," he said. "How about you playing some three-man ball with an old married man before you go back to school?"

"Sure," I said.

I met Eddie at the schoolyard on Saturday morning and we played for a couple of hours. He wasn't as graceful as I'd remembered him, but he could still jump—only now he knew how to throw his weight around and use his elbows and body and shoulders. He was murder under the boards and deadly with his jump shot and rough on defense. We played against some pretty tough high school and college and ex-college ballplayers that day and Eddie was the best of us all. Between games, we'd rest next to the fence together and Eddie would talk and joke and kid about the pot-belly he was putting on. When we played, though, he didn't smile and he didn't talk. He played hard and he played to win.

JAMES BAKER HALL was born in Lexington, Kentucky and now lives in Connecticut. His first novel, *Yates Paul, His Grand Flights, His Tootings,* was published in 1963. Mr. Hall is currently working on his second and third novels, and a collection of short stories. This is his first published story.

A Kind of Savage

FOR THE SECOND TIME in three weeks the housemother from Brewster Hall, Elizabeth Dickinson, class of '29, was sitting in the Dean's office yacking on and on about this girl from Lexington, Kentucky, who was going to wreck the entire dorm if something wasn't done. Knowing Elizabeth (dear old Elizabeth), the Dean halved everything she said and discounted the tone completely—which left little that could be construed as a dean's business. Courtney Pettit this, Courtney Pettit that! For lack of any other way to entertain herself, Dean Bradford leaned forward in her chair in a private parody of interest and attention.

Elizabeth Dickinson was a frail, nervous woman who whipped lickety-split along the campus walks with her head buried on her chest; every few yards her face would pop up, smiling, only to disappear again abruptly. For a while the Dean had thought that the housemother had a tic rather than any real interest in the world, but Elizabeth Dickinson knew as much about what was going on at Talcott College, from the lowest freshman right up through the President, as anyone around. The Dean often thought now that if you could draw her hair back while she was trotting along with her head down, you would find her ears standing at alert like a dog's. It wasn't simply Elizabeth Dickinson, class of '29, that brought out that sort of meanness in the Dean; it was

"A Kind of Savage" – James Baker Hall, *Saturday Evening Post,* Copyright © 1967 by James Baker Hall.

Elizabeth Dickinson as one of many. They were like the Chinese
Communists, these old alumnae still attached to the college; what
they lacked in equipment they made up for in dedication and
tactics and sheer number—they just kept coming in human
waves. A whole squad of them operated out of the very place
where the Dean lived and ate, and one or two evenings of every
week she fled straight from her office into New Haven; it was
either that or end up being insulting. Or, worse still, dead.

"If you and the girls can't handle something like this, what
can you handle, Elizabeth?" the Dean said. "I don't know this
Pettit girl nearly as well as you do, of course, but she impressed
me as a very quiet and accommodating little girl."

"That's the way she impressed me! That's the way she im-
presses everybody!"

What the housemother didn't understand, what very few of
the little old ladies around Talcott College understood, was that
the refinements and distinctions that meant so much to them
were largely lost on the girls, who saw you as either for them
or against them; either you were on the side of life, of freedom
and adventure, or you were some version of death itself. If they
ever got the idea that you were an old maid, you'd *had it*
as an influence in their lives. Not too many years ago Dean
Bradford would have tried to get Elizabeth Dickinson to see
that, but now she knew better than to try. Considering the
sort of women that Talcott was trying to cultivate, and the per-
sonnel they had to do it with (on paper, half the faculty was
male, but it was hard to tell sometimes which half), the Dean
was inclined to marvel at what success the college had.

Before the appointment was over, the Dean was feeling sorry
for Elizabeth and a little guilty about being unable to take her
problems more seriously. By way of making amends, she invited
herself over for a drink late that afternoon. She thought it was
clear that this would be a purely social call, but the housemother
misconstrued the whole thing; when the Dean arrived, expecting
to flop down in a chair with a drink, there in the living room
were three of Elizabeth's girls—Courtney's ex-roommate, the
dorm president, and the chairman of the dorm discipline committee—and the Dean found herself listening to the same garbage
she'd heard that morning. Courtney Pettit this, Courtney Pettit

that, all over again. Somebody was always having to get up and let her in after the doors were locked; she stayed up all night and slept all day and never seemed to study; penalizing her with extra duties simply meant risking further humiliation because it was hard enough getting her to do her own share in the first place. It all struck the Dean as enough to make you fall in love with Courtney Pettit, sight unseen.

The girls left, and as she was having her drink with Elizabeth, she said, "What's this I hear about you hanging out your laundry on Miss Finch's lawn?"

The housemother, taking her ritual walk about the campus on a recent Sunday morning, had discovered two undergarments —one male, one female—tied to the branch of a tree on the President's lawn.

"*What?*" Elizabeth exclaimed. "Where in the *world* did you hear *that?*"

"From Miss Finch herself. She said she happened to look out of the window, and there you were hanging things out to dry on her trees."

"I was taking them *down!* Lord have mercy, I—Oh, you had me *scared* to *death!*" The housemother, blushing, shook her head in bewilderment at the Dean's imagination. "No wonder the girls love you."

"I thought they were scared of me."

"Oh, underneath it all they love you. Dearly! You're really so young at heart. They *identify* with you."

"Let me catch one doing that! I haven't got a heart, Elizabeth, just a gizzard."

On the way home she grew conscience-stricken for having abused the poor timid woman all over again. Unlike some of the little old ladies on the faculty, Elizabeth Dickinson had no say in the college, so she was relatively harmless; what's more, compared with most of the old maids that the Dean was obliged to deal with day in and day out, Elizabeth was open and lively. That was cutting it pretty thin, aligning Elizabeth Dickinson with the life force, but as the girls would tell you, you had to get your kicks where you found them, and in a woman's col-lege you could end up sometimes cutting things pretty thin.

The Dean had nothing against the college or her job that being able to get away from it every night wouldn't have relieved—or so she was fond of telling herself. When she'd first come there, after the war (she and Miss Finch had been in the Marines together, a fact that still set everybody—students, faculty, alumnae—off in seventeen different directions at once), she'd promised herself, even told Miss Finch, that if she wasn't allowed to live in New Haven after a time, she would find herself another job. That was a good many years ago, and she'd never mentioned it again. For one thing, she found the way of life on campus much less sterile and parochial than she'd imagined. It was, in fact, very lively in a quiet way—the lake, the arboretum, the library, the talk—and she'd found it possible to live a deeply civilized life. Still, she would probably have moved to New Haven long ago but for the fact that more and more of the young faculty, especially the men, were trying to do that. The administration had not been forced to draw the line yet, but Miss Finch had gone out of her way on numerous occasions to let it be known that she didn't intend trying to run a residential college with a commuting faculty. If the Dean hadn't been a dean, she would have gone ahead anyhow, knowing that quite a few others were getting by with it, but being in the administration carried a special burden in the matter, as in so many others.

A lot of people were saying that Courtney Pettit would never fit in, that she was the most egregious mistake Talcott College had made in years, but when the Dean finally did agree to call Courtney in, it was more from curiosity than concern.

She was all prepared, when Courtney came in, for another of those full-dress debates in which the college was accused of being an oppressive reactionary matriarchy, but Courtney showed no interest in representing the forces of life and freedom. She was the first to point out that Talcott College was Talcott College, that she had known more or less what she was getting into when she came, and that she could always leave if she didn't like it. It was like interviewing a Girl Scout with bad grades, not a chick who was feared to have revolution in her blood.

"Gosh, Miss Bradford," Courtney said. "I try, I really do."

"What's so immensely difficult about obeying a few simple rules?"

"It's terrible, I know."

"You haven't been to English in three weeks. How long do you think you can keep your grades up without attending classes?"

"Probably not even one more day. I've been lucky on all those English papers."

"Why didn't you wait on tables the other morning when you were supposed to? Now don't give me that stuff about how ashamed you are. I want the reasons—one, two, three."

"I was in bed."

"My dear child, we were *all* in bed until we got *up*. Did it ever occur to you that if you came back to the dorm on time and went to bed at some decent hour, you wouldn't be so sleepy?"

"Yes ma'am, I know it. I've tried to go to bed early, but I always end up just lying there wide awake for hours and hours. I reckon it's my metabolism."

"Your metabolism, huh?"

"Oh, don't make fun of me, Miss Bradford. It's the truth, it really is!"

"You're driving Miss Dickinson to distraction, I trust you realize that."

"Yes ma'am."

There was a long silence.

"Well? Is that a matter of indifference to you?"

"No ma'am. I'm sorry about Miss Dickinson. I realize she has a hard time."

The Dean looked up sharply. "What do you mean by that?"

"Nothing," Courtney said. "Heavensakes, I don't have anything against Miss Dickinson or any of the girls, I really don't."

"Either you're going to learn how to get along in the dorm, or you're going to end up before the Student Council. Do you understand what that means? It's up to you."

"Yes ma'am, I know it," Courtney said. "I'm going to get a good night's sleep tonight and start working off all those penalties tomorrow."

She waited on tables three times a day all that week, and

when Elizabeth Dickinson called, wanting to know what in
the world the Dean had done, the Dean was tempted to suggest
that Courtney Pettit, far from being disrespectful of authority,
understood and appreciated it quite well, because she responded
only to the real thing; but instead, a little ashamed of the frequency with which she used housemothers and virgin girls to
take an attractive measure of herself, she told Elizabeth simply
that she'd done her bit and the whole thing was now back in
the laps of the powers at Brewster Hall, where it should have
stayed all along.

At the dorm, though, few believed that Courtney Pettit really
wanted to reform, and the first time she didn't show up for breakfast duty, they were laying for her. The word spread over
the dining room like news of an international crisis, leaving silence
in its wake. The girls turned their chairs away from the tables;
the waitresses, wearing their aprons like placards, lined up against
the wall in protest; everybody trained attention on the door,
waiting for the delinquent Courtney. A few girls got their own
breakfasts, boycotting the protest, but the rest just sat indignantly,
refusing to take a bite until Courtney Pettit reported for duty.
They waited five minutes. Ten. Fifteen. They couldn't sit around
waiting all morning—most of them had an eight o'clock class—
so they hastily assembled an *ad hoc* committee to roust Courtney
out of bed. The five girls boarded the elevator and waited in
grim silence, like a bunch of Marines in a landing barge, until
someone pushed the button. When the committee got back, somebody pointed out that it was no good getting Courtney up because
they had no way to keep her from going back to bed again.
Somebody else suggested that getting Courtney Pettit to fulfill
her responsibilities was considerably more trouble than it was
worth, and that the reasonable thing was for them to go on about
their business as though she didn't exist. Somebody else pointed
out that, yes, that was true, and it was probably exactly what
Courtney was counting on; she was putting them on no matter
which way they turned. A senior jumped up to say that she
had taken as much guff off a freshman as she intended to
take, that she personally had served that little bitch her meals
a half dozen times and would be *damned* if she would let her
get out of New England without paying her debts; there was

nothing personal about it, it was a matter of social justice. With
that the whole dining room exploded into factions, and the upshot
was that most of the girls had to go without breakfast in order
to make their classes.

It was midwinter before the Student Council got anywhere
near as worked up as the girls from Brewster Hall. The first
time they called Courtney in they contented themselves with
reviewing the trouble she'd caused and issuing rather severe
warnings about what would happen if she persisted in thinking she was a law unto herself. Courtney was contrite, and
left quite obviously chastened. Some of the Council members
were seeing her for the first time, and they agreed afterward,
despite the loud protests of the representative from Brewster,
that anybody who would be upset by that little girl was looking for
somebody to be upset by. "Just wait," the Brewster girl kept
saying, "just wait and you'll see," and the more she said it the
more fun they made of her.

For several weeks Courtney behaved herself, but then all of
a sudden everything was right back where it had started, and
this time the Council decided to confine her to the campus on
weekends for a month. For the first time since Courtney had
taken up residence in Brewster Hall the girls listened without
complaint, at least on the weekends, to the jazz she played
all night in her room. In fact, some of the more vindictive made
a ritual of going to her door at date time on Friday and Saturday
and Sunday nights and yoo-hooing good-bye to her. Everybody,
Courtney very much included, seemed more or less satisfied that
she'd gotten what she deserved, until she was seen in New Haven
late the last of those Saturday nights—while back at the dorm
the housemother and the Student Council representative, among
others, were listening to all that jazz. A quick investigation revealed the possibility that Courtney had been taking her privileges
all along, but it couldn't be proved, and so the Council, in-
fluenced again by Courtney's disavowals and pleas and resolutions, only repeated the original punishment. This time there
was no jazz at all; in fact, in a touchingly conspicuous effort
to overcome suspicion, Courtney kept out in the open in the
library virtually every night until it closed. But then, with even
the more skeptical admitting it was unlikely that she would

try to pull anything now, she was seen in New Haven again, eating breakfast one Sunday morning with a bearded fellow, and the Student Council called a special meeting to lower the boom. Before long they had her confined to her room night and day, seven days a week, except for classes—at least on paper they had her confined to her room—and the entire college was up in arms. The editor of the paper put the student government on the spot by pointing out what everybody was becoming more and more aware of—the Council had no power that couldn't be ignored by each and every student. One group within the Council wanted to salvage what prestige it could by trying to cultivate Courtney's impulse to reform, another wanted to pursue the hard line with ultimatums that even they weren't sure they could enforce. Finally, in frustration, the Council made an unprecedented request that the administration take Courtney Pettit off their hands.

"What choice have we got?" the President asked the Dean. "The girls have done all they can do."

"What about allowing the Council to recommend probation or expulsion? It would give them at least the semblance of some real power."

There was a long silence at Miss Finch's end of the phone.

"Subject to the approval of the faculty adviser or something like that," the Dean added.

Finally Miss Finch said, "No, that could end up getting us all in a lot of trouble. I don't think we ought to encourage them to think they've got anything to say about that at all. What is it about this girl anyway? You're fond of her, aren't you?"

"She's tremendously entertaining," the Dean said. *"More* than that, actually: she doesn't for a minute expect or even want the college to underwrite her behavior. It's extraordinary. I haven't seen a girl like that in all my years here. She can give a more intelligent and eloquent defense of the way things are around here than some of those Westchester girls on the Council. Their trouble is, they think they'd be immensely better off if they could get rid of Courtney Pettit, when the truth of the matter is that they'd have to invent her if she didn't exist."

"Does she want to be expelled? Is she just leading everybody on?"

"If she were a little older I'd be inclined to think maybe she was one of the world's great straight-faced comedians, but I really doubt it now. You know how kids that age are: there are probably three or four mutually exclusive Courtney Pettits crashing around inside that girl, and whenever one gets on top for any length of time, there's bound to be a palace revolution. She's like the wolfman—about once a month the Talcott gentility and respectability has a full-moon effect on her; it turns her into a kind of savage. It's an adolescent response to the same damn conflict that produces people like . . ." The Dean named several of the more publicly tortured and convoluted personalities around the college.

"Look," Miss Finch said, "you go ahead and handle it in whatever way you see fit. Just keep me posted. If we're going to let somebody wreck the college for the sake of being entertained, I don't want to miss any of it."

"I'm not going to let her go too far, don't worry about that."

When she put the phone down, the Dean began dictating a note requesting Courtney to make an appearance tomorrow at eleven, but then she grew impatient with all that formality and told her secretary to get the girl on the phone. And when Courtney came in the next morning, the Dean laid it on the line: She was going to have one more chance to respect the authority of the Council; after that she'd find herself confronted with the administration. By way of dramatizing that she meant every word she said, the Dean announced that there would be another meeting of the Council, and that she personally would be there, in the role of an observer.

"Well, how about it?" she asked.

"Gee whiz," Courtney said. "If I have to meet with those mixed-up girls many more times I'll go out of my mind."

After Courtney left, the Dean thought of calling Miss Finch to share that remark with her, but chickened out at the last minute. She tried to think of somebody she *could* call; there were plenty of people around who would appreciate what Courtney had said, but none that she could phone for just that. Finally she buzzed for her secretary.

The typing stopped, and the secretary appeared in the doorway, her glasses in her hand. "Did you want me?" Just the sight of her, another stolid well-meaning old lady for whom the college was life, suddenly moved the Dean.

"Guess what I told Miss Finch when she told me to have another talk with that Pettit girl."

The secretary confessed that she couldn't guess.

"I told her," the Dean said, "that if I had to meet with that mixed-up girl many more times I'd go out of my mind."

"You know," the secretary said solemnly, "just to talk to that girl, you'd never know she was that way. All these girls running around in sweat shirts and blue jeans, *they're* the ones who don't go to chapel."

The Council put off the meeting for a week in order to prepare for it; despite the Dean's disclaimers, they believed they were being called on to show cause why the case should be taken to the administration, and they weren't about to be made fools of again.

The meeting, when it came, was a solemn occasion. The Council president sat at one end of the great oval table and Courtney at the other, linked by girls around both sides, many with manila folders before them. One girl submitted the fact that, according to certain reliable sources at Yale, Courtney's bearded boyfriend in New Haven was a Communist. Another girl (the head of the campus chapter of Young Americans for Freedom, a girl who was fond of calling William F. Buckley Jr. "Bill" and of knowing exactly what he was up to whenever the fuzzy-headed liberals said he was up to no good) brought up the subject of what her father would think of Talcott College for condoning "a girl like that." Obviously no one at the table thought for a minute that Courtney had stayed out all night with a bearded Communist to eat ice cream at Ho Jo's, but all of them saw the need to stick to matters that were their business and to accusations that could be proved if necessary.

"Every girl on this campus takes the honor of the college with her wherever she goes," the first girl said. "She's desecrating us all! She's desecrating you, and you, and you"—she went around the room—"she's desecrating Dean Bradford, she's desecrating me!" She subsided into an emotional silence, her hand pressed to her chest.

"Courtney?" the Council president said.

"Gee," Courtney said, "I hadn't thought of it that way."

"Do you understand how we feel?"

"You mean 'desecrated'?"

"I mean, do you understand or don't you!"

"It's not a question of her understanding it," the first girl said. "Any degenerate can *understand* it. It's a question of whether she respects it!"

"Golly," Courtney said. "I can't respect desecration—that's sick. Desecration gives me the willies."

"That's not what I mean!"

"How am I going to keep somebody like you from feeling desecrated?" Courtney wanted to know. "If you feel desecrated, that's your problem, huh? Not mine. When it comes to feeling desecrated, it's every man for himself."

That did it. Up until then the proceedings had been fairly orderly, partly for the Dean's sake and partly out of the girls' recognition of the fact that things could easily get ugly if they weren't careful, but that last insolence loosed the hounds in them: They accused Courtney of being a dirty, drunken little slut. What they had been advertising as moral indignation was suddenly revealed to be nothing but hatred posing as righteousness. The Dean, assuming that Courtney was unaffected, that she would sit it out calmly and shame them all, was embarrassed for the girls and for herself too. She was about to leave the room, as a way of registering her protest and bringing the girls back to their senses, when the whole business took an abrupt turn.

Suddenly everybody was staring at the girl sitting there at the end of the oversized table, the fingers of both hands hooked over the edge. Courtney wasn't looking at anyone; she was just staring straight ahead, her round, innocent eyes sorrowful and hurt. She was close to tears.

"I try," she said, shaking her head, "I really do. I try as hard as I can. I don't want to cause trouble, I really don't."

No one knew what to say.

Finally the Council president pointed out that people had to be judged finally by what they did, not by what they intended to do. No girl there in that room had been admitted to Talcott College just because she'd tried hard, and no one would be graduated, no matter how hard she tried, unless she met certain objective requirements. It was just the right tone, conciliatory without being soft, apologetic without compromising the hard justice of the Council's position. All the girls nodded with relief and pride.

Then someone wanted to know, well, where did they stand? At which point, again to everyone's surprise, Courtney got out a typewritten statement and read it. No one, not even the Dean, doubted for a minute that she meant what she was saying. She spoke of the fall colors around the lake, the red and yellow and orange of sumac and maple, and of the fallen leaves scattered across the lawns and paths and parking lots; she called to mind the sound of the chapel bells, and the view of the lakeside tennis courts from the path up the hill; she spoke of the great rambunctious Brueghel scenes at dusk on a bitter winter day, when the frozen lake was crowded with skaters and dogs and racing children with hockey sticks; she spoke of the common rooms where some barefoot girl in a robe was forever ironing, of the long bull sessions with girls wandering in for a while and then back out again, of the transformation every weekend of teen-agers into chic young women in heels; she spoke of snowplows clearing the campus roads late at night, of the look of the lighted dorms on the snowy hillsides around the quad, of the couples courting outside those dorms just before the doors were locked, of the concerts, the plays, the readings, the lectures; she spoke of girls sunbathing on the roofs in spring, of the redwing blackbirds singing in the field below the gym, of the boys coming in from Yale and Wesleyan and Princeton and Amherst and colleges all over New England.

In closing she read the Donne passage about how no man is an island unto himself but each a part of the main, and when she finished the room was absolutely silent again. The Dean found herself deeply moved.

The Council president looked slowly around the room. "I don't think anything more needs to be said."

"I don't think anything more *could be*," someone said.

For several weeks the Dean waited for something to happen, but nothing did. She wasn't particularly comfortable with the idea that Courtney was on her way to becoming a thorough-bred Talcott girl, but it had happened before and no doubt would again. In time even Elizabeth Dickinson went on record as giving the girl a chance to grow up and become civilized. The Dean was about ready to chalk up another one for good old Talcott College when she got a note from the Dean of one of the sister colleges saying that she ought to know that some girl at Talcott, claiming to have the name and address of the greatest lover in France, was trying to organize a summer pilgrimage composed of one girl from each of the sister colleges.

And the very next Saturday, Courtney stayed out all night without signing out, and didn't return until a little before nine the next morning. The girls were pouring out of the dorms on their way to church when a bright red sports car, driven by a bearded man and followed by four motor scooters, idled in, deposited Courtney unceremoniously in front of Brewster, and idled back out again, the string of scooters wagging behind the sports car like a tired tail. The doors of the dormitory were wide open, but Courtney, who was still drunk, stood on the stone wall around the beech tree demanding to be let in. "Open up!" she kept shouting, as though it were late at night and the place locked up tight. "Open up!" Then she jumped off the wall, climbed into the housemother's car, which was parked near the door, and started blowing the horn, stiff-arming it with both hands. Before long every girl in the dorm was downstairs and out on the sidewalk. They had to wrestle Courtney inside and onto the elevator. Poor Elizabeth Dickinson spent the rest of the day under sedatives.

The next morning the Dean scotched all formalities and dialed Courtney's number herself. The phone rang and rang, but no one answered. The Dean sat there, elbows on the desk, and waited. There was something exhilarating in the fact that Court-ney hadn't become a Talcott girl after all, but it was the sort of feeling she knew she couldn't indulge. Finally Courtney picked up the phone.

"Courtney?"

"Yes, ma'am."

"Dean Bradford."

"Yes ma'am."

Silence.

"Your metabolism is rather sluggish today. I've been ringing for five minutes."

"Yes ma'am, you know, I heard something ringing, but I thought it was the alarm."

"It *is* the alarm, my dear." The Dean paused, but nothing came over the phone except Courtney's breathing.

"Can't you say anything but 'Yes ma'am'?"

"Yes ma'am. I mean, no ma'am." Courtney laughed. "Sometimes I reckon I just don't know what it is people want me to say."

"What does that mean?"

"Well, sometimes I just don't know what you-all want."

You-all, huh? The Dean stalled for as long as she dared, hunting for an oblique way to distinguish herself from Elizabeth Dickinson and the Talcott girls, but she knew that Courtney had her.

"What we-all want, my dear, is for you to abide by the rules. That's all, I can assure you."

There was a long silence, by which Courtney managed to insinuate—or so it seemed to the Dean—that she knew that was a lot of guff, and that the Dean knew it too.

"I'll give you an hour to get dressed and get over here, Courtney. If you're not here in an hour—don't come."

By the time the girl arrived, the Dean had spoken with her parents, with Miss Finch, and with the housemother. Campus life could no longer tolerate Courtney (even the girl's father wanted her expelled), but the Dean, despite her own qualms, finally persuaded everybody that Courtney should be allowed to finish out the few remaining weeks of the year by living, under dormitory rules, with an uncle in New Haven.

The poor uncle was an elderly lawyer who had seen her no more than a dozen times in his life—one day he and his wife were living the perfectly civilized life of a New England couple of means, and the next Courtney Pettit was in residence. The rules were hard enough for the Talcott people themselves to understand, so it was no wonder he found them utterly confusing.

Almost every day either he or his wife phoned to check Courtney's interpretations with the Dean's office.

The weekday eleven o'clock check-in, did that mean the girls
had to be in their rooms or merely on the premises? He was
asking because Courtney had sat in a car out in front of the
house the previous night from eleven until nearly one A.M. No,
the Dean said, eleven o'clock meant in the house with the
doors locked. So the next night Courtney brought her New Haven
friends in with her, five of them with three guitars. Neither
he nor his wife had anything against young people having a
good time, the uncle told the Dean, but he felt obliged to see
that Courtney kept her part of the bargain, and he was beginning to suspect that she was taking advantage of his lack of
familiarity with the rules. He hoped he wasn't being merely
old-fashioned, but to be quite frank neither he nor his wife
found much to appreciate in the young people she was bringing
into their house—they certainly weren't the sort one would expect a Talcott girl to be running around with. A few days later
he called the Dean the first thing in the morning and said that
if that girl wasn't out of his house by dinner time, he was
going to call her father to come after her.

The Dean got Courtney out of class to the phone.

"Guess who."

"Dean Bradford?"

"Guess what."

"I've had it," Courtney said.

"You said it, honey."

"What's the matter now?"

"You're attending classes at Talcott College, and you're no
longer a student here, that's what's the matter."

"Really?"

"Really."

"Gee."

A long silence. Did Courtney honestly not care? Hard as it
was for her to face, the Dean was afraid that this girl was
insisting on their differences, and she felt betrayed. She knew
that when it was all over, when she was left with those who
cared about nothing else, that she would want Courtney not to
have cared at all, that she would be drawn to the idea that

there was somebody out there in the world who appreciated everything that Talcott had to offer and was still able to toss it all away with ease. Now, though, there was something in the Dean that wanted to see a little chink in the girl's armor. "How's the pilgrimage to France shaping up?"

"How did you find out about that?"

"I just assumed that's what you'd be doing this summer."

Courtney laughed appreciatively. "It's falling through. I've got a Cliffy and a girl from Barnard, but the others aren't coming through. Everybody over at Vassar is shook about the school's reputation. I haven't heard a word from Smith—are there people still sort of moving around and breathing over there at Smith?"

"Some, sort of," the Dean said.

Another silence.

"Your bearded Communist boyfriend, don't you think that's going just a bit far? I mean aesthetically? You disappoint me at times, Courtney."

"He's not a Communist, Miss Bradford."

Okay, so he wasn't a Communist. She ought to have known— another point for Courtney Pettit.

"I suppose you were just too ashamed to admit it, though."

Courtney laughed again, and the Dean found herself responding to the girl's appreciation.

"I went out on a limb for you, I trust you realize that."

"Yes ma'am, I know you did."

A pause.

"Do you want to come over here and talk about it? There's nothing that can be done, but we can talk about it." The minute she'd said that, she was sorry.

"I will if you want me to," Courtney said.

A long silence this time.

The Dean was suddenly disgusted with her own naïveté and weakness. "Forget it," she said. "Just get the hell out of here, will you? I don't want to see you around here after today, do you understand?"

"Yes ma'am."

Late that afternoon Elizabeth Dickinson telephoned to find out what had happened, and as the Dean sat there at her desk listening to the housemother go on about the whole affair, she saw three girls pull off their shoes and walk across the lawn outside her window, dragging their feet sensually through the grass. Suddenly they tossed their books to the ground and raced up the long steep terrace, laughing and screaming, slowing as they approached the top, pulling their long shadows, until they were barely moving. Then, like stunt planes peeling off, they angled along the ridge of the terrace for a few yards, picking up speed again, and then they dove to the ground, one behind the other, and let themselves go, rolling like logs back down the hill. Their laughter rang out in the clear spring air; along the campus walks girls stopped and smiled and hugged their books and watched. Down they came, faster and faster, their supple bodies spinning through the lush grass, their skirts and blouses and legs and arms and hair a blur of freewheeling light on the green hillside. Unconsciously, the Dean lowered the phone against her neck, pressing Elizabeth Dickinson's voice out of hearing for the moment, and held her breath—held it for the girls' safety, for the sheer beauty of the life that was in them.

Elizabeth Dickinson said, "You know, there are some people who just don't appreciate Talcott College, and they just don't belong here—it's as simple as that."

"Maybe you're right," the Dean said. Why was it she couldn't acknowledge the claims those girls out there had on her without getting involved with the likes of Courtney Pettit? Sometimes her life seemed to be nothing but a crude mockery of the distinctions her mind lived on. "But nothing's as simple as that," she said to Elizabeth.

One drink that evening before dinner and she knew that she couldn't face the little old ladies in the dining room, so she just sat there in front of her TV in a kind of stupor, eating blue cheese and crackers and drinking bourbon. After a while she dozed off, woke, and struggled into the bedroom. Several minutes later she found herself sitting on the side of the bed with her shoes and stockings off and her blouse unbuttoned, but she couldn't figure out whether she was supposed to be dressing or undressing.

The phone rang, piercing her stupor. It was Miss Forman, the head of Physical Education, calling from the next apartment house. She needed the Dean's help with a little problem. The matron over at the gym had just phoned to say that the new young man in English, Mr. Klein, had played squash with a friend during the dinner hour and hadn't returned the squash-courts key. Since Mr. Klein was just across the hall there from the Dean, Miss Forman wondered if she would mind inquiring about the key. Why, of course, the Dean said, she'd be glad to. As it turned out, Mr. Klein hadn't pocketed the key—how could he? he said; it was wired to an old Ping-Pong paddle—he had left it, not at the matron's window, but around the corner on her desk, where he'd assumed it was conspicuous enough. The Dean phoned the information to Miss Forman and, though it was still early, went to bed.

It wasn't until the next morning that it hit her just how odd the whole business about the key really was. In the first place, what the dickens were they locking the squash courts for? Bravado? In the second place, with all the duplicate keys around, surely there was no immediate need to recover the one Mr. Klein had used—they were just antsy at the idea of a man (a new young man at that!) running off with a key to something they'd locked up. And even if they'd needed that particular key that very night, and been reasonable in suspecting that someone had run off with it, paddle and all, why had the matron called Miss Forman instead of Mr. Klein himself? And why had Miss Forman, instead of contacting Mr. Klein directly, carried the matron's foolishness just that much farther? And worse still, the Dean thought, what about herself? What really shook her up wasn't that she'd gone along with the whole silly thing, but that she hadn't seen anything silly about it. It had seemed a perfectly natural little problem being solved in a perfectly natural way—if a man runs off with one of your keys, then naturally you've got to get it back immediately, and naturally you can't just ask him for it. One doesn't go around insulting people, even when they do behave suspiciously! The Dean tried to make allowances for herself—she'd been drinking, hadn't she?—but she'd destroyed that excuse too many times in dealing with the girls. The real trouble, of course, was that all of it *was* perfectly natural—natural to the little old ladies at Talcott College.

The next morning, before she had a chance to change her mind, the Dean took an apartment in New Haven and informed the housing office that she was moving out; that afternoon she left her office early and loaded the back seat of her car with her belongings. If she got fired, well then she would just have to get fired, for it seemed clearly a matter of life and death to get some distance between herself and the college.

As she was waiting at the gate for a break in the rush-hour traffic, a horn beeped, and there behind her in a sleek little red sports car with the top down were Courtney Pettit and her bearded boyfriend. The Dean's heart jumped. Her eyes met Courtney's in the rear-view mirror, and they both smiled politely, the smiles growing steadily richer until, in unison, they burst out laughing. The moment was shattered, though, when the horn beeped again, this time with unmistakable mockery, telling her to move out or move over. The Dean's smile vanished, but Courtney only laughed that much harder. What they would infer from her loaded car the Dean didn't know, but she felt revealed before them, as though they were seeing something that she did not want them, of all people, to see. If they tooted that horn again, she would scream! No, she would just sit there, by God, until they quieted down, and then she would—— Suddenly they swung out behind her, and with Courtney's head flung back in laughter, proceeded to show her how it was done. The Dean had been thinking that she would get out and walk back there calmly and say that maybe *they* weren't intimidated by rush-hour drivers, but she was just a hung-up Talcott lady herself and there was no telling how soon she would find her way into that kind of traffic—and then they shot around her, bluffed their way recklessly in, and roared off toward New Haven, trailing Courtney's laughter like tin cans behind a marriage car, leaving her there alone at the college gate.

DAVID STACTON was born in Nevada and educated at Stanford and the University of California. He has written ten novels and three nonfiction works, the most recent of which, *The Bonapartes,* was published in 1966. Mr. Stacton's story, "The Metamorphosis of Kenko" appeared in the 1964 O. Henry collection.

Little Brother Nun

WE ARE on an old-fashioned paddlewheeler, and the water, as it drips from the scoops of the wheel, has the color and texture of meerschaum. It is a hot, hot afternoon in 1882.

In short, we are in the nineteenth century, the safe century, the comfortable century, the century when we have long since outstripped the life of unreason, and come to settle, at evening, during our flight, on that quiet and most protected of lakes. The bird tucks its beak into its breast, and need not fly again until tomorrow. It is safe here.

At the back of the boat there is an awning, striped red and white. There is very little wind, just enough not to flap, but to undulate, the awning. We are going up the river, through the flaccid, almost unwilling water. Progress is slow, and it is doubtful if anyone would want it to be any faster, for under the awning sits Ramakrishna, dispensing his wisdom, which is verbal and autobiographical. He has an odd voice, a double octave, deep and at the same time high pitched. It is a compelling voice. As he talks, the flies settle on his glistening face, but an admirer flicks them away with a fan made from the single desiccated yellow frond of a palm, set (he is a rich admirer) in a jeweled handle, and so disposable.

It is civilized here in Bengal. It is because we have had

"Little Brother Nun" – David Stacton, *Virginia Quarterly,* Copyright © 1967 by The Virginia Quarterly Review, The University of Virginia.

the British longer than in the other parts of India, and so have had ample time to become resigned to, and then emulous of, their decorous and exclusive propinquity. After all, if people bleed us, but treat us scrupulously, prevent us from bleeding each other, which is a great saving, and yet will not have us in their club, surely they know a secret we do not? They are recent, of course, and barbarous, but then so were the Muslims, and surely it cannot be denied that in some way they have grace?

What is it they know?

For all this Ramakrishna cares not a rap. He has had an interesting life.

"I was only a boy when I first determined to become a nun," he says, and pauses.

Yes, only a boy. He does not at first answer that respectful silence which he has come to expect, and therefore gets. It is hard for him to remember that he was once a boy, particularly as he is still a boyish man. He has enthusiasms; that is why. Such people are lovable because they are vulnerable, but he is not aware of that. He has been on an endless journey. What people love in him is not himself, but only what he has brought them back. And here it is, on the deck in front of him, in a glittering, invisible pile. What he has brought back is a special kind of wisdom which, being pressed hard, has carbonized and looks like a diamond.

"When I was a boy, I wanted to become a nun," he repeats, more or less, for the wise often repeat themselves, they cannot help it, they can speak only of what they know; and since he was a determined boy, he succeeded in his aim. He experienced this:

II

The company listening to him has come to see one of the curiosities of the day. No one is quite sure whether to laugh reverently or not, for he is a Holy Curiosity. The Master makes them uneasy, for one reason more than would formerly have been the case. For the Master is a holy lunatic attached to the temple of Kali at Dakshineswar, in suburban Calcutta; and the leader of the visitors, Keshab Chandra Sen, has not only in part adopted Western ways, he has attempted to adapt to them, and so has his friend, the doctor.

Keshab Chandra Sen is the leader of the Bràhmo Samàj, a colorless, well meaning, nervous, and therefore influential organization devoted to the reconciliation of Western and Eastern Thought, by leeching from both religions everything but their ethical content. Since the ethical content of any established faith is apt to be minimal, the result is inevitably pallid, but that, of course, is what they want. The question that does not bother them is, does India want it, too?

They are snobs in no man's land, but there is no harm in them, and they mean well. They are well dressed people in a country where English furniture and plumbing are still an unfamiliar but necessary nuisance. One or two of them have even contemplated eating beef at meals, though with repugnance, and with the feeling that to do so would be an irremediable act. The others say they will eat beef when they see horsemeat upon the Governor General's table, for the English are horse worshippers, are they not?

Sri Ramakrishnà would make them nervous, even were they not emancipated souls, for sacred freaks tend to be dirty. Though healthier than most, the Master has loose flesh around him, it has never absorbed; he has a big unweaned mouth and bad teeth; his beard is an uncouth blur, there is something shrewd, evasive, and unmistakably mad about his eyes. He has the pushy dignity of short self-made men (he is the son of penniless Brahmin peasants). To coin a verb, he ostentates, for though what he does is objectionable on its own terms, he is not pretentious. He is epileptoid, blinks in a strong light, and has found that trance states are not only enjoyable, but solve awkward social problems, and are an irrefutable answer to unanswerable dialectic. His voice is pitched too high, as though to reach for something. He is as mongrel as the temple he comes from.

Dakshineswar is a startling building. When the French military advisers came to India after the Napoleonic wars, they imposed their architecture upon the native Princes at enormous fees. India is dotted with these follies. The English confined themselves to a sparse late Georgian and complacent Regency. But whoever

designed Dakshineswar was mad as a hatter, with money to
spend. The main block suggests Nijny Novgorod, with Hindu
concessions, Palladian arcades, and a porte cochère. At either
end stand detached two-story pavilions in a strict frostbitten St.
Petersburg style. The complex stands back from the Ganges, in
no sense a flashing stream, though dangerous enough, and the
gardens had run to seed so soon as they were planted. Against
probability, and partly because of the ruined garden, the effect
is natural and pleasing. The detail is bad. It looks all wrong.
And yet it isn't. The same might be said of the Master.

"When I was a nun," he says, and it is true: he has been
everything: he is an actor. When he was nine, on Sivarati
Night, the actor chosen to impersonate Siva having fallen ill,
his friends made up Ramakrishna instead. Disconcertingly, he
was not only convincing, he was convinced. He had been Siva.

Children capable of empathy, and not themselves yet suf-
ficiently differentiated so that their ego controls their response,
cannot act, but they can become whatever they are told to become. While walking to the stage, and concentrating on doing
it properly, Ramakrishna became Siva, took the audience by
storm, his first audience, and dimly aware of the distant breakers
of applause, fell into a trance. The performance had to be
stopped. For him, it would never stop. He organized a dramatic
troop among the children, and played both Radha and Krishna,
god and milkmaid, as he felt like either part, in a mango grove
in his native village. He was slightly effeminate to begin with:
he did not find it difficult to become a woman.

Later, studying Vaishnava disciplines, he impersonated Radha
the more intensely to feel Krishna's love of the universe. This
spiritual transvestitism also allows one to free one's self from the
desires of the male body. Indeed, the anomaly frees one from
all sexual desires. One becomes Impersonal Spirit.

However, there are worse desires than the physical. He had
them. Krishna may be worshipped in two forms, depending upon
the age of the worshipper. Young women adore him as Krishna,
the lover; women past the menopause, as Krishna, the baby.

Ramakrishna's father died when he was seven. This was his
first experience of corporeal death. An astute child, he drew
the conclusion: men died; women did not. The death disturbed

him, and he took to sitting in the cremation yard, to think things
over. Man means well, but is transient and dies. Women, who
are there to provide food and affection, bear the survivor's burden.
So one must please women. He began to help his mother with
her chores. Brought up in a household of women, their standards
were his, so he knew how to please them. To please men, one
pleased what was womanly in them, the softer or gentler side,
which was in any event preferable.

He became a mimic, to the delight of the women of the
village. Your seeker after God is a man with a mania for
imitation. He does not parody others. He becomes others and
lets their voices speak. He leads parallel lives. If you listened
closely when Ramakrishna was sitting silent in any gathering,
you became aware of a soft rattling and clicking sound. This
was the Master as a boy, reproducing not their voices, but them,
by rearranging the muscular constrictions of his and their vocal
chords.

He had been Mohammed, the Buddha, Christ, Siva, Krishna,
Radha, even, with daring, Kali sometimes, so why not a nun?
The future saint or religious leader cannot have a father, for
he is in part divine, the birth can be observed, all mothers are
mortal, but the insemination cannot. At the age of sixty Ramakrishna's father, a dispossessed Brahmin, made a pilgrimage to
Gaya, and there had the vision that Vishnu had impregnated
his wife. When he returned, he found not only that she was
pregnant, but that she too had had a vision, during which some
God, she had not recognized which one, had done the deed. It
is possible. Life in small villages along the Hoogli is sometimes
disorderly at night.

It had puzzled the Master, in his worship of Kali as the
Black Mother, that she had no children in that avatar. But
while studying Christianity, he had been overwhelmed by the
radiance streaming from a chromolithograph, hanging on the
wall, of the Virgin and Child. The child nestled there, magnificently taken care of. The Virgin Mary was a previous avatar
of the Mother Goddess. Therefore there was no doubt in the
Master's mind that he had been, and was, Christ, for he felt
in himself, as had Christ, the longing for disciples. And do not
nuns long to be the bride of Christ? It is a chaste marriage,

but satisfying. His own marriage had been of the same order, and had much flattered his wife (when he allowed her to visit), for it meant she had been singled out, and conferred distinction. If one has been on top, one longs to be on the bottom; if one has been on the bottom, one lusts to be on top. So when he was a nun, he had had visions, of a kind difficult to secularize.

"When I was a nun," he began, blinking rapidly. The disciples were restless. As the Master himself had said, when the flower blooms, the bees will come to it. But bees discriminate between this nectar and that, and here was the Master peering out at them from among the tropic vines of Bengali superstition, with the soft bright eyes of a dormouse whose flanks heave. They had been told by Brahminical authority that he was a *true* Incarnation, but was that compatible with the latest Western science? They could not be sure. His talk flowed smoothly, but he was too much like the Ganges, beneath whose murky waters there heaved here and there an amorphous and therefore dreadful shape, ready to surface, which sometimes, though not often, did so. The Ganges is a sacred river, but not for that reason yet free of the sudden crocodile.

Chandra Sen suggested food and felt the need of a Western witness. The dishes were brought on, served by a steward eager not only for a glimpse of the Master, but also for the approbation of important people. The most important person there he did not notice, since, like most people, he had no talent for futures. This was Narendranath Dutta, the Swami Vivekananda to come, and so chosen by the Master to spread his gospel to the world. Narendra was a Bengali aristocrat and looked it. His manner lacked subservient bustle, so naturally he was ignored. Nevertheless, the Master, in his remorseless recapitulation of the world's religions and their leaders, had early recognized that no revelation will go far with a Propaganda Fidei, and had made his arrangements accordingly. Narendra was to be Ananda, Mohammed, and Sts. Peter and Paul as well. Matthew, Mark, and John had been compressed into Nahendranath Gupta, better known as M, who took the Master's words down in shorthand. Luke was provided by almost any passing photographer. The Master was not vain of his appearance, but thought of everything.

The circumstantial persecutions of neglect, though he was ab-

stemious, had left him with an abiding admiration for food. He
ate little, but liked to have it there. Moreover, in these later
years, he expected it to be there. As he said himself, Kali had
provided him with five helpers to wait upon his needs. There
was an old woman who brought him curry and fed him sweet-
meats, in the belief he was the reincarnation of the baby Krishna,
and should be coddled accordingly. There had been Mathur
Mohan, the son-in-law of the rich sudra woman Rani Rasmani,
who had founded Dakshineswar temple. He was dead now eleven
years. There had been Rani Rasmani herself (once he had convinced her of his sanctity by slapping her face during prayers).
There had been, until last year, Hriday.

Nobody ever lasted for good. It was always possible for him,
given time, to perceive their imperfections.

Hriday, the first of those comely devotees with whom the
Master liked to surround himself, though Hriday had been
genuinely fond of him, had been the helper assigned by the
Mother Goddess to support the Master's body when he was in
samadhi, to see that it was fed, washed, and taken care of,
while the Master was away on a trance journey. These sometimes
took six months. But as Hriday had grown older, somewhat fatter
in the face, and too jealous of his prerogatives to please the later
worshippers of the Master, he had had to be, not without difficulty, removed, on a trumped-up charge of indiscretion. It was
noticed that the Master took the removal in good part.

He not only liked the young, he liked new young. Those
observant shining eyes of his watched events, they did not com-
ment upon them. He had already seen many people go, and
every day a few more arrived. He was a shrewd judge, not so
much of character, as of obedience. If disciples seemed likely
to serve his purpose, he said, "Ah, you have come. I have been
waiting." If they did not seem likely to serve his purpose, he
said nothing, until they had gone away. He did not contrive these
matters. He let them happen, unless he did not wish to let them
happen. Only about a later disciple, Nityagopal, is he known
to have expressed bitterness. Nityagopal had done his own leaving.

Meanwhile, here was the food.

"I am the first born of the divine essence.
Whoever bestows me on others, thereby keeps me to himself.
I am FOOD. I feed on food and on its feeder.
FOOD they call death; the same Food, they call life.
FOOD, the Brahmans call growing old.
FOOD, they also call the begetting of offspring
    They feed on ME. I feed on everything,"

he intoned, quoting, from memory, for he could not read, the
Taittriya Brahmana. The quotation was designed to offend none,
but to please all, particularly the somewhat pedantic ladies and
gentlemen of the Bràhmo Samāj.

"When you were a nun," prompted Chandra Sen, who in
his younger days had had many women, and had often wondered
how they felt about it.

But the Master was rubbing his bowl for sauce, with a rolled,
bitten chapatty, and was not to be rushed. To watch him eat
was to remember his origins. It was not a pleasant sight. He
ate with the oblivious cruel self-satisfaction of a sly child and
the table manners of an idiot. Though scrupulous in oral hygiene,
he had a stench to his breath.

There was another reason for regarding the Master as holy.
It was plain that he would not live long. Holy idiots seldom do.
The religious explanation of this was (the Master gave it freely)
that though he had attained to highest enlightenment, the Goddess
had persuaded him to return to the earthly plane to the benefit
of humanity. He thus fluctuated momently between the lower
and the higher state, a boon unique in the history of faith, but
one day would not return.

It took him three days to become any religion or religious
leader, the first to attain to it, the second to enjoy it, the
third to begin the arduous labor of return. His time schedule
never varied, but he was tired of returning. So soon there
would be no third day.

The medical explanation was diagnostic. His history was
known.

The Master was born in a cluster of thatched huts, under
a fever tree, by a dirt road in the Hoogli hamlet of Kamarpukur,
the solitary delayed last child of old age (the women of that

district age rapidly, and his father was either the God Vishnu,
or else sixty). He had been brought up among matriarchs ("We
never regarded him as a man," said some of his female devotees
once, "we regarded him as one of us."). Since the artificial
boundaries between the sexes are not so publicly rigid in India
as elsewhere, there is a good deal of time for shillyshallying
across the border. There was no confusion in the Master, but
much ambiguity.

A local official had given a mango grove to the village. Here
the Master had been Krishna sometimes, but preferably Radha,
the loved one, not the lover. The Master's emotional responsibility
was limited to allowing himself to be loved. He thus differentiated
between two egos, the ego of Knowledge, devotion, and the
servant, which is edible, and ripe, and goes down smoothly; and
the green ego with the stubborn stem, which does not. As a ripe
and therefore healthy ego, Ramakrishna allowed himself to be
swallowed whole by one divinity after another, knowing himself
not only to be digestible, but as self renewing as the pitcher of
Baucis and Philemon.

His first ecstasy had occurred while he was eating. He had
been walking down a paddy field path, at the age of six or
seven, munching puffed rice. He had fallen into a fit. The
puffed rice shot every which way into the paddies, to float there
like the dead souls of the rice plant itself. A white light had
flared through his head, and then left him in joyous darkness.
If there is nothing agreeable in the lower room, you may ascend
the ladder to the loft, where all good things are stored. Some
villagers carried his stiffened body home.

In 1849, his eldest brother, then in his forties, went to Calcutta
to make his fortune, and in 1852 sent for the Master, in order
to induce him to learn some breadwinning discipline.

Ramakrishna did not take kindly to discipline.

"Brother, what shall I do with a mere breadwinning education? I would rather acquire that wisdom which will illumine
my heart and give me satisfaction forever," he said, in his
glittering, stubborn way.

There was living at this time in Calcutta, a rich sudra woman,
a creature of the lowest caste, by name, Rani Rasmani. Though
she was one of the untouchables, many were touched, which is

to say brought to the point of strong emotion, both by her ruthless business acumen and by her piety. Tired of giving money to the shrines of others, she decided to build a temple of her own, a spiritual money bank of whose solvency she might remain permanently assured. The result, dedicated to Kali, Radha, and Krishna as an aspect of Vishnu, also to Siva, (she meant to make sure), was Dakshineswar, dedicated in May of 1855. Sudras, in her opinion, should have their temples, too.

Rasmani was devout both by policy and conviction, for if you give to the rich, you may take from the poor with impunity. Her new temple was of the richest workmanship, and she endowed it liberally. Her piety was of the kind which longs for reassurance, but she could believe only in a sanctity with the courage to strike her, for nobody in this life had so far dared to, they preferred to sneer; therefore that sign must come from the other world.

Ramakrishna's brother became a priest at this temple. Though made uneasy at being fed food prepared by members of an inferior caste, Ramakrishna followed. Comfort made him amenable by degrees. Hriday came next.

The overseer of this temple was a man named Mathur Babu, that Indian figure, the sensuous older brother in search of a younger son.

Almost all human relationships are destroyed by being defined. Sensibly, this relationship was not given a definition. Ramakrishna recognized Mathur at once, as he recognized all people belonging to him. His appetite for being petted was inexhaustible. Not wishing to be eaten alive, Mathur felt the need of an intermediary. Hence Hriday.

It was amusing to come in from the estates, or from temple business, and converse with the Master, who was a little animal in those days, and like animals, combined with independence a desire to learn the house rules. The Master was sizing his keepers up.

And yet, though his deepest desire was so clearly to be a woman, he was not womanish, having no more than that degree of ambiguity about him with which Indian men soften all relationships into a gummy sweet mash, out of their desire to be neither one thing nor the other. It must remain indefinite.

A man such as Mathur Babu lives in the world and has not the time to live out of it. So he transfers his spiritual obligations to another, an ascetic whom he keeps about the house and pampers as he would pamper a good hunting dog. The Hindu ascetic is there to do what we would do, if we did not know better than to do as we wished, like the masochist who wants to be murdered, does not want to die, and gives the whole thing up ten minutes afterwards, only to start again.

Besides, the little creature was the most amusing talker, full of anecdotes of village life. "When I meditated, I used to think of the unflickering flame of a lamp set in a windless place." That was not only informative, it was charming and pretty. And then there were the stories.

"A man was angling in a lake all by himself. After a long while the float began to move. Now and then its tip touched the water. The angler was holding the rod tight in his hands, ready to pull it up, when a passerby stopped and said, 'Sir, can you tell me where Mr. Bannerji lives?' There was no reply from the angler, who was just on the point of pulling up the rod. Again and again the stranger said to him in a loud voice, 'Sir, can you tell me where Mr. Bannerji lives?' But the angler was unconscious of everything around him. His hands were trembling, his eyes fixed on the float. The stranger was annoyed and went on. When he had gone quite a way, the angler's float sank under water and with one pull of the rod he landed the fish. He wiped the sweat from his face with a towel and shouted after the stranger. 'Hey,' he said. 'Come here! Listen!' But the man would not turn his face. After much shouting, however, he came back and said to the angler, 'Why are you shouting at me?' 'What did you ask me about?' said the angler. The stranger said, 'I repeated the question so many times, and now you are asking me to repeat it once more!' The angler replied, 'At that time my float was about to sink; so I didn't hear a word of what you said.'"

That was so real you could touch it and see it. It had the Bengali poetry, and if it did not help much with the Infinite, at least it made you so curious about Mr. Bannerji, that you wondered about him for the rest of your life.

"And who was Mr. Bannerji?"

"Ah," said the Master. "He always wore a red turban. I don't

know why." And you would see the red turban for the rest of
your life, too.

The achievement of sanctity, however, was wearing for everyone.

The Master had become as inseparable from the Kali temple
as a child from its rag doll. Like most affectionate people of his
type, he was not above being a bully in order to be loved in
return. He had a horror of being touched, though he ran his
hands over others as eagerly as a man looking for something in
the dark. He did so like to become others.

The goddess Kali was wilier than most. Though he had no
trouble becoming her, he could never become all of her, there
was always more, *and she kept things from him.* Though she let
him in, she refused to give him her full attention. Her mind was
somewhere else. He did not like this. He was not accustomed to
being thwarted.

What she wanted, of course, was a child. Since that was what
he wanted her to have, he blinked and remained content. It was
curious about that blink of his. It was something he always did
just before swallowing, not food, but people, who were what he
really ate. He was now the chosen one. Since he had given in to
the goddess and consented to become her child, he was now free
to do as he pleased.

Unaware of these private treaties with Divinity, the Master's
brother summoned a Brahmin to instruct him, so he might qualify
for the priesthood, the better to send a little money home out of
his stipend.

The Master looked the Brahmin over with beady good humor,
hunched up his shoulders like a cat getting ready to pounce, and
at the first plummy praises of Immensity (the Brahmin had lips
like a camel), clapped his hand to his forehead, shouted, "I see
it all," and fell into a three-day trance. A better education had
been routed by a better mind, and never came back to tarnish
him again.

The next year the Master's brother died, perhaps of chagrin.
The Master had rather thought he would. Most people do. One
has only to wait.

The Master then became priest of the Kali temple, and, the
better to free himself of this world's snares, took to meditating

naked in a grove. One night, in a fit of despair, he picked up a sword and thought about killing himself. He was too excited to turn back. On the other hand, he had no real desire to kill himself. It was a quandary.

At long last Kali consented to appear. "Don't do it," she said. "The world needs you." And with a compassionate, understanding look, she folded him into her breast. He lost consciousness. It was at this time that he developed his theory of the ripe and of the green ego. Three days later, reviving, he said, "Mother," in a rather pleased if feeble tone, and consented to eat a few slices of ripened mango.

"She has allowed me," he told Hriday, "to come back. She says I must stay in this form for a while yet, for the benefit of humanity. Is there any shredded coconut?"

It was at this time that Hriday began to doubt, volubly, the sanity of the Master, who had also been caught feeding to the temple cat food meant for the Goddess. It was decided to marry him, for the sake of his health, to a five-year-old child.

"O Mother," he said. "I have taken refuge in Thee."

His health began to improve. He returned to the temple. An old woman turned up, dressed as a nun. She said he was not mad, but an incarnation of God. He was Baby Krishna, so she babied him.

"My son, everyone in this world is mad," she said. "Some are mad for money, some for creature comforts, some for fame, and you are mad for God. The other good things in this world will come later."

Even Mathur Babu was not ready to accept him as a living avatar. However he agreed to call in a council of experts. While the nun and the two experts talked things over, Baby Krishna, which is to say, the Master, sat on the porch, chewing spice from time to time, to sweeten his mouth, and spitting the pulp out on the ground.

Finally Vaishnavcharan, the elder of the two pundits, rose, cleared his throat, and said, with a thoughtful glance at Rani Rasmani, who was hovering, that all things considered, and here he looked round at the temple, that yes, the Master was undoubtedly that very rare thing, a Manifestation of God in Man.

"Ha," said the Master to Mathur, and looked boyish. "Just

fancy. He says so, too. Well, I am glad to learn that after all it is not a disease." For from time to time God gave him a head-ache.

Gauri, the second pundit, not to be outdone, said, "Is that all he has to say about you? Then he has said very little. I am fully convinced that you are that Mine of Spiritual Power."

"You have outbid Vaishnavcharan," said the Master. Gauri looked modest.

"The more I live the more I learn," said the Master, also look-ing modest.

He was launched.

The miracles, the disciples (some handsome), the female fol-lowers, the old woman who baked him a special kind of sweet-meat and liked to dandle him in her lap (he liked that too), came, as the nun had said, later. The Master sometimes spent so much time in a trance state, that it was necessary to beat him back into his body (that is, to beat the body like a soft gong, until he came back into it), in order to feed him. He became costive, and could suspend his bodily functions indefinitely.

He would die.

III

"It is all part of the pattern of a not unknown pathological type," said the doctor with Occidental training, a graduate of a western University, someone who had put superstition behind him, or seemed eager to believe he had. His manner was profes-sional, with brightly polished pointed patent leather shoes. He never went anywhere without them.

"Yes, of course," said Keshab Chandra Sen, no less contem-porary, and feeling out of place in his turban.

Together, from the stern of the paddlewheeler, they admired the meerschaum water.

Behind them, near the deckhouse, someone had lit a few lamps. The stench of kerosene discouraged the evening mosqui-toes, though not much.

A woman walked by, as though on eggshells, for she was one of the new emancipated women, and had to behave with a certain shocked circumspection. Though not particularly intelligent, she had the required thick horn-rimmed spectacles, and was too stolidly built to be graceful in her sari.

"We seldom looked on Sri Ramakrishna as a member of the male sex. We regarded him as one of us. We never felt any constraint before him. He was our best confidant," a woman said once more, afterwards, the Master then being dead at fifty-one, of cancer of the throat.

"And the wife? The child bride?" asked the westernized doctor, for it made him blush to see the same habits go on year after year. When no Occidentals were present, he blushed for himself.

"There was never anything between them. He calls her the Holy Mother. She has a shrine of her own at Jayrambati. . . ."

From the other end of the deck came the demanding quaver of the Master's voice.

"When I was a nun. . . ." He began to sing a song by Ramaprasad, in a high, quick, irritable, insistent voice. His eyes were on the stern. It was like being summoned by a snake.

"What does he do when he's a nun?" asked the doctor, who hoped one day to compile a small book of case histories, to be published, perhaps, abroad.

"He becomes one," said Keshab Chandra Sen. "It is quite remarkable. He can become . . ." and he looked at the jungle which covered here the many mouths of the Ganges, and which was impenetrable and much too green, "he can become anything." And here he gave the doctor not only an apologetic, but a challenging stare.

"But he's insane," said the doctor, with that small and unconvinced part of him that had been taken out and trained at University College Hospital, in cold London, a million miles away, not at all a healthy place, but they had conquered India, they must know something.

"Yes, of course," said Chandra Sen. "But what has that to do with it?"

For the Master was inhabited by something else, despite himself. No matter how much you congratulated yourself upon the dubieties of his history, you would never know enough to nullify that. And so. . . .

It was dusk now. At dusk the real world comes back into its

own. A bell rang, and as though in a panic, the steamer reversed its engines, and they were on their way downstream again.

The Master, whose hearing was acute, and who saw more than he was meant to, with a look of serene amusement, now began to tell the parable of the Doctor, the Widow, and the Sick Soul.

ELDON BRANDA was born in Port Arthur, Texas. After receiving a Master of Fine Arts degree in English from the University of Iowa in 1960, he lived in Ireland for two years. From 1963 to 1965 Mr. Branda taught English at the University of Texas in Austin and he is currently a research associate in the Department of Research in Texas History at the University of Texas. His stories have appeared in *Antioch Review, Texas Quarterly* and other magazines.

The Dark Days of Christmas

I

WHAT I CAN'T GET USED TO," said Billy Murphy, a little impatient, with getting the fire going in the ancient grate, "is that everything in Dublin is so old."

Billy lived in the flat below them. He was a student at Trinity College, and, like themselves, he was an American. What a good boy was Billy. Young and healthy, he still had time for them. Charming Billy. God love him.

"It's lovely the way you have with fires, Billy," said Annie McGovern. "Geraldine and I are no good at all."

Geraldine moved slightly away from her sister-in-law, for unobstructed warmth. "I love to watch a new fire burning," she said. "I've lit many in my time."

"It's all in using plenty of old coals to begin with," said Billy, pleased now that it was going well. "You can't build a new fire without the old ashes. But of course I cheat a little," he

"The Dark Days of Christmas" – Eldon Branda, *Texas Quarterly,* Copyright © 1966 by The University of Texas.

said, holding up a block of paraffin, "with ye olde instant fire-
lighter."

Geraldine chuckled, and Annie turned to her. "But you could
never start a fire without the paraffin, now could you, Geraldine?"

"We never had such things in Ireland when I was a girl. My
brother Thomas could start a roaring fire with only sticks and
paper."

"I can't imagine Thomas doing anything like that," said Annie,
"but in America, thank God, everything lights itself." She turned
to Billy. "It isn't as though my husband was really Irish. He was
only born here, God rest his soul."

Billy unstuck the new coals with a poker, spread them evenly
over the grate so new flames whooshed up the chimney. He
was afraid the ladies might begin to argue. "I hope this everlasting
rain will turn to snow, at least by Christmas," he said.

The ladies fell silent. Christmas. Children. Trim the tree, bake
the turkey, make mince pies.

"All the family was home in Texas last Christmas," said
Annie.

"The children . . ." said Geraldine, vaguely.

"They love their Auntie Gerald," Annie said to Billy. "And
the young ones, my son and daughter's younger children, they
still don't know, between Geraldine and me, who is their proper
grandmother."

Geraldine, forever unmarried, seemed to be wandering off.
"Jesus, Mary, and Joseph . . . Christmas is for children . . ."

Annie was looking into the fire. Her eyes washed the flames.

"Nonsense," said Billy Murphy. "You can have a real American Christmas in Dublin as well."

They looked at him. He was young, and he was there. He was
making things possible. Oh where will you be, Billy boy, Billy
boy, oh where will you be, charming Billy?

"We will bake a turkey," said Annie.

"And stuff it with oyster dressing," said Geraldine.

"Certainly," said Billy. Now he was committed. The room was
still cold, though his back was hot where he stood before the
fire. The whole country seemed hostile to him. He shivered.

"You ought to wear a sweater," said Annie.

"I'm roasting, really," he said. "But you'd think in a country with weather like this they wouldn't object to central heating."

"There's something cheery about an open fire," said Annie.

"Cheerier if there was some light and you could warm the whole room. How do you stand it?"

His sudden discomfort frightened them.

"It will be better after Christmas," said Annie. "The days get much longer."

"It's these dark days," said Geraldine.

"If you had it all to do over again," Billy said, "would you still come to Dublin?"

Neither of them looked up. It was like a children's game they had forgotten how to play. If you could be anything you wanted, what would you be? If you were lord of all the world, what would you do? If you . . . would you . . . Billy, dear Billy, keep the fire going, come to Christmas dinner, stay in Dublin.

The fire was settling down now to bright hot coals, and Billy placed a long piece of dry turf over them. The flames licked high.

"You do like it here, don't you, Billy?" said Annie McGovern.

"It's ever so nice when you get used to it," said Geraldine.

II

Annie McGovern had spent weeks secretly preparing their escape to Dublin from the oil-washed shore of Texas. She couldn't tell Geraldine because the nurses at Meadowlawn had a way of finding out everything. "Miss McGovern is doing fine, aren't you doing fine? just your lil' ol' self almost." Old self, *old* self, indeed. They no longer quarreled, wasn't that a sign Geraldine was better? Even Prunella, their colored girl, said it was not the same and was not right, taking Miss Geraldine off to that place. But Annie's children, and even the older grandchildren, said it was the only thing to do to eliminate the fusses.

They hadn't used to quarrel before Thomas died, or when the children were still at home, or even afterwards, when the grandchildren still came. The two of them had kept the large, empty house reasonably neat and seemed always busy baking and cooking, not to be caught without a thing in the house. Much food and effort were wasted. Annie's children agreed they needed someone to help them, someone to cook just what they needed, someone to watch over them. They had begun to quarrel when Prunella came to them.

What a good girl, Prunella. Dark-skinned, healthy, happy, she could do anything, everything. Just the way they would have done it themselves. Good Prunella. God love her. They followed her about the house, looking for chores to do.

"You know, Prunella, you're not so strong you can go on all day like that," Annie would say as she tried to help.

When Geraldine caught them together, Annie helping, she would go off to her room and wait for Prunella's quiet step, her soft knock, her wonderful voice. "Miss Geraldine, it sure would be nice if you could make a little tea now." Prunella, peacemaker. God love her.

Her patience with them was regal. She made little jobs for them, but she could not resist finishing them off. When they insisted she stop for tea or coffee she found herself between them, the prize of their competition. When Annie talked about her late husband, Geraldine carried Thomas further back to when they were children in Ireland. Prunella, with dark superstition, was amazed that Miss Geraldine came from that magical land, and Annie resented the association of the leprechaun and such foolishness with her Thomas. Their beloved husband and brother, never controversial in life, finally came between them.

On the occasional visits of the younger members of the family, Annie and Geraldine fell into alternate periods of silence, took them off in whispering huddles about subjects of seemingly no importance. Aunt Gerald's confidences seemed to have a strange ring of storytelling, mixing past with present.

But their usual day was confined to Prunella. They made her have coffee or tea almost every hour. Good Prunella. She did what she could. When one of them eclipsed the other, the darkened spirit turned to the telephone, to the absent family.

Anguished interruptions in the lives of the young. Something had to be done. When Aunt Geraldine ordered a second tele-

phone in the house and told the newsboy to leave two copies
of the daily paper, the family knew the time had come. They
sent her to Meadowlawn.

It was the last thing Annie had expected or wanted. She found
it difficult to talk about anything now. Except about Geraldine.
Dear Geraldine, her husband's only sister, why they had been
together practically all their lives. "It ain't right," Prunella would
say gloomily. "If she was mine, I'd take poor Miss Geraldine out
of that place in a minute."

All of the family was relieved. They didn't call it a rest home.
Annie's children encouraged her to visit Geraldine—Meadowlawn. Isn't it a lovely place, Mother? Of course you're still quite
able, yet.

It was the "yet" that terrified Annie McGovern.

"I was thinking," said Prunella one day, "how Miss Geraldine
would like it to go to Ireland again. Seems to me she was a
mighty happy child in that Ireland."

Thomas' Ireland! The Emerald Isle. The Island of Youth!
Good Prunella. God love her.

Annie went to the County Clerk's office. She was amazed at
how simple it was. Birth certificate, application, photograph,
immunization card.

She got permission to take Geraldine for a day's outing, and
they secretly took their immunization at the County Health
Clinic where no one knew them. Airmailed applications to
Washington, D.C.; passports returned. Air tickets to Houston,
to Chicago, jet tickets to Shannon—Dublin.

Prunella packed. "You want some warm things," she said. In
little over a month they were ready.

One fine morning Annie and Prunella picked up Geraldine for
another day's outing. "Out in that wild blue yonder," said Prunella,
laughing. Good, good, oh good Prunella.

The airport was a strange place to all of them. Suddenly Annie
and Geraldine didn't want to leave.

"You just take good care of each other in that old Ireland,"
said Prunella. "I can get me a job just about anywheres."

A voice over the loudspeaker was calling them—to Houston,
to Chicago. The ladies hesitated. To Ireland?

"You go ahead now," said Prunella.

And there they were, lifted into that wild blue yonder, as Prunella called it—God love her—off to the land of youth.

III

They stayed first near the center of Dublin, at a small hotel in Harcourt Street which they found cold and uncomfortable, then took a flat in the suburb of Dun Laoghaire because it was close to the sea and they thought it might be like their own Gulf of Mexico. But it was even colder there because they had to make their own fires, and neither of them was good at it. The most surprising thing about the whole adventure was that the children approved, scolding them only for their secret machinations. But it made a lovely story at home, their derring-do, and it was all very quaint and exciting to the younger generation.

Though their flat was furnished they went to the auctions on the Quays along the River Liffey, intending to bid on vases and candelabra, but they never succeeded in entering the competition. They told each other it was because they didn't understand the money. Who could tell if "two and six" means pounds, shillings, or pennies? They had no idea what things should cost unless they had time to compute them in dollars. They went to small, well-lit shops, carefully avoided antiques, and bought little figurines that looked curiously American.

With the ever-lengthening days of spring they took the city bus tours, scanning the crescent from the Hill of Howth to Dalkey. They viewed the city from the top of Nelson Pillar and could not imagine, from that height, just where it was they lived; for a moment it frightened them to be unlocatable.

They visited Dublin Castle, and its thirteenth-century antiquity seemed no more unusual than the Georgian buildings along Fitzwilliam and Merrion Squares. They sat in St. Stephen's Green near the pond, tore off pieces of fresh bread, and felt sorry for the seagulls because a sign told them only the swans and ducks could be fed. It was unfair, said Geraldine, to have such rules. But Annie supposed it was because the gulls could always take to the sea.

On Sundays they went to the zoo in Phoenix Park, stopping off first in the park to look at the residence of the American Ambassador. They understood that the homes of the President of Ireland and the Papal Nunciature were there too, but they didn't find them. They went in to the grounds of the zoo, where they watched the people looking at the animals.

They went one Saturday morning in June to St. Michan's Church, in the heart of old Dublin. Geraldine hadn't wanted to go, but Annie insisted. Below the church, there were vaults, so the guide said, that contained bodies which had lain for centuries without decomposing. Annie followed close behind the guide, taking Geraldine's hand; but when they entered the vault of the mummies it was Geraldine who went forward. The guide explained that there was something extraordinary about the air in the vaults which preserved the "Crusaders" from decay, and it was considered good luck to shake the hand of one of the heroic men. Geraldine placed her hand lightly on that of a withered Crusader and, holding it, she turned and smiled at Annie, who was backing away. "Oh you must, Annie, you must." With the guide assuring her that it meant good fortune, Annie stretched her fingers to touch the Crusader's. There. It was done. They moved out quickly, up, out of the earth, exhausted, into the open air.

It had begun to rain and the mid-day sky was dark. Neither of them was hungry, but they decided to have lunch at Jammet's in Nassau Street because they heard that Americans went there. They picked at their food, saying nothing, until Annie recalled with horror, "Geraldine, we didn't wash our hands!"

From that time they seldom left Dun Laoghaire. The seaside suburb was filled with English tourists, and when they walked along the bay each evening they pretended they were part of the holiday crowd. After all, they were not Dubliners. They reserved a table each evening in the dining room of the Castleross Hotel, where they could look at the sea, and were pleased when the summer crowd overflowed to their table. By September the days were noticeably shorter, the crowds thinner. Though their acquaintances were only nodding ones, they regretted the disappearances as though of old friends. They never quarreled now, and very often they held hands when they walked along the seawall.

Then, in October, came Billy Murphy, taking the flat below
them. What a good boy was Billy. He was the only American
they knew.

They could never do enough for him. He let them do everything. Each morning they made him come to a hot breakfast of
oatmeal, eggs and sausage, toast and coffee, while they themselves
ate sparingly. How they loved his eating, watching him eat,
feeling his sustentation at their table. They were sure that he
worked too hard at Trinity, and they would not leave the flat at
noontime until they were sure he would not come in for lunch,
then they would take their string bags to the shops in Dun
Laoghaire and buy all the things they thought Billy might like for
dinner.

Billy came in every evening cold and depressed from the everlasting wetness of Dublin, ready for the two ladies to look after
him. He had been deceived that first day in Ireland when the
sun gave a golden lie to the twinkling green shore. He seldom
lit the fire in his own flat because the ladies made him feel
necessary to theirs.

Then towards the end of November, Billy was held up in
Dublin occasionally, and Annie and Geraldine could not imagine
what was wrong. He explained there were things he had to do at
the University. They tried to keep up with his affairs at college,
but the academic world was lost on them.

In early December he stayed out later and more often, explaining at breakfast that there were some bright and useful lads
at Trinity who met at Neary's Pub off Grafton Street over a few
jars of stout, and that he got along famously with them.

They said he was beginning to speak like the Irish, and they
asked questions about his new friends in town and cautioned him
to be careful among foreigners. Nevertheless, they continued to
fix elaborate dinners every evening, on the chance that Billy
would be there. On those evenings when he didn't come Annie
and Geraldine were on the closest terms, and they calculated,
together, that the pubs closed at eleven, the last bus left O'Connell
Street at eleven-thirty (the last train was past), the bus took
thirty-five minutes to the stop a Lower Glenageary Road. At five
minutes past twelve o'clock they were listening for his heavy foot-

steps. Oh, where have you been, Billy boy, Billy boy? They were gratified, and they slept well, when they knew that Billy Murphy was home.

IV

The dark days of Christmas were full upon them. Why the light, observed Annie, was completely gone by four-thirty in the afternoon. It was never that way at home, said Geraldine. But neither of them really cared that the days were short. They could never be sure, anymore, when Billy was coming home. A young man has to get out sometime, said Annie. But I know he's not eating properly, said Geraldine.

Their one enthusiasm now was Christmas dinner. Billy had promised. They even talked about going in to Dublin for the Christmas shopping, but nothing came of it. Everything you could buy in the city you could find in Dun Laoghaire, they decided. They ordered the turkey five days ahead, then bought a few canned goods each day thereafter, saving the perishables until Christmas Eve. When the shopping list became too short they studied for long periods what they could add. Though they had already decided on the Aran Island sweater for Billy—one of those with the natural oils left in the wool—they put off buying it. Since there were so few things to buy, they didn't want to have it over with; but when Geraldine suggested that the shop might sell out, they rushed right down, desperate that their Billy's sweater might be gone.

On Christmas Eve they went to the shops and bought the perishable goods, striking the final items off their list. It was done. They lingered along Upper Georges Street, and when the Christmas lights came on they decided they had never seen anything so pretty, and they would not go home quite yet. They stopped to listen to a group of schoolboys caroling, St. Vincent de Paul's taking alms for the poor; they stared in the decorated shop windows, pretended there was something else they had to buy; finally they had a cup of tea at the empty Castleross. Then they walked slowly home to trim the tree and prepare the turkey, but all the

while they were listening for Billy. He had promised. They went
to bed, still wide awake.

At five minutes past twelve they heard him come in. Oh, where
have you been, Billy boy, Billy boy, Oh where have you been,
charming Billy?

V

"Shall we ask Billy to come in?" said Geraldine on Christmas
morning.

"Of course," said Annie. "The morning of our Lord's birth, and
poor Billy all alone."

"Breakfast will spoil the turkey," warned Geraldine. "He
wouldn't want to spoil it."

Billy came in, took only a cup of coffee. They gave him the
sweater—it was too small, swaddling him—and he had for each
of them a tiny Celtic cross, silver, with inlaid Connemara marble.
They both exclaimed over the fine workmanship, then quickly got
back to work.

"But you've done too much," he protested to the busy ladies.
"I should have taken you to the Castleross." He looked in the
roaster, smiled back at the fat turkey.

"Such nonsense," said Annie, elated, "to go out for Christmas
dinner!"

"They wouldn't have oyster dressing at the Castleross," said
Geraldine.

Everything was perfect. The ladies had a great sense of well
being with Billy maneuvering there between them. He moved
lightly about the kitchen pulling and stretching the heavy Aran
sweater in order to give his full body freedom, peeking into
things and having his hands slapped. Lovely, silly Billy. As he side-
stepped their charges from pantry to sink to stove, making wonderful little dance steps, they marveled at his lightness. Dear,
charming Billy. God love him.

"Everything is ready. Will you set Billy a chair?" said Annie to
Geraldine.

They sat down. Annie offered grace. Geraldine filled Billy's
plate; Annie saw to it that it was kept filled. His appetite was

enormous, and their own matched it in the pleasure of seeing him eat.

"A feast to end all feasts," said Billy.

The ladies McGovern beamed. Dear, charming Billy.

When Geraldine put on the coffee, Billy explained that he couldn't stay, that some people were expecting him, that there was a girl too that he had promised to meet. They didn't want him to go, but he said it was unavoidable. He lingered on for some time, telling about his plans, seeming reluctant to leave them. He told them he was going to join the Trinity Rugby Club soon, use the old muscles.

"I believe it's very rough," said Geraldine.

"But your studies . . ." said Annie.

"I lose a lot of time commuting from Dun Laoghaire to Dublin," said Billy. "The lads want me to take a flat with them close in to college."

Annie carefully laid all the used silver on one plate. Geraldine stacked the dishes.

"And . . . do you really like Dublin, after all?" asked Geraldine, quietly.

"Yes," said Billy, enthusiastically. "I want to see the whole country, take some hikes, maybe buy a bicycle. There's the Easter vacation coming."

While Geraldine was pouring the coffee, Annie took the mince-meat pie from the sideboard. "And . . . will you be moving in to town?"

"The lads are expecting me."

Annie cut the pie.

"All this," said Billy, "and then you bake a mincemeat pie."

"It was no trouble," said Geraldine.

"Almost no time at all—" said Annie.

Christmas had come and gone, quick as a cat can wink its eye.

Billy helped them with the dishes and then went in to Dublin. He had made a lovely fire for them in the sitting room, and now they sat watching it. From time to time they added a bit of turf, but they could never keep it going the way Billy did.

"It was a lovely dinner," said Annie. "I think Billy enjoyed it."

"He has a marvelous appetite," said Geraldine.

"I wonder, could he be serious about this girl."

"He's very young," said Geraldine.

They went over Billy's plans. Now that Christmas was over and the days would be ever lengthening, they could see him taking the walk to Dalkey on the footpath along the railroad tracks, a bicycle trip through the Wicklow Mountains, a hitch-hiking tour in the west of Ireland. He had such marvelous strength.

By four-thirty in the afternoon it was as dark as it would get, and the ladies continued by the slow burning fire.

"Funny how you get used to the darkening days," said Geraldine.

"Yes, it's hard to imagine that starting now the days will get longer."

Outside, from the direction of Dublin bay, they could hear the fog horns. They knew, without looking out, that it had begun to rain again.

"Shall I make tea?" asked Geraldine.

"I would love some tea." Then, sitting alone, Annie could see the ocean rising by the minute with all that rain. She saw the distant Texas shore about to be inundated, lost forever, and she heard the mournful horn.

> Do not think you can escape them
> From night 'til early in the morn.
> The eyes of Texas are upon you
> 'Til Gabriel blows his horn.

"You look cold," said Geraldine, coming in with the tea things. "Will I build up the fire?"

"No, I don't think so. It's late."

"Yes, it hardly seems worth it."

They sat side by side in the darkness with only a flicker of light on them, not speaking, hardly daring to let cup touch saucer. Clink! shattering. Silence invited them.

"Do you think we might go home?" asked Geraldine.

"I think we might just as well," said Annie.

They took the tea things to the kitchen, then went in to the bedroom where they got into their night clothes and began to make plans. It was simple. All was settled, and they were both very tired.

"Do you think Billy will be very disappointed?" asked Geraldine.

"Well now, Billy is old enough to take care of himself," said Annie.

He was such a dear boy, they agreed as they got into bed. Good Billy. God love him. But this dark Christmas night they did not wait up for Billy Murphy. Except for Annie's fleeting glimpse of seagulls high over the sea, they did not even dream.

JOHN UPDIKE has published three volumes of short stories, two of poetry, and one of essays; and his fifth novel, *Couples* is to be published this spring. Four of his stories have been included in earlier O. Henry Prize Story collections; "The Bulgarian Poetess" was awarded First Prize in 1966. Born in Shillington, Pennsylvania in 1932, Mr. Updike lives in Ipswich, Massachusetts with his wife and four children.

Your Lover Just Called

THE TELEPHONE RANG, and Richard Maple, who had stayed home from work this Friday because of a cold, answered it: "Hello?" The person at the other end of the line hung up. Richard went into the bedroom, where Joan was making the bed, and said, "Your lover just called."

"What did he say?"

"Nothing. He hung up. He was amazed to find me home."

"Maybe it was *your* lover."

He knew, through the phlegm clouding his head, that there was something wrong with this, and found it. "If it was *my* lover," he said, "why would she hang up, since I answered?"

Joan shook the sheet so it made a clapping noise like muted thunder. "Maybe she doesn't love you anymore."

"This is a ridiculous conversation."

"You started it."

"Well, what would you think, if you answered the phone on a weekday and the person hung up? He clearly expected you to be home alone."

"Well, if you'll go to the store for cigarettes I'll call him back and explain what happened."

"Your Lover Just Called" – John Updike, *Harper's Magazine,* Copyright © 1967 by Harper's Magazine, Inc.

"You think I'll think you're kidding but I know that's really what *would* happen."

"Oh, come on, Dick. Who would it be? Freddie Vetter?"

"Or Harry Saxon. Or somebody I don't know at all. Some old college friend who's moved to New England. Or maybe the milkman. I can hear you and him talking while I'm shaving sometimes."

"We're surrounded by hungry children. He's fifty years old and has hair coming out of his ears."

"Like your father. You're not averse to older men. There was that Chaucer section man when we first met. Anyway, you've been acting awfully happy lately. There's a little smile comes into your face when you're doing the housework. See, there it is!"

"I'm smiling," Joan said, "because you're so absurd. I have no lover. I have nowhere to put him. My days are consumed by devotion to the needs of my husband and his many children."

"Oh, so I'm the one who made you have all the children? While you were hankering after a career in fashion or in the exciting world of business. Aeronautics, perhaps. You could have been the first woman to design a nose cone. Or to crack the wheat futures cycle. Joan Maple, girl agronomist. Joan Maple, lady geopolitician. But for that fornicating brute she mistakenly married, this clear-eyed female citizen of our ever-needful republic—"

"Dick, have you taken your temperature? I haven't heard you rave like this for years."

"I haven't been betrayed like this for years. I hated that *click*. That nasty little I-know-your-wife-better-than-you-do *click*."

"It was some child. If we're going to have Mack for dinner tonight, you better convalesce now."

"It *is* Mack, isn't it? That son of a bitch. The divorce isn't even finalized and he's calling my wife on the phone. And then proposes to gorge himself at my groaning board."

"I'll be groaning myself. You're giving me a headache."

"Sure. First I foist off four children on you in my mad desire for progeny, then I give you a menstrual headache."

"Get into bed and I'll bring you orange juice and toast cut into strips the way your mother used to make it."

"You're lovely."

As he was settling himself under the blankets, the phone rang again, and Joan answered it in the upstairs hall. "Yes . . . no . . . no . . . good," she said, and hung up.

"Who was it?" he called.

"Somebody wanting to sell us the *World Book Encyclopedia*," she called back.

"A very likely story," he said, with self-pleasing irony, leaning back onto the pillows confident that he was being unjust, that there was no lover.

Mack Dennis was a homely, agreeable, sheepish man their age, whose wife, Eleanor, was in Wyoming suing for divorce. He spoke of her with a cloying tenderness, as if of a favorite daughter away for the first time at camp, or as a departed angel nevertheless keeping in close electronic touch with the scorned earth. "She says they've had some wonderful thunderstorms. The children go horseback riding every morning, and they play Pounce at night and are in bed by ten. Everybody's health has never been better. Ellie's asthma has cleared up and she thinks now she must have been allergic to *me*."

"You should have cut all your hair off and dressed in cellophane," Richard told him.

Joan asked him, "And how's *your* health? Are you feeding yourself enough? Mack, you look thin."

"The nights I don't stay in Boston," Mack said, tapping himself all over for a pack of cigarettes, "I've taken to eating at the motel on Route 33. It's the best food in town now, and you can watch the kids in the swimming pool." He studied his empty upturned hands as if they had recently held a surprise. He missed his own kids, was perhaps the surprise.

"I'm out of cigarettes too," Joan said.

"I'll go get some," Richard said.

"And a thing of Bitter Lemon at the liquor store."

"I'll make a pitcher of martinis," Mack said. "Doesn't it feel great, to have martini weather again?"

It was that season which is late summer in the days and early fall at night. Evening descended on the downtown, lifting the neon tubing into brilliance, as Richard ran his errand; his sore throat felt folded within him like a secret, and there was some-

thing reckless and gay in his being up and out at all after spending
the afternoon in bed. Home, he parked by his back fence and
walked down through a lawn loud with fallen leaves, though the
trees overhead were still massy. The lit windows of his house
looked golden and idyllic; the children's rooms above (the face
of Judith, his bigger daughter, drifted preoccupied across a slice
of her wallpaper, and her pink square hand reached to adjust a
doll on a shelf) and the kitchen below. In the kitchen windows,
whose tone was fluorescent, a silent tableau was being enacted.
Mack was holding a martini shaker and pouring it into a vessel,
eclipsed by an element of window sash, that Joan was offering
with a long white arm. Head tilted winningly, she was talking
with the slightly pushed-forward mouth that Richard recognized
as peculiar to her while looking into mirrors, conversing with her
elders, or otherwise seeking to display herself to advantage.
Whatever she was saying made Mack laugh, so that his pouring
(the silver shaker head glinted, a drop of greenish liquid spilled)
was unsteady. He set the shaker down and displayed his hands,
the same hands from which a little while ago a surprise had
seemed to escape, at his sides, shoulder-high. Joan moved toward
him, still holding her glass, and the back of her head, done up taut
and oval in a bun, with blonde down trailing at the nape of her
neck, eclipsed all of Mack's face but his eyes, which closed. They
were kissing. Joan's head tilted one way and Mack's another to
make their mouths meet tighter. The graceful line of her shoulders
was carried outward by the line of the arm holding her glass
safe in the air. The other arm was around his neck. Behind them
an open cabinet door revealed a paralyzed row of erect paper
boxes whose lettering Richard could not read but whose coloring
advertised their contents—Cheerios, Wheat Honeys, Onion Thins.
Joan backed off and ran her index finger down the length of
Mack's necktie (a summer tartan) ending with a jab in the
vicinity of his navel that might have expressed a rebuke or a regret. His face, pale and lumpy in the harsh vertical light, looked
mildly humorous but intent, and moved forward, toward hers,
an inch or two. The scene had the fascinating slow motion of
action underwater, mixed with the insane silent suddenness of a
television montage glimpsed from the street. Judith came to the
window upstairs, not noting her father standing in the massy

shadow of the tree, and, wearing a nightie of lemon gauze, innocently scratched her armpit while studying a moth beating on her screen; and this too gave Richard a momentous sense, crowding his heart, of having been brought by the mute act of witnessing perilously close—like a child sitting alone at the movies—to the hidden machinations of things. In another kitchen window a neglected teakettle began to plume and to fog the panes with steam. Joan was talking again; her forward-thrust lips seemed to be throwing rapid little bridges across a narrowing gap. Mack paused, shrugged; his face puckered as if he were speaking French. Joan's head snapped back with laughter and triumphantly she threw her free arm wide and was in his embrace again. His hand, spread starlike on the small of her back, went lower to what, out of sight behind the edge of formica counter, would be her bottom.

Richard scuffled loudly down the cement steps and kicked the kitchen door open, giving them time to break apart before he entered. From the far end of the kitchen, smaller than children, they looked at him with blurred, sheepish expressions. Joan turned off the steaming kettle and Mack shambled forward to pay for the cigarettes. After the third round of martinis, the constraints loosened and Richard said, taking pleasure in the plaintive huskiness of his voice, "Imagine my discomfort. Sick as I am, I go out into this bitter night to get my wife and my guest some cigarettes, so they can pollute the air and aggravate my already grievous bronchial condition, and coming down through the back yard, what do I see? The two of them doing the Kama Sutra in my own kitchen. It was like seeing a blue movie and knowing the people in it."

"Where do you see blue movies nowadays?" Joan asked.

"Tush, Dick," Mack said sheepishly, rubbing his thighs with a brisk ironing motion. "A mere fraternal kiss. A brotherly hug. A disinterested tribute to your wife's charm."

"Really, Dick," Joan said. "I think it's shockingly sneaky of you to be standing around spying into your own windows."

"Standing around! I was transfixed with horror. It was a real trauma. My first primal scene." A profound happiness was stretching him from within; the reach of his tongue and wit felt immense, and the other two seemed dolls, homunculi, in his playful grasp.

"We were hardly doing anything," Joan said, lifting her head as if to rise above it all, the lovely line of her jaw defined by tension, her lips stung by a pout.

"Oh, I'm sure, by your standards, you had hardly begun. You'd hardly sampled the possible wealth of coital positions. Did you think I'd never return? Have you poisoned my drink and I'm too vigorous to die, like Rasputin?"

"Dick," Mack said, "Joan loves you. And if I love any man, it's you. Joan and I had this out years ago, and decided to be merely friends."

"Don't go Irish on me, Mack Dennis. 'If I love any mon, 'tis thee.' Don't give me a thought, laddie. Just think of poor Eleanor out there, sweating out your divorce, bouncing up and down on those horses day after day, playing Pounce till she's black and blue—"

"Let's eat," Joan said. "You've made me so nervous I've probably overdone the roast beef. Really, Dick, I don't think you can excuse yourself by trying to make it funny."

Next day, the Maples awoke soured and dazed by hangovers; Mack had stayed until two, to make sure there were no hard feelings. Joan usually played ladies' tennis Saturday mornings, while Richard amused the children; now, dressed in white shorts and sneakers, she delayed at home in order to quarrel. "It's desperate of you," she told Richard, "to try to make something of Mack and me. What are you trying to cover up?"

"My dear Mrs. Maple, I *saw*," he said, "I *saw* through my own windows you doing a very credible impersonation of a female spider having her abdomen tickled. Where did you learn to flirt your head like that? It was better than finger puppets."

"Mack always kisses me in the kitchen. It's a habit, it means nothing. You know for yourself how in love with Eleanor he is."

"So much he's divorcing her. His devotion verges on the quixotic."

"The divorce is her idea, you know that. He's a lost soul. I feel sorry for him."

"Yes, I saw that you do. You were like the Red Cross at Verdun."

"What I'd like to know is, why are you so pleased?"

"Pleased? I'm annihilated."

"You're delighted. Look at your smile in the mirror."

"You're so incredibly unapologetic, I guess I think you must be being ironical."

The telephone rang. Joan picked it up and said, "Hello," and Richard heard the click across the room. Joan replaced the receiver and said to him, "So. She thought I'd be playing tennis by now."

"Who's she?"

"You tell me. Your lover. Your loveress."

"It was clearly yours, and something in your voice warned him off."

"Go to her!" Joan suddenly cried, with a burst of the same defiant energy that made her, on other hangover mornings, rush through a mountain of housework. "Go to her like a man and stop trying to maneuver me into something I don't understand! I have no lover! I let Mack kiss me because he's lonely and drunk! Stop trying to make me more interesting than I am! All I am is a beat-up housewife who wants to go play tennis with some other tired ladies!"

Mutely Richard fetched from their sports closet her tennis racket, which had recently been restrung with gut. Carrying it in his mouth like a dog retrieving a stick, he laid it at the toe of her sneaker. Richard Jr., their older son, a wiry nine-year-old obsessed by the accumulation of Batman cards, came into the living room, witnessed this pantomime, and laughed to hide his fright. "Dad, can I have my nickel for emptying the waste baskets?"

"Mommy's going to go out to play, Dickie," Richard said. "Let's all go to the five-and-ten and buy a Batmobile."

"Yippee," the small boy said limply, glancing wide-eyed from one of his parents to the other, as if the space between them had gone treacherous.

Richard took the children to the five-and-ten, to the playground, and to a hamburger stand for lunch. These blameless activities transmuted the residues of alcohol and phlegm into a woolly fatigue as pure as the sleep of infants. Obligingly he nodded while his son described a boundless plot: ". . . and then, see Dad, the Penguin had an umbrella smoke came out of, it was neat, and there were these two other guys with funny masks in the bank, filling it with water. I don't know why, to make it bust or something, and Robin was climbing up these slippery stacks of like half-dollars to get away from the water, and then, see Dad . . ."

Back home, the children dispersed into the neighborhood on the same mysterious tide that on other days packed their yard with unfamiliar urchins. Joan returned from tennis glazed with sweat, her ankles coated with dust. Her body was swimming in the rose afterglow of exertion. He suggested that they take a nap.

"Just a nap," she warned.

"Of course," he said. "I met my mistress at the playground and we satisfied each other on the jungle gym."

"Maureen and I beat Alice and Judy. It can't be any of those three, they were waiting for me half an hour."

In bed, the shades strangely drawn against the bright afternoon, a glass of stale water standing bubbled with secret light, he asked her, "You think I want to make you more interesting than you are?"

"Of course. You're bored. You left me and Mack alone deliberately. It was very uncharacteristic of you, to go out with a cold."

"It's sad, to think of you without a lover."

"I'm sorry."

"You're pretty interesting anyway. Here, and here, and here."

"I said really a nap."

In the upstairs hall, on the other side of the closed bedroom door, the telephone rang. After four peals—icy spears hurled from afar—the ringing stopped, unanswered. There was a puzzled pause. Then a tentative, questioning *pring,* as if someone in passing had bumped the table, followed by a determined series, strides of sound, imperative and plaintive, that did not stop until twelve had been counted; then the lover hung up.

PAUL TYNER was born in Indianapolis, grew up "in and around Washington, D.C." and studied mathematics at the University of Illinois. He is married and has two sons. His first novel, *Shoot It,* is being published this spring. Mr. Tyner is currently working on another novel, *The Family Album.* This is his first published story.

How You Play the Game

HERBY walked through the park and almost decided to stop and sit down for a few minutes before he went to the poolroom, but he kept on going, because he might be able to win a little money before he had to go to work. It was early in the afternoon, and hardly anyone in the park recognized him out of his uniform. They all nodded and smiled at him when he walked his beat, but they were just nodding and smiling at the uniform, the badge, and maybe the gun, too. That was probably it. The gun. He remembered an old immigrant he met one time when he was flat-footing it through the park without his gun, because he was on probation for the payoffs they found out about. The old man had asked him, "How you goin' to shoot anybody widdout a gun, hey?" and Herby had just smiled and said that he hadn't shot anybody up yet and probably never would have to. A *"Schutz-mann,"* the old man called him—the man that does the shooting.

So Herby kept on walking through the park and didn't smile or nod at anybody, because they didn't smile or nod at him. He crossed the street against the light and saw Sal's big Olds Holiday parked in front of the poolroom. Herby remembered the night Sal won it off Baltimore Whitey. Baltimore had heard about Sal—had

"How You Play the Game" – Paul Tyner, *The New Yorker,* Copyright © 1967 by Paul Tyner. From *Shoot It* by Paul Tyner. Reprinted by permission of Atlantic-Little, Brown and Company. Originally appeared in *The New Yorker.*

heard he carried a good stick, and wanted to find out if it was true. He found out. He lost everything that night—the night everybody knew Sal was the best.

Sal was about to shoot as Herby walked into the poolroom. Herby closed the door softly, nodded at Shorty, who was polishing the Coke machine, and sat down in front of the big window that looked out on the street. Sal was playing nine-ball with Jerry, and it looked as though Sal hadn't given up too many games to Jerry. A neat row of twelve wooden beads had been pushed across the wire. Herby guessed they were worth five apiece. Jerry wouldn't play Sal unless Sal spotted him the eight, and he still ended up losing every time.

Herby wished Sal would spot him the eight sometime. He would tear Sal up.

"Sal's losin' his goddam eye, Shorty," said Jerry in a mock whisper, loudly enough for Sal to hear him.

Sal never said much, even when Jerry was yelling at him. He was used to the tactics of punks like Jerry. The only time anybody could remember Sal losing his temper was about ten years ago, when Sal was just out of the Navy. Roger Woodward and Peanuts were the best then, and Sal beat Roger the second time he played him. Roger was getting old and losing his eye. Right after Sal beat Roger, somebody called Peanuts to tell him about Sal. Peanuts hustled down and offered to play banks with Sal for ten a ball, and Sal said O.K. Peanuts was the best banks player on the East Coast. He offered to spot Sal three balls to twenty-five, but Sal said it was O.K., he didn't need any spot. Sal beat Peanuts in about half an hour, twenty-five to seventeen. Peanuts gave him the money—eighty bucks—and everybody got a glimpse of the roll he carried. There must have been about a thousand in there. Peanuts suggested a little nine-ball, and Sal nodded. Sal really started wailing on him and was five hundred ahead when Peanuts really started to get rattled. He would make little mistakes, the kind that told you it was more than an off-day for him. He'd put just a little too much draw, or maybe take a dangerous shot at the nine when anybody half-decent could have run the table. Finally Peanuts decided it was time to hang it up, and Sal collected all but a hundred of that roll and put his stick away. He didn't even have his own stick at the time. When Sal got outside, Peanuts and two of his big buddies were waiting for him. Sal walked right past them and cut into the alley. He probably didn't even think they were going to yoke him. They followed him into the alley, and Peanuts pulled a knife and told him to hand over the roll. Sal turned around, and the way the story goes, when he saw the knife he just kind of exploded. Peanuts was pretty good with a knife and the two guys were big, but they never expected him to try anything. Sal just let out a roar when he saw the knife and dived on Peanuts. The knife went through Sal's forearm, but he didn't even know he was cut until later. When the cops came by they found Sal kicking Peanuts and his two buddies all over the alley, and Peanuts was already dead. The cops managed to quiet Sal down, and he had to go to court for murder, but the case was dismissed.

Herby watched Sal run the balls off the table. Damn, to shoot like that.

"Hey, Herby, Sal's losing his eye," Jerry said as Sal hung up the eight near the corner pocket, and laughed. Sal had to let Jerry win once in a while or Jerry wouldn't play him.

"Eight ball in the corner hole!" said Jerry. He chalked his cue and scrutinized the table as though he were about to make an almost impossible shot. He leaned over the table to pick off the eight. He shot too hard and nearly scratched in the side, but the eight fell. He yelled *"Rack!"* and shoved a bead across the wire, away from Sal's winnings. Then he said, "Hey, Sal, you losing your eye?"

Sal didn't say anything but racked the balls professionally, dropping them into the triangle, cradling them in the front crotch of wood, and swishing them neatly into place, then he deftly removed the rack and took his stick off the table.

Jerry broke the balls. "Fall, you bastards!" The eight went two rails up and down and was kissed into the corner pocket by the deuce. *"Rack!"* shouted Jerry. "Rack 'em up, Sal. That last rack was real nice. How about another one like it?" Jerry shoved another bead over.

"I ain't paying for the eight on the break."

"The *hell* you say. Rack 'em up, Sal!" Jerry shoved the rest of the balls down the table toward Sal.

"You know the rules I play. I don't pay for the eight on the break."

"Well Gee-zuzz Crice. O.K., Sal. O.K. If that's the way you wanna play. Just tell me about it next time. I know you're losin' your eye, but that don't mean you gotta make up the rules as you go along." Jerry shoved the bead back.

Sal racked the balls without speaking.

The door opened, and Mr. Clay hobbled in on his stiff leg. He nodded at Shorty, Sal, and Herby, and sat down next to Shorty by the cash register, thrusting his stiff leg out in front of him as he collasped in the chair. Then he clenched his old pipe deep in his mouth and puffed.

Herby had never liked playing with Mr. Clay. Mr. Clay took too long to get off a shot. His eye was bad, and he always warmed his stroke for half a minute before he finally jabbed at the cue. He whistled whenever he put his pipe down or knocked it out on the floor or packed it. And the only tune he ever whistled was "Make Believe," over and over. But Mr. Clay was still a pretty good one-pocket player, and it wasn't so long ago that he could beat Sal, although Mr. Clay never gambled. Herby would just as soon have Jerry yelling at him as have Mr. Clay whistling and taking so long with his goddam shots. Mr. Clay had once been one of the best in the country, and he still got off a good shot now and then. You didn't need good position for one-pocket, but you needed one hell of an eye to make up for it. Position controlled the game. If you could shoot good leave every time, you didn't need a great eye for the hard shots, because there wouldn't be a lot of them. You made the shots easy, and then you picked them off. That was what had happened to Mr. Clay. He had had a good eye but didn't know enough about shape. And once his eye started to give, there he was. Nothing.

Herby looked up and saw Sal running the table now—pow, pow, pow, just like ducks. It looked as though he was completely detached from the game, as though there was nothing there but the body, the machine, making shots and missing once in a while. He probably never felt the thrill of winning or the disappointment of losing.

Jerry was fidgeting nervously. He chalked his cue again and

again as Sal methodically put the balls in the pockets, getting just the right position each time for the next shot.

Sal banked the eight into the side for good shape on the nine and chalked his cue. The nine was the game.

The nine was something special. You could make them all but the nine and you'd still lose if you missed it. To Sal, though, the nine was just the last ball on the table, the ball that needed to go in the hole and leave nothing on the green skin but the cue. A situation that needed correcting.

Sal leaned over to drop the nine and was about to shoot when BBBBBBBRRRRRRRR AAAAAAAAAAAAA TTTTTT-TTTTTTT GGGGGGGG—Jerry had stuck his stick in the fan. Sal looked up from his shot for just a moment before he stroked the cue dead into the nine, making the nine roll neatly down the rail and into the corner hole.

Jerry was laughing so hard he nearly fell over on the table he was leaning on. Sal walked past him and put his cue away, and then he came back and stepped in front of Jerry and said evenly, "If you ever do that again when I'm shooting, I'll cut your heart out." And then Sal walked over and put a dime in the Coke machine.

"Just like my old man," said Jerry, his voice a little high-pitched. "Can't take a joke." He lit a cigarette and inhaled deeply.

Sal took the bottle from the cradle in the machine and snapped it open, then raised it to his lips without speaking. He was looking straight at Jerry.

Shorty stood up and walked over to examine the fan. "You still living with your folks, Jerry?" He said it casually, fingering the switch on the fan.

Sal finished his Coke and set the bottle in the rack next to the machine. "Give the boy a chance, Shorty. He can't go out into the cold world all by himself. The boy's only twenty-nine years old. You can't expect the lad to support himself."

"He can't be twenty-nine already, Sal. I heard him say just last week he was only eighteen, when Mike was going to bust him one," said Shorty, still ostensibly engrossed in the fan. Mr. Clay had laboriously raised himself from his chair and hobbled over to join him. They looked like two old women observing the first flower of spring.

"Hell," said Jerry. "Don't take it out on me because you're getting so old and losing your eye. You're the luckiest son of a bitch I ever saw in this poolroom. Your luck's gonna change one of these days, and I wanna be around to get my money back when it does."

"You ain't given me any yet."

Jerry pulled his wallet out and tossed it on the table. "I only got five bucks, Sal. Honest. Take a look."

Sal opened the wallet and looked in it. "Four."

"Oh yeah, I bought some butts."

"What happened to all that money you won this summer when you got hot?" Shorty asked.

"I heard he won over a thousand in one week this summer, when he got hot, not to mention the barbershop he won," Mr. Clay said.

"I lost it all. Honest," said Jerry, looking at Sal.

"You owe me thirty-five," said Sal.

"How about next week, Sal? We can play it off."

"Next week, hell. You give me the same story every time we play."

"I'd play you tomorrow, but I gotta get my wife a present."

"You ain't married."

"I got married last week, Sal. Honest. Listen, I'll tell you what." Jerry produced a quarter from his pocket and set it on his fist. "We'll toss for it, Sal. Double or nothing. You call it. Seventy bucks or nothing. Call it."

"O.K., kid. Heads."

Jerry looked at Shorty and Mr. Clay, who were watching, then at Herby, then back at Sal. He smiled at Sal. "The man says heads. How about tails, Sal—you think it might be tails instead? I'll take heads if you want, Sal. It ain't too late yet. I still haven't flipped it. You sure you want heads, now. You're getting so goddam blind you probably won't even see what it is. Hey, Herby, you want to place a side bet?"

"No."

"C'mon, Herby. Just because you're a cop don't mean you can't gamble. Don't be chicken. Sal ain't chicken, are you, Sal? Hell no, Sal ain't no chicken. Last chance, Herby, you want to get in on it? C'mon, we'll let you in for five. O.K., Sal? Sure, it's

O.K. with Sal. He don't care. O.K. Herby? Five bucks? No? O.K., Herby. You could bet five either way, then you wouldn't lose. You want to do that? Give your money to Shorty. Five on me and five on Sal. You can't lose, Herby. . . . Still don't want to do it? Christ, you wouldn't bet on the rain being wet, would you, Herby. O.K., everybody ready? Here we go."

He flipped it with a grandiose swing of his whole arm. The quarter landed flat on the table without bouncing or rolling.

Sal didn't move from his spot.

Jerry leaned over, obviously enjoying the suspense he had effected.

"Tails. See you." He picked up the shiny disc and replaced it in his pocket, walking to the door. "Better luck next time, Sal."

Sal unscrewed his cue and put it in the case of Spanish leather.

"Well," said Shorty, "I don't think he woulda paid you anyway, Sal. In fact, he coulda been lyin' just then, but I doubt it. I don't think he's got the guts to lie to you."

Herby lit a cigarette. "He doesn't have any guts at all. That's why he can lie so much. But I don't think he was lying then."

"He wasn't lying. I can tell when he's lying," said Mr. Clay.

"Well," said Shorty, "he mighta been lyin', though. You never can tell about Jerry. He's crazy sometimes. Ever since I first seen him come in here I've thought he was a little crazy. The way he stuck his cue in the fan. I never even heard of anybody doin' anything like that. There used to be a hustler named Kokomo Joe who'd do some pretty crazy things—that's what kept him out of the tournaments. He used to run all around the table yelling some of the dirtiest language I ever heard at whoever he was playing. It got so nobody'd play him. But he did it to win. I don't think he got no thrill or nothing out of it, like Jerry stickin' his cue in the fan. Jesus Christ, I never heard of anything like that. And Christ, he lies all the time, even about little things— about what he had for lunch or something. You can't tell about a guy like that. You never know what the son of a bitch is goin' to do next. I'd like to keep the bastard out of here, but what are you goin' to do about a guy like that. Why hell, he'd probably throw a goddam rock through the window some night. . . ."

"He was lying. I saw the quarter. It was heads," Sal said.

"It was? Why didn't you do anything about it?" Herby asked.

"I got my reasons."

"Well," said Shorty, "I thought the bastard was lyin'. Crazy bastard."

Sal sat down and began to read the paper, and Shorty dusted off the back tables. Mr. Clay had got his old cue stick out of the closet and was screwing it together. It was a nice stick, but a little too heavy for pool and also a little warped. When Mr. Clay held it he always made sure that the bend was going the right way.

Herby knew that Mr. Clay was going to come over and ask him if he wanted to play some Dudley with him. Dudley was Mr. Clay's favorite game next to one-pocket, and he had invented it himself. Herby did not like playing any kind of pool with Mr. Clay, especially Dudley. Mr. Clay changed the rules from one week to the next, and he always enjoyed explaining the new rules before the game. He would add impossible shots, and give them a value of fifty or a hundred points. Every third shot had to be impossible, and when Herby's turn to shoot an impossible shot came up, Mr. Clay would very slowly and deliberately stroke his ball into a corner, and then step back from the table and fold his arms, maybe with one hand on the pipe wedged into his jaw and with his chin down on his chest, looking like an old hawk up on a crag somewhere. Herby would disgustedly shoot as hard as he could, and Mr. Clay would stand there and watch until all the balls had stopped, and then he would hobble over and take an endless thirty seconds to get his shot off.

"Hey, Sal," Herby said, "you want to shoot some nine-ball?"

"O.K." Sal folded the newspaper and set it on the chair.

"Spot me the eight?"

"I don't care. O.K."

Herby went to the closet and pulled out his new cue. It was a beauty. It cost him fifty, but that was all he could afford since the Force started keeping an eye on him. It was almost as good as Sal's, but Sal's case was really fine hand-tooled Spanish leather. Sal didn't talk about it, but Herby took it out one time when Sal had gone home and looked it over. It was really nice.

Herby screwed his cue together and then walked over to the bench where Shorty kept the steel wool and talcum powder. He rubbed the steel wool a few times over the shank of the stick, watching the slight film of sweat-pasted dirt come off, to show the good clean wood underneath. Then he shook a little talcum powder into the palm of his hand and rubbed it over the shank, giving it a cool smoothness. He was careful not to put too much talcum powder in his hand, because later on it would cake up and make the stick gummy. He walked up to the front table. Sal had got his cue out and was racking the balls.

Herby pulled a quarter from his pocket and flipped it.

"Heads," said Sal.

It was heads. Sal broke the balls and the nine went in. Sal pushed a bead over and Herby racked. Sal broke and ran out. Sal pushed a bead over and Herby racked. Sal broke and ran out again, then pushed another bead over. Herby racked. Sal broke and the nine fell. He pushed another bead over and Herby racked.

Four games. Five dollars a game. Twenty dollars and he hadn't shot yet. A couple of high-school kids had wandered in and were watching Sal worshipfully, not daring to speak while he shot, not even whispering, just nodding reverently as the balls dropped —plop, plop, plop. When they finally got tired of watching Sal, they would listen to Shorty's stories.

The kids sat down next to Mr. Clay, whom they regarded as a kind of silent wizard, an omniscient patron saint of pool. They watched his reactions to the game with respect. When Mr. Clay nodded after a shot had been made, they knew it was a good shot. When Mr. Clay tilted his head back a little and puffed languidly, they knew that they, too, would have to think that shot over. And when Mr. Clay knitted his brow and exhaled through his pipe, they knew that the shot was not good.

And all this time Shorty would be telling the pool stories—the one about the hustler who came in one rainy night and lit up four cigars, setting one at each corner of the table so that he wouldn't have to walk around the table to take a drag; the one about One-Arm, who could run fifty balls at straight without using the crutch; the one about Kokomo Joe; the one about Hat, who was so called because he never took it off, until one night and everybody saw he kept a twenty-two there; the one about Crazy Johnny, who couldn't shoot a decent game unless he wore gloves; the one about Peanuts and Sal; the one about Raincoat, who wore the bottom halves of his trousers held up by rubber bands around the knees. And now Herby could hear him telling them the new one about how Jerry shoved his stick in the fan, and what Sal said. . . .

"Your shot, kid," said Sal.

Sal had missed. It was his shot. Herby chalked his cue. You had to have guts to play Sal, even with a spot. You had to have more guts to beat him. The kind of guts that told you it didn't matter that Sal was the best, that everybody watching would bet on Sal, that Sal made his living at pool and lived well, that Sal was ten years older and ten years smarter. That Sal was a machine whose function it was to put the balls in the pockets. A well-oiled, smooth-running machine that hardly ever made a mistake and was very quiet, so quiet it could almost scare you into losing.

Herby looked at the balls scattered over the green and felt the rush of excitement run through him. Six ball. Low left english off the rail, back behind the seven. Control the game. Don't let it control you. Just right. Seven in the side, follow it a hair, make the ball line up right. Easy, easy. And now the eight, the spot, the game ball. Run it right down the rail, right down into the corner.

And out again.

Sal stepped up and dropped the eight, drawing the cue the length of the table to stop just off the rail six inches behind the nine; then dropped the nine and shoved another bead over. Herby racked.

Sal broke, and nothing dropped. Herby dropped the one and hung up the nine with the cue; then sent the cue ball three rails off the deuce on the next shot to kiss the nine down the hatch.

"Nice shot," said Sal. He racked.

It meant something to Herby when Sal said nice shot. A lot of guys had said nice shot to Herby—the same guys that set the chalk down in your field of vision when you were shooting.

Herby pushed a bead away from the cluster. Five to go.

Half an hour later they had broken even.

"I'm gonna get some lunch. I'll be back in twenty minutes if you want to play some more," said Sal.

"No, I gotta get to work pretty soon anyway. Looks like we bust even. Let's play one more game so somebody comes out ahead. If we quit now, the only one that comes out ahead is Shorty."

Shorty smiled at this. He had heard it a thousand times.

"O.K.," Sal said. "How much?"

"Hell, I don't care."

"All right, kid. How about twenty?"

"O.K. Call it."

"Heads."

Sal won the toss and broke. The nine fell. Sal unscrewed his cue and put it back into the fine case.

Herby laid two tens on the table and walked over to Shorty. "How much I owe you, Shorty?"

Shorty looked at the clock and mumbled, "That's O.K., Herby."

"How much, Shorty? You can't eat if you don't charge anybody."

"That's O.K., Herby. You had bad luck today. Some days the balls roll for you and some days they don't. You looked pretty good today, but the balls just weren't rolling right for you. Even without the spot you woulda given Sal a run for his money."

Mr. Clay nodded his agreement.

"Sal was off," said Herby. But Sal wasn't off. He had given Sal a run for his money. "Here's a buck, Shorty. I got to get to work."

Herby put his stick away and walked out, nodding to Sal, Mr. Clay, and Shorty. He squinted in the sunlight outside. It was still afternoon. That was the thing about the poolroom—time. When you got back outside you never expected it to be any time at all.

If they hadn't found out about the payoff, Herby thought, he wouldn't be walking this cruddy beat. Through the park and around the block. Walk around and check the doors on the stores and smile once in a while to the citizens, to tell them the cop is their friend. No more payoffs. No whores in this neighborhood. No junkies, no crap games, no nothing. Only the poolroom, and there wasn't any payoff there—not between Shorty and him. Even though the gambling there was illegal and even though minors were a dime a dozen. No excitement at all. Nothing. Once in a while there were a couple of queers in the park, but you can't take them in just for being queer. They've got to do something. And on this cruddy beat, nobody did anything.

It was more exciting in the poolroom. At least you could get excited about winning or losing. The people were more exciting. People like Sal or Shorty or Mr. Clay or even crazy Jerry.

Twenty bucks this afternoon. Twenty-one, counting Shorty. He was still ahead in the long run, but it hurt to drop twenty just like that, especially if you were on. Where did it get him if he won? He blew it all the next day. But still, when you won, you won.

Not like Jerry. Maybe the guy *was* crazy. Jerry lost, but he never really lost, just like Jerry won, but he never really won, either. It's in the feeling of it. You've got to feel it, to feel you've done something. Jerry was out for what he could get. If he got paid for losing, he would probably lose. Jerry never felt anything about winning or losing.

How you play the game is winning or losing. And Jerry didn't really play the game, he just sat in on it, and yelled every once in a while, or stuck a piece of chalk down in your field of vision, or talked while you were shooting. And if you won, you were a cheater, or lucky, or anything but a winner. Jerry could never be a real winner, because the game controlled him.

Take Sal. Sal controlled the game, called all the shots. The balls didn't roll against Sal, because he made them roll. He made them roll the way he wanted them to roll and how far he wanted them to roll, until they stopped where he wanted them to stop. And then he made them roll again. But why didn't he get excited about it? Did he feel anything at all inside that machinelike appearance? He felt something when Jerry stuck his cue in the fan. It looked like he was really going to do something about it. He did do something about it. He scared the hell out of Jerry. But how could he keep from getting excited about the game, about winning?

Jerry got excited about the game, but in a different way. Jerry liked to think he controlled the game in a different way. He got his grins by jamming his stick into the fan, or by flipping the coin and dragging it out as long as possible.

Why the hell did Sal let him get away with that? Thirty-five isn't a hell of a lot to Sal, but it's thirty-five bucks. And he let him cheat.

Shorty got his grins out of telling the stories to the kids, to anybody who'd listen. Even old Mr. Clay got his grins out of acting like such a goddam expert in front of the kids, the high-school punks. And out of Dudley. Where the hell did Sal get his grins?

Herby was tired of walking already, and he had over four more hours of it to do. He walked into Heon's and sat down at the bar. Heon came over, smiling.

"How are you, Herby?"

"O.K., Heon."

Heon poured a cup of coffee and set it in front of him. "Not much business yet. It's early. The kids will start coming in later." He looked at the booths as if to justify his remark.

Herby put a dime on the bar.

"That's all right, Herby. Forget it."

"Take it, Heon. Coffee costs money."

Heon took the dime and rang it up. "You catch any crooks lately, Herby?"

"Nobody's a crook around here. Nobody to catch."

"You keep them from being crooks, huh, Herby?" the old man said, and smiled.

"No. They keep themselves from being crooks. They want to be crooks, but they never risk it. They keep themselves from being crooks."

"Yeh, Herby, but you keep them from being crooks. You got the uniform and the badge and the gun. They see that, they don't want to be crooks. Because of you."

"No, Heon. If they turn into crooks, I catch them. I get paid for it. That's my job."

"I know some crooks you can catch. Catch the crooks writing on the walls in my rest room here. I never seen such filth. Dirty pictures. This no poolroom here, Herby. This Heon's Restaurant. Who's gonna come in here to eat when they see that filth? I think it's the guys from the poolroom, Herby. I seen the pictures in the poolroom. Same thing. I heard the talk there. Same thing. I seen the calendar there. Picture of pretty girl naked, nice pretty body. What they do? They draw on her. They scratch her with their fingernails. They're crazy, Herby. Talk to them for Heon. Tell them Heon doesn't want it in the restaurant. Will you, Herby?"

Did Heon really think that talking accomplished anything? Did he really believe that people wouldn't write on the walls if he talked to them? He had seen the guys in the poolroom writing stuff on the walls. They did it because they wanted to do it, and you couldn't stop them from doing it unless you outlawed walls, and then they'd start in on the floors or something else. Herby drank his coffee down. "O.K., Heon. I'll talk to them." He got off the stool. "We'll see you."

"O.K., Herby. Good night."

Herby walked out into the city. It seemed darker than it had been when he went into Heon's just a couple of minutes ago. The darkness, that was nice. When they couldn't see you coming. If there was anybody. Of course, there usually wasn't. That was the trouble with being a cop. Everything usually wasn't when you were around. It always happened somewhere else or some other time.

He wasn't *doing* anything. He was just walking around, checking doors and listening to people's problems. But when and if something happened, and he was there, things would happen. When and if. If something happened, he would react, participate, call the shots, be there, do something real, if and when.

And then he heard the scream, coming from somewhere in the park across the street. He looked around, startled, and stood looking into the park before he realized he was a cop and had a job to do.

He got to her. She was a woman in her fifties who didn't care if she looked it. She was still screaming. He grabbed her by the arm, and she stopped. People were gathering to watch. He led her to a bench near the statue.

"Are you all right?"

"He scared me so. So big, so big and so black."

"What did he do? Did he hurt you?"

"He took my purse."

"Did he do anything else?"

"No. He took my purse."

"Which way did he go?"

She pointed behind the statue. He decided against blowing his whistle. The yoker was probably still in the park. It wasn't dark enough to escape detection completely. He probably stuck it in his jacket until he got a chance to check it out for money.

Herby ran to a clump of trees on the other side of the statue and looked around. Nobody big, nobody black. Hell. A yoker. He didn't even rape her, just took her goddam purse, with about five bucks in it.

He was walking back to the woman when he saw somebody big and black walking across the street. He began to walk faster, after the somebody.

He got to the corner, and the light changed to red. The big figure was moving into the mass of people on the sidewalk. He got a glimpse of the bulge in the jacket and knew this was it. He ran across the street in time to see the big somebody duck into the alley. Herby knew the alley. He knew every dead end and every fire escape in these eight blocks around the park. He ran around the block to the other end of the alley and entered it, ducking behind the fire escape where the alley doglegged. He heard the footsteps getting louder and felt the excitement mounting in him. The figure came around the dogleg. Herby took a deep breath and stepped out, unsnapping his gun.

"Hold it!" Herby yelled.

He was big. He was one big boy all right. And he had the bulge in his jacket.

The big face froze for an instant and then disappeared, and the body turned around and ran.

Herby jumped around the bend and levelled his gun on the big back.

"Hold it or you're dead, big boy!"

The figure stopped and raised its hands above its head.

"That's right. Just stand right there."

He walked to the figure and poked the gun in its back.

"Get over to the wall and lean on your hands." He poked the gun hard. The back jerked and the body lumbered to the nearer wall, where it leaned on its hands.

Herby frisked the big Negro. He unzipped the jacket and pulled out the purse. It was a cheap patent-leather purse. He opened it and dug through the pocket in it.

"Twenty-one bucks." He dropped the purse to the pavement.

"You want money, Jim?" said the Negro.

"Shut up." He drove his gun into the big back. He pulled a wallet out of the Negro's hip pocket and opened it. "Mark S. Johnson."

"You talkin' to me, Jim?"

"Shut up. That's a fairly common name. Mark S. Johnson. You know what a mark is, Mark?" He paused, then drove his fist hard into the back. It was solid. Mark grunted. "Do you?"

"It's a book of the Bible."

"Do you know what *else* a mark is?"

This time Mark knew enough to answer. "A mark is a sucker."

"That's right, Mark. A sucker. Which one are you named after? The sucker or the saint?"

"The saint. Hey, you gonna take me in or not? What you doin' with these questions? Whyn't you take me in?"

"Shut up. I'll take you in when I'm goddam good and ready."

"I just wanna know, Jim, that's all."

Herby drove his fist home again. "Shut up. You ain't got any right to know anything. *You're* a goddam crook."

"You're the boss, Jim."

"You're goddam right I'm the boss. Now just shut up until I want something out of you. I'll tell you what to say, Mark. Say this—say, 'I'm a crook.' "

"I'm a crook."

"Good, good. Now say this, Mark—say, 'I'm a crook and a sucker.' "

"I'm a crook and a sucker." The voice seemed amused.

Herby hit the back again. "Don't get smart, Mark. Say it right."

"I'm a crook and a sucker." He said it right.

"Very good, Mark. Now say something else for me—say, 'It's not whether you win or lose, it's how you play the game.' "

"What?"

"Go on, Mark, say it. It's not hard to say."

"It's not whether you win or lose, it's how you play the game."

"That's good too, Mark. Now turn around for me."

The evening traffic was just quieting down, and the evening people were just about all home, and the elderly woman was just sitting on the bench wondering how she would get along without her twenty-one dollars, and Heon was just serving a pitcher of beer to a young man and his underage date, and Shorty was just turning over a new page on the calendar with a new naked woman, and Mr. Clay was just lighting his pipe and nodding his approval, and Jerry was just walking into the poolroom, and Sal was just breaking the balls without a trace of emotion when Mark S. Johnson turned around for Herby, and Herby told him not to move a muscle, but Mark S. Johnson happened for some reason to smile at Herby, who happened for some reason to put a bullet through the big black grinning head and who for some reason was utterly convinced that he had finally accomplished something.

MARILYN HARRIS was born in Oklahoma City. She now lives in Norman, Oklahoma with her husband Edgar V. Springer, Jr. and their two children. She is the author of a collection of short stories, *King's Ex,* and is at work on two novels.

Icarus Again

KAY KNEW at first glance the place was uninhabitable but refrained from saying so. Old man Trammel's house reeled with age; three floors of spoilt, century-old interiors, depressingly unimaginative in the manner of the Victorians and unstintingly grim. The indecision of the architect—clearly a neurotic—was epitomized in the roof. Three turrets faced south. One faced east. The ceilings didn't fit the arcades, the arcades didn't fit the walls, and the walls slid about on the foundation in uneasy curves. The chimney fell resoundingly to the basement and connected with a coal furnace, circa 1867. It had to be stoked four times a day, according to Mr. Trammel, who explained the antiquated procedure in detail, encouraged by the cavernous look of interest on Cliff's face. Among her husband's assorted idiosyncrasies, this bludgeoning of total strangers with an urgent, all-caring interest mystified Kay to the point of annoyance, and she was on the verge of asserting herself into the fatal fog of antiquarian complacence when Trammel wheezed and addressed a question to her, the first since they'd descended to the basement. "And do *you* like a big house, Mrs. Devons?"

Kay blinked, her eyes momentarily rendered useless by thought. An unfair question! "Yes, I like a big house" would be interpreted as "Yes, I like *your* house." "No" would add another hollow to the wizened old face that was beginning to bear an un-

"Icarus Again" – Marilyn Harris, *The Malahat Review,* Copyright © 1967 by Marilyn Harris. From *King's Ex! and Other Stories* by Marilyn Harris. Reprinted by permission of Doubleday & Company, Inc.

canny resemblance, under the metamorphosis of a sunless New Hampshire twilight, to Robert Frost. Trammel was shorter, and lacked the disarming futility so evident in the last photographs of the old poet, but the wisps of white hair were there, and the head jutted forward, pulling the shoulders after it, a list that appeared to originate from little invisible weights attached to the corners of his eyes. There was a concealed sadness about him. Soon death would end his marriage to this world, and no one must know that love had died years ago. Trammel, like all old men, filled the air with gross superfluities: a blend of tobacco, a favorite dish, the size of a house, hoping somehow these things might matter again. Kay had no desire to add hurt to such a face, and fence-straddled as pleasantly as she knew how. "I've never lived in one, Mr. Trammel." She smiled. "Not this big. We've taken apartments before."

"Oh?" There was a hint of condemnation in the single syllable. Trammel's voice climbed with his eyebrows, and in the ensuing silence Kay moved back toward the coal bin. The chemistry of fatigue and apprehension produced sharp feelings of inadequacy, and she felt herself retreating, wondering what it was like to drown.

That their warmly uncharted odyssey, stretching over ten years, should end unceremoniously in Mr. Trammel's ugly basement seemed a perversity of the first order, and from her position of retreat Kay organized her thoughts into a series of heated protests, determined to be rude if necessary to convince her dreamer-husband that while the house was undoubtedly an ideal dwelling a century ago, it was not now, and would never again be inhabit-able. She might have said all this, and more, but a rat pushed over a coal clod in the bin behind her and with the spastic speed of one who slides across thick carpet to metal, she jerked to the opposite wall, became hopelessly ensnared in a cobweb, flailed arduously for freedom, and finally backed away to a position of safety near the foot of the stairs. There she waited out an un-gainly heartbeat, one gone berserk with fear, and concentrated on a wobbly green crayon scrawl on the wall eight feet above her that marked the height of floodwaters during the hurricane of '38, all the time hating.

The granite map of Mr. Trammel's face remained solid. Kay was certain the old Yankee had noticed her St. Vitus' dance to the foot of the stairs, and she felt that any expression of sympathy, even a jiggled eyebrow, would have been more civil than what she received, which was exactly nothing. In a splendid surge of wifely tolerance, she forgave Cliff his imperception of her discomfort since at that moment his eyes were trained in the opposite direction, on the innermost bowels of Trammel's dungeon basement. Cliff was wondering again. She knew it. Not even the subterranean light of smudged ceiling windows could mask the taut, half-mast stance of Cliff wondering. As wonderers go, Cliff had no peers. He wondered shamelessly, indiscriminately about all things: the construction work on Huntington Avenue, Karl Barth, water chestnuts, Tacitus, and now Trammel's outdated coal furnace. Resignedly, Kay studied the back of her husband's head and rested her eyes on the perpendicular canal beneath his hairline, a spot so pleasing that she left off hating.

Trammel stirred. "So you're the new professor," he said, thickening the air with unrelated conversation.

"I am," Cliff admitted, and turned his attention from the coal furnace to the kerosene water heater, still wondering.

"From the West, I hear tell," said Trammel. He patted the side of his water heater as he spoke, a gesture consistent with the feminine gender he'd employed to explain the workings of everything old and broken in his house. "She don't smoke on you," he said, of the heater, "if you treat her right. Just a smidgeon of kerosene and she'll warm you up good." Watery-eyed, Trammel bobbed his head up and down with an air of seeing beyond the object. Apparently the thick-lensed specs were barriers to his vision, for he tried vainly to peer over or under them, and Kay's dislike of the man grew sinfully though honestly, rooted in the fact that it was Trammel who owned this three-story, bilious yellow house, and was now trying to palm it off on Cliff for eighty dollars a month.

Cliff, still wondering and insulated from the coarse urgency of expired leases in Cambridge and house hunting in New Hampshire, ambled back to the coal furnace and bent low for a clinical study of the cast-iron lion's head handle. "I was wondering," he began, and Trammel stiffened, "why the manufacturers of these things used the lion's head. Remember, Kay? The potbellied stove in Provincetown? Same lion! Same head!" A "Eureka" light shown on his three-quarter profile. "Do you suppose—" and his voice had a gaunt cathedral sound to it. "There was Thisbe's lion, and—"

While Cliff retreated into a myth, Trammel, who'd stiffened into a pose of defense, confident that his furnace was about to be maligned, now raised his eyes to the ashy ceiling, found a god there and gave silent thanks that he, Marvin Trammel, was a man of common sense.

Kay leaned heavily on the slanted handrail and tried to massage through the accordion pleats of her forehead the dull ache lodged in the middle of her skull. Through the bars of her fingers she read the face of her platinum teardrop watch. Four forty-five! January nights came fast in New Hampshire. A gift from Papa, the watch, an expensive gift designed, she suspected, to make Cliff feel bad. The sun had scarcely shown its face that day and was now dying without protest. A cold grit hurled itself against Trammel's high basement windows. Noon's fine mist had frozen into sleet.

Trammel was saying, "Don't know nothing about lions," and he pushed out the words gingerly, like hot handles. "But I do know if you bank her proper, she'll keep you warm, warmer than the newfangled central heat. She served *us* well for over thirty-five years. Not a reason in the world why she won't last another thirty-five." Pride lifted the old man's voice and gave him confidence to cross his arms where patches showed at the elbow.

Shivering from the damp cold at the window, Kay found a warm pocket in a latitude of compassion, and regretted having to hold the man at bay. She'd met Trammel before in Frost's perverse long songs to the state north of Boston. Perhaps it was Trammel who'd told Frost that three foggy mornings and one rainy day will rot the best birch fence a man can build, and undoubtedly it meant nothing to Trammel to climb a mountain he'd worked around the foot of all his life. But these were Trammel's mountains, not hers, and Frost's men were paper men, not landlords threatening her with three floors of dim, dust-filled rooms where colleagues would come to pass judgment on "the new philosophy man" and colleagues' wives (nameless now) would come to see their unique furnishings. (Early Cal Coolidge, she'd joked with Cliff years ago when hope still made joking possible.)

Kay wavered in the dusk of Trammel's basement and steadied herself on the handrail eight feet below the floodwater mark from the hurricane of '38. She loathed the changes that had taken place inside her, the superficiality, the odious false pride. But more loathsome was the ugliness of a world that offered nothing in abundance except deprivation and debt. The stove in Provincetown? She remembered it, and more: the time in Boston when the rent money had purchased a fine set of Homer, and she'd cowered in the bathroom for three hours, counting cracks in the plaster, terrified at her first encounter with bill collectors, while old Mrs. Hartwell, Brahmin turned wino, had stood outside in the hall hissing, "She's in there. You keep knocking. They're transients, you know." Or the night in the condemned loft on West Eighty-fifth when the drunk had heaved in the lower hall, then lurched up the stairs, slurring through black whiskers mottled with regurgitation, "Someday I'll be a big man," all the time weeping.

She remembered a perennial vow, "Wait till the first teaching job. Everything will be new." She remembered ten years of day-old bread and endless gifts from home wrapped smugly in brown paper and reeking with charity. Ten years of cutting milk and corners, of sleeping in overcoats and shivering; Cliff gone, Cliff studying, empty rooms, budgets bleeding with red pencil marks, half-baked poverty peppered with self-denials and hollow stomachs, while hope, like lye, ate holes in the walls of her heart, and suddenly closing her eyes to the discord in her mind, Kay heard above the melee a woman's voice, too shrill for all ears save her own, crying, DAMN YOU, CLIFF.

The basement was quiet. Kay's flesh face was unalterable. The repose there was bred in. The ache, less dull, fanned out from the center of her skull to a spot above the right temple, and brushing her finger tips across the distressed area, she stood like Whistler's White Girl, compliant, obedient, waiting. Rectangles of sepia-colored landscape spilled through the four high windows, a frieze severed into quarters, wintry still except for the rustling of dead weeds and a blended baritone counterpoint of men chuckling.

"Yes, sir, that was a bad one, the blow of '38." Trammel pointed at the floodwater mark above her head. " 'Course not any of em's good, but that one of '38 was real mean. 'Bout eighty folks drowned."

Thrust unexpectedly onto center stage, Kay rose to the occasion with a contained, level eye. "It must have been terrible," she murmured, and tried to appear grateful for the information although she couldn't remember seeking it.

Cliff recalled the old man's attention by knocking on one of the hollow tentacles that sprouted from the top of the furnace and were designed to carry heat to the labyrinth of rooms above. "They're hollow," said Trammel, and turned his back on Kay. While both men knocked and listened, as rapt as boys with a sea shell, she hazarded a glance at the wall above her head, curiously obsessed with the green crayon mark. The hurricane of '38 had subsided, yet if she'd stood then where she stood now, the waters would have closed around her. If she'd fought her way to the top, acting in good faith on the psychologist's theoretical "will to live," she'd have met an even greater terror. The distance between the flood mark and the top of the ceiling was a scant six inches. Assuming the waters were tranquil, she might conceivably have dog-paddled to the thin layer of air and, tipping her head back, lived for a while. But hurricanes are not known for their placidity. The water would be angry and, under pressure of nature, slosh into the six-inch layer of grace. Assuming fear to be the last visitor before the void, Kay or any living creature would have assisted the death rite by flailing, filling mouth and nostril with wet suffocation, beckoning the end to come ahead of schedule, and confirming the psychologist's theoretical "will to die."

With imaginative ease she envisioned herself sliding down that wall into the next world. Cliff would mourn. Trammel would have to lease his house to someone else. Surely there are no transients in heaven. God would not permit weeping men to get drunk and heave on His doorstep. In the pathless velvet of dying, all men must be rewarded with peace unfettered by hope. The discontent within her vaulted. Hope! As suffocating as floodwater. Damn

Pandora! Damn Cliff, and Trammel, and hurricanes and all things that breathe on the world and make it ugly.

Her excursion into hate was too vivid, and she felt the breath contract in her lungs. She tilted her head back and scanned the ashy ceiling, and wondered what manner of god Trammel had found there. Then turning her eyes to the left, she spied at the top of the stairs, on high, safe ground, available to all for the grasping of a handle, the basement door.

All the while Cliff pursued his investigation of the basement with delight. The coal furnace had attracted his attention from the beginning and held it now. He encircled "her" slowly, stooping to examine bits of ornamentation, alternately shoving his hands into his pockets, content to look, then removing them eagerly, compelled to touch. Kay recognized the preoccupation on his face and made a conscious effort to understand it, appalled by the vast amounts of stranger in her husband. This much she knew. He was at home in all places. A dormant Mephistophelean strain, orphaned by recent and concentrated studies of the classics, prompted him to grasp the lion's head handle and peer inside the dead cold belly. When he emerged, his face was smudged with coal dust and blank with thought. His literatured and adolescent mind responded. Kay watched. Melville might be speaking to him now, warning him of the hazards of fire-watching, or, since the furnace was dead, Prometheus. A clue! Cliff wondered at all worlds, and knew all men, and his wonder led him to love equally, while she was unable to fathom the brief span between the date of her birth and the probable approximate date of her death. Although she stood less than three feet from him, she was alone, and envious of his ability to find delight in the interims of living, the moments that went nowhere and accounted for nothing, waste according to Papa, who since the beginning had equated Cliff with weakness.

A new futility sprang from an old conflict. Waste or weakness, she was tired of waiting, and moved toward him with the only weapon at her disposal, the woman's part of her. A campus clock tolled a distant five. She brushed lightly with her body against his arm. "It's late," she murmured. "Boston is two hours away— three with the sleet."

He looked up, surprised to see her as if she'd returned un-

expectedly from a long journey. A smile spread from one corner
of his mouth and warmed his eyes to an intimacy that died in a
wink. Having acknowledged her closeness, and grateful for her
gifts, which would come "later," he took her hand in a manner
at once provocative and tender, and reciprocated in the only way
he knew how, by pointing out the wonders and delights of a
hundred-year-old heating apparatus. "Have you ever seen anything like it?" he asked quietly. Then louder to Trammel, "And
you say she really works?"

"Absolutely—if you bank her proper." Trammel had found
temporary amusement in a loose cuticle, but now that the focus
of attention had been shifted back to his furnace, he bit off the
cuticle and shuffled forward. At the same time Kay retreated, twin
movements, smooth enough to have been choreographed. Cliff
remained fixed. An authority on coal banking, Trammel spoke
in the idiom of his state, eliminating *r*'s indiscriminately, adding
them where they didn't belong. "Now the idear is," he began.

Yankee frugality! With a degree of disgust she was afraid she
couldn't mask, Kay turned away from the two men and walked
slowly back to her place by the stairs. *Her* place! To have
touched death, even in the imagination, made one possessive.
Her wall! She wanted no part of it. Trammel's house loomed
above her like a three-story extension of the last ten years: the
same decay, time-crazed rooms scented with other lives, door-
sills worn thin from the passage of unknown feet, newel posts
cracked and rotting. Fatigue conspired with despair to release
a stinging moisture from her tear ducts. Her eyes rimmed, but
the dam held. She leaned heavily against her wall, needing it now
for support.

Trammel was saying, "—so that your coal slides down in
layers, you see, and catches on 'fore the others ash—"

Cliff nodded. "I see."

But Kay saw more. From her place beside the wall, she saw
night. It melted against the four high windows, swallowing the
sound of sleet and dead weeds. Her eyes widened in fear of the
nothingness, with such treachery corrupting the black contained
already within the confines of the submerged room. There was
no space for more, but it came anyway, black night marrying
forcibly with black coal, shrouding the two men hunched in

earnest discussion of fire and ash, came consuming, blinding, black on black. The timorous tears came civilly, one at a time. The day was obliterated. Her eyes closed. "Cliff!" she cried.

Trammel halted midstream in his laconic idiom to float his arm toward the ceiling. With a scant flick of his wrist he defeated the night. A forty-watt sun swung giddily from a frayed cord patched with friction tape. He giggled in her direction. "Let there be light, eh?"

Lacking a mirror, she perceived her own expression by noticing theirs. Surprise fell on both men in precisely the same pattern, as if splashed there by the swinging sun; eyebrows lifted, the skin above the nose folded in pleats of concern and amusement. Cliff ventured toward her, motivated by a vested interest of ten years. "You all right?" The modesty of his inquiry, as if she'd shamed him by crying aloud his name, seemed allied with the strong smell of masculine superiority that had invaded the basement room.

Trammel tried to help. "My missus don't like the dark neither. 'Course I spoof her about it regular, but she just gets madder and scareder." A crooked smile lit sparks in his eyes and revealed yellow teeth and good intentions. Unwittingly, in his own way, the old man *had* helped to dispel the taut embarrassment that had flowered magnificently from the seed of Kay's one cry.

With a modicum of relief, she risked another glance at the windows. Reason had returned. Night was no longer a foreboding, emblematic specter. Night was merely night, the death of day, and Trammel ceased to be the quaint-faced warden who shortly would lock her behind the legal bars of a two-year lease in a three-story prison of age and leftovers. Trammel was merely Trammel, an old man with an old wife who frightened easily, and who somehow had nagged her way out of this wooden remnant into one of those modern wonders with central heat, pointing out en route with probably horrendous repetition the dire inconveniences of a century-old dwelling.

A quiet dispatch marked Kay's resolution. When the moment came, as she knew it would, for Cliff to aim all the engines of his ingenuous charm in her direction and ask in that malevolently innocent manner of his if this place was "suitable," she would for the first time in ten years write a new finish to an old scene.

She'd smiled and said yes behind the vault doors of the abandoned loft on Eighty-fifth, and yes again to the gray splintered
beach shack in Provincetown, yes *sans* smile to the old barracks
in New Haven and yes *sans* everything to the smelly walk-up
over Romy's Cambridge delicatessen. As for Cliff, if he wanted
an argument, he could pick his spot; either here in front of the
rejected landlord, or in the cold car during the drive back to
Boston, or (here her new defiance blazed across her face, leaving
two puffs of blush on each cheek) if Cliff wanted, they could
discuss it in Romy's flat, loud enough for all Harvard Square to
hear. Romy, with his sly winks and ways, could paste his ear
against the wall and hear more than bedsprings this night. There
was in the soul of the wandering heiress an insatiable hunger for
one thing new and whole. The hair shirt was beginning to scratch.
Mammon was a soothing salve.

If Cliff was aware of the revolution brewing by the wall, he
gave no indication of it. Moments after her outcry, he'd fallen
into a warm discussion with Trammel concerning the price of coal
and kerosene. "'Bout forty bucks' worth three times a year
should do it," Trammel was saying.

Cliff stood with his arms crossed, nodding intently to the useless information. "That's reasonable enough," he said.

"Oh, it is," agreed Trammel, who stood with his arms crossed
in an exact duplication of Cliff's stance. From her position by the
stairs, they looked like a set of mismatched bookends, supporting
nothing. The time had come. Clothed self-consciously in her new
resolution, Kay ventured forth into the male camaraderie. "Cliff,
I don't think that—" The men turned as one. She wavered, then
compromised. "—that we should detain Mr. Trammel any longer.
We'll phone you our decision in the morning." Then to Cliff,
with ominous firmness, "I'll be waiting in the car."

The handrail quivered under her grasp as she took the stairs,
sedate, ladylike, in spite of the shrill silence that accompanied
her with each step, and averting her eyes from the floodwater
mark of '38, she grabbed for the basement door with such force
that the doorknob fell off in her hand.

"What seems to be the trouble, Mrs. Devons?" Trammel's
singsong voice at the bottom of the stairs mocked the metallic
sound of panic as she tried to rejoin the doorknob with the

narrow cylinder bobbling inside the door. "If you'll tilt it to the left, then ease up on it, I think she'll work for you."

Kay struggled against hysteria and endeavored to follow the old man's instructions. Why was everything worn and broken in Trammel's house referred to as "she"? This small thought, along with hundreds of others, all vicious, provided her with that surge of will usually equated with survival. The doorknob made the necessary contact, the door fell open and escape lay straight ahead across the cracked linoleum of the dining room, past the wainscoted kitchen, through the dingy back porch and out into the evening where their car waited, a patient black bug, inert but sensible. Trammel cackled his apologia after her. "Been meaning to fix the thing, Mrs. Devons. Will if you decide to take the house."

Disciplined to the end, Kay checked her impulse to run, aware that the sound of her footsteps would resound in the basement room. A stoic's measured tread carried her out into the air where winter slapped her face and a sleet-glazed windshield blurred her vision of the ugly world. Inside the car and unbelievably miserable, she slumped against the icy plastic seat covers and wept.

A few moments later the light went out in the basement. A single eye of light bounced crazily within the darkened kitchen. Trammel, a man with an affinity for small suns, had produced a flashlight. Cliff appeared first, a tall, blurry shadow. Next came Trammel, smaller, bent, waving the flashlight at her. "Nice to have met you, Mrs. Devons." No response was called for and none was offered.

Within the car, no words were spoken. At first the gearshift and sluggish defroster occupied Cliff's attention. Then the treacherous reversal out of Trammel's drive and down the street through winter's hieroglyphics. Kay huddled close to her side of the car, dry-eyed and desolate, and stared numbly at the passing campus. The buildings were empty now at mid-term, but on Monday the sons and daughters of mill workers would come streaming back, and listen with polite disinterest while Cliff expounded on his cherished Greeks. Was there any god on Olympus capable of turning away their eyes from their cold, impoverished backgrounds and setting them to wondering? Kay wondered.

For the first few miles, Cliff combated the storm and conversed with himself, covering a wide range of topics from the miracles that could be wrought with paint and elbow grease to the comfortable snugness of the beach shack after Kay had worked her special magic. As they were approaching Dublin Lake he got down to specifics. "Trammel's house might look better on a bright day, don't you think? Maybe the sun will be out when we see it again."

Conjurers worked beneath the black mirrored surface of Dublin Lake, filling her head for the second time that day with profound and frightening thoughts of drowning. Numbed by the cold and late hour, Kay opened her mouth, then closed it again, momentarily distracted by the reflection in the car window of a woman's face. Her heart raced in alarm for the ugliness, with such facility assaulting mouth corners, carving so consummately deep hollows to a soul depth. The sun would not shine. Its rays were as antiquated as hope and Trammel's house.

"Kay?" he tendered.

Her eyes lifted from the reflected ugliness to his face. To claim for now the distant promises of a future chimera, she became the architect of a private paradise, and slid the distance across the seat to beneath the arm that opened to her. The warmth there was rich. Her lips moved:

"Trammel's house will do nicely."

JOYCE CAROL OATES is the author of two collections of short stories, and two novels. Her second novel *A Garden of Earthly Delights* was published in 1967. Mrs. Oates' stories have appeared in many American magazines. This is her fifth O. Henry Award; "In the Region of Ice" was awarded First Prize in 1967.

Where Are You Going, Where Have You Been?

for Bob Dylan

HER NAME WAS CONNIE. She was fifteen and she had a quick nervous giggling habit of craning her neck to glance into mirrors, or checking other people's faces to make sure her own was all right. Her mother, who noticed everything and knew everything and who hadn't much reason any longer to look at her own face, always scolded Connie about it. "Stop gawking at yourself, who are you? You think you're so pretty?" she would say. Connie would raise her eyebrows at these familiar complaints and look right through her mother, into a shadowy vision of herself as she was right at that moment: she knew she was pretty and that was everything. Her mother had been pretty once too, if you could believe those old snapshots in the album, but now her looks were gone and that was why she was always after Connie.

"Why don't you keep your room clean like your sister? How've you got your hair fixed—what the hell stinks? Hair spray? You don't see your sister using that junk."

Her sister June was twenty-four and still lived at home. She was a secretary in the high school Connie attended, and if that wasn't bad enough—with her in the same building—she was so

"Where Are You Going, Where Have You Been?" – Joyce Carol Oates, *Epoch,* Copyright © 1966 by Cornell University.

plain and chunky and steady that Connie had to hear her praised
all the time by her mother and her mother's sisters. June did
this, June did that, she saved money and helped clean the house
and cooked and Connie couldn't do a thing, her mind was all
filled with trashy daydreams. Their father was away at work most
of the time and when he came home he wanted supper and he
read the newspaper at supper and after supper he went to bed.
He didn't bother talking much to them, but around his bent head
Connie's mother kept picking at her until Connie wished her
mother was dead and she herself was dead and it was all over.
"She makes me want to throw up sometimes," she complained
to her friends. She had a high, breathless, amused voice which
made everything she said sound a little forced, whether it was
sincere or not.

There was one good thing: June went places with girl friends
of hers, girls who were just as plain and steady as she, and so
when Connie wanted to do that her mother had no objections.
The father of Connie's best girl friend drove the girls the three
miles to town and left them off at a shopping plaza, so that they
could walk through the stores or go to a movie, and when he came
to pick them up again at eleven he never bothered to ask what
they had done.

They must have been familiar sights, walking around that
shopping plaza in their shorts and flat ballerina slippers that
always scuffed the sidewalk, with charm bracelets jingling on
their thin wrists; they would lean together to whisper and laugh
secretly if someone passed by who amused or interested them.
Connie had long dark blond hair that drew anyone's eye to it,
and she wore part of it pulled up on her head and puffed out
and the rest of it she let fall down her back. She wore a pull-over
jersey blouse that looked one way when she was at home and
another way when she was away from home. Everything about
her had two sides to it, one for home and one for anywhere
that was not home: her walk that could be childlike and bobbing,
or languid enough to make anyone think she was hearing music
in her head, her mouth which was pale and smirking most of the
time, but bright and pink on these evenings out, her laugh
which was cynical and drawling at home—"Ha, ha, very funny"

—but high-pitched and nervous anywhere else, like the jingling of the charms on her bracelet.

Sometimes they did go shopping or to a movie, but sometimes they went across the highway, ducking fast across the busy road, to a drive-in restaurant where older kids hung out. The restaurant was shaped like a big bottle, though squatter than a real bottle, and on its cap was a revolving figure of a grinning boy who held a hamburger aloft. One night in mid-summer they ran across, breathless with daring, and right away someone leaned out a car window and invited them over, but it was just a boy from high school they didn't like. It made them feel good to be able to ignore him. They went up through the maze of parked and cruising cars to the bright-lit, fly-infested restaurant, their faces pleased and expectant as if they were entering a sacred building that loomed out of the night to give them what haven and what blessing they yearned for. They sat at the counter and crossed their legs at the ankles, their thin shoulders rigid with excitement, and listened to the music that made everything so good: the music was always in the background like music at a church service, it was something to depend upon.

A boy named Eddie came in to talk with them. He sat backwards on his stool, turning himself jerkily around in semi-circles and then stopping and turning again, and after a while he asked Connie if she would like something to eat. She said she did and so she tapped her friend's arm on her way out—her friend pulled her face up into a brave droll look—and Connie said she would meet her at eleven, across the way. "I just hate to leave her like that," Connie said earnestly, but the boy said that she wouldn't be alone for long. So they went out to his car and on the way Connie couldn't help but let her eyes wander over the windshields and faces all around her, her face gleaming with a joy that had nothing to do with Eddie or even this place; it might have been the music. She drew her shoulders up and sucked in her breath with the pure pleasure of being alive, and just at that moment she happened to glance at a face just a few feet from hers. It was a boy with shaggy black hair, in a convertible jalopy painted gold. He stared at her and then his lips widened into a grin. Connie slit her eyes at him and turned away, but she couldn't help glancing back and there he was still watching her. He wagged a finger and laughed and said, "Gonna get you, baby," and Connie turned away again without Eddie noticing anything.

She spent three hours with him, at the restaurant where they ate hamburgers and drank Cokes in wax cups that were always sweating, and then down an alley a mile or so away, and when he left her off at five to eleven only the movie house was still open at the plaza. Her girl friend was there, talking with a boy. When Connie came up the two girls smiled at each other and Connie said, "How was the movie?" and the girl said, "*You* should know." They rode off with the girl's father, sleepy and pleased, and Connie couldn't help but look at the darkened shopping plaza with its big empty parking lot and its signs that were faded and ghostly now, and over at the drive-in restaurant where cars were still circling tirelessly. She couldn't hear the music at this distance.

Next morning June asked her how the movie was and Connie said, "So-so."

She and that girl and occasionally another girl went out several times a week that way, and the rest of the time Connie spent around the house—it was summer vacation—getting in her mother's way and thinking, dreaming, about the boys she met. But all the boys fell back and dissolved into a single face that was not even a face, but an idea, a feeling, mixed up with the urgent insistent pounding of the music and the humid night air of July. Connie's mother kept dragging her back to the daylight by finding things for her to do or saying, suddenly, "What's this about the Pettinger girl?"

And Connie would say nervously, "Oh, her. That dope." She always drew thick clear lines between herself and such girls, and her mother was simple and kindly enough to believe her. Her mother was so simple, Connie thought, that it was maybe cruel to fool her so much. Her mother went scuffling around the house in old bedroom slippers and complained over the telephone to one sister about the other, then the other called up and the two of them complained about the third one. If June's name was mentioned her mother's tone was approving, and if Connie's name was mentioned it was disapproving. This did not really mean she disliked Connie and actually Connie thought that her mother preferred her to June because she was prettier, but the two of them

kept up a pretense of exasperation, a sense that they were tugging
and struggling over something of little value to either of them.
Sometimes, over coffee, they were almost friends, but something
would come up—some vexation that was like a fly buzzing suddenly around their heads—and their faces went hard with contempt.

One Sunday Connie got up at eleven—none of them bothered
with church—and washed her hair so that it could dry all day
long, in the sun. Her parents and sisters were going to a barbecue
at an aunt's house and Connie said no, she wasn't interested,
rolling her eyes to let mother know just what she thought of it.
"Stay home alone then," her mother said sharply. Connie sat out
back in a lawn chair and watched them drive away, her father
quiet and bald, hunched around so that he could back the car out,
her mother with a look that was still angry and not at all
softened through the windshield, and in the back seat poor old
June all dressed up as if she didn't know what a barbecue was,
with all the running yelling kids and the flies. Connie sat with her
eyes closed in the sun, dreaming and dazed with the warmth
about her as if this were a kind of love, the caresses of love, and
her mind slipped over onto thoughts of the boy she had been
with the night before and how nice he had been, how sweet it
always was, not the way someone like June would suppose but
sweet, gentle, the way it was in movies and promised in songs;
and when she opened her eyes she hardly knew where she was,
the back yard ran off into weeds and a fence-line of trees and
behind it the sky was perfectly blue and still. The asbestos "ranch
house" that was now three years old startled her—it looked small.
She shook her head as if to get awake.

It was too hot. She went inside the house and turned on the
radio to drown out the quiet. She sat on the edge of her bed,
barefoot, and listened for an hour and a half to a program called
XYZ Sunday Jamboree, record after record of hard, fast, shrieking songs she sang along with, interspersed by exclamations from
"Bobby King": "An' look here you girls at Napoleon's—Son and
Charley want you to pay real close attention to this song coming
up!"

And Connie paid close attention herself, bathed in a glow of
slow-pulsed joy that seemed to rise mysteriously out of the music

itself and lay languidly about the airless little room, breathed in
and breathed out with each gentle rise and fall of her chest.

After a while she heard a car coming up the drive. She sat
up at once, startled, because it couldn't be her father so soon.
The gravel kept crunching all the way in from the road—the
driveway was long—and Connie ran to the window. It was a
car she didn't know. It was an open jalopy, painted a bright gold
that caught the sunlight opaquely. Her heart began to pound
and her fingers snatched at her hair, checking it, and she
whispered "Christ. Christ," wondering how bad she looked. The
car came to a stop at the side door and the horn sounded four
short taps as if this were a signal Connie knew.

She went into the kitchen and approached the door slowly,
then hung out the screen door, her bare toes curling down off the
step. There were two boys in the car and now she recognized the
driver: he had shaggy, shabby black hair that looked crazy as a
wig and he was grinning at her.

"I ain't late, am I?" he said.

"Who the hell do you think you are?" Connie said.

"Toldja I'd be out, didn't I?"

"I don't even know who you are."

She spoke sullenly, careful to show no interest or pleasure, and
he spoke in a fast bright monotone. Connie looked past him to the
other boy, taking her time. He had fair brown hair, with a lock
that fell onto his forehead. His sideburns gave him a fierce, embarrassed look, but so far he hadn't even bothered to glance at
her. Both boys wore sunglasses. The driver's glasses were metallic
and mirrored everything in miniature.

"You wanta come for a ride?" he said.

Connie smirked and let her hair fall loose over one shoulder.

"Don'tcha like my car? New paint job," he said. "Hey."

"What?"

"You're cute."

She pretended to fidget, chasing flies away from the door.

"Don'tcha believe me, or what?" he said.

"Look, I don't even know who you are," Connie said in disgust.

"Hey, Ellie's got a radio, see. Mine's broke down." He lifted
his friend's arm and showed her the little transistor the boy was

holding, and now Connie began to hear the music. It was the same program that was playing inside the house.

"Bobby King?" she said.

"I listen to him all the time. I think he's great."

"He's kind of great," Connie said reluctantly.

"Listen, that guy's *great*. He knows where the action is."

Connie blushed a little, because the glasses made it impossible for her to see just what this boy was looking at. She couldn't decide if she liked him or if he was just a jerk, and so she dawdled in the doorway and wouldn't come down or go back inside. She said, "What's all that stuff painted on your car?"

"Can'tcha read it?" He opened the door very carefully, as if he was afraid it might fall off. He slid out just as carefully, planting his feet firmly on the ground, the tiny metallic world in his glasses slowing down like gelatine hardening and in the midst of it Connie's bright green blouse. "This here is my name, to begin with," he said. ARNOLD FRIEND was written in tar-like black letters on the side, with a drawing of a round grinning face that reminded Connie of a pumpkin, except it wore sunglasses. "I wanta introduce myself, I'm Arnold Friend and that's my real name and I'm gonna be your friend, honey, and inside the car's Ellie Oscar, he's kinda shy." Ellie brought his transistor radio up to his shoulder and balanced it there. "Now these numbers are a secret code, honey," Arnold Friend explained. He read off the numbers 33, 19, 17 and raised his eyebrows at her to see what she thought of that, but she didn't think much of it. The left rear fender had been smashed and around it was written, on the gleaming gold background: DONE BY CRAZY WOMAN DRIVER. Connie had to laugh at that. Arnold Friend was pleased at her laughter and looked up at her. "Around the other side's a lot more—you wanta come and see them?"

"No."

"Why not?"

"Why should I?"

"Don'tcha wanta see what's on the car? Don'tcha wanta go for a ride?"

"I don't know."

"Why not?"

"I got things to do."

"Like what?"

"Things."

He laughed as if she had said something funny. He slapped his thighs. He was standing in a strange way, leaning back against the car as if he were balancing himself. He wasn't tall, only an inch or so taller than she would be if she came down to him. Connie liked the way he was dressed, which was the way all of them dressed: tight faded jeans stuffed into black, scuffed boots, a belt that pulled his waist in and showed how lean he was, and a white pull-over shirt that was a little soiled and showed the hard small muscles of his arms and shoulders. He looked as if he probably did hard work, lifting and carrying things. Even his neck looked muscular. And his face was a familiar face, somehow: the jaw and chin and cheeks slightly darkened, because he hadn't shaved for a day or two, and the nose long and hawk-like, sniffing as if she were a treat he was going to gobble up and it was all a joke.

"Connie, you ain't telling the truth. This is your day set aside for a ride with me and you know it," he said, still laughing. The way he straightened and recovered from his fit of laughing showed that it had been all fake.

"How do you know what my name is?" she said suspiciously.

"It's Connie."

"Maybe and maybe not."

"I know my Connie," he said, wagging his finger. Now she remembered him even better, back at the restaurant, and her cheeks warmed at the thought of how she sucked in her breath just at the moment she passed him—how she must have looked to him. And he had remembered her. "Ellie and I come out here especially for you," he said. "Ellie can sit in back. How about it?"

"Where?"

"Where what?"

"Where're we going?"

He looked at her. He took off the sunglasses and she saw how pale the skin around his eyes was, like holes that were not in shadow but instead in light. His eyes were like chips of broken glass that catch the light in an amiable way. He smiled. It was as if the idea of going for a ride somewhere, to some place, was a new idea to him.

"Just for a ride, Connie sweetheart."

"I never said my name was Connie," she said.

"But I know what it is. I know your name and all about you, lots of things," Arnold Friend said. He had not moved yet but stood still leaning back against the side of his jalopy. "I took a special interest in you, such a pretty girl, and found out all about you like I know your parents and sister are gone somewheres and I know where and how long they're going to be gone, and I know who you were with last night, and your best girl friend's name is Betty. Right?"

He spoke in a simple lilting voice, exactly as if he were reciting the words to a song. His smile assured her that everything was fine. In the car Ellie turned up the volume on his radio and did not bother to look around at them.

"Ellie can sit in the back seat," Arnold Friend said. He indicated his friend with a casual jerk of his chin, as if Ellie did not count and she should not bother with him.

"How'd you find out all that stuff?" Connie said.

"Listen: Betty Schultz and Tony Fitch and Jimmy Pettinger and Nancy Pettinger," he said, in a chant. "Raymond Stanley and Bob Hutter—"

"Do you know all those kids?"

"I know everybody."

"Look, you're kidding. You're not from around here."

"Sure."

"But—how come we never saw you before?"

"Sure you saw me before," he said. He looked down at his boots, as if he were a little offended. "You just don't remember."

"I guess I'd remember you," Connie said.

"Yeah?" He looked up at this, beaming. He was pleased. He began to mark time with the music from Ellie's radio, tapping his fists lightly together. Connie looked away from his smile to the car, which was painted so bright it almost hurt her eyes to look at it. She looked at that name, ARNOLD FRIEND. And up at the front fender was an expression that was familiar—MAN THE FLYING SAUCERS. It was an expression kids had used the year before, but didn't use this year. She looked at it for a while as if the words meant something to her that she did not yet know.

"What're you thinking about? Huh?" Arnold Friend demanded. "Not worried about your hair blowing around in the car, are you?"

"No."

"Think I maybe can't drive good?"

"How do I know?"

"You're a hard girl to handle. How come?" he said. "Don't you know I'm your friend? Didn't you see me put my sign in the air when you walked by?"

"What sign?"

"My sign." And he drew an X in the air, leaning out toward her. They were maybe ten feet apart. After his hand fell back to his side the X was still in the air, almost visible. Connie let the screen door close and stood perfectly still inside it, listening to the music from her radio and the boy's blend together. She stared at Arnold Friend. He stood there so stiffly relaxed, pretending to be relaxed, with one hand idly on the door handle as if he were keeping himself up that way and had no intention of ever moving again. She recognized most things about him, the tight jeans that showed his thighs and buttocks and the greasy leather boots and the tight shirt, and even that slippery friendly smile of his, that sleepy dreamy smile that all the boys used to get across ideas they didn't want to put into words. She recognized all this and also the singsong way he talked, slightly mocking, kidding, but serious and a little melancholy, and she recognized the way he tapped one fist against the other in homage to the perpetual music behind him. But all these things did not come together.

She said suddenly, "Hey, how old are you?"

His smile faded. She could see then that he wasn't a kid, he was much older—thirty, maybe more. At this knowledge her heart began to pound faster.

"That's a crazy thing to ask. Can'tcha see I'm your own age?"

"Like hell you are."

"Or maybe a coupla years older, I'm eighteen."

"Eighteen?" she said doubtfully.

He grinned to reassure her and lines appeared at the corners of his mouth. His teeth were big and white. He grinned so broadly his eyes became slits and she saw how thick the lashes were, thick and black as if painted with a black tar-like material. Then he seemed to become embarrassed, abruptly, and looked over his shoulder at Ellie. *"Him,* he's crazy," he said. "Ain't he a riot, he's a nut, a real character." Ellie was still listening to the music. His sunglasses told nothing about what he was thinking. He wore a bright orange shirt unbuttoned halfway to show his chest, which was a pale, bluish chest and not muscular like Arnold Friend's. His shirt collar was turned up all around and the very tips of the collar pointed out past his chin as if they were protecting him. He was pressing the transistor radio up against his ear and sat there in a kind of daze, right in the sun.

"He's kinda strange," Connie said.

"Hey, she says you're kinda strange! Kinda strange!" Arnold Friend cried. He pounded on the car to get Ellie's attention. Ellie turned for the first time and Connie saw with shock that he wasn't a kid either—he had a fair, hairless face, cheeks reddened slightly as if the veins grew too close to the surface of his skin, the face of a forty-year-old baby. Connie felt a wave of dizziness rise in her at this sight and she stared at him as if waiting for something to change the shock of the moment, make it all right again. Ellie's lips kept shaping words, mumbling along with the words blasting in his ear.

"Maybe you two better go away," Connie said faintly.

"What? How come?" Arnold Friend cried. "We come out here to take you for a ride. It's Sunday." He had the voice of the man on the radio now. It was the same voice, Connie thought. "Don'tcha know it's Sunday all day and honey, no matter who you were with last night today you're with Arnold Friend and don't you forget it!— Maybe you better step out here," he said, and this last was in a different voice. It was a little flatter, as if the heat was finally getting to him.

"No. I got things to do."

"Hey."

"You two better leave."

"We ain't leaving until you come with us."

"Like hell I am—"

"Connie, don't fool around with me. I mean, I mean, don't fool *around,"* he said, shaking his head. He laughed incredulously. He placed his sunglasses on top of his head, carefully, as if he were indeed wearing a wig, and brought the stems down behind his ears. Connie stared at him, another wave of dizziness and fear rising in her so that for a moment he wasn't even in focus but was just a blur, standing there against his gold car, and she had the idea that he had driven up the driveway all right but had come from nowhere before that and belonged nowhere and that everything about him and even about the music that was so familiar to her was only half real.

"If my father comes and sees you—"

"He ain't coming. He's at a barbecue."

"How do you know that?"

"Aunt Tillie's. Right now they're—uh—they're drinking. Sitting around," he said vaguely, squinting as if he were staring all the way to town and over to Aunt Tillie's back yard. Then the vision seemed to get clear and he nodded energetically. "Yeah. Sitting around. There's your sister in a blue dress, huh? And high heels, the poor sad bitch—nothing like you, sweetheart! And your mother's helping some fat woman with the corn, they're cleaning the corn—husking the corn—"

"What fat woman?" Connie cried.

"How do I know what fat woman, I don't know every goddam fat woman in the world!" Arnold Friend laughed.

"Oh, that's Mrs. Hornby. . . . Who invited her?" Connie said. She felt a little light-headed. Her breath was coming quickly.

"She's too fat. I don't like them fat. I like them the way you are, honey," he said, smiling sleepily at her. They stared at each other for a while, through the screen door. He said softly, "Now what you're going to do is this: you're going to come out that door. You're going to sit up front with me and Ellie's going to sit in the back, the hell with Ellie, right? This isn't Ellie's date. You're my date. I'm your lover, honey."

"What? You're crazy—"

"Yes, I'm your lover. You don't know what that is but you will," he said. "I know that too. I know all about you. But look: it's real nice and you couldn't ask for nobody better than me, or more polite. I always keep my word. I'll tell you how it is, I'm always nice at first, the first time. I'll hold you so tight you won't think you have to try to get away or pretend anything because you'll know you can't. And I'll come inside you where it's all secret and you'll give in to me and you'll love me—"

"Shut up! You're crazy!" Connie said. She backed away from

the door. She put her hands against her ears as if she'd heard
something terrible, something not meant for her. "People don't
talk like that, you're crazy," she muttered. Her heart was almost
too big now for her chest and its pumping made sweat break out
all over her. She looked out to see Arnold Friend pause and then
take a step toward the porch lurching. He almost fell. But, like a
clever drunken man, he managed to catch his balance. He wobbled in his high boots and grabbed hold of one of the porch posts.

"Honey?" he said. "You still listening?"

"Get the hell out of here!"

"Be nice, honey. Listen."

"I'm going to call the police—"

He wobbled again and out of the side of his mouth came a
fast spat curse, an aside not meant for her to hear. But even this
"Christ!" sounded forced. Then he began to smile again. She
watched this smile come, awkward as if he were smiling from inside a mask. His whole face was a mask, she thought wildly,
tanned down onto his throat but then running out as if he had
plastered make-up on his face but had forgotten about his throat.

"Honey—? Listen, here's how it is. I always tell the truth and
I promise you this: I ain't coming in that house after you."

"You better not! I'm going to call the police if you—if you
don't—"

"Honey," he said, talking right through her voice, "honey,
I'm not coming in there but you are coming out here. You know
why?"

She was panting. The kitchen looked like a place she had
never seen before, some room she had run inside but which wasn't
good enough, wasn't going to help her. The kitchen window had
never had a curtain, after three years, and there were dishes in the
sink for her to do—probably—and if you ran your hand across
the table you'd probably feel something sticky there.

"You listening, honey? Hey?"

"—going to call the police—"

"Soon as you touch the phone I don't need to keep my promise and can come inside. You won't want that."

She rushed forward and tried to lock the door. Her fingers
were shaking. "But why lock it," Arnold Friend said gently, talking right into her face. "It's just a screen door. It's just nothing."

One of his boots was at a strange angle, as if his foot wasn't in it. It pointed out to the left, bent at the ankle. "I mean, anybody can break through a screen door and glass and wood and iron or anything else if he needs to, anybody at all and specially Arnold Friend. If the place got lit up with a fire honey you'd come running out into my arms, right into my arms and safe at home—like you knew I was your lover and'd stopped fooling around. I don't mind a nice shy girl but I don't like no fooling around." Part of those words were spoken with a slight rhythmic lilt, and Connie somehow recognized them—the echo of a song from last year, about a girl rushing into her boy friend's arms and coming home again—

Connie stood barefoot on the linoleum floor, staring at him. "What do you want?" she whispered.

"I want you," he said.

"What?"

"Seen you that night and thought, that's the one, yes sir. I never needed to look any more."

"But my father's coming back. He's coming to get me. I had to wash my hair first—" She spoke in a dry, rapid voice, hardly raising it for him to hear.

"No, your daddy is not coming and yes, you had to wash your hair and you washed it for me. It's nice and shining and all for me, I thank you, sweetheart," he said, with a mock bow, but again he almost lost his balance. He had to bend and adjust his boots. Evidently his feet did not go all the way down; the boots must have been stuffed with something so that he would seem taller. Connie stared out at him and behind him Ellie in the car, who seemed to be looking off toward Connie's right, into nothing. This Ellie said, pulling the words out of the air one after another as if he were just discovering them, "You want me to pull out the phone?"

"Shut your mouth and keep it shut," Arnold Friend said, his face red from bending over or maybe from embarrassment because Connie had seen his boots. "This ain't none of your business."

"What—what are you doing? What do you want?" Connie said. "If I call the police they'll get you, they'll arrest you—"

"Promise was not to come in unless you touch that phone, and

I'll keep that promise," he said. He resumed his erect position and
tried to force his shoulders back. He sounded like a hero in a
movie, declaring something important. He spoke too loudly and
it was as if he were speaking to someone behind Connie. "I ain't
made plans for coming in that house where I don't belong but just
for you to come out to me, the way you should. Don't you know
who I am?"

"You're crazy," she whispered. She backed away from the
door but did not want to go into another part of the house, as if
this would give him permission to come through the door. "What
do you. . . . You're crazy, you . . ."

"Huh? What're you saying, honey?"

Her eyes darted everywhere in the kitchen. She could not remember what it was, this room.

"This is how it is, honey: you come out and we'll drive away,
have a nice ride. But if you don't come out we're gonna wait till
your people come home and then they're all going to get it."

"You want that telephone pulled out?" Ellie said. He held the
radio away from his ear and grimaced, as if without the radio the
air was too much for him.

"I toldja shut up, Ellie," Arnold Friend said, "you're deaf, get
a hearing aid, right? Fix yourself up. This little girl's no trouble
and's gonna be nice to me, so Ellie keep to yourself, this ain't
your date—right? Don't hem in on me. Don't hog. Don't crush.
Don't bird dog. Don't trail me," he said in a rapid meaningless
voice, as if he were running through all the expressions he'd
learned but was no longer sure which one of them was in style,
then rushing on to new ones, making them up with his eyes
closed, "Don't crawl under my fence, don't squeeze in my chip-
munk hole, don't sniff my glue, suck my popsicle, keep your
own greasy fingers on yourself!" He shaded his eyes and peered
in at Connie, who was backed against the kitchen table. "Don't
mind him honey he's just a creep. He's a dope. Right? I'm the
boy for you and like I said you come out here nice like a lady
and give me your hand, and nobody else gets hurt, I mean,
your nice old bald-headed daddy and your mummy and your
sister in her high heels. Because listen: why bring them in this?"

"Leave me alone," Connie whispered.

"Hey, you know that old woman down the road, the one with the chickens and stuff—you know her?"

"She's dead!"

"Dead? What? You know her?" Arnold Friend said.

"She's dead—"

"Don't you like her?"

"She's dead—she's—she isn't here any more—"

"But don't you like her, I mean, you got something against her? Some grudge or something?" Then his voice dipped as if he were conscious of a rudeness. He touched the sunglasses perched on top of his head as if to make sure they were still there. "Now you be a good girl."

"What are you going to do?"

"Just two things, or maybe three," Arnold Friend said. "But I promise it won't last long and you'll like me that way you get to like people you're close to. You will. It's all over for you here, so come on out. You don't want your people in any trouble, do you?"

She turned and bumped against a chair or something, hurting her leg, but she ran into the back room and picked up the telephone. Something roared in her ear, a tiny roaring, and she was so sick with fear that she could do nothing but listen to it—the telephone was clammy and very heavy and her fingers groped down to the dial but were too weak to touch it. She began to scream into the phone, into the roaring. She cried out, she cried for her mother, she felt her breath start jerking back and forth in her lungs as if it were something Arnold Friend were stabbing her with again and again with no tenderness. A noisy sorrowful wailing rose all about her and she was locked inside it the way she was locked inside this house.

After a while she could hear again. She was sitting on the floor with her wet back against the wall.

Arnold Friend was saying from the door, "That's a good girl. Put the phone back."

She kicked the phone away from her.

"No, honey. Pick it up. Put it back right."

She picked it up and put it back. The dial tone stopped.

"That's a good girl. Now you come outside."

She was hollow with what had been fear, but what was now

just an emptiness. All that screaming had blasted it out of her. She
sat, one leg cramped under her, and deep inside her brain was
something like a pinpoint of light that kept going and would not
let her relax. She thought, I'm not going to see my mother again.
She thought, I'm not going to sleep in my bed again. Her bright
green blouse was all wet.

Arnold Friend said, in a gentle-loud voice that was like a
stage voice, "The place where you came from ain't there any more,
and where you had in mind to go is cancelled out. This place you
are now—inside your daddy's house—is nothing but a cardboard
box I can knock down any time. You know that and always did
know it. You hear me?"

She thought, I have got to think. I have to know what to do.

"We'll go out to a nice field, out in the country here where it
smells so nice and it's sunny," Arnold Friend said. "I'll have my
arms tight around you so you won't need to try to get away and
I'll show you what love is like, what it does. The hell with this
house! It looks solid all right," he said. He ran a fingernail down
the screen and the noise did not make Connie shiver, as it would
have the day before. "Now put your hand on your heart, honey.
Feel that? That feels solid too but we know better, be nice to me,
be sweet like you can because what else is there for a girl like you
but to be sweet and pretty and give in?—and get away before
her people come back?"

She felt her pounding heart. Her hand seemed to enclose it.
She thought for the first time in her life that it was nothing that
was hers, that belonged to her, but just a pounding, living thing
inside this body that wasn't really hers either.

"You don't want them to get hurt," Arnold Friend went on.
"Now get up, honey. Get up all by yourself."

She stood.

"Now turn this way. That's right. Come over here to me—
Ellie, put that away, didn't I tell you? You dope. You miserable
creepy dope," Arnold Friend said. His words were not angry but
only part of an incantation. The incantation was kindly. "Now
come out through the kitchen to me honey and let's see a smile,
try it, you're a brave sweet little girl and now they're eating corn
and hotdogs cooked to bursting over an outdoor fire, and they
don't know one thing about you and never did and honey you're

better than them because not a one of them would have done this for you."

Connie felt the linoleum under her feet; it was cool. She brushed her hair back out of her eyes. Arnold Friend let go of the post tentatively and opened his arms for her, his elbows pointing in toward each other and his wrists limp, to show that this was an embarrassed embrace and a little mocking, he didn't want to make her self-conscious.

She put out her hand against the screen. She watched herself push the door slowly open as if she were safe back somewhere in the other doorway, watching this body and this head of long hair moving out into the sunlight where Arnold Friend waited.

"My sweet little blue-eyed girl," he said, in a half-sung sigh that had nothing to do with her brown eyes but was taken up just the same by the vast sunlit reaches of the land behind him and on all sides of him, so much land that Connie had never seen before and did not recognize except to know that she was going to it.

MAGAZINES CONSULTED

ANTE – P.O. Box 29915, Los Angeles, Calif. 90029

ANTIOCH REVIEW – 212 Xenia Avenue, Yellow Springs, Ohio 45387

APPROACH – 114 Petrie Avenue, Rosemont, Pa. 19010

ARARAT – Armenian General Benevolent Union of America, 250 Fifth Avenue, New York, N.Y. 10001

ARIZONA QUARTERLY – University of Arizona, Tucson, Ariz. 85721

ATLANTIC MONTHLY – 8 Arlington Street, Boston, Mass. 02116

AVE MARIA – National Catholic Weekly, Congregation of Holy Cross, Notre Dame, Ind. 46556

CARLETON MISCELLANY – Carleton College, Northfield, Minn. 55057

CAROLINA QUARTERLY – Box 1117, Chapel Hill, N.C. 27515

CHELSEA REVIEW – Box 242, Old Chelsea Station, New York, N.Y. 10011

CHICAGO REVIEW – University of Chicago, Chicago, Ill. 60637

COLORADO QUARTERLY – Hellums 118, University of Colorado, Boulder, Colo. 80304

COMMENTARY – 165 East 56th Street, New York, N.Y. 10022

COSMOPOLITAN – 1775 Broadway, New York, N.Y. 10019

THE CRITIC – 180 N. Wabash Avenue, Chicago, Ill. 60601

DECEMBER – P.O. Box 274, Western Springs, Ill. 60558

THE DENVER QUARTERLY – Denver, Colo. 80210

DESCANT – Dept. of English, TCU Station, Fort Worth, Tex. 76129

ENCOUNTER – 25 Haymarket, London, S.W. 1, England

EPOCH – 159 Goldwin Smith Hall, Cornell University, Ithaca, N.Y. 14850

ESCAPADE – 529 Fifth Avenue, New York, N.Y. 10017

ESPRIT – University of Scranton, Scranton, Pa. 18510

ESQUIRE – 488 Madison Avenue, New York, N.Y. 10022

EVERGREEN REVIEW – 64 University Place, New York, N.Y. 10003

FANTASY AND SCIENCE FICTION – 347 E. 53rd Street, New York, N.Y. 10022

FOR NOW – Box 375, Cathedral Station, New York, N.Y. 10025

FORUM – University of Houston, Tex. 77004

FOUR QUARTERS – La Salle College, Philadelphia, Pa. 19141

THE FREE LANCE – 6005 Grand Avenue, Cleveland, Ohio 44101

GENERATION, THE INTER-ARTS MAGAZINE – University of Michigan, 420 Maynard, Ann Arbor, Mich. 48103

GEORGIA REVIEW – University of Georgia, Athens, Ga. 30601

GOOD HOUSEKEEPING – 959 Eighth Avenue, New York, N.Y. 10019

THE GREENSBORO REVIEW – The University of North Carolina, Greensboro, N.C. 27412

HARPER'S BAZAAR – 572 Madison Avenue, New York, N.Y. 10022

HARPER'S MAGAZINE – 2 Park Avenue, New York, N.Y. 10016

HUDSON REVIEW – 65 E. 55th Street, New York, N.Y. 10022

IMPULSE – Rockland Community College, Suffern, N.Y. 10901

JOHNS HOPKINS MAGAZINE – Baltimore, Md. 21218

KENYON REVIEW – Kenyon College, Gambier, Ohio 43022

LADIES' HOME JOURNAL – 641 Lexington Avenue, New York, N.Y. 10022

THE LAUREL REVIEW – West Virginia Wesleyan College, Buckhannon, W. Va. 26201

LILLABULERO – P.O. Box 1027, Chapel Hill, N.C. 27514

THE LITERARY REVIEW – Fairleigh Dickinson University, Teaneck, N.J. 07666

MADEMOISELLE – 420 Lexington Avenue, New York, N.Y. 10022

THE MALAHAT REVIEW – University of Victoria, Victoria, British Columbia, Canada

THE MASSACHUSETTS REVIEW – University of Massachusetts, Amherst, Mass. 01003

MCCALL'S – 230 Park Avenue, New York, N.Y. 10017

MIDSTREAM – 515 Park Avenue, New York, N.Y. 10022

THE MINNESOTA REVIEW – Box 4068, University Station, Minneapolis, Minn. 55455

THE NEW MEXICO QUARTERLY – University of New Mexico Press, Marron Hall, Albuquerque, N. Mex. 87106

THE NEW YORKER – 25 W. 43rd Street, New York, N.Y. 10036

NORTH AMERICAN REVIEW – Cornell College, Mount Vernon, Iowa 52314

THE PARIS REVIEW – 45-39, 171 Place, Flushing, N.Y. 11358

PARTISAN REVIEW – Rutgers University, New Brunswick, N.J. 08903

PERSPECTIVE – Washington University Post Office, St. Louis, Mo. 63105

PLAYBOY – 232 E. Ohio Street, Chicago, Ill. 60611

PHYLON – 223 Chestnut Street S.W., Atlanta, Ga. 30314

PRAIRIE SCHOONER – Andrews Hall, University of Nebraska, Lincoln, Nebr. 68508

PRIMIERE – P.O. Box 8008, Mobile, Ala. 36603

PRISM INTERNATIONAL – Dept. of Creative Writing, Vancouver 8, British Columbia, Canada

QUARTERLY REVIEW OF LITERATURE – Box 287, Bard College, Annandale-on-Hudson, N.Y. 12504

QUARTET – 346 Sylvia Street W., Lafayette, Ind. 47906

THE QUEST – P.O. Box 207, Cathedral Station, New York, N.Y. 10025

RAMPARTS – 1182 Chestnut Street, Menlo Park, Calif. 94027

REDBOOK – 230 Park Avenue, New York, N.Y. 10017

RED CLAY READER – 2221 Westminster Place, Charlotte, N.C. 28207

THE REPORTER – 660 Madison Avenue, New York, N.Y. 10021

SAN FRANCISCO REVIEW – Box 671, San Francisco, Calif. 94101

SATURDAY EVENING POST – 641 Lexington Avenue, New York, N.Y. 10022

SEQUOIA – Box 2167, Stanford University, Stanford, Calif. 94305

SEWANEE REVIEW – University of the South, Sewanee, Tenn. 37375

SHENANDOAH – Box 722, Lexington, Va. 24450

SOUTHERN REVIEW – Drawer D, University Station, Baton Rouge, La. 70803

SOUTHWEST REVIEW – Southern Methodist University Press, Dallas, Tex. 75222

THE TAMARACK REVIEW – Box 159, Postal Station K, Toronto, Ontario, Canada

TEXAS QUARTERLY – Box 7527, University of Texas, Austin, Tex. 78712

TODAY – 221 W. Madison Street, Chicago, Ill. 60606

TRACE – P.O. Box 1068, Hollywood, Calif. 90028

TRANSATLANTIC REVIEW – Box 3348, Grand Central P.O., New York, N.Y. 10017

TRI-QUARTERLY – University Hall 101, Northwestern University, Evanston, Ill. 60201

THE UNIVERSITY REVIEW – University of Kansas City, 51 Street & Rockhill Road, Kansas City, Mo. 64110

VENTURE (for Junior High) – 910 Witherspoon Bldg., Philadelphia, Pa. 19107

VENTURES – Yale Graduate School, New Haven, Conn. 06520

THE VIRGINIA QUARTERLY REVIEW – University of Virginia, 1 West Range, Charlottesville, Va. 22903

VOGUE – 420 Lexington Avenue, New York, N.Y. 10017

WASHINGTON SQUARE REVIEW – New York University, 737 East Bldg., New York, N.Y. 10003

WESTERN HUMANITIES REVIEW – Bldg. 41, University of Utah, Salt Lake City, Utah 84112

WOMAN'S DAY – 67 W. 44th Street, New York, N.Y. 10036

THE YALE REVIEW – 28 Hillhouse Avenue, New Haven, Conn. 06520

COLLEGE OF THE SEQUOIAS
LIBRARY